Call My Name
the Wind

Call My Name the Wind

DAVID OSER

BEACHCOMBER RD PRESS
NEW YORK

Epilogue quotations are reproduced with the kind permission of Fulcrom Publishing.

Cover photography design by Allen B. Oser
Book production with assistance of Patricia Rasch.

Beachcomber Rd Press Ltd.
Beachcomber RD Press
PO Box 168
Massapequa Park, NY 11762
Email: **beachcomberpress@verizon.net**
Beachcomber ISBN: 0-9755392-1-3
Printed in the United States of America

This book is dedicated to those of you who told me about your lives, hopes, aspirations, nightmares, and dreams that inspired this novel. It is for all of the suppressed spirits that are waiting for the right moment to surface, to ignite your dreams, and to define your destinies.

Acknowledgements

The young people whose histories invaded my mind with their passionate dreams for freedom inspired the writing of this book. This work could not have been possible without the patient editorial assistance of my wife Rhoda. Thanks to the *New Yorker* magazine for providing their report on the Tompkins Square Park incident that played a part in the transformation of this book's "hero." A long search for the cover material landed close to home with the photography of my son, Allen and the co-operation of Patricia Rasch. Thanks goes to the production staff of Fidlar-Doubleday.

Thanks also to the participants in the many workshops and reading clubs for asking the simple question, "How do you write a whole book?" The answer is simple. Just begin on page one.

Prologue

Told Around the Campfires

In the eleventh summer, phantom lights streak out of the north sky, gather lost warriors and raise them peacefully to campfires frozen in time. This has happened since the beginning of the world and will happen until the last fearless hero is free.

These words are heard around autumn campfires, when night's blanket is pulled across the sky, when cinders reflect in old, knowing eyes, and smoke fills pulsating nostrils of young lovers. Old men speak softly and nod approval at the story of Tern Harbor.

They used to say the rains would clean the world and they used to say the wind would whip the rain against the earth, drive away all the sins and they used to say devils would go into hiding and evil spirits would drown in the deep waters.

At the campfires, they tell about the young warrior who was to protect the land and the waters, and the woman who was to protect the animals. Together he and she would keep the earth pure and safeguard the true ways.

The story is told that sailors from giant boats stole the man and the woman. The sailors tied the warrior into a small boat and forced the woman into the back of another boat.

A storm heard what had happened and sent East Wind to drive the sailors into the fog. The sea rose up to force them far from their ships and toward the rocky shore. Fierce gusts and waves tormented the boats until the one carrying the warrior began to sink. As the sailors wrapped an anchor around a huge rock they were catapulted into the dooming water.

The anchor's rope spun around the rock; the boat, pitched from side to side, smashed violently against the boulder, and splintered. Terror blazed in the warrior's whitecap drenched eyes, and then softened as he prepared to meet his ancestors. The warrior's body rose and fell yielding to the sea's whims. His head beat with the waves' rhythm. The ropes, that had held him captive in the boat, lashed him to the rock. His mouth locked open. His lifeless eyes fixed on the enshrouded cliff.

Sailors in the second boat dug oars into uncompromising waves, stretched muscles against competing currents, and pleaded with horizontally slashing rain. The woman's eyes focused as a sea hawk on her mate. She raised the small anchor, crushed the skulls of two sailors, and hurled the anchor into a third man's chest. The sound of his cracking ribs and piercing screams were buried by the disharmony of whistling winds and booming waves that grabbed and swallowed him. The woman, draped in blood, leaped at the last sailor. The boat rocked, overturned, and tossed them into the thundering breakers.

They tell around the campfires that chattering waves decided to save the woman. Splashing tides, moaning like mourning women, rolled onto the beach, then foam raced back like white men's children caught swimming naked.

Surf licked at the woman's feet. She scrambled forward to escape unseen enemies and pulled herself to the top of the beaconing hill. The warrior stared toward her; his outstretched arms fluttered against the boulder that held him captive and his body joined the steady tempo of swells.

She scratched deep into the earth under her, pulled her hands across her face making marks of mourning and hiding her true face from the moon and the sun. She howled to frighten away evil spirits and to call for the white shadows to come from the sky.

Her weeping hid the rustling sound of the sailor lunging toward her. He slipped, grasped vacant space, and screamed for help. His fall delivered him to the sea and his crewmates. The woman stumbled on the dirt she had scraped and skidded down the slope. Rocks reached out to save her but she was impaled on a devil rock.

Her mouth froze open in final song to her lover. Her eyes locked onto his watery gaze.

They say night despised day, and they say that the morning chased the night's storm. Terns returned to the beach. They pecked at fish remains, clams, and the eyes of the lovers. The birds' excitement turned to frenzy as they plucked the eyes from the couple, flew to a secret place, and hid their treasure.

The story is told that the spirits of the blinded couple search for each other and it is told that the terns will stay there forever guarding the secret hiding place.

The story is told that one day, if the eyes are released, the lover's spirits will fly up as white shadows to join warrior ancestors in the Northern Skies.

They say that if you are on the Sound during an autumn storm, you can hear a chilling song coming from Devil Hill or that big rock in the middle of the harbor. That's what old men say around the campfires.

1

The Palmers

Coast Guard and Fire Department rescue beams and searchlights dueled in frantic patterns across Tern Harbor Bay. Needling rain, rising tide, and salt spray, collided with howling autumnal winds obscuring the beach and bluffs. Firemen and volunteers braved ear-piercing thunder and crackling lightning as they searched for Steve Palmer.

"Over here." A voice bellowed through the fog. "Here. Hanging off the cliff. Oh God, it's his wheelchair."

"Down here," one of the firemen yelled from the foot of the cliff. "A rifle. Right here. Under Devil's Rock. Those bastards better find him fast. Where the hell is he?"

"Keep Gloria inside." Men splashed through tidal pools that flooded the beach. A small boat's light wavered, and then steadied on the red buoy's bell tower.

Intertwined layers of seaweed circled the buoy and cloaked the body that hovered below whitecaps. Human sounds stopped. The ratchety harbor launch clicked away time. The rescue crew harvested the tenacious sea grass and laid the body onto a stretcher.

"Look at this. His head's pulled all the way back."

"Oh crap." A young fireman pulled slimy green dead man's fingers from Steve Palmer's mouth. "Couldn't have breathed but must have been dead before this stuff got into him. Look how tight these weeds wrapped around his neck. Coulda' drowned or maybe the weeds got the old man."

"I thought weed was something you were using at Belle's the other night."

"No time for jokes."

"Poor son-of-a-bitch, must've suffocated."

"How could he of gotten all the way out here?"

"These wild currents. He must've put up some battle to stay afloat."

"He couldn't swim. Couldn't even walk after the friggin strokes."

"Shoulda yelled."

"Don't be friggin' stupid. He couldn't talk. Told you he had them strokes."

"Hey." Butch Moulder commanded from the top of the hill. "You dumb bastards get him up here. The van is on the way from my place."

"The funeral parlor? You sure?" The fire chief was standing next to Butch. "Shouldn't we get him over to the fire house or the hospital?"

"Easier for Doc Felder to check him out, privately."

"Butch," the chief wiped the rain from his face. "Who's going to tell Gloria?"

"Leave it to me. She's up there in the house." Butch motioned toward the dark windows. "She's strong like the old man. Won't let anyone see how she feels."

Butch Moulder lit a cigarette and leaned against moss covered boulders. Small plants and algae, plastered against the rocks surface by time and weather, blended with boulders Steve Palmer had imported from Vermont to lend the appearance of undisturbed centuries to the cliff. Oak trimmed glass windows filled the wide arc of the family room that emphasized the old house's dominance.

Butch lit a second cigarette. "Damn. Those bloody idiots are racing up the road with lights flashing. Probably have sirens wailing. Damn." He smashed his cigarette against the wall and started toward the front of the house.

Headlights flashed intermittently as police cars passed Baron-Palmer Acres and moved along Diablo Beach Road. Oversized houses with rarely used front porches were referred to as Barren Acres. The land had been stripped of anything that could grow to accommodate Victorian style homes.

Two vehicles turned past the barbed wire entrance to the Coast Guard Station and the hidden driveway to the Utility Company power plant. The police car's orange and red spinning lights flickered through the short expanse of woods, past the Goose Island Road that led to the wetland island. A decaying wood sign was the only indication that the place was an abandoned Army Corps of Engineers project. Goose Island, once a desolate marsh, was now divided into two acre building lots with entrances hidden by poplars and hedgerows.

The cars moved along the narrow road, past the small rocky beach. White clapboard houses, that created a bright border during daylight, were hidden in the stinging mist.

Butch Moulder was about to knock at the front door when the cars screeched to a halt on the wet gravel driveway. He slammed a cigarette on the police car's windshield.

"Cut the damn lights and the siren. Want to bring every one of these jerks out of their houses and up here to gawk at what's going on? You guys seal off this place so no one, no one of these nosey neighbors sneaks around here. No one has to know that we already moved Steve to the Funeral parlor. Head back to town, go about your routines, and do it quietly!"

———✦———

Gloria Palmer, tucked into a green afghan, rocked gently and rubbed her arms to stay warm. The glass encased room yielded an uninterrupted harbor view. Rain-splattered windows diffused the rescue vessels' light beams into ricocheting shadows that moved helter skelter over framed family pictures. Ghostly, gilt framed ancestors danced across a silent grand piano.

"They must be having the last laugh," Gloria said to the photograph of her mother and father. Gloria turned to a picture of her mother holding a birthday cake and pursed her lips as if to blow out the ten candles.

"I love you Momma. It was a beautiful party Momma and you asked Amanda to add those wonderful colors. The girls at the party were all pretty, neat, and well behaved. I couldn't stand that bow in my hair."

Gloria smiled, remembered how she followed a group of skinny boys who were sneaking away from the party, waited until they climbed down the hill to the beach, waited until they were in the water, and grabbed their clothes. Gloria dusted the picture frame and held it close to her chest.

"Hey," I yelled at those boys, twirled their clothes over my head and laughed while they hid their little bottoms under the water. Can you imagine how pathetic they looked, hiding in the water and screaming up at me? Those pale naked boys yelped like puppies.

"Beg," I jeered. "Bet you won't come out of the water if I sit here all day."

"Momma, then I saw a boy with rusty hair. I knew he wasn't one of them, didn't know him at all. He swam from the other end of the beach, swam all the way to Target Rock, climbed naked onto the rock, stood spread eagle and waved his arms over his head to me. I waved back with one of the white shirts and then tossed the clothes to the beach."

"You acted so angry, Momma, but you let me blow out the little flames and then you hugged me."

"I wanted to find Poppa," she thought. "Wanted to have him hug me too, but he wasn't there. You made some excuse about business. It was always the same, wasn't it Momma? Did you really believe him? I knew he wouldn't be there when we needed him, just like he's not here now. You never wanted me to see or hear unpleasant things, always tried to protect me. I wish you were still here Momma. I'm going to need you."

Gloria pulled her mother's afghan closer around her shoulders. She heard the men shouting "Don't want her to see this. She shouldn't see this."

Gloria approached the window, looked toward Target Rock. "I never did forget those boys," she thought.

Butch Moulder edged quietly into the dimly lit room, dragged his hand across the piano, dusted one of the frames, and sat on the piano bench.

"Gloria, I . . . they found him." Butch put his thumb nail between his front teeth.

"I know Butch. Thank them for me." Gloria sank into the leather arm chair.

"Sent Dad to the funeral parlor. Doc Felder will take care of the paper work. I'll arrange for the wake and anything else that you want. Sure he'd want to be up high on the hill." Butch recited the list as he always did with grieving clients.

"No wake. Don't want everyone staring down at him. Want him cremated and scattered into this harbor. He built it; let him stay here. You'll know what to do Butch."

"People will be upset." Butch coughed.

"Tell everyone it's what he wanted, and it's what I want. They can come to a memorial service."

"I'll move next week's Tern Harbor Day Committee meeting over to the Yacht Club instead of here. They'll understand." Butch started to leave. "That's quite a beautiful sight," he nodded at the pictures on the piano. "All those relatives. He must have been very proud of them. They would have been proud of him."

"Don't change the meeting. It's always been here"

"You're terrific, Gloria. He'd be proud of you." She twisted away as Butch reached toward her shoulder.

"You take care of it yourself, Butch. He would want things done right." She stared into the funeral director's eyes. "That's why he made you Mayor. You always knew what he wanted."

"Right, Glory. I'll take care of it. It'll be fine." He tapped each of the bells that lined the front hallway. "Steve loved these bells. Will have church bells played all over town for the memorial."

"Yes. Those bells." Gloria squinted, massaged a flashlight, flipped it on and off, scanned the family pictures, then moved rapidly through the front hallway, past the brass bells, opened a polished oak door, and made her way down the stairs to the old section of the house.

She tapped on the door, entered the dark room, and listened to Amanda's plaintive chant. Fireplace embers flickered red shadows across the small squatting woman whose face drifted in and out of the soft orange light. She had spread her fingers through the dust under the flickering logs, spread ashen lines across her high cheekbones so that sunlight would not find her during the mourning time. Gloria had seen Amanda shield her face with ash when Rosa Palmer had died and once when she had returned from her home. Gloria had avoided asking why she seemed to be in mourning then. A single clamshell shaped silver and ruby earring was covered with ash as it had been when Rosa Palmer died.

Gloria sat next to the woman who had been her mother's surrogate, rocked with her, tried to hum the same chants, and then held her hands in silent communication. She imagined that Native women had echoed the same sounds throughout their history, and it must have been the same sounds made by the mythical woman clinging to life on Devil Rock.

"Why, Amanda, why the ash?" Gloria asked.

"It's our way." Amanda whispered.

Gloria rolled her finger under the logs, smeared gray ash across her face, squeezed Amanda's hand, and left the room. She felt her way up the dark stairway, fingered each of the bells as a blind person might, brushed past the leather couch and chairs, and straightened the racing sloop painting that hung over the mantle. Tears cascaded over the ash markings on her cheeks as she reached for the empty space where her father's wheel chair would have been. She tried to inhale his absent medicinal smell but only recalled the odor of smoke, liquor, and the perfume of women who would have been in the boathouse.

A candle flickering on the piano cast old family pictures into a historic stereograph. Gloria held her parents wedding picture, rubbed the glass front with her loose blouse, took it from its frame, tore her father's face from the photo and replaced the frame on the piano.

"You son-of-a-bitch," she screamed. "Even now, even now you have it your way." She put the head torn from the photo over the candle, watched it ignite, and then dropped it into a glass ashtray.

The full moon's light, breaking through thinning cloud cover, girdled Target Rock. Gloria pressed her nose against a cool window, thought about the bay, the beach, the rock where she had seen the boy, and the tenth birthday party. "I never forgot the colors, the laughter," she looked back at her Mother's picture. "Those ridiculous boys and that boy standing on the rock," she hunched her shoulders. "And Momma, you never do forget the first time you see a boy naked."

2

Gloria

Droning black fans tumbled rotating shadows along Harbor Light Diner's patterned tin ceiling. Freckled grease residue, splattered from the flat grill, amplified smoky odors of bacon and toasted muffins. Worn octagonal floor tiles, set during the building's brighter days, added to the nineteenth century ambiance that attracted tourists. Sally's sense of style included assorted tables, chairs, and booths rescued from decaying Maine bars.

Jack Greeley, editor of the *Tern Harbor Journal*, swirled his coffee, pushed bacon onto the last square of toast, checked the bill, and dug into his pocket for the tip. Town cronies buzzed with gossip and advice for this week's edition of the paper. Ned and Cindy Gross, blotting tears of laughter, pulled Jack into a seat and repeated the story they had just heard; Sally Bastone had whispered a nasty tidbit about a woman who was passing the diner.

Jack blushed, smiled, "Don't think I could use that. Her old man would probably show up with a pitchfork and I don't run too fast." He got up to leave.

"Don't rush out, Jack," Sally put her manicured hand on his shoulder. "The boss won't be in yet, so soon after the memorial. Anyway, it's the beginning of the month and she wasn't even around collecting rents."

"No way. It's Wednesday. Gloria'll be in the office early checking every word for Friday's edition." Jack nodded to Sally. "And you know she's not like Steve. Tenants mail the rent these days."

"God forgive me, that old son-of-a-bitch knew how to collect rents right up to that blessed stroke. Would've rolled down here in that wheelchair if Gloria let him. He'd never let us, Billy and me, be late with a dollar. If times were tough, he'd get his somehow. Guess I oughtn't mention the wheel chair."

"What do you think about that, Jack," Ned Gross peered over his horn rimmed glasses. "What do you think about how they found the chair?"

"Don't know any more than you do. Really bad accident. He'll be missed." Jack tried to leave.

"Come the end of the month," Sally interrupted. "He'd be right on time to collect rent. Palmer would go right past the Diner, up those rickety stairs, and open the door to my Billy's rooms. Wouldn't even knock, just go right in. Billy was afraid of him." Sally continued her monologue as she clicked salt and pepper shakers into place, cleaned the counter, watched the waitresses, and worked the cash register.

"Yeah that old bastard, I know all the beautiful words the minister and all them suck-ups said at the church, but he was always trying to get a look at Billy's six pack. Oh you know Cindy, the stomach muscles. Palmer could be really nasty when it came to any kind of sex. You gonna put any of that stuff in your story about him, Jack?"

"Don't think I can."

Sally looked into the mirror behind the counter and adjusted a loose strand of hair. "Best thing that ever happened around here was when he had those strokes and Gloria came home. No, best thing is when the old son-of-a-bitch kicked the bucket."

The Grosses crossed themselves.

"Gloria knew about the old man, don't you think? Took good care of him through all them strokes. Wait outside, Jack. I'll tell you how she saved my Billy. Jack, really, want to talk to you."

Sally handed a menu to a young college student seated in a raised booth. His legs surrounded the table's chrome pedestal.

Sally dropped her pencil close to the young man who was sipping orange juice and reading the *Daily News Sport Section*. She fumbled for the pencil, and stared at the tattoo of a spider's silky thread climbing past his knee into the loosely hung khaki shorts.

"He never tried to touch me," Cindy Gross blurted. "I'd have stuck this old hat pin up his, his six pack."

"Whose? The geezer's or Billy's?" Ned Gross hissed.

Sally's scowl stopped the laughter.

"Well, I think Gloria had her own ideas about her father," Jack smiled. "And Sally, you sure drop a mean pencil."

"Didn't you see that tattoo? Like spiders creeping up to a web." she shuddered. "Wait outside though, Jack."

The counter clock's little cuckoo, silenced by some early morning drunk, spun out trying to crow eight o'clock.

Jack patted Sally's shoulder. "Steve should have made a pass for you, Sally old girl, and then you wouldn't have had to pay any rent at all." He waited in the shadowed vestibule. A gray cement keystone over the terra cotta arch displayed the fading legend, *1878*.

Sally lit a cigarette. "Have to smoke out here these days." She blew the smoke in a relaxed oval. "You going to write some pretty pages about him, ain't you?"

"Do what's right. This town wouldn't be what it is if he hadn't made it." Jack glared at Sally.

"Maybe. But I know what he did to a lot of people, even Gloria, and I love that girl for how she helped my Billy."

"She gave up a lot to come back here, took charge, just like him." Jack turned to leave.

"No way she's like *him*. She's an angel."

"Humph." Jack breathed in the last of Sally's smoke.

"He tried to hit on Billy. Did you know that? End of every month I'd see the clothesline. White underwear all month, and then end of the month, those black gym things he liked Billy to work out in. I knew what he would try. I'd call up so he'd think I was coming and all he'd do was look. But Billy was scared. I knew when I saw that clothesline. But you know Glory, that angel, she saved Billy. Got him a place of his own, out East, his own café. Go ahead. Write the sweet stuff about Palmer. I hope the ghost of that Indian princess grabbed him, got him for screwing up her land." Sally wiped her hands on her apron and went back into the diner.

Jack shrugged, gritted his teeth, and looked back toward the diner. "Doc called it a heart attack and stroke caused by the accident." He passed his thumb across his chin. He turned toward the newspaper office, inhaled the crisp air drifting in from the harbor; he avoided his usual walk toward the village dock, didn't want to see boats that were beginning to file past the buoys, and turned to blot out the sounds of snapping sails that were reminders of Steve Palmer.

Jack read the bronze sign mounted on the corner of the *Journal* building.

Village of Tern Harbor

founded for tranquility

Guiseppe Palmieri, 1870

"Yeah," Jack thought. "Heart attack. Accident. Yeah, right!"

———•———

"Good morning, Nessa. Boss in yet?" Jack didn't wait for the secretary's answer.

"I can't believe she's coming in so soon after the memorial. Hear she took the ashes out on the boat herself, God knows where, and she's . . . ."

"Yeah. She's strong like her father." Jack looked at the note pad on his desk. "You know she rebuilt this paper better than it ever was. Did you know that? Did that, and all the time looked after Steve. She's had her share of mourning," he leaned on the secretary's desk. "So don't rock her boat. When she comes in, it's just another day. Get it?"

"She's already here," Nessa grinned.

Gloria's perfume wafted gently around the office as she opened her door. "Been here since five, Jack. Wanted to get this place in shape." She held a teacup and clicked her tongue in rhythm to the jazz radio station.

Jack had learned to read Gloria's twitches, the little nervous snapping of her bra, the slits of her eyes when she got angry, and he recognized her inherited temper. He appreciated the way she had transformed the business from the stodgy small village gossip sheet and printing business into a first rate newspaper. Computers had replaced typewriters and the inadequate telephone system. Gloria had replaced old *Journal* pages that had covered the front windows with green café curtains.

"I stopped by Austin Strong's Anthro class to select this year's intern," Gloria smiled. "I was a little late just like when I was a student, so had to sit through his lecture about the old myth. He started with that tired joke about his being Indian, then he said his usual oops, and that he means Native American, and goes on jabbering about the Indians."

"Isn't he exciting, the Professor?" Nessa continued shuffling files.

"Why not just send Nessa?" Jack sneered.

"It was forever until I was introduced, and then only as Steven Palmer's daughter; imagine still can't introduce me as Gloria Palmer. I asked for volunteers for the festival and the race. I wound up leaving a note for Strong telling him which student I selected to intern for the *Journal*."

"Welcome." Austin Strong began the session with the same patter with which he had captured students during the duration of his tenure. Gloria thought about the discomfort of sitting in that musty classroom, wearing large round sunglasses, trying to sink into the sallow room itself. It was the same seat in which, as an undergraduate, she would sit erect pretending to take notes.

Gloria sat, eyes closed, mouthing the lecture she had heard so many times, trying to stay in rhythm with the worshipped professor. She didn't pay attention until she heard the new part of the lecture.

"And it is told around the campfires, that one day the wind will come from a new direction, wild, strong and unafraid. The wind, it is told, will discover the terns hiding place, repair the lover's eyes and they will be free, borne up into the white sky mist to find their freedom." Austin Strong paused, closed his eyes, drew a deep breath, then nodded his head to the back of the room and told them Steven Palmer's daughter would like to talk about the upcoming festival.

"Imagine that Jack. He would only refer to me as Steve's daughter; wouldn't even mention my name. Probably never forgave that I dropped his class. Did I say the intern would be coming in today? Show him around, okay?" Gloria retreated into her office signaling the beginning of the press run.

Jack dropped into his swivel chair, lit a cigarette, looked over the phone memo's stacked under his telephone dial and glanced over his glasses when he heard the tinkling bell over the office front door.

"Hello. I'm looking for Miss Palmer. Professor Strong . . ."

"Oh. You're the intern," Nessa became interested when she saw the good-looking young man enter the shop.

"Uh, yes. James, just Jim Meredith"

Jack looked up, recognized the young man he had seen in the diner, wondered if Sally knew that he would be a frequent visitor and if she had gotten a good look at him when she dropped her pencil.

James Meredith's black hair was tied into a ponytail. A small silver hoop hung from his left ear and there were the marks of a small spider web tattoo on his right wrist. He wore a short sleeve white shirt, the khaki shorts that had interested the diner crowd, white socks, and moccasins. It was not the dress code Jack would have expected and not the fashion Steve Palmer would have allowed.

Gloria was informal, concerned with mind not appearance. "It's the intellect that has made this into a better paper," had become part of her talks to civic groups. "Not the color of a tie or the length of a skirt, and I hope nobody cares about how I dress." Besides she thought, it's my choice.

"You'll like working here." Gloria said to the intern who was standing at attention in her office. She continued looking through the copy for Friday's edition of the *Journal*.

"Yeah. It's great. I was sorry to hear about the accident, your Dad," the young man shuffled uneasily.

"There are files in the basement that you ought to start with," Gloria disregarded his fumbling response. "You can use any of them you think you need for your research. Jack'll get a key for you in case you work late, and you can order stuff delivered from the Diner, just tell them to add it to our tab."

James fidgeted until Gloria said he could begin work as soon as he wanted to. Relieved, he asked if he could begin immediately.

"You'll find boxes and boxes and a stack of loose files. They are dated and some have detailed notes on them and they're pretty dusty so good idea to take some paper towels with you. I'll catch up with you later. I have a Kiwanis luncheon that I never miss. You see, I'm the first woman they ever let in. Can't let the old boys think they can out drink me. Jack," she called over the intercom. "Come on in, I'll introduce you to James."

"We've already met, that is I saw him at the diner."

"Please help him and introduce him to Sally. Have her set him up on our tab."

"Oh, I think Sally has already had a good look at him." Jack and James shared private smiles.

———————

Gloria was late getting to the Kiwanis Luncheon at the Black Stallion Café. She knew the drill, prepared to pay the dollar when Buzzy O'Donnell saw her, knew he would lead the group in singing "She's our girl true and true." Butch Moulder was holding a seat for her. She ordered her usual Bloody Mary. Gossip and private jokes circled the table along with Kiwanis news. Announcements and correspondence were followed by more singing, then with a prayer, and *God Bless America* led by Buzzy.

As the others were leaving, Butch motioned to Gloria.

"Have something really important to speak to you about"

"Finally get caught in the sack with some dentist's wife?"

"No, nothing like that. You know I wouldn't get caught doing anything like that. Especially because of what I have to speak to you about."

"All right Butch. Get it out. I'm really busy at the paper."

"Guess the best way to say it is to just say it. I plan to run for Congress. Been suggested by the Party leaders and really considering it. But Glory, I would like to have your support and help. Support means bucks, help means from the *Journal*."

"Wow! That's a big order. First congratulations on being considered. Have to think about the paper. Money, depends on how much."

"I figured I could count on you. Your dad would have wanted you to help get a congressman. I knew it when I told him day before the accident. I could see it in his eyes."

"He always had a way of saying things with those eyes." Gloria grimaced.

"It was tough on the boys finding him out there. I could tell how he must've struggled when we got him back to my place. The expression in his eyes though, like terror, I knew that something was funny, almost like he was looking for something. And his hands, tight, like he was holding his rifle. I think I was the only one to spot . . ."

"Butch, I said I would help. Can't promise the paper until you are really nominated. I do know how to express my appreciation for all you did that night, keeping it neat."

"Great. Knew I could count on you."

Gloria watched Albert "Butch" Moulder swagger toward his car. "How," she thought, "would anyone really think of this penguin for Congress."

———•———

The perfume that had floated through the *JOURNAL* office blended with late afternoon quiet. The staff left early to avoid the forecast squall. James Meredith thought the basement, where he was sorting old files, smelled like an old wine cellar. He dusted them with a soft brush as if he was finding bones or cracked dishes on an archeological dig. Ancient vibrations from those crackling folders seemed to be talking to him. He opened old manila envelopes, looked through handwritten documents, brushed them as if they had been stolen from a pharaoh's tomb, and then placed them into new cases for safekeeping. "Unreal," he said to whatever spirits might be in the basement with him. "Look at these papers that someone must have taken from the old Riverhead Township books. They date back to the 1600s, are still just sitting here, and that the handwriting is so crisp."

———•———

Gloria won her race with heavy rain drops, ran breathless into the office, smiled and waved to Jack to go home before he got caught in the deluge. She checked her phone messages, signed letters, and savoured the quiet of the empty office. The clicking of files from the basement reminded her that she was not alone. "Hi, James. How are you doing? Need any help?"

Gloria hesitated on the narrow stairs that led to the basement where as a child, she had often hidden in the dark, pretending she was alone in the Village, and playing a secret children's game. She would swim into a cave where she would find the myth's lost eyes. The basement was mystical and she suspected the old documents held answers to mysteries.

"You know," James volunteered, "There are some folders tucked way in the back corner on top of those old wooden shelves that I thought might break if I stepped on them."

"Check the store room for a ladder. I guess Jack didn't really give you the tour. Probably figured you could find things on your own. Sometimes that works better, finding things on your own."

Gloria concentrated on files dated 1860-1870 and another dated 1947, wrapped them in a large brown envelope and tapped lightly as if she had discovered a scoop for the *Journal's* next issue.

An accumulation of dust flew into James's face. "This is a real mold bin. Don't think anyone has looked at these in years."

As he handed down one of the files, Gloria saw the spider web tattoo on the intern's wrist and the tattoo on his shoulder. She recognized the marks she had seen elsewhere.

She stacked a file marked "Confidential, S.P." with the others.

"Storm must be getting close." Gloria had spent many stormy sessions hiding from her father in this basement. Thunder rattled the storefront windows; the lights flickered then went dark, air conditioning sounds stopped, computer screens went black, and the intern slipped down the ladder. Gloria reached up to help him but the ladder gave way and they were on the floor. The lights came on as quickly as they had gone black.

The intern reached across to help Gloria, saw the demanding authority he had seen earlier in the day. "Oh hell," he thought, "I'm probably out of here."

"James, come to my place on Friday afternoon, bring your files, and stay for dinner."

"Friday? Dinner?"

"Yes! Come early. My father always likes, that is liked, me to have ... the interns come to the house"

The intern hesitated. "Did your dad help when you guys were working?"

She smiled. "Watched, them, just watched. He sat in his chair, couldn't talk, just watched the interns. Be sure to come Friday and bring your files and summaries."

James Meredith started up the stairs. "Why?"

"Because I want to know how you are coming with your work."

"I mean why was he watching?"

Gloria turned back to the files she had set aside. "Because, just because."

Why indeed, she thought. Tease him. Plague him. Revenge.

.

3

Family Pictures

Gloria stroked the stained documents that had been rescued from the basement hiding place as if they were deserted kittens. They interrupted a new myth she had conjured; Steve Palmer had been released from his pain, his daughter was free to leave Tern Harbor, and this time she would never return. But these old papers imposed truths that she knew would trap her, would force her to keep control of her father's business, and would finally take control of her.

She read the carefully scripted note on the bottom of the blemished paper bill-of-sale. There it was, that ominous promise made to T. Steelehart, "this is sacred land, never develop it." The Indian woman's haunting song echoed past Devil rock, reverberated through the document, and seared Gloria's fingers. "Never develop this land. A promise is a promise."

"*Broken promise*", she wrote in the margin of a Xeroxed copy of the deed and slipped it back into its folder. "*A promise is a promise Steve*. Broken here like a twig." She set the file into the roll top desk, and locked it as a pirate might hide precious treasure.

Deluge turned to soggy mist. Gloria turned off the office lights and leaned against the closed front door. She turned toward Belle's Saloon, allowed the rain to roll across her face, then moved to her car, set the radio to a local station, and watched silhouetted movements inside the tavern.

"He would have been in there tonight," she talked to the car radio. "But not in that wheel chair; to proud to come here looking old. Baymen's night." She lit another cigarette, and listened to the Beatles "Long Day's Night".

That night, like all Tern Harbor Tuesday nights, was alive, loud, brawling, bright, red and orange, smelled of cheap beer and blared with orchestrated bravado in Captain Belle's Saloon. Baymen roared their virtuous declarations of recipes for Clam Chowder.

Gonna beat the crap outta all you this year. Putting Belle's new beer in the chowder.

Bull. Got something better. Gonna make the judges want mine and no one else's. They get a snort of the vodka, it's all over.

Yo! Not even telling any of you drunks what I put into mine this year. Not some of that New England shit, but real Island specialty.

Yeah, probably Island shit.

Each of the baymen boasted that the secret ingredient in his chowder would guarantee victory in Tern Harbor Day's chowder contest. Beer, cigarette smoke mixed with occasional sweet smell of marijuana got confused in reflecting pools of drug soaked eyes.

———

Seasons have their own calendar in Tern Harbor. When sails appear in mid-April, it's Spring. Racing formations coursing like swarming white moths flying into the wind mark late Summer afternoons. Sleek launches move around Long Island Sound with young tanned bodies in tee shirts and shorts. Fading water activity and shadowy shorelines play codas to Fall from mid-October until Thanksgiving. The park bandstand and winding paths provide secluded territories under wintry skies that become teenagers' property. Night terns pick at fish heads, crumbs left by tourists, and bay morsels they swoop from the water.

Tourists frequent the village most seasons, but antique shops, restaurants and bars belong to the locals in December when Christmas decorations wink across Main Street to Santa Clause with a bell and red bucket outside the Island Commercial Bank.

Streetlight reflections flicker across the waterfront from West Tern. The amber lantern in the Harbor Master's shack teases the unborn morning.

Clammers proliferate during late spring and summer when high school seniors try to find an easy way to earn money. They pull up one or two count, one hundred clams per count, quickly tire of the back wrenching and redundant dropping of the rake, pulling against the sandy bottom, pulling up weeds, cans, sand and clams. The same boats appear throughout the season with changing casts. A sole clammer, though, starts work at four-thirty, repeats the drill every day, every season, controlled only by prevailing winds or storms, changing his routine in tandem with tides.

The lone clam boat's chugging motor leaves a foamy trail along the beach. The purring flat boat, with its rakes, pails, empty canvas bags and sole occupant, passes the red buoy, leaves the safety of the harbor, and ventures into the deep clam fields of Long Island Sound.

———

As Gloria sat smoking and listening to the car radio, watched as Chris Verity and two others were tossed out of Captain Belle's. They threw themselves back into the bar, and were quickly ejected onto the rain-slicked sidewalk with Belle staring after them.

"Don't come back until you're clean. Hear? Don't bring any more of that crap in here. I'm not going to lose my license because a few screw-ups think you can do more business in here than me. Keep that crap outa here, or..." She shook her head and watched them move into the shadows. "Bunch of druggies."

Two of the men crept into the wooded park. Chris Verity stumbled to his boat, splashed his head with cold water and moved out to the clam fields. He poured water over his eyes and cleared his head of the drugs' euphoria. His elixir, work, made him sweat and cleansed alcohol and drugs from his body. On nights like this, he would escape his demons, stay on the boat until he could sleep without dreaming; he pulled clams until the rakes ripped open his callused palms.

Bound to the Harbor, as Prometheus to the rock, Chris Verity's daily reward was five or six hundred clams. His skill and daring at working with long rakes in dangerous clam beds was ingrained into every sinew and muscle in the days when his father kept him out of school to work. That was before Chris and the tides had exchanged blood and brine, had forged the bond of common natures; it was before he and the currents ever shared the comforting resonance of the bells.

The morning peel of St. Peter's measured tome, rolled across the gently lapping bay. Mid-week morning bells cautioned neighbors a funeral was in progress. Bells from the white clapboard Presbyterian Church on Main Street had a high pitched quick tempo in counter point to St. Andrew's basso profundo. The alto bell from West Tern Unitarian completed the choir. Church bells were indistinguishable to strangers sailing on the Bay. They sounded one way rolling over the water, another on land.

Those church bells were not like the gentle tinkle of the red buoy marker, the tinkle like some gentle messenger calling, not loud, but carefully, "Don't disturb the fish. Don't unnerve the waves. Announce the Harbor, the joy, the sadness." The red buoy bell clanged night or fog, sometimes a friend, sometimes a screaming warning, sometimes a casual temptress.

Main Street Episcopal played dolefully, as if Chinese guards were pounding gongs whose intonations reverberated through mountain passes until all of China was on guard.

The clanging of the red buoy's bell, soft, delicate, comfortable, is most fearsome of all. The red buoy marks safe passage, its bell declares safe home during erupting August storms. Deceptive protective sounds of that bell conceal mysteries, warnings, danger, and haunting screeches of the terns.

The young clammer peeled off his jacket. Early morning sun flashed on a red thermos. He wrapped his hand around the steaming coffee cup; he squinted across the thin plume of steam, cleared his eyes, and inspected the coastline from the harbor opening eastward to the utility towers. He had pulled more than his usual quota of clams, took a coffee break, stripped down to black turtle neck sweater and faded red shorts. Now, he could be seen, not as an older, crouching man, but as young man who might sit in a college classroom.

He watched cars circle into Chloe Beach's parking lot; watched coolers, blankets and umbrellas being set up, and the fading colors of autumn tucked into hidden cracks along rock jetties. He saw a dog leaping after a Frisbee, children playing in the sand, and a small fire being lit in a beach barbecue grill.

A line of cars lumbered past the beach, disappeared behind blazing sumac, and reappeared as they turned onto the gravel driveway of the Palmer's house.

Gloria Palmer, immune to most warning bells, shuddered at the sight and sound of the red buoy. "I should have blown that damn buoy out of the water when I had the urge," she thought. "Wouldn't have to hear it now, wouldn't have had to listen to him, and wouldn't have had to wonder if Steve would still be bragging about all the bells."

"This room, these windows, I created them, and they command this Island's most rapturous views of eternity," Steve Palmer would boast at the Tern Harbor Day Committee organization luncheon. "That marker," he would say, "is more than a navigation marker. It keeps this harbor a safe, pure place. It keeps good things in and danger out. Just listen to that bell."

"Should have done it long ago." Gloria fantasized about being twelve years old, sailing out to ring that buoy's bell, clanging it long and loud until her father would look down from that glassed-in perch; she would wave a greeting to him and set a torch to that damn buoy.

The long windows panes, like delicate prisms, ensnared rainbows and views of the harbor beyond the red buoy, past the Long Island Sound, across to Connecticut, and back to the eastern landscapes of Tern Harbor beyond the power plant's belching smoke stacks.

Soon after he bought the property in 1867, Gloria's great grandfather Guiseppe Palmieri built a cottage on the rocky cliff overlooking the bay. Now it dominates the approach to Tern Harbor and has been the center for local society since Steve Palmer expanded the house in defiance of the ominously eroding cliffs. Gloria wondered if someday, when she is very old, the house would surrender to the winds, fall into the bay, and return the land to its source. She wondered if the house would resist the whims of nature.

She wondered if Amanda, who seemed as permanent as the building's pillar and post foundation, would remain a part of the house as she had for as long as Gloria could remember. She had been with the family; nurse and mentor to Gloria, cook and overseer of the house, caretaker for Rosa Palmer through her sick days, and remained faithful to the family and the house.

As Amanda prepared for the Festival Committee's luncheon, she avoided looking into the cove where Steve Palmer's body had been found. The buffet tables were alive with jonquil colored linens; small tables were covered in white cloths, rose napkins, and antique luncheon silverware. Sparkling glasses were filled with ice water and lemon slices. The menu included choices of bisque, chowder, stuffed clams, shrimp, crab cakes, salads, raspberries, chicken in mushroom sauce, desserts and champagne cocktail.

"It's wonderful, as usual, Amanda," Gloria sampled the bisque.

"Wouldn't have it any other way."

"Why don't you stay? See how they love it. Stay, stay."

"No. This is your day. What would a Tern Harbor Day Committee be without a Palmer in charge? Someday, though, I'd like to stay to see that old Butch Moulder grab someone and it turns out to be one of those baymen in drag."

"Would be fun. I'd rather grab one of those baymen in his tight jeans, you know like someone else I used to know." Gloria reached under her loose over blouse and unconsciously adjusted the bottom of her bra.

"Someday you'll . . . Oh here they come." Amanda faded into her section of the house, as if she hadn't been there, as if she belonged to the old house as much as the posts that support up.

Dressed in uncertain late summer and early autumn colors, the committee members greeted one another as they tracked across the gravel driveway and the wide entry doors. They filed past the polished bells. Sandra Nelson carried a planter of begonias; someone else had brought a bouquet of fresh garden flowers. Helen Delaney gasped when she saw the wide main room, its view, its decoration, the buffet and the antique silver service.

"You know," she said to the blond woman next to her. "I really volunteered for this moment. The Palmers have done this for years and always start with this luncheon. Isn't it great?"

"Just terrific," the wide-eyed blond woman lurched forward when Butch Moulder brushed his hand across her as he paused briefly behind her.

"Hi folks. Help yourselves to the buffet and please enjoy the champagne cocktail." Butch grinned at the blond woman.

Lunch was noisy with polite chatter of community people impressing each other with their wonders of summer travel, visitors from abroad and their children's college tours. After coffee, tea, and dessert, the clanging of one the porch's brass bells called the group to attention.

Alice Kelly hovered over the family pictures on the piano. "Aren't these beautiful? They must tell a history of the Village."

"Don't see any recent photos, though," Fannie Delberti held a picture of Gloria in her ballet costume.

"Must have been so hard for her, so stoic at the memorial service." Alice Kelly dusted one of the frames. "She was wonderful, just standing there, talking to everyone."

"Did you notice the tall young man, auburn hair, real cute? Never saw him here in town before. Never even went over to pay respects to Gloria." Fannie Delberti squinted. "Just stood in back. Couldn't miss him. Dark suit stood out against all that white of the walls and pews and railings. Isn't it something how white that church is? Must cost a fortune to keep it up."

"Think he was there with the Indian lady who works for them. He spoke to her outside and then drove off in that fancy little car."

"Yes," Alice smiled. "He was cute wasn't he? I think everyone in town was at the service. Did you notice they kept the front row empty like they were waiting for someone? I'll bet no one showed up from the family, you know the Brooklyn part. Well you know! I guess Butch wants to get things going."

Butch Moulder made the usual announcements, organized the plans for Tern Harbor Day which would take place in May at the end of the College's exams. Committee chair people were appointed. Alice and Tom Sloves would organize the marathon, which would end with a turn around the park.

Claire Furley, short, stocky, rosy cheeked, was the obvious choice to chair the chowder contest. "Bet she always wears an apron and grins over pots on her stainless steel stove or bends over her food preparation island." The blond woman's hands gave away her avoidance of kitchen work. She watched Butch throughout the meeting.

"Butch'll get his," sneered the blond woman. "I'll never forget that he stood behind me and pinched me. He'll get his."

The group left with the chatter of accomplishment that turned to polite laughter. Butch was placing the meeting paraphernalia into his car when the blond woman passed behind him. He plummeted dumbfounded into the open trunk. The blond woman held her hand high, snapped her fingers, and shouted, "Returned your favor, Butch honey."

———◆———

The afternoon was peacefully quiet. Gloria sampled the shrimp salad, then settled onto a reclining deck chair and fell asleep, cumulus clouds, heaped onto each other like cars in a highway accident. White sails raced back to the safety of Tern Harbor as the bright afternoon turned dark shades of gray. Flattening clouds blotted out resistance from the cerulean sky. Billowing black clouds twisted angrily from the northeast preparing to release their rage on the Sound and the Island.

Gloria, folded the green afghan into a square cushion, placed it on the piano bench, reached over the fireplace mantle, lifted the driftwood framed seascape from its hook, and dropped it behind her father's club chair. She rearranged furniture, moved chairs and lamps until they occupied their original spots, and waited for the coming evening gale. She grimaced with the same agony that had contorted her stomach when she heard of her father's first stroke.

Gloria walked to the windows and shuddered at the sight of the red buoy; imagined her father rising and falling in the surf; imagined him pounding against the rock; and imagined the rescuers' sounds as they called to one another during that treacherous storm. She imagined the mythical warrior waiting to rise to his ancestral paradise and of the woman, impaled on devil rock, singing her final hymn toward the sea. She shrugged and rubbed her hands as she watched the red buoy being tossed by the darkening bay and listened to the endlessly clanging bell. Treacherous storms kindled her passionate hatred for that red marker. She felt rising fury at the bell's clanging and the feeling that her father's triumphant stroke had sentenced her to Tern Harbor.

"Miserable bastard! Must have paid someone to cause the stroke, just to get me back. And now . . . now . . . this. Damn him."

Nighttime pitched the house into welcome darkness. The front hallway's faded amber light crept along the brass bells as if to clang them for the deaf, leaped across the piano, and family pictures that had always frightened Gloria when she was a child. She imagined the people in the pictures could come to life, capture and pull her into one of their silent frames.

There was Guiseppe Palmieri with his arm around Tomohawk Henry Steelehart, from whom he had purchased this land that became Tern Harbor. Together, they had paced off the boundaries that extended from Long island

Sound on the north to the South Woods, west to the big bay and east to the steep cliffs. Guiseppe Palmieri promised to use the property for hunting, fishing, and a small house on the land which he promised to keep forever unscathed.

Judge Caleb Winston, owner of waterfront property west of Tern Harbor, made a series of court rulings and paid his friends to divert the emerging Rail Road away from the coastline and far enough south so that it would not interfere with the private estates.

T. Henry Steelehart, knowing that if he did not sell the land, he would lose it by some white man's trick, moved his family to the safer ancestral home on the North Fork of the Island. The Steelehart children and grandchildren married Steeles, Harts, Saunders, Merediths, Palaskis, VanHagels, and an alloy of other names.

The narrowing strip of crop-yielding land became a sacred trust; clean water in the streams, bays and wide Long Island Sound promised food from Nature; the air and sky remained the playground of the birds.

Obscure books of original foreclosure documents dating into the 17th century filed in the Riverhead Town Clerk's office, trace the methodical taking of those properties from unprotected and illiterate Native Americans, taking lands that had been inhabited for more than 30,000 years.

Old T. Henry's stories of the island, the water, and the wind encouraged his descendants to buy land and adapt to "white Joe's" ways. Old men repeat those stories around the campfires and together recite his caution. "No one ever owns land. Our people will never own land. We use it. We hunt on it or farm it. We keep the land. But we never own it. We never own anything, only have the use while we are here. We are the caretakers. Only white Joe thinks he owns anything. But when you adopt his ways, remember who you are. He will. And beat him at his own game."

"White Joe has taken everything from us. Someday, take it back. His way! If you are like him, buy it from him. Beat him at his own game, but remember who you are."

Steve Palmer roared "Garbage," whenever he heard this story. Now Gloria had the bill of sale that had been pulled from the dusty archives and understood how her father had violated his family promise.

"If this land was sacred to Old T. Henry, then by God it will be kept that way," old Guiseppe Palmieri had written. "Besides who the hell wants to build anything here in this forsaken place."

"But that," Gloria murmured, "was 1867."

———————

Thunder shocked Gloria back to childhood days when she would huddle alone in this room. Ghosts would emerge from those photographs, ghosts of children, their parents, and grandparents; phantoms of relatives who had lived at different times, in different ways, came alive, sharing habits, food, laughter, and tears. Children grown into their parents, emerged from different photographs. They mingled as if they were at a celebration, as if they were an orchestra waiting for the conductor, and tonight they seemed confused and pleased that the conductor was missing.

In the midst of the collection of relatives, Great-Grandpa Guiseppe Palmieri sat stiff and erect, overseeing the tumultuous gathering from his perch in a gnarled, high backed chair; Great-Grandma, wearing her one fancy white dress, stared beyond the photographer announcing the moment of her triumph. From that wedding moment she would be Rosetta Palmieri, mistress of the Palmieri household. The seated patriarch could do anything but she, Rosetta Palmieri, would have Guiseppe's children, keep his house, and determine the Palmieri future.

Grandpa Alphonso wore his white suit, white shoes, and white lapel flower. His broad smile revealed evenly sized, straight teeth; Gloria had inherited that smile which she knew could be more potent than any of the drinks served in the family's Brooklyn restaurant. It shielded the trait that was passed to his eldest son and from him to Gloria.

She had repeatedly heard the word "familia" lovingly from her mother who described Grandpa Alphonso. Everyone who worked for Grandpa was made to feel like "familia". Their problems were his, their joys were his, their welfare was important to the business success. When new people arrived from the "old country", Grandpa was there to greet them, help them find their families, or get settled if they were alone. Everyone knew him, loved his smile, everyone, except perhaps his children.

Steven Palmieri choked acrimoniously at the word "familia". As the oldest son in this Italian family, he expected to be treated with respect, inherit his father's admiration, and the lion's share of the family fortune. He worked in the restaurant until he went to New York University where he learned to enjoy things beyond the family, found the joys of beer, smoking, and sex.

Gloria bit her lip as she thought of her father, crippled, angry, and helpless in his wheel chair. She imagined him, useless, with a harem and speculated at his unquenchable thirst for conquests. She guessed that in his college days he would bring young women to the country house for torrid weekends. She thought of his learning to hunt, use that rifle, fish, and become free from family constraints. "So why were you such a control freak, why did you do that to me? Gloria wondered if her father had developed his plans for Tern Harbor during those early days, she wondered if he had contrived to take his revenge. She wondered if he did that while hunting or making love.

Steve's younger brother Alphonse was the family favorite. He managed the development of the seafood market in Manhattan while assisting their sister Marie's expansion of the Palmieri restaurant. His smile and personality reinforced the tradition of making all the customers feel like they were coming to visit; "when you have visitors," he insisted, "they must always be welcome, respected and treated as if they are in your home."

"I am my family's Esau," Steve would say. Privately, he had plans beyond the "familia" heritage. After his father's death, he felt that he had been disinherited and changed his name to Palmer. Alphonse inherited the family fish market in New York; his sister Marie managed the restaurant, and inherited the family's Brooklyn house. Steven had been given the "useless" land on Long Island. Each of the children was to take turns with Grandma until she joined Gramps in Heaven. She would jokingly shake her finger at Grandpa's picture, "We'll go back to Italy and when I find you up there," she crossed herself and scolded. "Then you'll have to stay home and eat my pasta."

———◆———

Gusting wind, pounding rain, and lightning startled Gloria. The Connecticut shorefront went dark. Rain lashed the windows erasing the family picture reflections. She listened to a car approaching, then speeding away, its sound trailing with the wind. A triumphant stream of light crashed into the bay, exploded across power lines and turned the landscape, the houses, and Gloria's room into impenetrable darkness. Thunder muffled the sound of a car rolling across the gravel driveway.

Tapping on the front door punctuated the dark silence. Gloria opened the door and extended her hand to the shadowy figure. "Glad you're here. Almost forgot it's Tuesday."

4

Billy's Café

The white BMW convertible defied Wednesday morning's blazing sunrise, sped east along Route 25A, turned onto Orient Village's South Road, and cornered abruptly into Billy's Sweet Shop parking lot. Matt leaped over the car door, zipped the toneau cover, and headed for the corner table that had been reserved for him since the café opened.

"Hey Billy, how's it going?"

"OK Matt. How's about some coffee? It's that new mixture, forgot its name, but it sure is delicious. Here, try it. One of the girls will be out to help you in a few minutes. They just got in, guess they had a big night."

Billy Bastone's copycat ability to open the café, clear tables, get the cook and waitresses busy at their jobs was learned at Sally's diner.

He chattered to friends or the empty shop, mimicking his mother.

"Do you ever see Gloria Palmer? Now there's a classy lady. Helped me get this place. Holds the mortgage. Did you know that Matt?"

"Had an idea she did."

"Of course. Cheez. You sold me the place. Never could figure how she got the price down or even found this place."

"Well she's a sharp business lady. In the blood, I guess." Matt sniffed the coffee as a connoisseur exuberant over old brandy. "Coffee smells good Bill. What did you call it?"

"Forgot its name. Forget a lot of stuff that doesn't mean much anyway."

"I have a very good memory. Remember details about things that happen."

"My mom's like that. She can remember the dress she wore for confirmation or for the prom or anything at all."

Matt sipped his coffee. Billy's perpetual motion stopped, time froze, his gaze locked onto Matt Steele. Billy was heading up that rickety staircase, staring into Mr. Palmer's nefarious eyes, eyes that commanded, eyes that were hungry, eyes that angered and terrified Billy. He remembered Gloria Palmer's soft, helpful and compassionate touch.

He stared at Matt, saw the same compassion, the authority, and the wonder Matt had for Billy's accomplishment and well being. He saw the eyes that would protect him from all predators.

Billy shook his head and heard Matt, "Really? Bet you can't remember the color of your underwear."

"I always can," smiled Billy. "White."

Fishermen, straggling from a night casting from the shore, jammed into the café. Some were silent, some noisy, smiling revealing success of the night's efforts and some showing the results of flipping open cans but all were ready for the hearty breakfast specials and for Billy's chatter.

"Some night you guys had. Waited out the storm, I guess. Didn't think you'd make it."

"Well, I got on a buzz before old man moon chased them clouds and let us out on the beach. Must have been, what guys, about 2 o'clock."

"Help yourself to coffee. Girls are a little slow this morning. Any of you guys keeping them busy last night? Yah! Right! Ferne would have knocked you on your butts if you tried." Billy chuckled as he motioned to his backside.

"She's some piece of . . . work." The fishermen went into conversations about women they would like to have.

"What would you do if that Kidman babe gave you the nod?" Each of the men continued to spin fantasies.

"Well guys," Matt shouted to them as he backed out the front doors. "Sometimes I'll tell you about it." He revved up the convertible motor, and drove off grinning.

"Enough listening to their BS," he mused. "Listened to enough of that from too many people. Can't wait to have a place away from everyone, looking out over the water, or the mountains, or looking at the stars. Can't wait to escape voices from the past. Can't wait to be free of all these damn things.

Matt talked into the tape recorder on the car seat. "Publication day. Look over the papers' financial reports, work with Larry at Island Commercial, and put together the funds to finish the job.

"One more newspaper will complete the circle, one more parcel brings home all the land, then if only I could release the lovers, let them fly free, let me soar with them to the sky warriors. OK Matt, get real."

——◆——

The fishermen watched Matt speed out of the driveway. "Yeah, like Matt ever had any big movie star in his car."

"Or anywhere near his, well you know."

"Think he's still a virgin?"

"What kind of stupid thing to ask? Look at the guy. You think there's not some babe's going to grab his ass? I'd like to spend one week in his bedroom."

"With him?"

"No stupid, in bed with the women who probably parade though there. You know with his background and his dough."

"I'll put money on it, he's not all that good. Heard some, uh, some stuff about that wise ass, flying out of here trying to make us look stupid."

"Yeah, what you hear?"

"Well, you know his Uncle George. Everyone knows he's a real chicken fricassee, fruitcake. He doesn't hide it. Well I heard they once, maybe still do, well had a thing going. Just heard. His old man, when he was around, used to hang out in bars and tell how he found the two of them feeling each other up. Nobody believed it then. But you know where there's smoke." Saul's erotic smile curled his lips toward his left cheek.

"Saul," Salty ventured. "That was when Matt was fourteen, or was it twelve, and anyway don't spread old rumors."

Challenged, Saul leaned forward. "Okay. Did you ever notice that George works close with Matt? When Matt takes off, who's in charge? And I hear they sometimes go into Matt's office, close the door and ... well you can guess as well as the next guy."

Billy was chattering with two young girls who were left over from the summer at a local cottage. "Hey Saul. Come into the kitchen so I know how to save those fish of yours."

As Saul walked into the back room, the door swung closed behind him. Billy put his right hand under Saul's chin, pressed against his Adam's apple and lifted the man against the white tile wall. "You ever talk that way about Matt Steele, here or anywhere and I'll put you up on a hook in the freezer with those damned fish of yours. Don't ever spread those nasty rumors about him. His old man was a no good drunk. Everyone knows it. If he's good to his uncle, it's because George is his uncle and because he does a damn good job." Billy's grip tightened around his prisoner's neck. "You go out there and you tell them you were fooling. And by the way, where do you think he goes when he's out of town. Don't you think he has some great women waiting for him?"

Saul had never seen Billy get angry. He felt the hook sinking into his back. He retracted his gossip. "Just chatter guys. Heard he's a real stud."

"Hey Billy," whispered Salty. "Did you ever have any of them summer dames?"

"Outta here you guys. Taking up too much space. Pay your bills first."

"Any of them know the color of your underwear?"

"They all do," Billy hummed as he counted out change and looked out the back window at his clothes line.

"White."

5

Matt

Burnt umber and pumpkin orange blanket the landscape after summer people leave the East End for their playgrounds in the cities. Hypnotic shades of crimson, dark green, yellow squash, cauliflower white, black berry stain, and bare brown grape vines waft autumn's perfume across Long Island's North Fork. The annual encampment reunites Native families that have been blended into the white man's community, estranged from their ancient language, and separated from their heritage. Vagrant summer flowers, dying leaves, drying pine needles, toadstool shrouded fallen limbs, and damp, deserted springtime nests congeal into the subtle mist that rises from the same forest beds that once slipped under the feet of Native children.

Late night campfires, exuberant youthful dancing, and stories told by glossy eyed old men buttress uniting traditions. Beyond names imposed by European settlers and beyond belonging to the American dream, blood pounding through pulsating veins revives the Native experience. Ancient blood that runs deeper and longer than the earliest European settlers appearance, responds to the hushed call of Autumn, the smoke of the campfires, and the bond to the earth.

The wind had called Matt home to fulfill the destiny his mother had indelibly tattooed on his soul, to rebuild ancient blood lines into a cohesive family intent on self help that would enable them to become a nation within a nation. It was Autumn, the time for family leaders to meet in the walnut paneled room overlooking the narrow strip of land between Great Peconic Bay and Long Island Sound.

Matt moved to the arched northeast windows, extended his arms, grasped the top edges of the window frame, and blocked the silver morning light of the rising sun. A halo surrounded his body reinforcing the aura of authority.

He surveyed the cornfields, orchards, vineyards and the undisturbed forest that extended past the main road, imagined secret things under the trees where the old Indian trail lay hidden from unknowing eyes. He imagined he could feel tall grass brush against his face as he would run barefoot through the woods. He imagined the slipping sense of coarse sand and small rocks as he threw off his clothes and dove into the rising tide.

The forest concealed the house and land that could be traced from old T. Henry Steelehart in a direct line to his mother.

Matt scanned Peconic Bay's coastline to the promontory where he had built the new house that resembled a teepee, round in a circle that had no beginning and no end, the same as the figure formed in the ground when young people danced around the campfires. It was an emblem of the universal continuum of land, sea, and family and the obligation to welcome and protect the natural world.

Wind gusts advancing from the West blew a windsock to stiff attention. He heard the wind whispering, "I am breathing faster and faster and heading your way. Prepare your boat and we will play before the East and the West begin their battle. We can fly across the bay."

Matt sailed with powerful winds, skied defiant slopes, and ran over untried trails. Challenge had become the cement of his foundation, had invaded his psyche, became reinforced by years of enduring pain, dominated years of survival in a hostile world, and strengthened the Native core that enabled him to endure the constant needs of those who drafted him as leader. Challenge had brought him home, carried him to this conference room, dared him to rebuild the Native American conclave, and defined his mission to save the land.

"It's been a long trail to get where we are," he spoke in the subdued voice learned around the campfires.

The family leaders, gathered around the oval table, heard the soft spoken words. Dynamic changes to the families, reuniting them with common goals, had followed Matt's return. He echoed, for them, the voice of old Tomahawk Steelehart.

Most of the counsel elders retained marks of their Native heritage. Some had the dark eyes of their ancestors, high cheekbones, and the sharp nose and long nostrils that allowed them to inhale perfume of the woods and water.

"Strange," elders would tell at the campfires. "Strange, Tomahawk would say that the white man would pay for the land and think he owns it. We own nothing." That's what the elders would tell at the campfires.

Matt understood that generations of marriages had changed family names but the genes cling to the blood, are constant as the sky, and ancient spirits still infect their communal souls.

"There's another reason we are here," Matt turned to the family leaders. "We must take back everything that was taken from us. Remember old Tomahawk's words. Beat them at their own game. Some of you, remember my mother's husband, remember what he was like, and how he tried to take everything from her and me. We beat him at his own game. And we, our families, have done a good job so far, but there's more to be done."

"Matt," Harry Meredith broke in. "I'm interested in buying that tract along Peconic Bay near Sag Harbor. Could probably buy up the cottages along the beach as long as no one knows that it's going to one owner."

"Speak a little slower, Harry. I can't keep track of the agenda and take the minutes if you talk so fast," Lloyd Feather admonished.

"We'll have to get you a tape recorder," Harry smiled.

The motionless family members nodded approval. "Figure out how much you need. The family fund is available. Remember, no interest, but pay it back."

Lloyd Feather read the agenda in all its detail. First item was the families' private fund which had been established to advance ownership of property, business, banking facilities, and farming.

"Lloyd. We all know about the agenda. Can't you just give us each a copy," Harriet Barrett scolded.

He glared over his glasses. Passed copies of the agenda and yielded the floor to Matt.

"Matt," Harriet Barrett got his attention.

"Harriet, you're looking beautiful. What's up?" Matt returned her smile.

"You know, some of the family members, John Montagne's family, haven't made any real efforts or contributions but want money for a house and land. I don't think we should do much if they haven't, well, haven't done anything, and haven't got anything."

"No one, I mean no one," Matt flushed as he pounded the table, "no one is excluded. No one is to be made to feel apart, separated. They, the ones who don't know what it is like to feel excluded, to be outsiders, they won't help. We will. No one, no one, no one with a trace of Indian blood is not one of us."

Harriet raised her hands in surrender. "Okay. You're right. Let's get on with the list."

Lloyd Feather smiled at Harriett, meticulously read each item on the agenda, and waited for Matt to end the meeting.

Matt hesitated, "I have one more project. One more thing to do to really beat them at their game, one more parcel that needs to be retaken; but this has been a wild stormy season and I intend to have fun. Tourists are gone, and this land, this end of the Island, is ours."

"In case of rain, we'll move the picnics into the Polo Lodge," Prentis Falwek mumbled as his palsied head wobbled. "I'll take pictures. Lots of pictures."

"Prentis, love," Harriet hugged him. "Try not to jiggle when you take my picture."

The room was empty and Matt flipped through his life as one might through a family album. "Never had any pictures," he mused. "Just images, just memories."

Matt was born Matthew Xavier Christopher Steele Donovan. The pandemonium of father-inflicted beatings turned to melancholy acceptance, then to the sense of deserved punishment for the guilt of ever having been born. It prepared him for the years during which rage beat his Native sense of destiny into recessive corners of consciousness. He became the most feared football player in the Island's East End Junior League. Sean Donovan smashed fists into his son so he would know true fear and would enjoy drawing blood from opponents. Matt's father boasted to his bar stool associates about his son's bravado and conquests.

Matt considered himself a failure when he couldn't compete at basketball with High School blacks.

"Don't want you playing with them niggers." Sean Donovan would throw Matt against the wall, push his huge hand around the boy's neck. "They're not real Americans. Think they're so damn good. Like them Indians. Think they're so frigin good." He lifted Matt off the floor so they were nose to nose.

"But, I'm . . ." Matt tried to talk, but the thumbs pressed against his throat.

"You're what? One of those damn Indians, like your mother? If you're really my kid you're not Injun. Irish like me. Hear. They're as un-American as some fucking Jews or Niggers, just a bunch of mix bloods. You ain't none of them!"

———◆———

Matt could mumble his family tree while elders, gathered around campfires, recited stories of things that used to be, told myths of giants and devils, and breathed freedom. They told the saga of the lover's tragedy. Matt dreamed of the day he would be the hero to set them free. He dreamed of leading tribes and defeating invaders and dreamed of freeing the land and the sky. He dreamed of being free.

A gray haired elder uttered the old stories as if he, personally, had known the common ancestors and as if old Tomahawk Steelehart had spoken directly to him. "Remember," Tomahawk would have said to him, "remember that when you become like them, remember who you are and beat them at their own game."

———◆———

When the conclaves were over, Sean Donovan would stumble into the log house. "Tie the little dick up," he'd shout at Amanda. "Tie him to the side of the bed with those Indian knots so I can get good shots at him." Sean Donovan would finish a can of beer. "Teach him what happens if he cries when he gets hit by one of them niggers anywhere! Teach him to take any crap from that kike coach. Not be a sissy, no son of mine, even if he ain't, teach him."

"He's yours," Amanda whispered.

"Tricked me, yeah, bitch, tricked me. Tie him now," Sean screamed. "I friggin married you. Got nothing. Not a damn dime. Keep him ready or I'll tie the two of you together and slam the hell out of both of you." Matt held out his hands so he would be tied and become her surrogate.

"Just don't let him hit you." Matt pleaded with his mother.

Matt anticipated whippings, nightly terror, and was relieved when he finally experienced the pain. He transferred hatred for his father to all authority, all who could inflict pain, and to anyone who he envisaged as an enemy.

His father's ranting was welded to Matt's consciousness. "I'll whip your ass so ya' never even think about hanging around with boys. Ever come home with one of them fag earrings, it'll be the last time ya' hear. Can't have another one of them in the family. You ever let my brother George in here, I'll, well just don't."

Matt waited to defy his father until the day when his Uncle George would leave Christmas gifts on the front doorstep and quietly leave.

"Now I can get back at the drunk," Matt tightened his fists, grinned, and ran out from behind the house. "Uncle George, how's it hanging?"

"Don't get wise with me young man."

"No. Really Uncle George, how've you been?"

"Fine. What've you been up to?"

"Collecting baseball cards and some really good magazines. Old man doesn't know. Come on take a look."

Matt led George to his room, shut the door behind them, clicked the lock. He pulled out the cards, handed them to George and then felt under his bed for a copy of PLAYGIRL with the centerfold fully extended. He handed it to George, held onto the magazine and placed his hand on George's hand. The two held silent for a few minutes, then Matt leaned over to his dresser, found a roll of electrical tape and started to wind it around his Uncle's wrist.

George leaned forward, placing both hands behind his back and Matt continued winding until he had the man tied to the chair by hands and feet. He wound the tape around George's exposed chest and was amazed that the man, as muscular and clearly as strong as his father made no sounds, no objections, just seemed to wait for what might come next. It was as if he had done this before.

Matt raised a thick black belt and whacked at his uncle's chair, once, twice, three times, expected to hear screams of protest, but heard nothing. Then, Matt moved close behind the chair leaned over his uncle. "Turn you on George. Your brother will be here soon. I can't wait to see what happens when he thinks we were … He keeps screaming at me, but he's really afraid he's like you. Can't wait 'til he thinks we were screwing around."

Matt hid the magazine and the cards. Unlocked the door and started tying himself to the bed. He had learned to do the task on his own, knew the knots, knew he could break loose if he wanted to, knew he would not because the savagery had become habit and he told himself he was saving his mother. But tonight would be worse. He knew it and waited.

He pulled his bound uncle to the floor next to him. The pickup truck rolled across the gravel yard, his father kicked open the front door and started yelling, "Hey creep. Where's some food? You were supposed to have it whenever the Indian isn't here. Where the fuck are you?"

Adrenaline raced through his young body that waited for the whip that was sure to split open his back. He wanted to calm the struggling, quivering body of his uncle George lying next to him. He was exhilarated with the ecstasy of awakening his father's worst fears. As his father came near the room, Matt placed his free hand on his uncle's leg.

"Jesus! The gene went from George to the creep. The fag gene got the both of you. Well, all right then. It ain't me. Thought you'd get me angry, eh! Show me some of your stuff. Go ahead creep. Feel him good or is it over? Creep, get yourself loose then cut the fag loose. I'm going to teach you a few new tricks. You gotta try it sooner or later," Matt's father smirked and hiccupped. "I'll get the barbecue going. You stay, George, for a good fag dinner."

Matt freed himself and his uncle. Deadly fear overcame him. "The old bastard won't let this go. He'll wait for us and do some shit when he's good and ready. Matt's father loaded the grill with charcoal and poured flammable liquid over the pit. "Drop a match on this and get this son-of-a-bitch going," he screamed at George. "Got to get something from inside."

"Old man's up to something. Better get outa here George," Matt urged.

"Nah! Seen him like this before. What makes you think he's never seen me, watched before? What makes you think he's not afraid it could be him? The fucker is probably part gay himself."

"Found some great stuff to really get this fire going." Sean Donovan approached the glowing coals. "Paper burns good."

He flipped baseball card after baseball card into the blaze. Matt grabbed his father's arm. "Those are mine. You know it," he grabbed for the flying cards. Sean Donovan laughed louder and louder, knocked Matt to the ground, kicked the base of his back, kicked his groin, tossed the remaining cards onto the fire.

"Cut it out Sean. Leave the kid alone or I'll . . ." George moved toward his brother.

Sean Donovan hurled his brother to the ground and started flailing both victims with the stiff leather belt. "Did you think I'd let you two get away with crap like that?" Whack! Whack!

"Sean, nothing happened. The kid's straight. He wanted to get you off. He did!" Whack, Whack, Whack.

"The little bastard." Whack, whack.

"You're the bastard who trained me to handle pain, never cry. C'mon man, C'mon." Matt smiled when he recalled George's words, "The fucker is probably gay himself." He smiled. "One of these days I'll swing the belt and maybe break the old bastard's arms."

<hr />

Matt, Stan Welsh and Bill Robins were the High School football team's dangerous trio until Matt got speared by one of his own teammates during a scrimmage. He smashed his helmet into his assailant's face, forgot the pain, pulled the other boy to the ground, wrapped his forearms around the boy's neck, and squeezed. He squeezed until the other players jumped on top of him, spiking his legs and ankles. Matt was dragged to the ambulance with blood still seeping through his uniform. From the stretcher, he stared at the smiling coach congratulating the tackler and high-fiving the rest of the team. Matt was accused of starting the fight, was barred from athletics, and forced to attend classes in a room separated from the rest of the student body.

Stan and Bill, consoling their friend, were finishing a six pack while sitting along the old Indian path. Matt's legs had healed, and he was able to lace the black boots, which had become part of his wardrobe. The high boots helped hold his legs in place and gave him a new sense of strength, and a feeling of invincibility. Stan and Bill were talking about their girl friends. "Stella is great," Stan was gesturing her curves and puckering his lips.

"Yeah," Bill leaned back. "She can really . . . oh can she ever!" He pushed his hips back and forth while rubbing his thighs.

"Cut the crap," Stan protested. "She's my girl."

"Oh yeah!" Bill continued the action. "Yours and mine and let's see."

They started a beer-teased argument, one of those nonsense things that teen boys do, starting as a joke, then got tougher. Bill's forearm came flying forward smashing into Stan's cheek. The crunch of bone was accompanied by the painful blurt, "You damn nigger. I'll bust your black ass for this."

The words rang through Bill Robins's head. "Damn nigger. Black ass." He had read those words on the school bathroom walls, seen the cartoons drawn on his gym locker and now they came from someone he had called friend. "Nigger. Black ass." He searched Matt's eyes for reassurance.

"There it is!" Bill swung at Stan. "See! One lousy thing and what you really think comes out. I was warned. Stay away from me white boy, honky."

Matt had never used those words to a friend or heard them from his friends. If Stan was a "honky" and Bill, a "nigger", what was he? No one had ever thought of him as anything but a white boy. He was accepted as a white boy, heard all the chatter about the stupid Indians and feared the day when his classmates might turn on him. His heritage had been screened behind generations of Steeleharts, Merediths, Harts, and now Donovans. His mother, always working with families away from home, or too battered to appear, never attended any games or public functions with Matt. No one, he told himself, would ever find out what he really was.

It had been a long time since the Indian blood was pure. Matt's mother, direct descendant from Old Tomahawk Steelehart, was pure. Why would anyone think of him as anything but white, a Donovan, burnt umber hair, dark at the roots, more auburn as it got longer, pale green eyes? But now, if Stan was "honky" and Bill was "nigger", would he be discovered? Would everyone know that he was by blood and in his heart, Indian?

Panic hammered the message. He knew his enemy, the one who could reveal his ancestry, was the friend who had just called him "honky." He knew anyone who could give away his history, his secret, was an enemy.

Matt and Stan tackled Bill, smashed his body with fists, kicks and tree limbs. Matt took out his pocketknife and scraped the letter "N" along his former friend's forearm. "Stay away from me forever, stay away, stay away."

Tears filled Matt's eyes, blood trickled down Bill's arm, Stan looked on with awe and Matt ran.

He ran through the woods, ran like his ancestors would have run through these woods, ran until he fell onto the cool sand, buried his head and cried.

He cried as he had when his father started those regular beatings, he cried after seeing his mother whacked into submission by his drunken father, cried knowing he would be next. Cried knowing he would be whipped with a black belt when his father found out what he had done. Then he stopped crying. Leaned against a cypress tree and tossed stones into Peconic Bay.

"No more crying. Should have run away long ago except for Old Tomahawk telling me to stay, telling me I would have to stop the old bastard when he really went after my Mom. He won't ever lay a hand on me again. If he does, it'll be the last time."

Matt climbed to the roadway, walked along the dark silent path home. He saw the shadow of the belt swinging through the air. As he opened the door, he was ready, reached up, grabbed the belt, pulled it and his father through the doorway. Matt had the belt, whirled it over his head, lashed at his father's legs, beat his head with a tree limb. Matt pointed a knife into Sean Donovan's alcohol soaked mouth immobilizing the terrified man. "One move, one, and you'll never speak again. Never touch my mother or me again. Get your stuff together, get out and never come back."

Sean Donovan hobbled to the yellow pick-up, dropped his tools and knapsack into the back, and fumbled with the keys. He drove to the front of the house, brought a gray glob from the back of his throat and blew it at Matt.

They say at the family picnics that Sean Donovan took off with some rich woman, they say at the picnics that he walked, drunk, into the Long Island Sound. They say at the campfires that the blind woman mistook him for one of the sailors and no one ever saw him again.

Matt expected Bill Robbins and his black friends to come looking for him and despite his dislike for joining any groups, found his shield.

It was a hot Friday night when he wandered through downtown Riverhead, followed the odor of Pizza, ordered a slice, grabbed the strip aproned man who asked to see his proof of age and refused to sell him beer. The restaurant erupted in teen age battles; one black clothed boy pulled Matt out of the store before the screaming police cars blocked the street, handed him a bottle, and said,

"C'mon, I'll show you a cool place. Oh yeah, I'm Greg Clement."

Matt hesitated, then followed Greg to a brightly lit house that was alive with loud music and boys and girls in black clothing. The blaring sounds stopped, a crew cut, athletic looking man stepped up to the microphone, and then Matt saw the unfurled Swastika.

Carl Gohrman spoke about rules set up by those who would control these young people, the minorities who were taking over their society, and the Jews who controlled their schools and their futures. He exhorted them to take America back, to learn what it meant to join the skinhead movement, and to be part of something really big.

Matt shaved his head, wore black clothes and high boots, went through the indoctrination, and was recognized as a natural born leader.

6

Good Italian Boy

"Matt, Matt," Harry Meredith burst into the room, shook his young leader who was trembling against the window. "Matt, You OK?"

"Yes, OK. Just thinking."

"Storm is coming in fast. The boys are moving loose stuff and equipment into the barns and sheds. Anything else you want done?"

"Yes. Come with me onto the Hobie. Fun time."

"Are you nuts? Look at those windsocks. Going to be wild!"

"Seen it before, Harry. Only way to go. I'm on my way. Now! Come on!"

They sped along the dock, untied the catamaran, set up the sails and moved slowly along the sheltered sand bar. They pulled in ropes, adjusted the sliding seat, lay flat on the canvas, waited for the moment when rip tides circled the pontoons and they tilted at forty-degrees into the open bay. They jerked into the wind, Harry high up on the sliding board. Matt tore off his life jacket daring the waves to do him harm.

"We're going to drown. We shouldn't be here. Let's get back," Harry yelled while holding tight to the main sail rope.

"Don't worry, Harry. The wind is my grandmother. It's not worth being here without being in harm's way."

"Tell your grandmother to screw off."

Wind, water and memories battered the sailors. Matt stripped his shirt and shoes, allowed spray and waves to whip his straining body.

"This is a pain in the ass," Harry yelled as he slid from one side of the craft to the other to balance its changing direction. Matt worked sail and rudder, held his head back, shifted his body in unison with the shifting sails.

"Wheeehah, Wheeehah," Yell at it Harry. Don't worry man, I've been here before. Once in a gale like this with George. He dropped a package right in the middle of the Sound. Coming about."

"I may do that in my pants," Harry hissed into the wind.

"Different kind of package," Matt yelled.

The wind stopped as if listening for a confession before howling absolution.

"It'll be quiet for a few minutes and then watch your backside Harry. Wicked Wind," Matt smiled to the West. They lay flat on the canvas.

"What the hell kind of package did George have? What were you dropping out here, with . . . well with him?"

"He did something special for me once and he needed a favor." Matt lowered his hand into the lapping waves.

"I thought George was tootie fruity. He did you?" Harry taunted.

"Don't be a wise ass. Did something for me and then I had to help him. Did something for him and that's when I had to leave here."

Matt glanced toward the Connecticut shore then back to the Island, felt the soft breeze telling him there was time before West Wind and East Wind would come out of hiding.

"You know, Harry, how when they cremate dead guys, they drop their ashes into the sea? Well, what if you bypass the cremation? Just supposing now! What if my old man had come back to the house, and what if he was whipping away at my mother when I came home? And what if George got there at the same time? And what if the old man wound up with his brain splattered? And what if there was a storm coming and George wrapped his brother for burial at sea? What if we bypassed the cremation and just fed him to the crabs? Now just, what if?"

"As I said before" Matt's eyes were slits, he spoke through clenched teeth while he pulled tight on the main sail. "I helped George and he helped me."

"Here it comes, Harry." Wheehah, Wheehah, Wheehah."

The boat tipped sharply to the Sound, raced back to the sheltered bay. The two men focused on sailing, Matt screamed at the wind, rain, lightning, and thunder.

"Now Harry, remember I said, just suppose"

"Matt, come to the house, have dinner with us. Like to have you there." They sailed slowly toward the dock.

"Can't tonight, Harry."

Matt sat on a decaying rowboat. The tempestuous return had ripped unwanted memories from hidden recesses.

He closed his eyes and felt his stomach muscles tighten as they did on the day he helped his uncle George. Matt had been working as the night cleanup boy at the *Blueclaw Bulletin*. During his breaks, he sat at the computer, practiced writing football stories with himself as the hero. He wrote about the coach who sent a player to spear him and created the image of himself rising with a broken back, binding his legs, and racing onto the field to score the winning touchdown. He finished his work, turned off the lights, and walked home. He walked, then ran through the sumac-surrounded path. Thumping sounds came from the house. He hesitated at the edge of the clearing. The yellow pick-up, its driver side door open, seemed bigger than the house.

"Where's the son-of-a-bitch?" Matt screamed as he raced through the open front door and clicked his knife open. He turned into the center hallway and stopped. Sean Donovan was sprawled the width of the hallway, his head splattered against the wall, a baseball bat dropped across his back. Matt's mother sat on the edge of her bed, folding and unfolding a skirt she had been ironing. Matt could see beyond his mother's bedroom window to the shoreline where his uncle George was pulling a small boat toward the surf.

Matt looked from his mother to the splattered head to his uncle George, ran into the bathroom, put his head over the toilet and vomited, and then moved into the hallway. Blood covered his hands as he pulled the body onto a large canvas sheet that was spread outside the front door. George wrapped the body; they lifted it into the boat and moved into the turbulent Sound. The boat rocked, the body slid overboard as George brought the boat about and they raced through the battering rain.

Amanda scrubbed the floors and the walls with bleach obliterating the signs of violence. As Matt held his trembling mother, he saw the bruises on her back, neck, and shoulders.

"Mom, go to your job in Tern Harbor, and Mom, stay there. Nothing happened tonight. Nothing. I love you Mom. Go. Go." Matt and his mother stared into each other's eyes.

"George, I'll have to leave too. If anyone sees the truck they'll start looking for him and it'll bring trouble. Can't let that happen. Can't stay. Hate this place any way, and hate all those wise bastards at school. What're they going to be now that they graduated, garbage men, store clerks, truck drivers? Big shots up to now. Not me. I'll be better than any of them. They dumped me fast when they couldn't use me; black boys want to kill me and those nice white creeps think I'm a stupid dirt bag."

Matt tossed his clothes and boots into a duffel bag. "That's why I got into this stuff, and you know I really like it. They don't want me around, are scared of me. I'm not like them and they know it. They're afraid of me and they should be." Rage pounded against his throbbing temples. "I got to go. I'll take the pickup. No one will ever know what happened to him, won't even think about him. People will just think he took off again. No one even cares about me."

George wiped his hands on a paper towel. "Your Mom owns the truck, owns everything. She never put Sean on the house deed. She would never let Sean have it, no matter how much he whipped her. If she dies, it's left to you in her will. Did you know that?" George waited for an answer.

Matt stared silently as if his mother was looking at him. Anyone with Indian blood, he thought, would understand and feel his silent answer. "I'll head for New York. Have some friends there and will stay with the kid who got me into the skin head stuff."

"Where'd you meet such a guy? Does he know who, what you are?" George handed Matt a twenty-dollar bill.

"I am only what I want to be. I create what I am. Forget it, George, forget it. Thanks for the cash."

"Hope they never find out. They could kill you. If you ever need me, call. Collect!" George added.

"Tell Mom I'll get in touch in a while. Don't talk to her about him. Don't talk to her about our little sailing trip. Tell her I took one of the clam earrings. She'll understand."

———•———

The aging yellow pick-up truck raised eyebrows as it moved along the Long Island Expressway past Forest Hills. The swastika and iron cross mounted on its bumper drew raised fists, silent epithets from behind closed car windows, and laughter from teenagers who tossed foaming beer cans from open car windows.

The Manhattan skyline raised Matt's energy level; he parked the car on 28th Street and Eighth Avenue and sauntered up the ten floors to Greg Clement's apartment, expected to be welcomed by a shaved head, black clothes, boots, loud music, and German beer. The young man who greeted him wore sandals, denim slacks, short button down sport shirt, and held lemonade. Greg Clement was no longer the arrogant young Hamptonite who had introduced Matt to the skinhead culture.

Matt had been energized when the recruiter, Helmut Gohrman, spoke of leaderless groups with each individual acting on his own, imposing terror, and inflicting pain on enemies of America. He easily adopted the idea that each individual would be responsible for his own acts, a tenet that would motivate his actions. Matt reminded himself "Not until later I found out what I was being sucked into and understood that being on my own meant there was no one to come to help me. It was all for them, nothing for me. Yeah, found that out later."

He hardly recognized the young man who opened the door, wearing sandals, button down shirt, neatly combed blond hair, not the aggressive confederate he expected to find.

"Greg?"

"Matt? Hi kid. What a surprise."

"Well you said you would be here if I ever needed a place. Need a place!"

"Alone?"

"Sure. I travel light. Staying here in New York and thought I could stay with you."

"Sure you're alone? Yeah. Come in. What a jerk, keeping you here in the hallway. Come on in. My folks got up tight, worried about the way I looked. Said the neighbors would go nuts, and I'd never get into any decent college. Started NYU, even taking an art class at the New School, they have these great models, bare ass, unbelievable."

Matt muscled past Greg into the clean smelling apartment, ran his hand across the dustless dining room table, and looked into the mirror at himself and his host. "Just another jerk out for thrills," Matt thought. "Dumped it all at the end of summer when it was not giving him the kick, not giving him the rush, not giving him the drugs or sex or whatever the hell those bare ass models could."

"Okay if you stay for tonight, Matt. My folks are in the Hamptons and will be back tomorrow. I can help you find some of the . . . some place you might be able to get a room, cheap. Down in lower Manhattan, near the East Village." Greg seemed uneasy as he looked out the window.

"One of those gay joints? Forget it."

"No! Straight as an arrow. Maybe a mixed neighborhood. You know, Spics, niggers, and some of those nice people who want to show how cool they are living close to the others. Not far from a park where everyone hangs out. You'll like the music. Jamaicans bang those drums. Yeah. I'll get you in touch with Terry Halleran. Tell him your name is Donovan and you're in."

"Tell him my name is . . . okay . . . Donovan. "

Matt parked the yellow pick-up in front of the four floor tenement building. The entrance stairs decorated with chalk graffiti marked that this block belonged to a Puerto Rican gang. Matt could read signs, "I sprayed enough of these. They better stay out of my way. Live and let live. They better stay out of my way."

Terry Holleran's top floor apartment was smaller than Matt expected. A swastika poster and large picture of Hitler covered one of the living room walls, leaflets condemning the scourges of America, a bong, empty beer six pack, half empty bottle of cheap smelling liquor, a carton of Camels, and a hunting knife completed the decor. The room was furnished with a plump couch, an overstuffed tub chair, a bridge table, and a single floor lamp.

The softly lit apartment was a welcome sight to Matt. He dropped one duffel bag and carefully set down a second, heavier bag.

"Who're the Spics who massacred the front door?" Matt moved his unopened bags behind the couch.

"The PRS. That's the Puerto Rican Society. Keep clear of them until we can get a group together. Then we'll cut their balls off." Terry made a slashing gesture.

"They'll know who I am. Won't forget me. Don't need anyone else." Matt demonstrated the stooped stance, the stare he had developed and the steel tipped Doc Martens boots that could be defense, offense and intimidate prospective antagonists.

"Yeah, but not these mothers. Don't give a damn about getting hurt. The pussies never move alone, never act alone, ever."

"We'll see." Matt pulled his two duffels close to the couch and massaged the heavier bag.

"Have one of these. You'll enjoy the party." Terry offered a joint, wrinkled his round tipped nose and squinted.

"Never smoke the stuff. Never use dope. Dulls the senses."

"God damn, don't go stupid on me. You'll learn soon enough."

"What did you say?" Matt was face to face with his host.

"I said God damn don't . . ."

"Don't ever say that. If you guys are really skins you know there is no God. No religion. No leader. Only us, one by one working together, but no leader, no organization, no group that can be . . ."

"Can be what?" Terry snapped. "So they won't find out who we are? You must have smoked too much weed. They already know who we are. One day they'll blow us away. Yeah! In glory. Heil, Heil, Heil."

"Never use dope," Matt repeated.

"We'll see," Terry returned Matt's scowl. They had both learned the terrifying look. Both knew how to intimidate.

As they exited the building, Matt heard a shrill whistle, then the calls from somewhere in the graying street.

"Hey look. He's got a girl friend."

Hey chooch. Pft, pft, pft."

"Hey maricone."

Matt heard the clicking, then the bat against the garbage can, then they appeared, one, two, and then more than twenty of the PRS pounding sticks and bats. They tapped and moved threateningly toward Terry and Matt. "Hey chooch, what you doing in our street. Don't want you skin fags here. Gonna show you what happens to people we don't like."

"Terry, back into the house."

Terry froze, fear stained his dope-burnished face.

"Back upstairs, NOW! Damn it, move."

Terry recognized command and knew he had met his leader. They scrambled up the stairs, slammed and double locked the door.

Matt tore open the heavy bag.

"Shit," whispered Terry. "That's a fucking arsenal."

Matt found the AK47, snapped the magazine, put the gun carefully inside his front pant top, tightened the laces on his boots and checked the curved knife he had strapped to his right leg.

"Okay, let's go. Party time." Matt looked at his reflection in the window.

"Not going out that way. Over the roof and out the back. Just us two and a dozen of them." Terry pointed to the steel roof door.

"Move your butt. We're going out the front." Matt pushed his new roommate.

They moved into the street, heard the whistle, heard the same chorus. Matt pulled Terry to the front steps and waited for the PRS to come close, "A little closer." He breathed. He pulled out the gun and started firing, close to sneakers, close to bats, then into the air rapidly enough to scatter the PRS. He fired, reloaded and screamed, "Hey chooch, hey puss, puss, now you'll know who you're jerking around. Never forget me, I'm nuts and you never know when I have a gun and will blow you away.

"Oh shit," Yelled Terry into the empty street. "You're all bullshit."

"They'll leave me, us, alone. That's what skins are about. Let them know we fear nothing." Matt glared at Terry. "and they'll be afraid of me. Let's go party."

Terry passed the word rapidly, told everyone about Matt's arsenal, how "We took on and whipped the PRS." Matt was easily recognized as the natural born leader.

Ear straining heavy metal chords blared from the stage built under the East Side highway. The louder the music, the wilder the mash pit dancing by copycat teens. Matt watched beer guzzling and was repulsed at the sight and smell of dope. The group was excited about meeting at Tompkins Square Park for some real action.

He grabbed drug soaked Terry, led him back to the apartment. He checked his undisturbed truck and chalk mark on the curb that indicated, "this one OK. Hands off."

"Made my point, buddy." Matt pointed Terry's head toward the curb marking.

Dropping Terry onto the bedroom floor, Matt ordered, "Find your bed yourself." Crawl through this mess. It gets cleaned up in the morning."

Matt cleared the living room of empty cans, wrappers and cold pizza, dropped couch cushions on the floor, and checked the door and window locks. He placed a gun under the couch, fell onto the cushions and listened to the unfamiliar late night sounds of the city. He embraced sleep for the first time in the two days that started with one storm and ended the violence that had become part of his core.

He dreamed of the young boy swimming out to Target Rock, hanging his bathing suit like a claiming flag from the red buoy. He dreamed of looking up at the young girl waving someone's shirt. He dreamed of finding the terns' hiding place. He dreamed of finding the lost eyes, freeing the warrior and the Indian woman. He dreamed of seeing strange white clouds in the night sky. He dreamed of being free. Then he was asleep and there were no dreams.

Crashing sounds snapped Matt's slumber, he grabbed the gun and moved behind the couch, ready for any attackers. Unfamiliar noise bellowed through the apartment.

"No broken glass, what the hell?"

He slithered along the floor to the fire escape window, looked past the empty alleyway to flickering truck headlights. The call of "hup, hup" followed by clanking metal cans and the whirling of machinery preceded the garbage truck's crushing sound.

"Better get used to the claque, don't want to wet my pants at every new . . .What the frig is that?"

The truck had moved forward, followed by a street-cleaning wagon.

"Terry! Terry! When do they clean this side? What happens to my truck? Do I have to move it? What happens if I don't?"

"Umm. It's the friggin middle of the night. They come in the morning."

"It's tomorrow. I come alive at night, in the dark. What about the truck? When do I move it?"

"Check the street sign. How would I know?"

Terry lunged to his bed, took off his shirt, exposing the iron cross on his left biceps and the swastika on his left shoulder.

"Clean this mess in the morning or you'll need more than a tattoo to save you. Big deal tattoos." Matt pulled off his shirt, examined the muscular body developed from sports, weight training and working on farms and boats. He examined the elaborate spider web on his left elbow, the web earned for acts performed while still in high school and for the act he knew had driven him from home. "Still room for a few more."

He stared the stare at himself. Pulled a silver loop from his coin pocket. "There baby, find the mark, right above the clam. Bang. Blood feels warm, just a little pain. What the hell, deserve some pain, needed something new."

The curved knife slipped from above his boot. Matt had traced the letters S and H on his shoulder, traced it gently first with the sharp knifepoint, then drew blood and made the scar permanent.

"Where the hell does he keep peroxide or anything but aspirin? There, just cold water. There now that's Matt Steele, just for now, here comes, Yeah! Matt Donovan"

"There goes the phone. Hello," Matt's voice softened.

"Hello, Terry."

"No. He's still sleeping. Who's this."

"Tell the drunken Mick to get his backside out of bed and get to work. You need a job? We need a lot of help."

"I'll get him, but who the hell is this."

"Al. Get the Mick down here. You need a job? What's your name?"

"Matt. Matt Don..." he paused suspecting this guy did not want to hear another Irish name.

"How do I know," Al was shouting to someone. "All the damn noise down here. It's Don something. Probably Donitelli, a good Italian name. You know anyone with a truck?"

"Yeah! I have a pick-up. The name is St ... Matt hesitated, that is Don ..."

"Yeah good! Bring it. We need someone to make deliveries. You know how to use a knife?"

Matt glanced in the mirror, put out his tongue, and stuck the point of his knife toward his mouth. "Yeah!" He fantasized using the weapon that might hurt one of Al's slow paying customers.

"Yeah! What you need me to do?"

"Same as Terry. Work on the fish. Cut em up. Then you can make deliveries. We pay cash, off the books."

"Where are you? Who are you?"

"Fulton Market. Palmieri Supply Co. Terry knows where. Matt Donitelli? Ay! How'd that turkey hook up with a good Italian boy?"

7

Harbor Brews

Gloria opened the green door to Belle's Tavern, twirled her hair tossing raindrops onto the worn oak floor which was counterpoint to the beer aged oak counter.

"Ya look like a drowned rat," hooted Belle. "Here, use this towel. I'll get you an iced tea."

"Thanks." Gloria wrapped the towel around her head, sucked in her cheeks, pulled her stomach muscles tight and set one hand on her hip. "Do I look like a Dior model?"

"More like a two-bit whore," Belle scoffed.

"Better be worth more than two bits." They giggled together.

"You ain't been here for a while. How've you been?" Belle wiped the bottles on the shelf below the smoky mirror and turned to polish the tap handles.

"Not since my father died. I know. Sorry Belle."

"It's all right. This place remind you of him?" Belle squinted.

"Only when baymen fill the place. I walked past the other night, heard all the noise, the bragging, and the brawling."

"Must have been Tuesday night. They got rowdy." Belle shook her head and lifted her tongue against her top lip.

"You were in pretty good form yourself."

"Yeah," Belle winked. "Had to dump a couple of 'em out of here. That Chris is a pistol. But I like the kid."

"I don't know his family. They must be new." Gloria sipped her tea.

"New? Shoot. His old man grew up here, took off, left here kind of suddenly. I don't remember why, but it'll come back to me. Heard he got killed on a motorcycle, hit by a bus."

Belle checked inverted beer glasses, rubbed the white menu board, and added fish and chips to the specials.

"Belle, would you do me a favor?"

"Sure honey, what you need?"

"Get those guys to be serious about this clam chowder contest, first one since he died. I heard them the other night and they sounded . . ."

"That was a bunch of kidding. They'll be perfect. First, they'll do it for your old man. Second, they'll do it for you. I'll talk nice to them"

"Promise?" Gloria asked.

"I can talk nice. Sure. I promise. How about a brew?"

"Just some chips," Gloria turned toward the door.

"Understand you can hold booze as good as those Kiwanians. How about that brew?"

"Just iced tea. I can probably out distance anyone of them, but it's strictly show. Prefer the tea."

"They'll respect you for that, not showing them up."

"No, not respect. They fear me. That's better. You sure I don't look like a model?" Gloria leaned forward on the bar, propped her head on the palm of her hand, and pouted for the smoky mirror

Belle leaned across the counter and snapped her towel at Gloria's thigh. "Remember, young lady, I knew you when you was a sweet little girl in ballet class. I seen those eyes like your father, always trying to look tough, intimidating. He never scared me, so don't you try to fool me with that hoodlum crap."

"It's a front, Belle."

"I know. Don't have to tell me." Belle sat next to Gloria. "I really knew your old man. Used to hang out in here on clammers' nights. Wanted to buy this place."

"Wouldn't he pay enough?" Gloria sipped her tea.

"He couldn't. I'll never sell to him, that is, wouldn't have. Not after all I knew about how he treated people, how he ran that Chris kid's father out of town. Oh yeah! That's what it was. You must have known him, that Conrad Winkler."

Gloria swirled chips around the dish, dipped one into salsa, then sucked it off the chip.

Two young couples piled into the Tavern. Belle checked their ID's, and seated them in one of the wooden booths that separated the bar from the dining area.

"Gotta get busy."

Gloria looked at the music box hidden behind the brass cash register. The little ballerina, dressed in pink leotard, stood ready to spin. It had been the same type of award that Gloria had once received.

"See you next time Belle."

Belle appeared in the kitchen doorway. "Ought to get a guy, Gloria honey. You need a man. Don't wind up alone like your old man."

Gloria smiled, shook her finger at Belle. "Don't worry. I'll never be like him and what makes you think I don't have one?"

Rain water dribbled along Main Street's rusting trolley tracks. Gloria walked past a storefront shared by Kydd's Karate class and Miss Gayle's Dance Studio. She looked at mothers and fathers gossiping in the waiting room while little girls were standing in front of full-length mirrors.

Gloria massaged the back of her neck, stared at the children, and remembered her mother sitting there watching, making sure her daughter did everything right, making sure Steve Palmer would be proud. He demanded that his daughter, anything he owned, be first, undefeated, and unchallenged.

Gloria had enjoyed listening to her mother talk about art in the "old country" and sat in wonder when her mother and Amanda exchanged stories about Italy and the Indians who once lived near Tern Harbor. Rosa talked about going to the opera and to the churches of Rome. Amanda talked about the woods, the land, the beach and the sea. They talked about the sky they both could see and they talked about their children. Rosa would talk about her dream that Gloria would be a great artist and run off with a ballet troop. Amanda talked about a dream that her son would be a great chief and would defend the wonders of Nature.

Gloria listened when they thought she was asleep and wondered about where she would go with the ballet troop and she dreamed about a great chief stealing her away.

——•——

Gloria adjusted her purse's shoulder strap and continued walking toward the park. Avoiding puddles, she stepped up onto the bandstand, turned toward the harbor, then looked back toward the ballet studio. She leaned against the white center post. Pink and green ribbons used to fly from the bandstand cupola during the Tern Harbor Day festivals.

Gloria folded her hands across her chest as she recalled her father's rambling about "his" Tern Harbor on that last day . . . "Damn that day, damn him," she said as she remembered his slobbering monologue.

He boasted "Tern Harbor Day was the best damned thing that could have happened for business and for building this place." He chuckled as he babbled about how he had made everyone think that the festival had been going on since Indians lived on these "friggin hills. People eat it up," he snorted. "They suck up old fashioned charm of any place. Those poor little bastards, makes their little houses worth a bunch of money, so they just suck it up." Gloria shuddered, twisted her fingers as if she were still wiping the white foam from around his mouth and looking into his terrified eyes.

Steve Palmer, shaking, his lips opening and closing, spoke in guttural, moist, clipped phrases while his daughter cleaned his chin. Panic invaded his face as if at that moment he understood that she had control over his body in the same way that he had controlled her mind. They understood each other. They were not father and daughter, not adversaries, but partners in a desperate struggle for sovereignty.

Steve Palmer moved his wheel chair toward the windows. He searched Tern Harbor, nodded, waved his hand, and continued the search but was no longer aware of what quarry he hunted. Tears rolled across the hollow cheeks that once rose in a smile that charmed friends, women, and those who were repulsed by his behavior.

He perceived himself as a hideous toy to be hidden in a dark corner when visitors came. He could not talk, charm, and delight his company with fine wine. He felt defenseless, odiferous, and offensive. He mumbled short responses to visitors questions, hated them for hiding their views of him as a fouled wreck, a fool, a disabled ship crashed on the rocks.

"Saw Fatso today," he gazed at the bay.

"Who?" Gloria adjusted her father's chair.

"Fatso. The mayor," Steve's head shook violently.

"Oh, Butch. Thought you liked him." Gloria steadied his head.

"Yeah! Useful, useful. Wants to be big shot. Congress." Steve Palmer tried to laugh. "Wants help."

"Okay. We'll help him," Gloria sighed.

"Can kiss my ass. Screw the no brainer."

Neither of them laughed nor spoke.

Steve Palmer became animated; his scrutiny of the bay turned to terror. "That clammer shouldn't be here." He coughed, raised his hand to his chest, and coughed again.

He turned to Gloria, pointed at her and said one clear sentence. "If I catch him, I'll kill him, this time I kill him."

Butch Moulder and Steve Palmer initiated the Tern Harbor Festival, organized committees, and forced real estate agents to offer prize money for the race and clam chowder contest. People came from all over the northeast to run the race, buy souvenirs, crafts, antiques, food, watch the clam chowder contest, marvel at the harbor and buy real estate.

Steve restricted clam chowder contest entries to local baymen with whom he partied at Captain Belle's. By Tern Harbor Day, the baymen were ready to put on a good show for Steve.

Gloria vowed she would not be like him, would not drink with the clammers at Belle's, but thought about high spirited sounds on Tuesday nights. She wondered what it might be like if she could be in a pub somewhere else, if she was free of this place.

She moved away from the bandstand, walked along the dock to the Harbor Master's shack, and skipped small flat stones across the water toward the red buoy.

The shack had the warm smell of wood that had hosted high tides, storms, and remnants of fish and clam fluids. The past lay buried in the layers of layers of tall fish tales that had encircled old men who would sit in here waiting for new adventures about sailing, fishing and women. Gloria cleared the smudged window, pressed her cheek against the wall, and scanned the brass-framed pictures that covered the wall. Steve Palmer signed each of the photographs in which he presented trophies to contests winners, regatta champions, men with trophy fish, and groups of nondescript visitors. The wall was a history of winners and a monument to Steve Palmer.

----◦----

Gloria was twelve on a bright and promising morning of the Tern Harbor Day Festival. She performed with her class at ballet recitals in front of the bandstand, was proud to be known as the boss's daughter, but sank into melancholy when she thought about having left her mother. Rosa Palmer, lay propped in bed, her breathing labored like someone who knows long nights and short days and fears the cold.

"Gloria, I want you to have a good time," her mother had waved at her.

"Momma, I'll stay here with you. You need help. Should Amanda call the doctor, take you to the hospital? Should I get Poppa?"

"No, No. The day would be nothing without him. Amanda will be here with me. I'll be fine. You'll see."

"Momma, I think I must be like you. You seem so pale. You lost so much blood." Gloria pressed against her mother's hand.

"No, sweet heart. You mustn't be like me."

"But Momma," Gloria sat on the bed, pulled her mother's arm around her. "I'm going to be pale, too. I have been bleeding a little. I didn't want to tell you."

Gloria's mother pulled her arm away, gently raised it and with sudden strength slapped Gloria across the face.

Gloria jumped away, ran to Amanda. "I had to tell her. Had to." She looked back at her mother who seemed to be asleep.

"She had to do that." Amanda held Gloria close. "They always do that, at her home, to girls when they become women. One of their old ways where she comes from. One of their myths."

"But this is her home," Gloria cried.

"Come here baby," Rosa Palmer stretched her hands out to her daughter. "Always the first time. I love you baby. Don't cry, you'll stain your dress."

"I love you Momma. I can't leave you, I'll stay."

"I want you to go. Gloria go. Amanda will be here. Look out the window at the lovely day. Go now."

"Promise you'll be all right. Promise."

"I promise. And, Gloria, you promise you will always look after your father. Promise."

"I promise Momma. I promise."

Amanda moved toward the bedside, and placed a wet towel on Rosa's forehead.

Rosa Palmer smiled. "Go."

Rosa Palmer watched her daughter leave the room. "She mustn't be like me."

Amanda touched Rosa gently, and then as she touched her own single clam shell earring, she said quietly, "No. Like him."

Parents and friends applauded the Tern Harbor Day ballet. Birds swooped into the water after unsuspecting fish. The girls changed from their swirling costumes to jeans, sneakers, short sleeve tops, sunglasses to try to make themselves look older. Visitors had lined Main Street applauding the colorful racers, handing them cups of water, and waiting at the finish line for their friends.

The Park was filled with craft and antiques booths, tables with twirling feathery toys on sticks, home made dolls, patch work quilts, wood bird houses, the smell of pop corn and hotdogs, and in the center of it all the clam chowder contest. Multi-colored pendants, spread across the bay to mark the regatta finish line, emphasized the carnival atmosphere. Merry-go-round music mingled with the rock sounds of a high school group and the laughter and noise of the visitors to Tern Harbor.

Judges had started tasting the baymen's presentations for the clam chowder contest. Gloria fidgeted behind her father, whispered then pleaded with him to go home.

Steve Palmer smiled, nodded to one of the judges and told Gloria that he would send Doc Desmond. He turned to her and whispered that Rosa never wanted to come to this feast and always found a way to get sick.

"Don't have time to get you home now. I'm busy. Now cut it out." Steve smiled while he chastised his daughter.

Gloria watched her father move back toward the baymen. He wrapped his arm around a blond woman who was tasting one of the chowders, then they moved to the next table where the woman, giggling, pried Steve Palmer's hand from her. She swirled a spoon around the dish then lifted it to her lips. The woman jerked back with the first taste, offered it to Steve. He turned to the bayman, moved stealthily toward him, and unloaded the full mouth of vodka laced chowder onto the bayman's cheeks. Judge, chowder-maker and Gloria's father embraced as if they had shared a secret rendezvous. Steve Palmer kissed the judge, whispered something private to her, then they kissed the bayman's chowder covered face.

Gloria raced home. Amanda had propped Rosa Palmer into a sitting position so she could see the colorful sailing events through the opened window, turned up the music from the opera *Tosca*, placed a cold towel on Rosa Palmer's forehead, and sent Gloria to get a glass of juice. Festival music was faint background to Maria Calas's final aria from that fatal opera. Rosa Palmer was staring toward wispy clouds, her mouth open and set into a smile.

Gloria moved her fingers along her mother's clenched fist and massaged the smooth knuckles. The Vicks odor, that had been a comfort to her mother made Gloria's eyes tear.

"I'll call for someone to come," Amanda spoke almost inaudibly.

"No. I'll call," Gloria reached for the telephone, dialed the number she had memorized, and called Butch Moulder's office. "Can you please get my father? It's important. My mother just died. Please get him."

Gloria waited on the porch, waited for her father, waited for night to safeguard the house, waited for her father. She wrapped herself in her mother's afghan, and waited for her father.

Cars pulled into the driveway. Doors slammed and Gloria waited for her father to come into the house. A woman was laughing, a bayman's deep voice was shouting at a barking dog and her father was urging them into the boathouse. Their shadows filtered through the darkened windows. Gloria wrapped herself in the afghan that held her mother's soft perfume smell, and she waited for morning. The visitors left, shadows ended, and Gloria waited for Steve Palmer. She hated him, knew she would hate him forever; wondered if someday she would have her turn making him wait; but knew she would always be there when he really needed her because she had promised her mother. "Oh that promise Momma, just one more promise."

—————

Gloria moved away from the Harbor Master shack's rotting odors, past the bandstand, past the dance studio and into Belle's tavern.

"I'll have that brew now Belle."

8

Bleached Ghosts

Matt sat cross-legged in his mother's darkened house for the first time since he and his uncle George had delivered their sanguine package to Long Island Sound. He stared past the open door, imagined he could see through the miles of cliffs and hills, imagined Gloria Palmer sitting in her glass encased room looking eastward at him, and thought of the first time he had been to the Palmer's house.

He thought of the boys sliding down the hill, stripping their clothes and jumping into the protected cove. In defiance of the myth of that haunted hill, he had jumped into the water and swam to the unprotected rock, scrambled to the top of the rock, raised his hands skyward, and stood exposed to the wind.

In those days, he sat in the back circle around the campfires, absorbed the lessons of the young men simultaneously leaping, howling, and stamping the ground to drive away satanic ghosts and appealing to the stars to send windblown heroic spirits. Back then, his father's vicious tirades forced him to matriculate from the smell of his own fear and to divorce his consciousness from bodily torture.

Matt recalled the days when he would plead with his mother to stay away from Sean Donovan, to remain in Tern Harbor caring for Rosa Palmer and her family. He remembered the stormy nights when he had run through shielding woods to the house where Momma Robins would hide and care for him, where he was safe.

Matt broke out of his daydream as lightning cracked the sky like shattered windshield glass. His breath quickened as he stared through the open doorway. Shadows danced with enveloping winds that trespassed shamelessly through woods where goblins and devils had haunted him, and where demons had trailed after him as they tried to embezzle his Indian spirit. He glowered at his father's apparition bending in the waves, crashing onto a stone jetty, then shrieking formlessly along the spitting surf.

He slammed the door, turned exhausted and saw a shadow fly past the kitchen window. He imagined the smell of Momma Robins' house where he was able to take cover until by chance, by accident, by disaster he had yelled that word "nigger", cut the letter "N" into Bill Robins arm, and turned away from his friend. He heard himself repeat that violent word "nigger", it had fallen easily from his lips, he had built the emotional barricade so that he could hide from himself. He used it to drive his Indian spirit into hiding, and that word "nigger" had altered his life; he could no longer smell the bleach odor of both mothers' houses that existed in a world where his image was that of the leader, the protector, and bravest of men. It was the bleached odor that had made him feel comfortable working at the Palmieri Fish Market.

———✦———

Saturdays at the fish market, he ran steaming water into the stainless steel sink, cleared the counters with clear bleach, pulled off his gloves, dropped the last of the garbage bags into the dumpster, locked the Palmieri Fish Market Van, tossed his apron into the laundry bin, and checked his pay envelope.

"Hey, finish what you're doing and come have lunch." Vincent Palmieri had cleared the stainless steel table, set out two plastic plates, cloth napkins, and a basket of freshly steamed clams. A platter of sliced cheeses, green peppers, mushrooms and tomatoes, and a basket-encased bottle of wine added color to the table. "Come on, have a drink. It's Saturday and you deserve a good lunch for what you did the other day."

"That was fun," Matt sat across from his employer. "Couldn't believe how easy it was."

"Here take some of this bread, fill it with cheese, the vegetables and sauce. Just place one of these clams into your mouth and then drown it with some wine." Vincent Palmieri waited for his guest to eat first.

"Couldn't believe how easy." Matt smiled. "When you asked me to go to collect money from Rosen's Restaurant, I thought I would have to bargain or something, maybe even tell them we wouldn't make any more deliveries."

"I knew who to send. Before he died, old man Rosen always paid on time. He was as honest as my father, never any bull, always straight as an arrow in business. That's how those old guys built these shops back then. But when he died and his son took over the restaurant, phhtt. He pays, but when he is good and ready. When he is pushed."

"Why do you let him get away with it?" Matt filled his glass with iced tea.

"Because they are good old customers and I promised my father I would honor the old Jew's business and family no matter what, and they always pay, they won't go no place else. We supply the best fish, keep it separate for the kosher customers and they know they can trust us."

"But why did you let Rosen get so far behind?"

"Never had a good collector before and now we also have a new bookkeeper who let's me know when they owe us too much. Good girl, she also does some job for my sister at the restaurant."

"It was funny when I walked into the restaurant. Everyone turned and looked, even the waiters who jabbered in Spanish. Then this fat guy, Rosen, came around from the back. Tried to look tough like he was going to kick me out. I gave him the squinty eyes, the look I have learned to use, and I thought he would drop it in his pants."

"Matt, you have to learn to be gentle with some people."

"Of course, but the one who is feared the most, wins. They recognize that look, they see tattoos, and they don't know what to think. From then on it's easy. It's a good thing I went on Thursday, though."

"Of course, they close early on Friday. It's the Sabbath." Vincent Palmieri crossed himself. "You're an honest kid, Matty. I counted the money. Six thousand fifty four dollars, forty-seven cents. Not a dime missing. You know I don't trust none of them bubbleheads who work for me. Take that friend Terry of yours; don't think he even knows how to count. I only keep him because he was smart enough to bring you here, almost three years now, right?"

"He didn't bring me, you told me to come."

"Anyway, I like the idea of a good Italian kid working here. I don't trust any of them others. Want you to do something for me today." Palmieri looked at the food on the table. "Here, finish these clams. I want you to lock up for me today and maybe every Saturday. Anyway, here's a set of keys."

Matt caught the keys, looked across to his boss. "Thanks," he said.

"I have to leave early." Vincent Palmieri twirled the wall safe dials. He scratched the back of his balding head. "We're having a party for my niece. She came to live with my sister, has done wonders for the restaurant and does my bookkeeping. I'd invite you but it's a family thing." He waved his hands in front of his face. "Her father, my brother, we don't talk. Sad. I should invite you. Like her to meet a nice Italian kid, but this is family. Make sure everything here is clean. Okay? And Matt, I give you a twenty-dollar raise. Good job with the Jew."

"Thanks, Mr. P. Anytime."

"And have some wine. That tea will kill you."

"Never drink." Matt locked the door behind Vincent Palmieri. "Never be like my mother's husband, that old bastard drunk."

———

Matt cleared the table, dropped the trash into a bag near the back door. He spotted something under a sink, lay flat on the floor and retrieved the errant bottle cap. He cradled his face on his arm, closed his eyes and inhaled bleach smells rising from the scrubbed floor. He lay there almost asleep. Tentative breezes from the rotating ceiling fan caressed his head and neck.

It was the same way the wind, tapping at tall grass, brushed his body when, stripped to the waist, ready to dive into the bay if his father caught up to him, he used to run barefoot along the beach.

Hidden by the reeds, he would lay flat, the wind would find him under the tall grass but his tormentor would not. When it was safe, he would run to the Robins' house. Mamma Robins would hide him inside the wood frame cottage, make him eat some grits and drink a large glass of water. Then he would lie on an olive colored blanket, try to sleep while he sniffed the bleach that had been used to clean everything in the house.

Matt ran from his mother's house, ran from the smell of bleach that filled his nostrils when her husband would push him onto the floor and hit him with the broom handle or a steel tip boot or kneel beside him and pound fists into his back. He ran to the Robins' where the smell of bleach rising from the floors taught him to sleep but remain on guard.

The smell of that cleanser filled his nostrils as he now lay still on the Palmieri's Fish market floor. A shadow, not a large hulking one, but a fleeting phantom darted into the corner under the sink. Matt stayed still, did not breath, watched the changing shape. In other days, he would have believed it was one of the little people he had heard of in Indian legends that were told around campfires. He would have believed he was one of the giants who formed the rivers and lakes and the little people were the witches he could destroy.

He watched the shadow. When it twitched, he lunged and held the motion-less mouse. Black circle eyes stared into the blank of space, waiting for the moment to escape or die. Matt held the terrified creature close to his face then lowered it to the bleach-smelling floor and set it free. The shadow fled into a dime-sized hole. The mouse had never hurt him; he remembered his mother preaching about the sacred nature of animals, and he remembered her words "save the animals and the land."

Matt finished his work, and drove the yellow pickup truck to its reserved place in front of the building he now called home. There were no more whistles or sound of bats. There was the genuflecting silence of respect.

He changed to the black clothes that identified him as someone to be feared and hid him as a shadow that could strike at unsuspecting prey. He slipped a knife into his steel tipped Doc Marten boot, brushed his hair back, and lowered his head as if driving fear into the face of any victim.

He walked past the pickup truck, past steel blinds hiding store windows, rounded the corner and saw the fluttering tree tops of Tompkins Square Park. He aimed steadily toward that target, wound his way past people standing in groups, or wandering indifferently, or leaning against brick walls and smoking. He entered the dimly lit park and sat on a shrub-shrouded bench.

Matt touched the soft boxwood leaves that had overgrown the seat, felt like he was hiding in a thicket from which, invisible, he could watch for an enemy or prey. He watched as joggers in the park passed singly, or in groups.

He sat snake still, poised to strike, when a shadow slithered onto the other end of the bench, raised a brown bag and emptied a bottle of wine.

"Offer you some but all gone," the bearded man leaned toward Matt. "Got any on you?"

"No." Matt turned away from the old man.

"Got a cigarette?"

Matt sneered at the derelict.

The old man lifted his head, stroked his beard then blew his nose in a curled cloth. "Just trying to make conversation before bedtime. Look at those folks in their cute little running stuff."

Joggers meandered across the cement pathways through the old European designed park.

"See those two. The one in the gray sweats and his friend in the sweatshirt and those little shorts slit up the side. They're very good friends if you get what I mean." The old man licked his lips.

Matt moved closer to the shrubs.

"Get a load of the bounce of that one's boobs. Think she's interested in running? Bull. She thinks she's gonna make it with the kid with the slit shorts. She's in for a surprise. Wow! Here comes the real winner."

"How do you know so much about these people?" Matt continued to survey the park.

"Live here. Been here for months. See all, know all, say nothing." The old man laughed.

"This bench ain't private, but you're getting in my way." Matt turned toward the runners.

"I live over there," said the old man. "Behind the bandstand. Convenient. Has running water. Keep my house folded up during the day with my stuff. Rent is cheap, actually free."

"Why don't you clean up, get a job and a real place?" Matt whispered in disgust.

"Sometimes I have company," the man smiled revealing stained teeth behind the yellowing beard. "Getting some later tonight and gonna have more next week. These cuties who think they own the place, well they're new here too. Moved in because it was cheap and kicked the rest of us out of them houses. In for a big surprise."

"Do you know that guy running with the young girl?" Matt nodded at the jogging couple.

"Call him Stud. He lives in that house with the fancy glass doors. Married. Not to her. Never saw her before. Seen him. His wife, think it's his wife, she travels a lot. Soon as she leaves, he bops down here and jogs along bouncing that back end of his and moves in on some little cutie. Lots of laughs. Don't take long. They head out of the park and up to his place. See. The one with the little flag in the window."

"How do you know so much?" Matt tossed a condescending grin at the man as a guard had done to him in a Riverhead jail.

"Told you I live here. Always keep tabs on my company." The old man leaned over toward Matt. "Like I know about those black clothes you wear, seen you here before. I figured out the tattoos."

"How do you know about, what did you call him, Stud?"

"You watch. See them going into the house. Wait a few minutes." Matt and the old man looked up toward the flag in the window. The man appeared from behind the curtains, raised the flag so it hung from the middle of the window.

"See," the stranger smirked. "It's his victory symbol, sign of conquest, I think it is a sign to his wife to stay away. Saw her once coming back from one of them trips. She looked up, saw the flag and kept going. She knew."

"Does she ever fool around?" Matt looked back at the flag.

"She travels a lot. I'd like to raise the flag with her. Here comes one of my roommates."

A shadow moved behind the bandstand. "I've seen you people here all summer. Police leave you alone?"

"Not for long. Make us move every once in a while. Having a big meeting next week, the neighbors who live around the park. Going to get the mayor and the cops to get us out of our homes. Again! In for a surprise!" The man rose from the bench. Matt saw the man's tattered army fatigues that bloused over his giant frame.

"What did you do before?" Matt whispered as the man slipped into the shadows.

The man paused, looked back at Matt, "Served my country. Found my way around the jungles. I can deal with anything these bastards can hand out. Vet. Vietnam. Fucked there. Fucked here. But you watch. Come back and see how we take this place." He disappeared under the hedges.

Matt deserted the shrub and stepped carefully across the grassy meadow. Victorian lamps cast shadowy breaches in the twilight. He knew the Indian way crossing the grass without being detected by an enemy.

The slowing parade of joggers was followed by a boy and girl, dressed in the familiar black, walking toward Greenwich Village.

The jogger who had picked up the girl and raised the flag was now dressed in the black sweat suit, slowed, then sat next to Matt.

"Stays light late these days," the man nodded to Matt.

"Sometimes," Matt answered.

"Treating you okay at that job?" The man smiled at a passing girl.

"Real good. Good Guy Palmieri. Trusts me." Matt shook his head.

"Good. You kids going to have some fun tonight?" The man adjusted his running shoes, then pulled a small package from his pocket.

"Yeah. We're heading to a club for some kidding around and dancing."

"They've straightened out and done good work since you took hold. Used to think it was a big deal to get together, act tough, bang around a mash pit, draw a swastika, and break a window." The man brushed his receding crew cut.

Matt straightened his back so he would be taller than his visitor.

"This is a nice place. I like to come here. Very pleasant for joggers and all the pretty girls who live near here." The man handed Matt a package.

"Something going to happen." Matt looked toward the bandstand, and then counted the twenty-dollar bills in the package.

"How did you know?" the crew cut man asked. "No one supposed to know yet."

"They're planning a meeting to have things all their way." Matt rubbed the spider web tattoo on his elbow.

"So. You have to do what I tell you sooner than I expected. Blacks are opening an office on Broad near Wall Street. That's where we need a job done." The man smiled at a young girl who passed them.

"Are we talking about the same thing?" Matt snapped his head toward the man. "They want to get rid of those homeless people who hang out here. Want us to do something about it?"

The man chuckled. "Who cares about them? Homeless creeps can go to Penn Station or something. Not my business as long as they don't piss on the lawn. We have real business. No. Don't care about this. But it would be a good diversion."

"What's happening downtown?"

"Told you, some smartass blacks are trying to become brokers and open an office for niggers to trade with them. Disgusting. Enough we have hotshot Jews in the business." The man spit through his teeth.

"What do you want me to do about it? I don't have any money to invest with them." Matt smirked.

"Scare the hell out of them. Nobody to really get hurt, just scare the hell out of them. Let them know skinheads intend to keep the place clean, odor free, and white. That's what you are to do. We can't have every immigrant in the world running things down there. Get this done then we have important work for you over in Jersey." The man rejoined the joggers alongside a girl who he led to his building, then adjusted the flag in the window.

Matt slipped the package of twenties into his pocket. "Two thousand dollars. What the hell can we do with two grand? Can blow this in a couple of hours at the club for those kids. Son-of-a-bitch. Probably costs you more than two hundred for your own entertainment tonight."

Drizzle scattered the park's temporary inhabitants, the homeless took positions under the bandstand, mist rolled across the grassy mall and Matt slipped out of the Park and trotted through an alley toward Greenwich Village.

A cleaning lady, carrying a bucket of sudsy bleach smelling water, bumped into Matt as she exited a building hallway. "Sorry," she said. "Gonna dump this in the street. You should watch where you are going. Did I get any on you?" She smiled at him.

He was face to face with her. "No. Missed this time. Want another shot? You better watch it when you come out like that, not up to me to look out."

He gritted his teeth, held back spitting at the fat woman, turned into the shadow drenched alley and continued toward the brightly lit street.

He did not turn back toward the woman until he heard her taunt, "Here turkey," she shouted. "Here." She raised the bucket she had been carrying and spun the last drops of dirty water along the alley. He smelled the familiar bleach, jumped out of the way, and smiled at the woman.

"Bitch. You're lucky I have something to do or I would . . ." He stopped, whirled and ran toward the rain diffused streetlights.

New York's Greenwich Village is the playground for young people, the gathering place for writers, artists, students, and people hunting for other people. It is the host of coffeehouses, pubs, and intimate restaurants boasting exotic global foods. Tiny boutiques are cluttered with used and new clothing. People, walking with determination, fill the Street from the East End to Sheridan Square and then to the Hudson River Drive. The Village borderlines careening east and west, north and south, is limited only by its tenant's exuberance.

When most city streets are deserted, the Village's streets are alive. Umbrellas protect racing men and women from heavy rain while neon lights ignite emotions of late night inhabitants of dimly lit pubs.

Matt maneuvered through the sea of umbrellas, tucked his left forearm toward his chest, his right hand was down, extended ready to ward off any interference like a quarterback heading for the end zone. He moved steadily toward the neon sign, BLUES CLUB. *Yeah, he thought, not gonna be blues tonight. Fun time.*

He brushed past the body builder whose shoulders and neck stretched the white shirt and blue jacket that identified him as the club's bouncer. The couple he had seen walking past the Park was huddled in a dark corner of the café, tapping in time with the drum and piano set on the small stage.

Matt pushed his way close to the bar, bumped two men who crowded next to him as he ordered a draft. He lowered his eyebrows and glared at the two men. They lifted their drinks and moved to the other end of the room.

"Better not brush me again. This spot strictly for any cute girl who wants a beer." Matt smiled at the bartender, turned so he could see who was coming in the front door, pointed his tongue toward the blond girl entering the club, and waited for her to squeeze next to him.

Lightning collided with a utility pole and dropped the Village into temporary darkness. Sirens sounded in the distance, quiet overtook friends and lovers packed against one another, beer lingered in the hushed darkness.

Crackling lightning spears slashed overhead and demanded the revelers' silence. The young girl moved away from Matt allowing others to fill the void. Streetlights flickered and the purple of the café reinvented life at the bar. A neatly dressed, crew cut man played his own form of jazz at the piano to the delight of the girl who had snuggled up to Matt.

The black clad couple came out of their corner, winked at Matt and shoved the man from the piano stool. They began to pound shrill, unmelodic notes from the ivories. The jazz player insisted they give back the seat. A tall man pushed the couple off the piano bench and started playing soft torch songs. Suddenly, black clothes, boots and ominous tattoos, surrounded the couple.

Matt hurled himself on top of the piano. "Let that couple play or I'll jump into the middle of this thing, wreck it and piss all over the bunch of you."

"Fuck you," screamed the man who had been playing jazz. "Fuck you and your friends. We'll beat the crap out of you. Get off the piano now."

Matt vaulted from his pedestal, smashed his fist into the man's face. Blood spun from the man's nose and cheek as he beat wildly at his attacker. The smell of blood obliterated the acrid beer smell that had entertained the crowd.

The bouncer rushed into the room, placed one hand under Matt's legs and one around his neck, lifted him, and shuffled toward the front door.

"Going to toss you the fuck out of here." The bouncer shoved his way through the cheering crowd.

"Are you thinking of tossing me out of here?" Matt chortled.

"Throw your ass so far you'll never walk close to this place," retorted the body builder.

"Well you had better take a look around." Matt coughed.

The bouncer had lifted Matt over his head, turned to see ten violent screaming skinheads moving toward him. Their Doc Martin boots threatened the bartender, customers, and the bouncer.

"Now whose ass is going to go flying? Better set me down nicely before this place is history. Going to kick me out? Right." Matt was standing face to face with the bouncer. One of the skinheads landed his boot into the bouncer's knee, another boot found his groin. Matt put a dollar into the tip glass on the bar and walked out the front door.

The crescendo from the pounding of piano keys ended and the laughing skinheads scattered.

"Going to toss me out? Just try it." Matt scowled as he disappeared into the alley shadows. He walked quickly, passed the doorway where he had confronted the cleaning lady, hesitated, waited for any sound from within the building, then, avoiding the doorway from which she might toss cleaning water, continued slowly toward the Park.

Cool breezes that ruffled yellow tinged leaves cast surrealistic images over secret creatures asleep in box caves in the Park. The homeless had invaded the province of young joggers in their fashionable sweats who had earlier ignored Matt sitting in the protection of the shrubs. They had avoided his gaze, his black clothes, his tattoos, and the danger he might present. They passed him, passed the ragged inhabitants of the boxes, and passed the cadaverous maple leaf shadows; they had created safety zones from which things that are not seen become harmless.

Steady mist drenched everything in its way as Matt raced back to the apartment he shared with Terry. Thunder slogged across Manhattan and echoed through deserted streets. Matt double locked the door, turned out the lights, fell into half sleep on the couch and waited for street sounds. The steady drumming of drizzle had the comforting sound of his regular heart beat; he pulled a blanket close around his shoulders and rolled into that sleep when demons and three-headed guardians of the underworld used to assault Matt's consciousness, battled ferocious winds and became blinded by sylvan pods driven from aging grasses.

It was that same sweat drenched sleep that was now reassuring as he lay covered by Indian blankets in his mother's house. He listened to rain screech across Long Island Sound and slap frantically against the windows. Matt felt curiously safe, secreted from the furies, and protected from the past in his mother's house.

Howling storm noises disrupted his semi-sleep, and Matt dreamed he was running through the alley with the black cleaning lady racing after him, dousing him with her cleaning water. He wanted to see Momma Robins, but this was not her house.

He folded the blankets on the end of the couch, felt in his pocket for the car keys, raced the white convertible through the rain to the place where Momma Robins' house had been.

The hospitable, safe house had been replaced by a neat row of Cape Cod houses that were separated by chain link fences. An oak tree jutted into the street as a remnant of the past. The mailbox, glistening black and gray letters under the street light, held the familiar name *ROBINS*.

Matt parked under the tree and listened to the scraping of a distant bug calling for a mate. He had not spoken to Bill Robins since he had cut the letter "N" into Bill's forearm. He had avoided his old friend since he returned to carve his niche into the Indian culture and restore the land. He watched the dark and silent house.

A woman peeked from behind sheer curtains of a second floor window, pointed at the white car to a man who was silhouetted against a triangle of light that trickled down the staircase. The man appeared in the doorway tapping a baseball bat against his palm.

Matt rolled the car forward so he could see Bill Robins, and then he jammed the car into gear and sped toward the dark driveway that led to Billy's.

"Hi, Matt," Billy called from behind the counter. "Just getting ready to blow out this last candle and close up. Get you something to eat?"

Billy's innocent smile had the effect Matt wanted. He smiled, put his arm around Billy's shoulders. "Nah. I'll get a cup of coffee and just sit nice and quiet. You finish closing the joint."

"Joint my backside. Work hard making this a cool place. Couldn't even get to Tern Harbor for old man Palmer's memorial. Shoulda gone. Couldn't." Billy made pretense of cleaning the sparkling counter.

"OK Billy. I was there, at the memorial, for Gloria's sake. Don't know if she knew, but I was there." A candle sputtered as Matt smothered it with his finger.

"But I shoulda. Knew what she done for me. Knew what he was like. Mighta said the wrong things, though. Mighta said what he was really like, what he did. Couldn't come this time. How's the coffee? Can make fresh pot." Billy moved toward the coffeepot.

"It's OK Billy. I told you, I was there. Stayed in the back with Amanda. People probably think it was just another harmless Indian. Go on home Billy. I'll close up." Matt moved his chair into the dark corner, away from the window.

"Ought to toss you the hell out of here." Billy laughed.

"Yeah just try it. Better have a look around." Matt smiled. Billy was gone and the café was dark.

"Yeah just try it."

Matt flipped open his cell phone, touched the number 2 and waited.

"Hello," came Gloria's soft voice.

"How are you?" Matt whispered.

"Just fine. Saw you there. Thanks for coming. I knew it would be tough for you to stay."

"My mother needed a little support. No one knows me, would think it was one of her Indians"

"Yeah. High cheek bones and all." The voice answered.

"Wish I could be there, with you, now." Matt moved toward the window.

"It's alright. Storm is settling down and I am going to change some of the pictures that he has, that is had, hanging around here."

"Well. Goodnight. One of these days, I can get there to see my mother. Get some business done. Hope they settle all the talk about the old man and you can get away from there. Matt moved the phone closer to his mouth.

"Don't think so," she answered. "More involved than I could ever know. Especially now. Glad you were able to help. Thanks. Got to go."

Matt slipped out of Billy's café and drove the white convertible onto the main road.

Orange and white lights flashed on a Suffolk County patrol car that was angled in front of a battered gray pickup truck; one of the policemen checked the young black driver's license; the other policeman, right hand ominously over his hip holster, examined the back of the car.

Matt drove past the two vehicles, mouthed the words as if to warn the driver, "leave, get away from here, drive anywhere but get away from here." He waved but avoided eye contact with the police; then instinctively turned onto a side road, turned off the headlights, and waited for the cars to leave.

"Ghosts." He said. "Just ghosts."

9

Gloria

Tender sounds of Handel's "Water Music" drifted across the room as Gloria moved the violent seascape painting that used to hang over the fireplace mantle.

The melancholy storm departed as suddenly as it had arrived. Gloria grimaced at the missing painting's gray outlines that marked time's erosion. "Can't have a little picture, it'll show all those picture hook holes. Need something bold, colorful, and anything but the sea." She opened a large flat box.

"Now I have the place for you." She lifted the oak-framed Western desert lithograph. An Indian woman was holding her skirt close to her body during a windstorm and looked past vague images of sagebrush floating over the fading horizon.

"Someday, and soon, I'm going to have a real Georgia O'Keefe painting, someday I am going to go where these were painted and I am going to be free as that sagebrush. Someday."

Gloria packed the family pictures that had resided on the piano into a shoe box, then she sat on the piano bench and started to play the Beethoven concerto while listening to a Bernstein CD. "I can play chopsticks in time with your baton Leonard, that way we can create a whole new kind of music. Very New Age," she chuckled.

Amanda, in her nightgown, bathrobe, and fuzzy blue slippers, was staring into the room. "Why are you so busy in here this late?"

"Rearranging things in this room. Make it cheery. What color do you think the walls should be?"

"You always liked pink."

"Yes, pink. Remember how Momma loved to see me in pink." Gloria's mood softened. "Did I ever thank you for being here, and for staying? Poppa, well, poppa, well I couldn't love him after we lost Momma. It was hard to love after that."

"Of course you could, you did. It was hard for him to let you know."

"Amanda, he never loved anyone except himself. Everything was for him. Always."

Gloria adjusted the Georgia O'Keefe desert painting. "Amanda, there's a strange light out in the Sound, over there near Goose Island. See it? Have you ever seen it before?" They strained to see the pinpoint of light that faded behind the tall grasses.

"Probably someone out on a boat or some kids playing around out there, damn fools. Going to get in trouble in this weather." Amanda turned off the lamplight and stared into the blackness toward the flickering beacon. "Whoever it is, he will be safe. And you should really get some rest, Gloria. If for no other reason, so that I can."

"How do you know it is a him, only a him?" Gloria backed away from the darkness.

"Amanda," Gloria's voice sounded like the young girl who would ask her mother's surrogate for help. "Amanda. How come you stayed?"

The woman who had nursed Rosa Palmer through her illness, who had cared for Gloria until she had run away from Tern Harbor, stood silent in the hallway.

"Amanda, how come you stayed here with him?" Gloria placed the last of the family pictures in the cardboard box.

"For you. I too made a promise. Promised her I would stay for you." Amanda shook her head affirmatively.

"But I left."

"Knew you would be back. A promise is a promise." Amanda smiled at the words. She had heard those words many times when she sat behind the elders at the campfires. She had written those words to her son many times in letters she never mailed. "I knew you would be back, as I knew the wind would always bring fresh rain."

"Amanda you sound like some old Indian story and I love you for it. What would I have ever done without you?" The two women looked at each other, Gloria smiled and Amanda started to laugh.

"Probably gotten a lot more rest. Goodnight."

"Heard that word already," Gloria repeated goodnight to herself as she picked up the phone, was about to tap a single number, set it back into its cradle after she gently caressed the phone and said "goodnight."

She gazed into the dark night, down at the hidden beach, and thought of her high school science class that was usually marked by Gloria's late entrance. "Well I guess we can all begin now," her teacher droned monotonously. Samuel Weinberg was noted for his thin red tie, white lab coat, and shiny bald head that gave the appearance of a spinning thermometer. Toward the end of the first quarter, Mr. Weinberg changed his opening remarks, "Miss Palmer would you stay a minute after class?"

"Guess the mercury finally blew out the top of his thermometer," she giggled with her friends.

He suggested she visit the guidance counselor, told her she would fail his class and perhaps it would be a good idea to make some kind of change. Gloria knew that Steve Palmer would never let her drop a class, would never let her fail a class or stand for her being less than perfect. She had never wanted to follow her friends into science and calculus classes or English classes that prepared her for a test to get into one of those super colleges. She had asked her father to allow her to take journalism classes, and business classes; she wanted to learn to type, take shorthand, and do accounting.

"Bull. Those crap courses are for kids who're going to become baby sitters or bums. They're for white trash not for my daughter." Steve Palmer would shake his daughter. "You will not only be in those classes; you will be numero uno like everything else around here."

Mrs. Tesoria's office, away from the grade counselors cubicles stacked with files and booklets, was clear of individual files except for the single folder she had opened with Gloria Palmer's records.

Gloria sat in the plastic bucket chair next to the desk, her hands clasped in her lap, her ankles crossed, and her lips tight. She exposed the commanding appearance she had learned from watching her father.

"You know Gloria," the guidance chairperson began. "I'm your counselor because of your father . . ."

"Yes I know Mrs. T, because everyone else is afraid of him." Gloria drummed her fingers on the desk.

"I think we have a little problem," Mrs. Tesoria continued. "Mr. W. thinks you might do better with a different teacher, in fact some other class. What seems to be happening?"

Gloria turned away from the woman who she had accepted as a confidant. "I don't know what his problem could possibly be."

"Gloria. He says you're always late, never do homework, and fail every test. Aside from that I guess there isn't much wrong. Do I sound sarcastic?" The counselor peeked over her glasses at this remarkable young girl.

"Well, you know I never wanted that class." Gloria watched boys playing knock hockey on the front lawn. "I won't do well in any of my courses. I could, but that is what my father wants. Can't you convince him to let me change? Won't he listen to you?" She stood up, walked to the window and watched one of the boys kick the little sack into a tree.

Gloria had seen the boy in the cafeteria, knew his name was Conrad, knew he was one of those who took shop classes, went to work, and one of those who her father would call "trash."

She enjoyed playing in the Spring musical's orchestra, watched Conrad working on set construction, and waited for the pleasant moments when she would hear Steve Palmer rant about her hanging out with the musicians and actors.

"What are you going to waste your time for in that loud band? You need that time to take a course preparing for the SAT's. Not wasting time with a bunch of losers." She wanted to tease him about Conrad.

Mrs. Tesoria kept talking about how difficult it would be to convince Mr. Palmer about course changes, Gloria watched the boys climbing the tree to retrieve the hockey sack; then she heard the suggestion.

"Mrs. Oberlin is willing to add you to her typing class during fifth period which means you would have to give up lunch. If it works out, you could take a beginning shorthand class in the Spring."

Gloria hugged her counselor. "But please don't tell my father. I'll take those classes without it being on my report card, I'll never cut, always be on time. Oh, what about the science?"

Mrs. Tesoria agreed to replace the Advanced Placement Science with Accounting as long as they could somehow avoid dealing with Gloria's father. "For the time being anyway," the counselor shuddered.

Parents waited impatiently for cast and band members at the end of the dress rehearsal. The stage crew moved props and stage settings into place and then hurried to waiting pick-up trucks. Conrad Winkler checked the set for the opening night performance then closed the stage door. He saw Gloria locking the orchestra store room. She fumbled with and then dropped the wide ring of school keys. Conrad leaned over to pick them up, got up slowly, and dropped them again as he was handing them to Gloria. He scrambled to one knee, retrieved the keys, placed them carefully in her hand, and fumbled with the words, "Sorry. Been a long night and I saw you in the back of the band. They ought to put you up front."

"Thanks, for the keys. They always keep the flute players where I am, so it's okay."

"Yeah but it would look better with you up front." he grinned. "You walking home?"

"Yes. It's not that far and I like to walk."

"Hey, it's cold out there and dark. I can give you a lift. I'm safe. Hope you don't mind a little clutter and I hope it doesn't smell like clams." He climbed into the driver's side of the pickup truck, leaned over and opened the door for Gloria.

She had wanted to meet him, had wanted to talk to him; she wanted to find out if he was really different from the boys she knew in advance placement classes.

She wanted to see Conrad again and wanted her father to see her in this little truck with Conrad, but knew that would not be the thing to do.

Her head erect, Gloria faced the road ahead, but her eyes watched Conrad as he shifted the gears. She wanted to touch his smooth forearm that glistened with the sweat from his work. She wanted to move closer to this boy, but kept her head and body pointed forward as they maneuvered the dark road along the rocky beaches and row of hidden houses.

"How do you know where I live?" she asked as they stopped beyond the gravel driveway.

"You kidding? Everyone knows Palmer's place." He angled his head toward the house. "What's he really like? Some say he's great, really built this town; some say stay away from him."

"He's okay." Gloria opened the door and started to leave.

"Hey, let's break a leg tomorrow night. That means good luck in theater talk. Everyone calls me Conrad, you can call me Connie," he winked at her. "Can I drive you to the cast party?"

"Maybe," she flirted. "If I break a leg."

Gloria and Conrad sat unobtrusively at the cast party, drank Cokes, and talked. He talked about things he was making in the school wood shop and about working on sets for the plays and about his working as a clammer. He talked about the bay, the beautiful feeling of being alone, of stripping to his waist, and of feeling the sun on his back as he tugged rakes filled with clams. He talked about going to secret places on the bay and around the point to Goose Island; he talked about the deserted duck blind where he spent warm summer nights wondering about each of the stars.

Gloria listened and wondered why she had never before been with Connie. She listened to him and wondered if any of the boys in her math class had met Conrad or talked with him or could ever be like him. She wondered what her father would say if he knew that she was with this boy.

She reached across the space between them and put her arm inside his and held his cool forearm. She moved closer and listened to him talking about his home, how he loved the Winklers and how good they were to him. He talked about the Easter morning when the Winklers found the basket on their front porch, he talked about the baby inside the basket, he talked about how the older couple, who never had any children, treated him as their own, and were proud of him.

"They're the only ones who are proud of me. You know they keep us over in the shop area away from the rest of the building, afraid we'll pollute it or something," he grimaced.

"Like everyone else, though, you have to go to the cafeteria and other classes." As she said the words, Gloria knew she was wrong.

"We have all our classes down there. Works okay for me. I can get out early to go to work and if I don't show up for a few days, well no one calls to find out where I am. They just wait for me to come back."

"Did you ever feel like never coming back," Gloria sighed.

"No, have to get that diploma. The Winklers deserve it. Let's get out of here."

They drove to Florio Beach, jumped barefoot through the surf, then hidden from the road, sat against the rock retaining wall. Gloria rolled her fingers over the wall's moist, spreading moss and gazed at the stars.

"Never been with anyone like you," Conrad said. He skipped flat stones across the beach to the edge of the bay where they hesitated like children nearing the waters' edge temporarily afraid to get their feet wet and cold.

"Never been to the beach at night, alone or with anyone." Gloria felt the cool breeze that blew across the booming surf filtering through her hair. She shuddered when a sudden gust snapped at her shoulders.

"Here take my sweatshirt." She smiled, moved closer to him, felt the warmth of his body close to hers. She looked up the hill toward her father's house, saw the light-less, lifeless porch and wished Conrad would surround her.

"Never been here with anyone like you," he said. "Never been here with anyone." He turned toward her, held her close, kissed her and pulled her close to him. They were in a close embrace, then they moved away, embarrassed at the moment they had just discovered.

"That's okay, Connie," Gloria whispered. "I've never been here or anywhere before, like this."

"I better get you home. The old man'll be looking for you."

"He's not home. It's Friday night and he's playing poker at the firehouse or hanging out somewhere in town with Butch Moulder or one of his other cronies; probably with some woman he just met; definitely not at the house. Don't have to be afraid of him."

"But he could screw up the clamming business; controls the wholesaler and could even get in the way of my license. If he knew I was with you, well, the heck with it. I never spoke like I did tonight to anyone."

"Connie, let's see each other again." Gloria felt as if she was in a cold lake, unable to swim, and waiting for rescue.

"How about next Friday? I'll be down here." Conrad widened his deep-set brown eyes and shook his head yes anticipating her answer. "We could go for a ride somewhere else and get a hamburger or something"

Gloria twisted her earlobe. "Only if you keep the clams in the back of the truck," she teased. "I like French fries and I like my burger rare." Promise, she thought, promise that you'll talk like you did tonight. I think I'm falling for you Conrad Winkler and you're right, my father would throw a fit.

"Gloria," Conrad was suddenly loud and excited. "Look there, over those stars, see it."

"See what, Connie," Gloria ran to be next to him.

"Look see those shooting stars. I'm naming them the Gloria comets. That's better than a star, you know. Can you guess why?"

"I give up," she said.

"Because they keep moving, don't belong to anyone, and only we have seen them. Look, another one."

"Will they still be there next Friday?" she pleaded.

"I'll make sure they are." The rising tide and tickling sand cemented their feet to the beach, held them outlined against swirling constellations bound together by fiery meteor showers that filled the late night sky.

They held onto a fugitive kiss, gently moved their hands along each other's back, then holding hands, walked back to the small truck.

"I'll make sure those stars will be here," he said. "Will you be here next Friday? I'll bring the greatest clam chowder. Will you be here?"

"Yes. Every Friday," she answered.

Every Friday, sure every Friday were the same words she had used to order the intern to bring files to the house.

———•———

Gloria knocked on Amanda's door, waited to be called into the room, moved to the small round chair near the end of the bed. Amanda clicked off the late night news. "It must be hard for you," she said. "It was a terrible way for him to have to die. I know you don't talk about it, Gloria, but maybe you should. Wouldn't it be better?"

"That's not why I came here. No I can deal with it. I dealt with it ever since I had to come home, wipe the spit from his face, clean his bottom, and listen to his venom. Gloria bit her bottom lip. "No, another reason."

"Okay. What then?"

"Once you said something that I didn't understand then and still don't." Gloria looked directly at Amanda. "When I was going with Conrad, you told me to be careful."

"That was so long ago." Amanda folded the end of her blanket.

"But you said that things can happen, things can happen and hurt a person. I thought you meant my father could hurt Connie. But I think there was something else. I think you meant he would hurt me."

"Conrad wouldn't have hurt you. Not on purpose."

"I don't think you were talking about Conrad. I thought you meant my father."

"Maybe I know what happens to people who go with young boys who they should stay away from. Maybe I once knew a girl who met a tall young boy who would never be accepted by her family and maybe hurtful things happened. And maybe that's why I warned you. And maybe things happened." Amanda leaned forward, "and maybe it all happens because we're meant to do something else."

"Look what happened to me Amanda, and I never did anything except fall in love. Momma had to leave, Connie left, left, just left me, no goodbyes, just left, and never even gave a damn. I promised myself, made another dumb promise, promised never again to fall in love so easily. Promise me Amanda, that nothing will happen if I do."

"Can the wind promise?" Amanda hugged Gloria. "Can the sea promise? Only you can make that promise."

"But Amanda, I fall in love too easily."

The two women retreated into their own thoughts. In half-sleep, Amanda wondered how she could help Gloria; Gloria, curled into a cushioned arm chair, wondered what had happened to Amanda.

Amanda sat up, "Friday I will make a wonderful clam chowder, you know that young man always brings clams around for sale on Fridays, and I'll order some lobsters. You get one of those wonderful pies from Village Bakers. We'll have a feast."

"Sounds fun, Amanda. Like the pilgrims and the Natives and not even Thanksgiving." Gloria added, "Oh yes we will have a guest, the new intern." Gloria smiled. "Like old times, clam chowder on Friday. Goodnight Amanda. Don't let the bedbugs bite."

10

Chris Verity

Chris Verity dropped folded burlap bags in the cab of the old Camaro he had purchased from Moulder Funeral Home. In kinder days, it carried flowers from wakes to cemeteries. Chris had converted it into a utility vehicle for carrying clams, equipment, an occasional lost dog, groceries, and any girl who was immune to empty beer cans, and clam odors.

He walked across the top beam of the jetty that divided the clam boat moorings from the bay, tossed two bags at a time onto the dock, sealed each bag with a yellow tag required by the State, moved his boat to a mooring, and secured additional bushel bags of clams under the boat to keep them fresh.

Chris delivered the day's count of clams to the wholesaler's shack where a grumbling old man waited to close the shop. The stringy-haired man signed a receipt, walked to the back of the shack, lifted a paper bag from behind an ice bucket, and tapped it with his bony forefinger. "Fair catch," he said as he threw the bag to Chris. "Now you sign for this. Use too much of this stuff and you'll forget to protect yourself, wind up with AIDS. Maybe, wind up with no brain like your brother Freddie. Screwed his self up. Don't let him in here no more. Ye'd be better off selling it than using it. Bunch of customers where you make your deliveries. Bunch more at that hangout of yours. Just sign for it."

Chris returned to the dock, parked his car, opened a can of beer, and watched the sunset.

"Another Tuesday," he said shaking his head. "Another night at Belle's, another night to have some fun, get stoned, and try to make it with one of those dames. I think I can catch the attention of one of them with this stuff I bring along. Think I can make it if Belle doesn't get up tight again. Hell, some fancy dudes who never show up at her place pay good money for that stuff."

Chris rattled a beer can, then sipped and talked to the foam bubbling from the top. "That Belle sure smacked me one with that big frying pan last week. Hell, I was just having some fun, trying to forget how hard it is to make a buck, trying to forget this damn bay, trying to have some fun. But she's cool. But does she have to take after me so hard? Says it's because she likes me and doesn't want to see me get messed up like my bro. Too late Belle old girl. Too late."

He locked the car and walked to the small apartment he had rented over the motor repair shop. He looked out the kitchen window from which he saw his car, boat, and bobbing mooring. He munched on an apple while cooking pasta and the sauce from a half-empty jar.

Tuesday nights were especially alive for Chris Verity. He delivered clams to regular customers in the neat ranch houses near the beach, collected cash for the clams and anything else he delivered.

Tuesday nights Chris had cash to play at Belle's and to pay for the drugs he would use and sell. He knew what to expect from Belle, and knew he would end the night on his boat. He would sail to the clam beds, to a place where he could talk to his boat, his motor and to those kindred spirits that belong to the salt marsh, are nurtured by it and in their turn, protect it.

Tuesday night, close to midnight, Belle opened the green doors of the saloon and without any help tossed Chris and his friends into the street. She stood there, large black pan in her hand, and waited until they were out of sight.

———•———

"Don't know how many more kicks in the ass I can take from Belle. It's painful but it's a blast." Solitary days intensified Chris Verity's monologues and conversations with his boat and motors.

"Funny as hell last night. Eight-balling in the back with those jokers, popping stuff 'till I didn't care about much except I was crying a lot. Offered some to the big brunette, that's when Belle slugged me. Grabbed my belt and spun me around. I couldn't stop laughing even when she tossed me out with the other dudes. We wanted to go back, but Belle was ready with that black pan. I can still feel the sting, asked her if she wanted to do that again and if she wanted to flop into bed. That's when she really got mad. Don't know what she was saying but knew it was time to stay out of there."

"Head still hurts, my back is red and black from that pan. My Mom never did that. She wanted to but couldn't lift a pan like that, half the time didn't know I was there. Just looking for big bro' Freddie. He was so mellow or blown out he couldn't help, but he was number one."

"Hey, motor, don't kick out on me when I'm telling you something important or if I'm dragging a rake."

"I'm there to feed everyone. Cinderfella! Good name, huh? Yeah! Get the clams, sell them, and pay the rent. No. Give Mom the money to pay the rent. Let her have the bucks, move every few months so she don't have to pay the last month. Probably never pays any except the first month's rent."

Chris Verity was relieved that the coming deluge would interrupt his long hot day's clamming.

"That old Palmer, though, he got wise to her. Wanted my brother Freddie's ass. Thought he was cute. Mom would have given me to him for the asking, but not big bro."

"There was the time, hear this you friggin rakes, when Pig, you remember the big kid, not too bright, good worker, well Piggy called me home from school. That's when I still lived with all of them. Said something bad was happening. Figured they were taking Mom to the hospital again but the sheriff was there this time. Old Palmer had done it. Had us tossed out, everything on the sidewalk. I ran up the stairs to try to save my things, had those records and stereo, but they were gone. Out the window onto the street, every bum in town had picked what he wanted. No one around to help so I ran down the stairs, spun the sheriff around, and broke his nose. All it took was a light tap; the son-of-a-bitch didn't know how to cover up. They slammed me into the cop car, cuffed behind my back. It hurt but I wouldn't let them know. Never let them know it hurt, anything hurt."

"Pop made me promise to take care of everyone. He knew I could do it even if I was drunk, didn't know about drugs. Loved my old man. Friggin bus driver hit him on the Harley, wiped him out. Poor bastard, I mean really, never had a chance his whole life. He once had a girl friend, some rich dame I bet. Her old man shot him. My old man must have been something else with broads."

"Toughest thing about it was me going to tell his old man. I met old man Winkler a few times, old lady Winkler too; they never wanted my Mom around, just because she held onto her family name. The old man scared the hell out of me, they're real creepy, those old people. Imagine that, they wanted me to be a Winkler. I picked my last name off the side of a truck. Made everyone really pissed.

Chris brought the flat boat onto the small island. Crouching in the deserted duck blind which had been used by hunters and bird watchers since the 1800s, he reviewed the fading carved letters GPalmieri and a carved spider that hid the initials TSteelhart. Chris dreamed of the day he would be secreted in the blind, watch the terns return from winter haunts, discover their hiding place, find the eyes, and set the couple free.

"Maybe then I'll have the rush of free flight. No more Tuesday nights. No more Mom blown out on the couch. No more carrying Freddie home too stoned to remember where he lives or his name or anything except that he needs more and swearing that everyone is a dick. No more worrying about HIV or if some girl is going to have another baby by some cheating bastard who pays a few bucks and disappears. Just floating. Floating free."

West wind drove black clouds racing like the Reapers retinue across the bay. Defiant gusts of the East wind prepared to ignite the clouds and electrify the sky.

Chris had waited out storms in the blind before. He waited for the moment when lightning would hit the bay and he could leap on top of the blind, strip to the waist and scream, "Here I am. Here I am. YaYaYa. Still here. WooWooWoo.." Connivance with nature's forces bubbled his plasma, impelled a rush from his toes to his shoulders, caused joyful and sanguine pain. He waited for the ultimate exhilaration of conquest. It erupted with the brawn of colliding ironclad warriors. He scrambled to the top of the protecting hut, stripped naked, hurled his clothing to the ground and Yayayad.

He dropped to the ground to recover his clothing, felt for his cell phone and yelled, "Damn you wind." He scrambled among the weeds, scratched the sandy shore, dug into the ground feeling for his cell phone. He dove into the dark surging tide, felt among the rocks, weeds, and sandy bottom, pulled up the cell phone and a large chowder clam. He rolled back into the shelter, tucked the drying phone and clam under his shirt and tried to sleep.

This lingering storm tore through power lines and knocked out the lights along the Connecticut shore. Chris saw cars race along the road and saw lightning reflected on the windows of the house where he delivered clams on Friday.

Lightning reflected on the cell phone, along the crystal algae growing along the Island's rocky shore, and on the worn side of the clam shell. Chris knife could not penetrate the muscle on the back of the clam that seemed to be fighting for its life. An impromptu wave shook the shell from Chris' powerful grip, rolled it into the water.

"Piss," he yelled. "I'll be back. I'll get you." He rolled back into the protected duck blind and slept until his wet phone buzzed with its preset alarm. "Now you work. Ought to toss you back sucker."

Chris slipped into the tentative sleep when the same dreams rolled in geometric formations, sometimes crossing on a diagonal, sometimes wiggling at a tangent, sometimes seeping into other dreams, but never different. "Dreams, damn dreams are like the rest of my life. Never start, never end, always the same crap. Not dreams about what's going to happen. Dreams like a book about things that have been and then just start the same damn book over again. One of these days, one of these days, going to end that book, maybe start a new one, maybe not have a book, only keep moving."

Chris dreamed about Belle, about Tuesday nights, about sliding across the sidewalk, coming back and getting tossed out by Belle, but ready to go back for her love and punishment.

Different from Sally in the diner. No freebees from her. Money on the table or F... off. Think she'd be better to him, knowing about Billy. Chris would sometimes wish old man Palmer had hit on him so that his daughter would have taken him in like she did Billy. Then he could be out of here, too.

Wonder if she ever really did it with Billy or just made the old man think so. She looks like a pretty cold dame, but I'll bet she could be something else.

One of these Fridays, maybe she'll have pity on a poor little clam boy.

His dreams were subject to their own vertigo, their own way of colliding with other dreams, of becoming fantasy within nightmares that churn at his groin and crunch his stomach muscles.

Chris flicked his flashlight on then off, then repeated the action as if he were a lighthouse or a savage buoy manipulating a safe harbor. Using his own clammer's code, he signaled the house on the cliff, "One of these Fridays."

11

Giant Tracks

Salmon-colored napkins complemented the gray tablecloth, silverware, stark white dishes, and red carnation centerpiece. Amanda polished the edges of the glasses, adjusted the flowers, and then returned to the steaming pots in the kitchen.

Amanda walked to the edge of the cliff, spotted the small clam boat returning to the harbor, set her two fingers near her lips and whistled; birds flapped and flew away. The young clammer waved his shirt acknowledging the call. She thought about another young clammer who once waved his shirt to Gloria.

She checked the things she had prepared for her clam chowder, called the Tern Harbor Market to remind the owner to deliver the lobsters promptly at four o'clock. Without knocking, Chris Verity brought two sacks of clams into the kitchen as he did every Friday, picked up a fresh baked cookie and waited for Amanda's harangue about not waiting to be invited into the house. He smiled and wagged his head, feigned apology until she stopped talking, paid him for the clams, and offered him a cup of coffee.

"Thanks. Got to make my deliveries. This is payday from the restaurants and bars, all my customers." If the Palmer dame was around, he thought, he might stay a little longer.

The intern set the canvas backpack on the front hall table, followed Amanda into the semi-circular porch, stretched his body and neck to see the dramatic view of the bay and Long Island Sound. He accepted a glass of wine along with one of Amanda's cookies.

"Thanks," he squinted. "I didn't know Miss Palmer's mother was . . ."

"Part Indian? No! I am not her mother, just an old friend." Amanda smiled at the young intern.

"Oh, sorry," he blushed. "My name is James Meredith. Should have introduced myself," he tried to change the subject.

Amanda looked through the circle of her forefingers and thumbs, moved them from the spider tattoo on the intern Meredith's wrist, to his square chin and wide jaw, the shape of his head, and broad shoulders. She looked at the black hair that had been tied into a neatly brushed ponytail. "A Meredith from Greenport, right? Harry and Beatrice's boy. I recognize a Native just by looking at you."

"How? I haven't said anything about where I come from." The intern spoke in the mellifluous tone Native men learn from childhood.

"I always know. Forecasting breezes whisper soft lullabies telling me what needs to be known."

Amanda motioned the young man into the kitchen. "Have some cookies while I finish my work. Miss Palmer will be home soon."

So he's the one Gloria picked from that new bunch at the College, Amanda thought. She must have known who he is; she doesn't just make choice by accident. Couldn't just have been a convenient wind blowing in her ear, must have been something else blowing in her ear. Too convenient.

"How long you had that tattoo?" she asked.

"A year ago. Got the earring when I was in Junior High. The spider web copied someone I know, someone important to my people." The intern stood at attention as if in the presence of a leader.

Amanda splashed potatoes into the large steaming pot. *Good model, she thought. Hope it's for the right reasons.*

"I brought these papers for Miss Palmer. Is it okay if I go over them before she gets here?" He began to sift through the rubber-banded files.

He started to set the files on the piano, saw Amanda shake her head, and then moved them to a table.

"When did you see the guy with the spider tattoo?" Amanda called from the kitchen.

"Used to work at a little restaurant in Orient. He's one of my people, like a shaman, more like a chief, a renegade who returned. He brought East End's Native families together like we haven't been, I guess forever. I saw him there, at the café, and decided to get this tattoo.

"All I asked was when did you see him. But sounds like you have a hero, or at least someone to look up to." Amanda retreated to her kitchen. *Yes. You have a beautiful role model. No, I'm not Gloria's mother, just an old friend. What would you do if you knew who I am? What would you think if you knew why your hero ever left? What will you do if you find the truth about Steve Palmer in those files of yours?*

"Come in here and help me with these chowder clams," she ordered. "You open them slowly, as if each one has a secret."

The intern hummed an old Native melody then switched to a rap beat as he speeded his work on the chowder clams.

"Amanda insisted on a party tonight," Gloria seemed to appear out of nowhere and handed the intern two pastry boxes. "Very informal though. Hope you like chowder and lobster." Gloria left the room as quickly as she had arrived.

The intern listened to the slow tinkling of the bell on the red buoy, and became narcotized as the sunset's magenta streaks and the moonlight's silver lines entered temporary conjunction across the horizon. Day and night, usually driven from one another like magnetic poles, converged around that sliver of time when neither was in command. The shimmering rock created the mystique of Lorelei beckoning sailors to exhaustive pleasure and nefarious catastrophe.

The intern became aware that Gloria was in the room reviewing the files. She had set aside the old copies of the *Gazette*, carefully examined each of the yellowing documents in the second folder and was about to open the folder marked "FINANCE" when a soft bell announced dinner.

Gloria was animated as they talked through dinner. They talked about the intern's experiences at the College and at the newspaper office. He joked about the secretary and her unexpected appearances in the basement. They talked about clam chowder and lobster and blueberry pie and ice cream. Then they talked about the bay.

"I never realized how many little inlets and small islands there are from here out to the Sound and then along that beach to the cliffs." The intern moved his forefinger along the window, outlining a map.

"All kinds of stories about how this place came to be," Gloria hesitated. "You do know that glaciers formed it all."

"Well maybe, but," The intern looked at Amanda who continued with her pie. "But there are stories I have heard about how it was formed. They tell at campfires. You know I'm Native American, right?"

"Yes. Go on." Gloria shrugged her shoulders in a form of noblesse oblige.

"They tell that the whole earth was once water and that after many years Giants came and raised the land from under the water. They say that one of the Giants pulled his fingers along the surface of the land and where he pressed hard he created lakes and rivers. They say that when he was tired, he put down his thumb and made the great bays and the body of water we call Long Island Sound. Then he drummed his fingers up and down making inlets and marshes. Another giant pulled together parts of the land into the hills and fields. The first giant walked into the water, and wherever he stepped he crushed the old shells of clams, crabs and other sea animals and made sand. The other giant walked along the shoreline and wherever he walked, he crushed stone and made pebble beaches. That's how they say this place was made so beautiful. That's what they say at the campfires.

"It's said," The intern continued. "When the giants' work was done they spun around very fast and turned into pillars of white dust, rose up to the star-filled sky canopy. That's what they say."

Gloria thanked Frank Meredith for the wonderful way he told that story of the Island's creation. She thought of how Tern Harbor Village had been created, how her father tried to be the giant, how he had put his thumb print on it and kept it there until he could no longer be in control. She thought of the difference between the mythical giants' magnificent end and the lonely despair of Steve Palmer's last moments.

"Oh, by the way," The intern was preparing to leave. "something odd about that financial material. Your father must have been a very careful person. Kept track of everything. Every check in those bank statements is carefully marked and every statement is perfectly reconciled. But there are a few checks that aren't clear."

"He made notes on everything. I think he made notes on bathroom tissues." Gloria looked at Amanda.

"Well there are a few kind of large checks, oh it was a while ago, that are written to the same person with no memo showing what they are for. I thought you should know just in case someone owes you money." The intern thanked Amanda for dinner and for helping make it easy for him to talk about his heritage.

The intern put on his helmet, straddled his mountain bike, and turned onto the dark road.

12

Winklers

Chaotic cologne blends adhered to everything in Steve Palmer's room. Gloria opened his closet door and adjusted the jackets and shirts. The top bureau drawers were tidy assemblages of gold rings, watches, cuff links, clothing arranged by color and season as if he was preparing to get dressed, as if he had never suffered a stroke.

"Don't move a damn thing," he would shout in undecipherable grunts. "Want it all where I can get at it when I get out of this damn chair. Don't you mess with it."

Gloria was uncertain about when she would get the courage to clear it all out. She folded a towel in the bathroom, closed a squeezed-dry toothpaste tube, and lined up bottles of after shave lotion and cologne. She moved to her own study at the end of the hallway, dropped the folders on the shag rug, opened the small refrigerator, and opened a bottle of beer.

"That's more like it," she said as she sat on the rug and opened the first file with its series of maps and charts showing the water route from Tern Harbor along the Island's north shore east to Orient Point. Small private Rail Lines, that serviced the agrarian economy, formed spurs to the developing towns and eventually combined into the Long Island Rail Road with its track extending east to Greenport on the North Fork of the Island and to Montauk on the South.

The intern had marked the Indian trail on the earliest maps that, on newer maps, became the pathway for horse drawn wagons and then the main road listed as 25A. The new highway followed the shoreline from New York City to Tern Harbor, then dipped south avoiding large North Shore estates. The intern had covered each of the maps with a clear overlay and marked sites of British massacres of Indians. Maps of emerging villages were accompanied by copies of deeds, small drawings and letters.

Gloria tried to avoid the finance folder, sipped the last of the beer, then looked at the notes summarizing the bank statements, mortgage notes due to Steve Palmer, the list of properties he had purchased, and the businesses in which he had investments. "Everything in precise order," The intern wrote. "A few unclear checks in separate envelope."

Gloria examined her father's small check marks that approved the bank statement numbers. There were statements for each month since Steve Palmer had arrived in Tern Harbor. Gloria sighed in boredom until she opened the last envelope of checks, marked *unaccounted for*.

Five $2000 checks were made out to cash with no descriptive memo were simply endorsed *Moulder* with the remark *Winkler, for CW*. Gloria spread the checks on the rug, turned them from front to back, then over again.

"Why Winkler," she murmured. "Which Winkler?" She checked the dates, put the checks back into the envelope, wrapped a rubber band around the file, walked past her father's room, and ran down the stairs and to her car. She drove past the beaches, past wavering trees, past Village bars and up the short hill to Stillwater Avenue. She stopped at the old blue-shingled Winkler house. She clutched the envelope, started toward the house, saw the flicker of a cigarette lighter on the front porch, inhaled the dry smell of a cigar that was lit for a second time.

"You can come, young lady." A soft old voice acknowledged her.

"Mr. Winkler? I am . . ." she tried to continue.

"Know who you are. What you want?"

"I'm not sure. How are you?"

The old man drew on his cigar, sent blue smoke up in the air and coughed. "I asked what do you want?

"My father died."

"So'd a lot of people."

"I was going through some papers and found some old checks that had something to do with you."

"Never saw any checks from him."

"Well no. Made to someone else and marked for you."

"Better come inside. Have to smoke out here. Wife too sick to handle these."

Gloria followed Kloss Winkler through the side door into a dimly lit room; the house had the smell of a sick room that had been scrubbed of vomit, vaporub in a hissing humidifier, and spilled cough medicine. Veronica Winkler was asleep on a pale yellow pillow that competed with her sallow complexion.

"Come in the other room. Don't want her disturbed." Kloss Winkler walked ahead of Gloria.

"Told you never had any check, never got any money. Wasn't for me." He offered her a cup of coffee. "You know what it was for."

Gloria looked around the barren room, saw two unframed pictures on the dining table.

"We never had much fancy stuff. No time. Too busy working in that psych hospital. Worked hard, honest; taught us to keep quiet about our work. No checks for us."

"My father was a very careful and precise person. I guess everyone who lived around here long enough knew that." Gloria tried to impress Kloss Winkler. "Those checks were marked for Winkler."

"Not for us. You know what they did to Conrad. You know why he didn't get to the graduation, get his award." The old man coughed from years of smoking stale cigars. "You know? Because he was in the hospital, that's why. And you knew about it, knew he was there because he got shot," he said. "By some dumb hunter."

"I never knew."

"Some hunter my ass," the old man shook with growing rage. "He was no place near that Goose Island. It was in the Harbor, doing what he always did near that friggin buoy. Getting through to you yet?"

"You mean someone from the beach?"

"Then that wasn't enough. They made him leave here or he would get it again. Lost our Conrad. Lost him."

"Oh my God," Gloria got up, walked toward the door, turned back toward Kloss Winkler. "The money was for him. They gave him money to get away from me. And he took it," she whispered. "That was all it took, $10,000."

"Never that much. He left here and went off and got married."

"Where is he now?" Gloria leaned on the wood dining room chair.

"Gone up on the same hill as your father." The old man turned his head to hide dry tears.

Veronica Winkler called from the sick room. "Is that her? Told you she's never to come into this house, that drunken whore."

"Not you," the old man waved his palm at Gloria. "Shh. I'll tell her who is here."

Gloria heard the gurgle of vomit, the intermittent sounds of running water and paper towels scraping at the floor. She controlled the gagging sensation instigated by the foul odors.

"So, at last you came here. Should have run away with him. Then he would be here not with that bitch." The old woman wheezed. "She has those boys, probably not even his, not the first one. The second one's a good boy but afraid to come in here. You should'uv run with him instead of chasing him away." Veronica Winkler coughed, then drifted into sleep. Gloria looked at Kloss Winkler as if pleading to understand what happened.

He told her that Conrad had gone to upstate New York, near Cortland, had a small farm. "He became a wild boy up there; drank, smoked, other things, rode a motorcycle," the old man said. "Married this little fat lady, she already had one boy, no father, and then they had another. Once, Conrad tried to win money at a traveling rodeo. Had to show he could do anything, afraid of nothing, tried to win. Got gored by a bull. High up in the hip," the old man put his hand on his own hip. "In the same leg where he had been shot. That ended his farming."

The old man motioned Gloria toward the front steps. He lit the cigar he had stored in the dead plant along side of the porch, told Gloria that Conrad returned to the Island, "asked your father for a little money, was going to start some small business, but never got any. Was riding his motorcycle when he got side swiped and slammed into the front of a bus. That's what put him up on the hill. Never found the car that hit him. I always figured it was the same folks as that shot his leg, but never any way to prove it. They made sure Conrad wasn't going to be around.

"And that's what happened. The old lady's going to be up there with him soon. And some day, maybe, me too."

"Can I help?" Gloria reached across to touch the old man.

"No." He pulled away. "Don't come back. Leave us in our own peace and anger. Your father is dead. Hah! And how much did he take with him? Same as my Conrad!"

Not what he took with him, she thought. What he took away from us, and how he tied me to this damned place. She drove home, stormed up the stairs toward her father's room.

"Bastard," she called out. "It was you. You shot him. You paid him. You took him out of my life, took away everyone I ever really loved; you're still doing it."

She entered the brightly lit room, pulled clothes from the closet, piled them in the center of the floor, emptied dresser drawers onto the stacked clothes; then she walked into the bathroom. She threw toothbrushes, razors, boxes of band aides, medicine containers, and mouthwash into the trash can. She reached for the bottles of after-shave and cologne, twisted the cap from the bottle of Eternity cologne, then, as if someone had grabbed her arm she stopped and replaced the bottle in the medicine cabinet.

Gloria left the house, walked across the driveway, turned on the lights of the studio that had been Steve Palmer's office and meeting place. She pulled files from the desk and cabinets, and dumped all the papers into a plastic bag. She found one drawer filled with pictures of bare bosomed women, an unopened box of shotgun shells, photos of clam chowder day contests, lists of cash donations, and scribbled notes of women's names and phone numbers. There were pictures of the Harbor taken from the glassed in porch including photos of a single clammer moving past the red buoy and waving his shirt up toward the camera. There was a picture of a clammer grimacing in pain, holding his blood-covered leg.

"You did it," she screamed. "That's what you meant, if you see him again, this time you'd kill him." She held the photos up to the light then put them in the envelope with the canceled checks. "You, you did it."

She ran along the road to Fazio Beach, leaned against the warm moss covered rocks, scraped her nails through the gentle plants that filled the cracks between the rocks, cried under the starless sky, listened to the receding tide, and skimmed a flat stone across the quiet bay.

"I needed you Connie. You took his money and just left. I've been afraid to get close to anyone after you. You just left me. I've never again wanted to fall in love, I fell in love too easily."

Gloria waded into the shallow water, tied her sneakers over her shoulder and walked along the beach. She thought about the void after high school and during her freshman year at Tern College. She thought about the lonely days without friends or Connie. She thought about becoming eighteen and taking control of her own money. She kicked sand into the water and watched clouds streaking from the west.

As if divorced from herself, Gloria envisioned a young Gloria Palmer during sophomore year. She stumbled from classes to boring Tern Harbor roommates to weekends listening to her father rant about the newspaper or the real estate deals, or the kind of people who were trying to move into town. Steve Palmer boomed through the jasmine smell of July nights.

"Would be no College if I didn't knock myself out at that newspaper, or racing around collecting rents from deadbeats, or going out to be sure this town remained clean and pure. I have an appointment with Butch Moulder, probably be late, meeting him at City Hall. Made that man mayor. Be nothing if I didn't do it for him." The black Jaguar screeched out of the gravel driveway.

Amanda appeared whenever Palmer would leave Gloria alone. "You know Amanda, I don't think Poppa spends his night like the avenger or a cop. He's probably making sure the single ladies at the bars get home safely. Bet he takes them home, theirs or that studio. Bet Butch has some young cop working tonight."

"Gloria. You shouldn't talk about your father that way."

"Come on Amanda. You were here when Momma died. You know what he is. I know how he collects rents. Amanda, I loved those earrings you used to wear. Are they silver?"

"Silver. Those little hoops, delicate, so nice, your Momma gave them to me. Did you ever see the little open clamshells? You know what they are?"

"They must be the myth. But that's an Indian story."

"Yes. Didn't you know?"

"Momma said something about it, but."

"Yes. I am Indian, my ancestors used to live here. Right here."

"Who do you think Poppa will rescue tonight? Maybe one of the interns working for the paper."

"It's a young man this year," Amanda nodded.

"That might be interesting for him." Gloria thought of her mother's death and her father's visitors that night. "He can talk about all he is doing for me. He isn't doing things for me, it's always for himself. Aunt Marie invited me for Thanksgiving." She paused, stared at her mother's surrogate. "Amanda, you have a son, don't you? What is he like?"

"Well, he's tall, with beautiful auburn hair, black eyes. He loves fun, was star of his high school football team. He loves me and I love him very much. One day he'll come home, he'll take over my house."

"Where is he now? What college?"

"He's your age, not in college. Lives in New York, trying to make his way there. He's helping set up a new business and preparing to expand into New Jersey."

I should get away too, Gloria wished. Escape from my father, way from here. Why did I ever make that promise to Momma?

"It must be hard for you. Your husband gone, your son away, but you seem at ease. You always had those shallow eyes like you had hadn't slept whenever you came back to work here. You seem happier since your husband, well you know."

"I do miss my boy, but he'll come home. Been away for a few years, but he'll be home. Please excuse me, I'm tired."

"Was he ever here? How come I never saw him?"

"Only once. Told him to stay out of the way. He has a way of getting into trouble." Amanda gazed toward the bay.

Gloria stared down at Target Rock and imagined that young boy standing there, planting his flag on the buoy. She reached for the telephone and called her Aunt Marie.

13

Hawk's Game

"Hi Aunt Marie, this is Gloria."

"Gloria. What's happened? Has my brother done something? Is he dead?"

"No poppa's fine. He went out as usual."

"Shame. So what's going on? Come here for Thanksgiving, right?"

"Yes, but I want to ask a favor."

"For you, yes. If it's for him, forget it. Will it upset him?"

"For me. I have to leave here. This week. And I need a place to stay. I mean to stay for a long time. Can't stand staying here, watching him, listening to him, and being his property. I have to be myself and I can't if I stay here."

"Bravo. Come here. I'd love to see the old bastard's face when you tell him. Stay here as long as you like. Don't worry about money, we can help with that."

"Not going to tell him. Might not make it."

"Will he try to stop you?"

"I'll be gone before he knows anything. Will leave everything here. Aunt

Marie, can you do something else for me?"

"Name it princess."

"Can you make an appointment for me at a beauty parlor? Need a cut and styling and whatever they do. Then can you come with me to Bloomingdales?"

"Everything OK except Bloomies. You'll come shopping with me. Get away from that little suburban girl stuff. We'll get you dressed right. Don't worry about money. The tight wad probably never let you have enough."

"I have my own money from Momma's estate; it became mine when I was eighteen. I switched the account from the Tern Harbor Bank to the College branch to make it easier to use privately, without anyone telling Poppa."

"We'll get you set up here at our bank. You'll keep it there and let me take care of you this once. You know he never invites us out there, never comes here except when he has to show the restaurant to his friends. He's always been angry with us, always been busy with his friends and his money. Enough of that. Get here. Can't wait. When?"

"Monday. He'll be busy. Amanda is going home to take care of some of her own business. I'll be there Monday."

"Glory. One question. He always used to . . . does he still fool around?"

"Whenever he can. More than you know."

Gloria, wearing dark glasses, huddled into the back corner of the train to avoid being recognized by any of the Tern Harbor commuters,. She watched as suburbanites, who boarded at local stations, sat reading newspapers, fidgeting or looking out the windows. She tried to count the men and women who daily boarded the train at each local station, reached their destinations and then dispersed like lava spewing from an overwrought volcano. She counted them as they fled in a quiet diaspora of broken dreams, returning at night to places they called home. She wondered how many of them had ever lost or found love.

Gloria paid the cab driver and pushed the guitar case in front of her as she stepped tentatively toward the low privet hedges that fenced the sweet smelling rose garden in front of the brownstone house.

"Oh my beautiful baby," Marie Palmieri hugged her niece. "You're the image of your mother. Where are your bags?"

"Nothing. I left it all. Just this one case."

"A guitar? You look like what's-er-name in that movie, *Sound of Music.* Do you play?"

"No. It's all the cash I took out of the bank. I couldn't get a bank check. He'd know how to stop it."

"Good girl. Let's get it inside before any of the street idiots get any fancy ideas."

Hissing sounds rising through steam radiators played skittish counterpoint to the soft rock music from the radio in Gloria's butterfly wallpapered room. She marveled at the humps of snow buried cars that were victimized by the Thanksgiving blizzard that was decorating Brooklyn.

She joined the family at the breakfast table. Spice odors of a slowly roasting turkey, the whirring sounds of a food processor, and the gentle touch of her Aunt Marie delighted Gloria. She looked cautiously at the twin cousins, who she remembered as those fat little boys in one of the piano's pictures. Home from college, they were no longer fat but handsome, dark haired, young men who were her age, and who she wished were not her cousins.

"You remember Thomas and Guiseppe don't you Gloria?" Her Uncle Vince tapped each of his sons.

"I'm Tommy," one of the young men bowed. "That's Gis," he tapped his brother on the neck. "Oh yeah, I'm Mom's favorite because I'm the oldest."

"I thought you were twins," Gloria squinted.

"Right, but I was born first and am older, so I'm the favorite."

"I'd bounce this wooden spoon on your head," Marie shook the spoon at her son. "But won't waste this good sauce. There are no favorites."

"Oh he's the favorite alright," smiled Gis. "He was the first to get ice skates, first to get driving lessons, first to be accepted to Dartmouth, and oh yes the first to have a girl friend."

"What girl friend?" Marie and Vince both stopped their activities in the kitchen.

"Told you to keep quiet," Tommy glared at Gis, who covered his mouthful of eggs.

"What girlfriend and how come you didn't say anything?" Aunt Marie showed her teeth in a broad smile that Gloria recognized as a danger signal.

"Well, thought I would tell you about her later." Tommy shrugged at Gis.

"She's a great girl, Mom." Gis came to his brother's defense. "Elizabeth is pretty, smart, an honor student and she's from Brooklyn. What more can you ask?"

"You left out an important word." Uncle Vince twirled the knife he had been using to shred lettuce.

"Yes," Marie tapped the wooden spoon on the sink. "What part of Italy, her family?"

"Very north part." Gis chuckled.

"She's from Brooklyn, Mom. Her parents are from here. Thought I would ask her to join us for Thanksgiving, if it's okay." Tommy put his arm around his mother.

"So what part of Italy, or did they come on the Mayflower?" Vince demanded.

"Not the Mayflower, Pop. Her grandfather came from Poland and her grandmother came from Nebraska." Tommy sat down and moved his fork around the cold eggs on his plate.

"Where the hell is Nebraska? They have snow and buffalo. So when do we meet this young lady?" Marie interceded.

"See, Gloria, he's the favorite," Gis laughed.

Gloria followed the animated banter. She had never heard the wonder of family activity before, wished she had always been in this family, that she could have argued about who is the favorite. She wondered if Gis had a girl friend.

"I asked Elizabeth to come for Thanksgiving. Knew you would want her to, Mom," Tommy put his arm around Marie's shoulders.

"And what about you, Gis? Am I going to hear another shoe drop, maybe another, what's her name, Elizabeth?" Marie bent her head toward Gis.

"Nope. Just me and my books."

"Sorry Gloria," Marie turned to her niece. "Never know what's going to happen next around here." She waved her cooking spoon toward each of the boys. "And I want you to introduce your nice friends to Gloria."

"We don't know any *nice* boys, Mom." Gis scratched his cheek. "But she could meet cousin Piggy."

"Don't call him Piggy. It's Francis. And she has already met him at your Father's office. And by the way, he is a very nice young man." Marie turned back to the counter.

"Oh yeah, Piggy, Francis, is a very nice young man. Right. He came up to visit us on campus one weekend and filled in a bunch of letters on his alphabet card." Tommy coughed.

"What's an alphabet card?" Gloria asked.

"He has this card he keeps in his wallet that has the alphabet with a girl's name next to each letter after he, uh, spends time, oh hell after he sleeps with her." Gis blushed.

"Yeah. So far he has a Yolanda, Wanda, Sally and when he was on campus he started from the front of the alphabet. Nice guy. Up to F the last time we saw the card. Decided to find excuses not to invite him again." Tommy shook his head as if in disapproval.

"So what do you do at the restaurant?" Gis asked Gloria.

"Answer phones, say hello to customers, and keep the books. Just have to keep track of cash receipts, who pays rents in the apartments and stores, make sure the bills are right and paid and make out the payroll. I'm trying to convince your Dad and Mom to get computers. They have these new programs and . . . I'm boring you."

"No. I think it's terrific," Gis moved his chair closer to his cousin. "But don't get into that with any nice guys we introduce you to. Hey Mom. There is one guy from school who is in New York and has no place to go for Thanksgiving. Should I contact him? He's staying at the Y."

"Why at the Y?" Vince asked.

"Well he's from Idaho and wasn't going to spend the money to go home, so he's staying in the City." Gis shrugged.

"Stupido." Marie smacked Gis with the cleaned wooden spoon. "What d'ya mean leaving him in the city alone. You call him and get him out here. Make space for him in your room. What's his name?"

"William Hawkclaw. We call him Hawk." Tommy spoke softly.

The twins took turns describing their tall, well structured friend, who had the strong Native American features that defined his character. They described his speed on the track and skiing, and then they described the singular feature that defined his name, his small sharp nose.

"Get him here. So we will have a guest whose family was here before the Mayflower and one whose ancestors came on the Mayflower." Marie checked the roasting turkey.

The afternoon and evening were full of smiles and food; Gloria and Elizabeth helped Marie in the kitchen; the twins and Hawk drank beer and screamed through a football game; Vince opened bottles of port wine and liqueurs to go along with the desserts. Logs crackled in the family room fireplace.

Tommy and Elizabeth went out for the evening, Marie and Vince went to their bedroom, and Gloria, Hawk, and Gis sat in the dimly lit family room. They talked softly about television shows they liked, skiing, ice-skating, music they enjoyed, and the wine they were drinking. Gloria wanted to know about Hawk's home, but didn't ask because she didn't want to talk about hers.

Hawk closed his eyes, moved his lips in a silent chant, crossed his arms across his chest, and held his fingers extended oblivious to his friends watching what seemed to be an ancient rite.

"Hawk," Gis whispered. "You okay?"

Gloria leaned forward. "Is that a Native prayer?"

"Yes praying." Hawk stretched out his hand, took hold of one of the empty bottles. "Praying for another beer. Gis. You ever see me do that before. Good trick isn't it? Got you going, but not fast enough. Any more in the fridge or should I go out to get some?"

Gloria left the room, came back with arms full of beer bottles, walked behind the couch, and placed them behind Hawk. "Answer to your prayers. Now your turn to guess mine."

"First we have to chug-a-lug." Gis opened the bottles, offered one to each of his co-conspirators and they started to drink from the short stem jugs.

"I believe you are praying that we were closer to the bathroom." Gis raised his eyebrows as he drained his beer, then left the room.

"I guess that you pray, let's see," Hawk placed his hand on Gloria's forehead. "You pray to be flying over a beautiful mountain, diving into a lush green gorge, soaring over the desert, and landing on an island in the middle of a serene northern lake." He stared into the fireplace embers.

Gis entered the room, raised his beer to the mantle, "I pray for the ability to see the world. I pray to be done with college, wander through all of Europe, ride camels in an African desert, sail across an ocean, and land on an island in the middle of an inland-sea."

"And what about you, Hawk. What do you really pray for?" Gloria touched his shoulder.

"Don't pray, not here, not until I go home, to my real home, not the one where my family, my people live, but where they should be. Then I will dance around a large fire. I'll show you how to do it. The table with the empty bottles is the fire. Now follow me."

Hawk removed his boots and socks, stood erect, spread his arm and turned his palms upward. Gis and Gloria, single file, trailed Hawk's steady rhythm as he moved around the table, expanded the circle around the room, then leaped onto the back of the couch with arms outstretched so that he appeared ready to swoop down on unsuspecting pray. "That's how I will pray," he smiled as he dropped onto the soft cushions.

The friends drank more beer, spoke again of music, books they had read, and paintings they had seen.

"How come you left home Gloria?" Hawk asked as he emptied the last bottle.

"Had to get away from there. Have to find something new, find a new life." She curled into her chair. "What about you?" She nodded toward Hawk.

"Was sent away. Sent to schools and then to Dartmouth. I will go back, need to find something," his hair fell softly around his neck then brushed his shoulders. "Want to find something old, sad, and real when I go home."

Gloria had other dreams than Hawk's. He never mentioned parents, brothers or sisters, only spoke the word family, only spoke of going to a real home. She wondered if she would ever spend a day or night without thinking about her father. She knew how the Native Americans had been pushed from one place to another, had been promised one thing and then another. She knew how land had been taken, she knew that she had lived in a place that should have remained free, and she knew how Steve Palmer had built a town on sacred land.

"Not me who prays to fly over the mountains," she said. "That's you, Hawk. Are we out of beer guys?" They sat with bare feet on the coffee table that had served as the campfire; they sat with eyes closed, and with their own dreams. They covered their feet with a plaid blanket, slept in the warmth of the dying embers, and slept with their private prayers.

The following Thanksgiving Marie invited family from New Jersey, the Bronx, Florida and several neighborhood friends. She recited the family relationship of each of the guests. "I even invited your father," she said without looking at Gloria.

"Is he coming? What did he say? Did he ask about me?"

"He hung up, as usual. Asked him last year, too. Only thing he ever asked was when is his daughter going to be returned to him."

"Never." Gloria tried to block Tern Harbor but was haunted by pictures on the piano; she remembered people on the train; she thought of her struggle to escape, and wondered if she would ever be free of her father.

During dinner, she sat next to her Great-Uncle Benito whose silver hair flowed freely caressed his neck. His dark marble-like eyes demanded attention when he spoke in the deep baritone that rose from his barreling chest. His wrinkled hands were the only part of his imposing presence that hinted the secret of age.

He sipped an espresso, then turned to Gloria. "I hear you are studying journalism at Brooklyn College."

"Yes," she fumbled. "I learned so that I could write the Restaurant newsletter. People really look forward to getting it; I think it has brought in new business."

"Hmm. Yes. I heard. You should come to see my little paper in Forge Creek, New Jersey. Not too different from the one your father has, I think. Someday I will steal you away from here to come work for me. But I will make sure my niece doesn't see me do it." He laughed. "Happened to them once before when Stevie stole your mother."

Marie glared at Benito. He sipped his cognac, winked at Gloria and turned away. It was the first time that she felt uneasy about living in her Aunt's house. She wanted dinner to be over, the sounds of Italian relatives to be muted, and the blaring noise of cousins' children to end. She wanted to be in front of the fireplace, bare feet on the coffee table, talking with Gis and Hawk, talking about music and football and anything but the past.

She dropped onto the couch between her cousin and Hawk, who was unusually quiet. "Still praying, Hawk," she opened a bottle of beer for him.

"No, decision-making. Time to make a change." He turned to Gloria.

It was the second time that day that someone had made her feel uneasy.

"Leaving Dartmouth after this semester. Going back to the family." Hawk ran his nails through his long hair, brushed it straight back and bound it with a rubber band. "Going home."

"You never spoke about your parents before." Gis spoke without looking at either his cousin or his friend. "Who's sick?"

"Never had parents, brothers, sisters, cousins, only family in a place where I grew up and then was sent to school."

"But, your mother and father. What happened?" Gloria wanted to pull back the question.

"My father is the sky and my mother is the earth. Not mystical, just the way it is. All I need. Do you really want to know about my family?" Hawk sat up on the back of the couch; his shadow filled the wall opposite the fireplace.

"Long ago my people were forced to leave their land in what you call Nebraska, were forced to walk to what you call Oklahoma, and were kept in a new place that was not their home. They were forced to work, give up their customs, and send their children away to school to become "civilized" white gentlemen. But the children were always Indians and not real people. One day a chief ran away, back to his home so he could bury his son on his own land. He was captured, put in the brig, jail, until a judge ruled that Indians are people under the law. But the judge's ruling was not applied to any other Indians. I must go home, find my spirit, my soul, and live with my family again."

"But Hawk," Gis pleaded. "That was a long time ago. We are all one people now. We are friends, like family?"

Hawk grasped Gis and Gloria's hands. "We are friends, but I have to go where I will be free. Have to go where I can breathe the air mixed with the desert dirt and the mountain snow. Where the sky embraces the earth."

Then they drank beer, talked about music and football and skiing and sailing and running. "Look at this photo album," Gloria spotted the small book under the coffee table. "We have most of these old family pictures on our piano. These little chubby boys must be you," she showed them to Gis and then to Hawk. "But where are Marie and Vince? I don't recognize the baby sitter."

"Not a baby sitter," Gis grimaced.

Gloria tried to remember the woman.

"Our mother." Gis held the book, then closed it. "Thought you knew. Tommy and I are adopted. Our parents were killed in an auto crash by a drunk driver. My parents were Pop's cousins. They adopted us, there was no one else. Vince and Marie have become our mother and father. Never knew anyone else. So you see, Hawk, we are not that different. Vince is my sky and Marie my earth."

"What about you, Gloria?" Gis squeezed her hand. "What are you searching for?"

"Not searching," Gloria blushed. "Running. My mother died." She mouthed a bottle of beer. "I am running away from who I was. You know the Native Americans where I lived were also shoved off the land, and hardly exist anymore. Don't know much about them, except that there is a myth about the place where I lived," she paused. "Some other time guys."

Tern Harbor, the view from her mother's window, sordid mixtures of opera and rock, fear of her father's controlling demands, and suspicion he had violated sacred trusts toward the land, careened in nightmare rapidity across her closed eyelids.

She reached for the beer bottle, began to sing "Ninety-nine bottles of beer on the wall. Let's talk about football."

Marie and Gloria wore simple black suits in contrast to the bight Christmas lights of the Palmieri Restaurant. "Be simple and stay in the background so the women customers shine more than usual this time of year," Marie advised. The two women greeted guests by name, asked about the family, the friends, commented on new hair-styles or jewelry and moved around the dining room to assure the cordial restaurant atmosphere.

Vince ran the kitchen like a top sergeant. He mixed instruction with demands and praise for the staffs. He marveled at the smooth operation that resulted since Gloria brought in computers but he avoided touching the "damn machines. Like a fast food joint," he complained. "But they work."

Gloria, working with the accountants, organized the computer system, for the Palmieri finances including the restaurant, fish market, and real estate. She spent time avoiding cousin Francis, "No way I'm going to make it onto his alphabet card."

She wondered if Gis had one in his wallet, squeezed his hand as they sat in front of the fireplace that Thanksgiving evening. Gloria wanted to say something about understanding to Hawk, but knew that she could not understand; she wanted to say something to help him, but she knew he had to find his own destiny; she knew she would have to find her own freedom.

"Hey guys. Let's talk about football." Safer she thought.

14

Gloria

Marie and Vincent kissed Gloria, left last minute instructions, and then left for their sons' Dartmouth graduation. Marie used the car phone to call the fish market and asked the young assistant to be sure that her brother had already left.

"Lucky he has that good Italian kid at the market," Vince said as he paid the tunnel toll. "Shame he has no background, would be nice to introduce a nice young man to Gloria. But that one's a little strange. Definitely not for her."

The flawless catering staffs were delighted with the gratuities they received from the weddings, glad there were no drunks, and parking was easy for the valet staff. The unflappable chef, informed that there were to be additional guests for one of the weekend weddings, phoned the Palmieri Fish market for an added delivery, met with his sous-chefs, and wagged his finger so that Gloria would not interfere.

Families visited the restaurant during the afternoon, lollypops and small toys were on a child level table, dining room staff gathered around to sing happy birthday for one family who celebrated a grandmother's birthday, a small group at a corner table serenaded the grandmother with a romantic interlude from *La Bohème*, and Gloria celebrated her short break before the dinner session. Cousin Frank arrived with a dark haired young woman whose eyes moved in tandem with her bosom. She was introduced as Gina. Gloria was glad that her cousin had finally filled in the "G" on his alphabet card.

As last rays of sun drew curtains across the Friday night sky, a line of limousines pulled up to the front of the restaurant. Passersby crossed themselves anticipating the vehicle occupants to have arrived from a wedding or a funeral. Dressed as if they had been rounded up at art classes, street fairs and rock concerts, men and women of various ages emerged from the chauffeured cars. Uncle Benito, wearing beret and painter's smock over army fatigues, led the entourage along the side aisle. He pointed to the autographed photos of celebrities and to family pictures in the entranceway. He accompanied his friends to the room he had reserved.

The troupe walked jubilantly toward the reserved room. When one of the men, smiled and raised his eyebrows toward Gina, a green haired woman rushed her hand into his back pocket and squeezed a sign of possession; a couple two-stepped toward the wall then turned back toward the dining room. A pregnant woman and a pony tailed man brought up the column's rear. His sleeveless khaki shirt hung loose over his patched denim pants. His muscular arms cradled a baby who he hugged close to his neck, occasionally nuzzling the child with gentle kisses.

—————

Gloria watched delivery trucks arrive Saturday morning, heard the commotion of waiters, waitresses, barmen and busboys setting up for the day. She turned to her computer to write the newsletter.

Coffee and donuts were set on a checkered tablecloth near the delivery dock behind the restaurant every Saturday morning. Deliveries of fresh fruit, vegetables, barrels of beer, milk, cream, flowers, fresh white linens, and special orders by the chef caused noise, rapid movement, laughter, shouting, and general chaos.

A yellow pick-up truck turned into the driveway, waited for the wooden boxes marked Palmieri Fish Market to be unloaded. The chef called Gloria to explain that her uncle's manager had to make the delivery himself. "Some Italian kid, they hired. Unbelievable, he can't understand a word of Italian. Might as well have hired some Spanish kid or an Indian." Weddings and dinner parties added joyous Italian music that reflected laughter and noisy conversation during the entire weekend.

Sunday morning, Uncle Benito called for an evening reservation for twenty or thirty, but suggested that the room be set for forty.

Gloria took her post near the front door on Sunday evening so she could talk with arriving guests. She asked about families, friends, and made new customers feel like lifelong Palmieri relatives.

A slow moving school bus, decorated like a graffiti mural, stopped in front of the restaurant. The bus windows were darkened and each of the tires was a different vibrant color. Uncle Benito was the first to emerge, this time leading men in tuxedos and women in evening dresses. Benito stopped at tables, greeted old friends, kissed several women, and walked back to the front of the dining room. He picked up Gloria's hand and kissed it gently.

"Thank you for being so gracious Friday night," he said. "They were very special friends of mine. Please join us later. I must talk with you." He bowed and rejoined his guests in the private room.

Sunday nights ended early at Palmiaris'. Waiters and busboys quickly cleared their stations, setup for Monday, tallied tips, and checked out at the back door. Benito's friends had left on the bus; bartenders polished the bar and dimmed the front lights. Gloria was moving toward the office when she realized Uncle Benito was still at the table where he had been the vociferous host. He moved his fingers as if conducting an orchestra, interrupted his motion by lifting a cordial to his lips, sipped slowly than continued the muted concert.

"Ah, Gloria," he sang while motioning her to sit near him. "Everything tonight was wonderful as usual." He folded his hands for a perch under his stubbled chin. "You know that this restaurant was no bigger than this room when it was first opened. Long before my time. You know how old it is?"

He related the history of the restaurant and the fish market. "You know the market came first. Your great grandmother, maybe her mother, decided to open a little restaurant right here near where they lived. The old house was back there," he pointed to the kitchen. He continued with a litany of the family tree, who was who in the family, pointed in the direction of the pictures on the dining room's wall.

"How's your father?" He vaulted into the present. "Haven't seen little Sal, does he still chase the girls, haven't seen him since he was a little wimp in school. Sorry about your mother." He crossed himself.

Gloria tried to correct Benito about her father's name; the old man coughed, drank another the cordial, held up his hand and cleared his throat. "Salvatore was quite a ladies man until he stole your Mamma from here. Was jealous that they were able to bring such a beauty from Italy, and wanted to keep her here for one of the cousins. So he stole her away, married her and then you came along. But it has been a long time since I saw him."

"Did Marie tell you I want to steal you? I told her I do. Not to get married, have had enough of that, three times. Now it is enough to have lovely women come with me to art shows, concerts, dinner, Europe, and just to have some fun."

"You saw all those newspapers I sent you. That's what I want to steal you for. You must know about Salvatore's newspaper and you have a good business head. I need someone for the papers and the business. I am getting too old and have other things to do."

"I was in your Tern Harbor once when I was a kid, went with my father and my uncle," he waved his hand. "My uncle is somewhere in your family tree. You know there was a lot of incest in that group. He took us to see his place. I was scared of that Indian story, about the ghost who was always hanging around. That old man, older than I am, told everyone to get out of Brooklyn, to see all of America. Told me to grow up and go somewhere else. Never wanted to see that Indian so I went to New Jersey."

Uncle Benito spoke rapidly, did not allow time for Gloria to say that her father's name was Steve. She thought the old man was drunk, making up some of the family history and the story of his visit to Long Island.

"Think about it, Gloria. I watched you since you came here, a beautiful young girl, now a woman. Is this what you will do with all your time, greet people, manage the restaurant? I know where you come from; I know you cannot live tied down to such a mediocrity. A time comes to make a change and it is your time Gloria. Think about it."

Gloria sat silent.

"My driver must be outside right now and I have to go to the men's room before I leave. I will haunt you until you make up your mind to come to my shop. And Gloria, I know he calls himself Steve, I was at his baptism, I know the truth, and once a Palmieri always one of us."

Benito faced the ceiling, shook so that his hair fell in silver contrast to his black jacket, and he scratched under his collar.

"It's your time Gloria. Think about it and then join me. You can be some-one. He became Steve Palmer but never got away from being Palmieri. Yeah, Palmieri, Palmer, all the same. Start with a P. Reminds me I have to go to the men's room."

He lifted Gloria's hand to his lips and gently kissed her knuckles.

Gloria closed the door, slid the chain lock shut, turned the knob for the dead bolt, and walked to the kitchen. She poured a glass of milk, spilled it into the sink, took a bottle of beer from the refrigerator, walked into the family room, sank into the deep couch, turned on the television and watched, without hearing or seeing the Yankee baseball game.

She thought of those football games she had watched with Gis and Hawk; she wondered what had become of Hawk, what Gis would do now that he was finished with college, wondered why she had remained hidden in the safety of Palmieri house and restaurant. She tried not to think about Benito, his charm, his strange selection of friends, his wide range of interests and his total disregard for convention.

Gloria daydreamed about her childhood, wondered if her mother ever really loved her father or if she paid reluctant homage when he made love to her, wondered if she ever really had a childhood or if those lonely years were as foreign to her then as Tern Harbor was now. Her childhood no longer existed, faded as if it had never been. She felt as if she was wandering in a strange place, a timeless savanna, as if she was in the Tern Harbor Race without a finish line, without a goal, without any space that was her very own. That childhood was as gone from her as was her father. She felt like a mystical child who would one day be freed by those damn birds who guarded the secret hiding place of the fabled spirits.

Suddenly the front door's dead bolt lock slid open. "Oh no," she thought, "Benito has come to get me, said he would haunt me, or someone is trying to break in." She grasped the top of the beer bottle, jumped as the beer trickled to the floor, and she prepared to hit the intruder. She watched a man's fingers reach for the chain lock, then disappear. The door was pulled closed and then pushed open, but the chain held.

"Hey Gloria," she heard the familiar voice. "How about letting me in."

"Oh God, Gis, you scared the hell out of me." Gloria peeked over the chain, then opened the door. "Where is everyone? How come you're home alone?"

"Well if you'd rather, I can go." Gis laughed as he tugged an overstuffed duffel bag into the house. "Folks stayed up in New Hampshire, Liz and Tommy are getting engaged, and guess who was at the graduation?"

"Hawk. Did he really get to the graduation? Wish I had seen him in one of those gowns. Would have hugged and kissed all of you." Gloria blushed.

"No. Not sure where Hawk is right now." Gis pulled one more duffel into the house. "No more guesses for you. Liz's folks were in from Nebraska, and Marie and Vince were staying to spend some time with them. Thought I'd be in the way, so I drove home. Let Tommy have the fun of riding home with Mom and Dad."

"You must be hungry," Gloria turned back to Gis. "Here's the hug and kiss anyway." She held close to her cousin in order to hide a tear trickling down her cheeks. "Must have been a sight, the Brooklyn Italians meeting the Nebraskans. How about something to eat?"

They took sandwiches into the family room, sat sipping wine and talking about college, restaurant, Frank's letter G, Hawk's disappearance from campus, his single letter and then his silence. Gis talked about going to Europe, backpacking through Germany, Italy and France. He talked about spending time traveling wherever he could for a year before coming home to work.

Gloria told him about Benito, talked about becoming a newspaper publisher, talked about getting away again; she talked about roaming around New Jersey and wondered if that was the purpose of her flight from the Terns. She talked about Benito's version of the family history. "He would have to be a few hundred years old to have seen all those people, especially the Indian who he talked about. Do you think he's all there?"

"Ever read his column in his papers? People love it because he talks about

Jersey history, goes back to before the Revolution, talks about it in the first person, present tense. He just does that. Doesn't mean he was there, but in his head, who knows." Gis shrugged.

They talked about their need to be free, even for a little while, and then they drank more wine and huddled close to each other.

"I could love you Gloria," Gis whispered.

"Yes. I really love you Gis, but can you imagine what would happen if we had kids. Cousins, distant, but we're cousins. The kids would be either idiots or wild or like, oh man, like my father." She shuddered.

"Yeah, we could be in love, make love like this," he bent over and kissed her. They held close to one another. "But you know, we're really not cousins. Told you we were adopted."

Gloria imagined they were on the beach with meteors filling the sky. She closed her eyes and remembered the smell of the bay, and the warmth of the moss covered rocks. He held her close, felt his body tighten as they moved closer to one another.

"But what if we were really cousins? Could you still love me?" Gis leaned away from her.

"I always will love you, Gis. But you know we're not keepers." They drank more wine, talked about Europe, talked about New Jersey, talked about Hawk, held hands, and talked about the baseball game.

"Better get my stuff upstairs. See ya later," Gis placed his hand on Gloria's shoulder. "Always love ya, Gloria. Maybe in some other time . . . cousins could love, really love."

"Some other time," she thought about what Benito had said. "It's time Gloria," he had said. It reverberated until all she could here was those words. Time Gloria, time, time, it's time, time it is, Gloria, time, time, time Gloria, it is time, time, time, tick tock, tick tock, time. Time, time,. Gloria's time. What will you do with time, it's time, Gloria.

The explosive crowd noises from the television were background to the announcer screaming, "Home Run, Grand Slam." Gloria watched the spectators smiling, hugging, and leaving the stadium as if they had played the game, as if they had run the bases, as if they were headed to the showers, as if it had been their time. She thought of the men and the women on the train from Tern Harbor; she thought of the clicking sound of the train doors shutting and opening; she was suddenly aware of Gis standing in the family room doorway. She tossed one of the couch cushions at him, "Not keepers, she laughed."

"But," He glowered then smiled, "If you ever need me, you know how to get me. Just put your lips together and whistle."

She threw a barrage of cushions at him as he ran up the stairs. "Don't know how to whistle," she yelled. "But I know how to tell time," she thought, "and it is time, my time, Gloria's time."

15

Fountains

Sultry heat steamrolled across New York throughout the summer of 1988. *DieHard* was the movie box office smash; *A Nightmare on Elm Street 4 The Dream Master* was playing at the New Line Cinema; the Southampton Antiques Show was drawing record crowds of New York's wanabee social set; weekend craft fairs surfaced on Long Island's North Shore. New York and New Jersey beaches were closed sporadically because of medical waste mysteriously washing up on shore. Mayor Ed Koch was barraged with complaints about mistreatment of carriage horses that circled Central Park. On Manhattan's West Side, the Chelsea neighborhood was the in-place to be on weekend evenings. Long-time tenants were being displaced as a result of gentrification along Tompkins Square Park on the East Side of Greenwich Village.

Young people inhabited overheated streets, couples found romance in cooling breezes along New Jersey's Palisades overlooking the Hudson River; the hum of window air conditioners mingled with soft jazz sounds and punk rock in heat trapped New York ghettos.

Matt Steele slept in his truck parked along the Jersey shore. He had spent Friday night moving through small towns like Jersey City where he met disaffected teenagers – as he did every weekend – gaining their confidence, bringing them into skinhead and punk rocker activity, while keeping each group independent of the other. This Friday night he had distributed flyers about the coming weekend at Tompkins Square Park and blamed all the problems with America on the "Jews, Niggers, and immigrants". He spent time imbuing his small army with a picture of a better life, a better America that was being stolen from them, and spreading the word to punk rockers that the skinheads were their allies and could protect them from nerds who would beat up on the kids with green or orange hair.

Morning blinked across the Hudson as Matt crossed the George Washington Bridge to Manhattan's West Side. He stopped at a Broadway donut shop, smiled at the Spanish-speaking clerk, ordered two donuts and a black coffee.

Matt glanced at the Straus Memorial Fountain that was built in 1914 in memory of two New York philanthropists who vanished with the Titanic. A draped, reclining bronze figure, gazing sadly and serenely over a lead-lined pond, seemed to be waiting for someone or something to appear.

Matt imagined he could still hear the gentle flow of the creek that had been trickling down the Palisade then splashing over rocks and tumbling into the Hudson River. He thought about the gentle caress of Long Island Sound against the rocky beach. He looked back at the sullen bronze figure. The lifeless fountain, waterless for years, mocked the summer swelter.

He made a U-turn, drove to 110th Street, across the north end of Central Park, turned onto Fifth Avenue, passed hospitals without looking at them, parked the truck, and entered the Park. He stopped near the Conservatory Garden, took off his boots and stepped barefoot onto the soft, wet grass.

He pulled his sweatshirt over his head and walked toward the three fountains that had been carefully designed to bring a sense of peace, relaxation and pleasure to the upscale part of the City. Geysers gushed from the center of two fountains. Matt dipped his hands into the cold water, splashed his face and chest, looked up at the cloudless sky, ran across the grass, and then through the wooded areas of the Park. He ran silently, unaware of the scratches he received from shrubs. He crossed a stream and circled the ponds at the North end of the Park. He imagined he was running over the old Indian path through Long

Island's forests. He returned to the truck and drove further downtown. The fountains in this part of New York, which catered to wealth, were pristine, alive, full, and shiny from the coins that were tossed into them.

In the early morning silence, Matt could hear the music from vest-pocket park waterfalls that graced condominiums and atriums of towering glass buildings. The enormous geyser in the center of Washington Square Park was shooting up as if to catch and torment birds living in the crevices of the Park monuments and arch. During the heat of the day, visitors would cool their feet in the large pond that encircled the splashing geyser.

The yellow Ford pickup truck meandered past Washington Square Park, headed south along Broadway, then passed two police cars that were parked out of sight of Tompkins Square Park. Matt Steele propped his feet on the passenger seat, bit into a donut, and sipped his coffee.

Conflict over ownership of the Park ignited nightly arguments among new young residents who wanted to bring their children to the Park, joggers who did not want to be accosted by beggars and addicts, the neighborhood's old people who wanted to spend hours in quiet conversation or playing chess, and visiting friends. Police made irregular rounds chasing undesirables.

As the summer progressed, the homeless occupied the Park as if to recover some lost fort from conquering armies. The Park resembled a tent city.

Matt waited for the moment when he would be involved with the brewing conflict. He knew that the skinheads he had organized would be blamed for the problems that the police were not able to control. He plotted the best ways through the Park's winding pathways and leave burdened trees, and he mapped the best escape routes.

Tenement buildings, that once housed anxious immigrants, reached up in stark silhouettes against the slit of dawn. Homeless squatters hid behind refaced facades of buildings marked for reconstruction.

Matt frowned at the signal flag usually laid flat against the closed window two floors above the familiar glass doors; it meant victory when the pennant would pulsate in the breeze. He sighted over his big toe as if to fire a bullet through that open window. A fly drifted across the windshield , disappeared behind the driver's seat, then positioning itself in line with the flag. Matt aimed his fierce grin at the fly, waited for the creature to be in place, and then smashed it with his large toe.

Abrupt pounding on the truck window brought Matt to rapid attention. He automatically reached for his boot, saw the Vietnam veteran, and drew his empty palm from the hidden switchblade.

The veteran was dirtier than Matt remembered, his hair was longer and turning gray, his crusty hands bore marks from scraping dumpsters in competition with other desperate creatures.

"Told you didn't I?" the Veteran said. "Told you we would take it over. No one has been able to keep us out. You were here. You saw the gendarmes last Sunday. Chased everyone out. Yeah bullshit. We came right back."

"Not their place," Matt stared at the man.

"Yeah, but you and your punk rock kids got to learn to keep quiet when me and my friends want some sleep once in a while. I know they're your friends. Got the same haircuts, or whatever you call them spikes."

Matt wanted the man to get away from his truck. "We got as much right as anyone," Matt yelled.

"Ain't said you don't. But they're gonna try again to kick us out. Imagine. They're going to try to shut us down at about one o'clock. You tell some bar owner to shut down at one. Fuck 'em. I know how to fight a war, been to the jungle." The veteran saluted at attention.

"They'll try to knock off the drug dealing," Matt smirked. "And shut down the Jamaicans playing their drums on the bandstand.

"Only drug dealing in the Park is down the corner, they gotta go to those damn empty buildings on 6th, that's where the trade is." The veteran spit on the sidewalk. "How come you still look like one of them kids? Are you a narc?"

"Get off my truck. I have to get to work. Yeah, right, a narc. Funniest thing I heard in months. See yah." Matt flicked the dead fly out of the window, drove to the front of the glass-doored building, entered the lobby, removed a brown envelope from a mailbox, and returned to the truck. The envelope contained money and instructions left by his mentor.

Carl Gohrman, who conducted the clandestine skinhead indoctrination in Riverhead, gave the impression of Nazi invincibility that first attracted Matt. It was at one of those meetings that he developed the need to hide his Native background, the night he decided to become the most feared at his school, the night that cleared away fear of his father, and to his becoming an accomplice in the fearsome event that led to his flight from home.

The August morning sky turned pink, then light blue and evoked his spirit of running along the old Indian pathway, watching the dawn sky, listening to the rustling wind, feeling the cool water as he leaped into frothy waves.

He shuddered as he saw the flag removed and the window closed, turned as two people walked past the truck, recognized the black woman who had tossed water at him in the alley, and wished he were on Mama Robins' comforting floor. He finished his coffee, made some notes on his clipboard, and scanned the park for signs of human movement.

Sleeping homeless, tenuous as Native Americans before being mutilated and massacred by invading British troops, snored in sleepy defiance of the ongoing gentrification in the Saturday dawn. It had been two years since the Vietnam veteran had cautioned Matt about how his people would "show them bastards how to win a war." Homeless people occupied one end of the Park; drug addicts and run-aways inhabited bed rolls, hammocks, cardboard boxes and grassy mounds that surrounded blackened campfires; foul odors rose in steamy swamps behind crowded shrubs that had become outhouses for homeless inhabitants of the Park. Matt saw the familiar army fatigues stop behind a decaying bush, turn toward the deserted bandstand, and splatter it as he relieved himself.

Matt looked back at the flagless window in the comfortable apartments with scrubbed bathrooms; a bare foot jutted out of a large cardboard box on the upper level of the scaffold erected outside one of the gutted tenements. Early morning light erupted through unkempt building windows as if to flow over the sleeping homeless.

Dust filled rays evaporated moisture from damp grass, swept across the Park in search of life, whispering a warning of imminent danger.

Joggers began to make their ways around the Park that they considered their property, a safe place to exercise, meet friends, and that they wanted free of the homeless, the vagabonds, addicts, and beggars all of whom had become an irreconcilable nuisance. New residents of the renovated tenements were determined to eradicate the intruders.

Matt read the note in the envelope, wrapped it in the sport section of the *Daily News*, circled the date August 24th 1988, counted the money that had been in the envelope, sneered, and quickly put the truck into gear and headed for his job at the Palmieri Seafood Market.

He was angered by the command in the note, thought of himself as one of the small fish that latch onto the back of a whale. When he met Gohrman in Riverhead, he thought he was moving with a dynamic leader who would carry him away from his past to a bright new world. The more he had to wait for signals from the fluttering flag and was given assignments, the more he understood he was following a bottom sucker of humanity. Matt vowed to become more than a parasite, to find a way to become his own leader in the world he had envisioned.

———————

Matt was surprised to find Al Palmieri's Cadillac in back of the market's open gate.

"Where the hell were you yesterday afternoon?" Al waved his hands as he bellowed at Matt.

"Told you I had to take the time off. What happened?"

"That stupid friend of yours nearly lost half my customers. If it wasn't they knew me better we'd be in the toilet. Fired the little son-of-bitch."

"Fired him?"

"Yeah. Fired, sacked, wanted to kill the bastard." Al Palmieri was flushed and sweating. "Tried to call you, but no answer. Get a friggin beeper."

"What did he do?" Matt spoke softly in an attempt to calm his boss.

"What'd the dick do? I told him to make a delivery to a new restaurant on 125th Street. You know what he said. He said no. No! Said he couldn't make any deliveries to a bunch of Niggers in Harlem. Said he didn't want to be the only white face in that there crowd. I looked at him as if he was crazy and then realized he meant it. Then came the winner."

"What else did the little jerk do?"

"What else? I sent him to make a delivery to Rosen's."

"Yeah, he's done that before. So?"

"So! He bumps into Rosen's kid nephew. Kid's just back from Cincinnati, a funeral for his grandfather. He pushed next to the kid and whispers. Heard your grandfather died."

"He was being sorry."

"Sorry my ass. He says to the kid, you know when they bury Jewish people they throw some dirt onto the casket in the grave. Did you do that? The kid looked up at this hulk and says yes. Then this Nazi says to the kid, I understand that after the Rabbi says blessings he pisses on the casket. Did you do that too?"

Matt stood silent.

"See! Even gets to you. Well the kid takes a swing at your punk skinhead friend and your Terry shoves the kid across the floor, knocks over two tables, breaks glasses, leans over the kid and laughs in his face. Then he comes back here and tells me everything went okay. Okay. I almost lost all my Jewish customers, but I was able to fix it by telling Rosen I fired your friend and that I would take care of any bills for the damage. I made the Harlem deliveries myself."

"I'll beat the crap out of the little moron. Make him get out of the apartment. Don't care if it was his. It ain't no more." Matt turned to leave.

"Where you going? I'm cooled down now. What anyone does away from here is his own business, but anyone works for me has got to be one hundred percent on the job. No bullshit. Whatever the help does away from here, strictly their business. I'll close up here today. Do me a favor, there is one delivery I got a call for from my sister's Restaurant in Brooklyn. Drop it off there for me."

Al Palmieri carried a box to the yellow pickup truck and picked up loose papers that became wedged under the box.

"You should have beaten the hell out of the stupid bastard. I'll catch him later and whip his butt. He'll never do that again."

"Don't need that little Nazi working here. Shows up stinking drunk or God knows what and then pulls a stunt like that one."

"He's not really all that bad, Al"

"I only kept him working here because he was your friend. I told you I'm not stupid. I know what goes on in the city, but whatever people do away from here, as long as it stays away, not my business. I know you hang around with them Punk rock kids and maybe some others who are trouble. You should get better friends. But what happens away, not my business."

"Al, I promise he won't pull any more crap like that. I need to have him working so he can pay his share of the rent. I straightened him out in the apartment so he's not a pig anymore, I'll straighten him out for you."

"We'll see. I'll give him one shot, but you are his boss from now on."

Always was, Matt thought.

"See you Monday Al."

"Yeah, Yeah." Albert Palmieri walked slowly into the shop, closed the door and unfurled the papers he had taken from the truck. He read the flyer announcing the Saturday rally in Tompkins Square Park; then he stared at the anti-Semitic poster that he was about to throw in the garbage. He leaned against the stainless steel counter and read it again.

"Now what do I do?" he said.

16

Whose Domain

Children were splashing through the torrent flowing from a fire hydrant; young men wearing lavender tank shirts, were sitting on concrete steps drinking beer, smoking cigarettes, and calling to young women who were swaying to the music blaring from a boombox. A stream of water flew from an upper floor window from which a toothless old woman wagged her finger and yelled, "Get away from my house and shut off that noise."

Her exhortations were drowned out by the boom box carried on the shoulder of one of the men. He pursed his lips, rolled his eyes up in the old lady's direction, blew her a kiss, then turned and danced across the street shifting his behind in her direction.

Shiny green, white, and blue cars lined one end of the street. Matt turned into the street, parked in one motion, slowed long enough to return the smile of one of the passing girls, and then ran up the stairs.

He unlocked the double bolted door and yelled, "Tim. You stupid son-of-a-bitch. Get out here. This place stinks, what the hell you been doing."

He threw an empty beer can at the quiet group sitting on Tim's bedroom floor. They smiled at Matt, broke into laughter, and then waited for their host to speak. Tim waved his hand to Matt, shook his head, tried to use his intimidating stare, then started to laugh.

"All you suckers, get out of here." Matt grabbed the nearest boy by the back of his shirt and tossed him down the stairs. The others crawled through the open doorway, some walked, some fell down the stairs. Matt slammed the door, propped Tim against the bed, and was about to drive his fist into the face that was smiling at him. He shook as he pictured his father beating him, beating his uncle, beating his mother and the final battle that ended with blood soaked walls. Matt pulled Tim from the floor, tightened his choking grasp, then let him crumble unconscious to the floor.

"Stupid little bastard," Matt murmured as he picked up the party residue, flushed the remains of white powder that lay across the low coffee table, and scrubbed the bathroom and kitchen with clorox. "Get rid of this stench, get away from this place, dump this joint. Never trust this idiot."

Matt dragged his unconscious roommate to the bathroom, put his head over the tub, and turned on the cold shower. Tim shook his head like a dog coming out of the rain. He started to shiver; his dark eyes, sinking under scowling eyebrows, reflected the void of a robot separated from its control panel. He shook his head again, reached for a towel, sat leaning against the tub, looked up at Matt, raised his hands to avoid more cold water splashing across his head, and said "*sorry*."

"Forget it," Matt left the room. "Just remember to be there tonight. Going to be one hell of a party."

Matt looked back into the room, smiled then turned his face into the threatening skinhead look he had mastered. "And better bring a stick; those other guys will have some pipes." Matt packed his duffels, counted the guns to be sure they were all there, folded his clothes, made sure there was nothing left in the drawers that could indicate he had been there, or who he was, or where he had come from. He carried the duffels down the stairs, hid it behind the truck seats, then drove to the Palmieri Fish Market.

After hiding his duffels in his locker, Matt checked the work schedule he had posted, replaced Tim's name where it had been crossed out, locked the steel door and the gate. He drove back to Central Park where he ran through the park, circled the fountains, and then sat on a hill from which he could observe the Sheep Meadow.

Children were running and playing games at one end of the meadow. These were not children who would be running through water streaming from fire hydrants, the young people lying on blankets and towels would not be victims to an old lady's cannonade of water, their radios and music would never boom across the Meadow to annoy or interrupt the dancing of young girls or boys. Matt focused on a man spreading oil on a tanned woman's back. Her bikini bottoms revealed light skin where a longer bathing suit had been, her bra top had been untied so that lying in the sun, two peach-like bubbles spread from under her chest. The man slowed his motion as he smeared the oil over her sides, then he lay next to her. The woman lifted her hand and started to smear the oil over the man's chest and forehead. Then they lay still in the sweltering sunlight.

Matt wondered if he would be there with that woman if he had not been born part Indian and part creep. He wondered if he could be there with a girl like the one he had seen long ago at Tern Harbor when he swam to a rock and stood naked while she waved at him. He wondered and then he got up, tore off his shirt, wrapped his boots around his waist, and continued his private movement back to the old truck. He moved slowly with the traffic on Fifth Avenue, took time to watch the women in their off-the-shoulder summer dresses, the children in their colorful clothing, men in khakis and button down shirts, tourists and New Yorkers moving into air conditioned museums to enjoy the art and escape the August heat. He drove past Washington Square Park, no longer the peaceful fountain-centered park he had circled that morning, but teaming with college students, artists trying to sell their paintings and visitors hoping to glimpse the pretty parts of New York.

Matt parked the truck in its usual spot of 4th Street, started to enter the apartment house, turned and walked into the street. He walked past his former antagonists, smiled at one of the girls who was dancing to mambo music, stared across the street at the leader of the purple shirted boys. They nodded to one another and Matt grabbed the young girl and started to dance with her. When the music stopped, the leader of the PR's walked up to him and shook his hand.

"I like all kinds of music," Matt said.

"Like you skinhead. When you going to dump that skinny little faggot you live with. Bet he's pretty good, eh?" The dark haired man grinned.

"Don't get funny with him. He's straight as an arrow, and so am I. Bring your girl friend to the Park tonight. It's going to be a big party. This one is real cute. Can I buy her a drink?" Matt recognized the authority of the man who he once expected he would have to shoot.

"No messing around with her. Don't care how many guns you have. Mess her up and you're touched," the man pointed to his knife.

"Just like to dance the mambo," Matt smiled and the man grinned.

"You dance pretty good for a white boy," the girl giggled.

The music changed to a sultry soft Latin melody. Matt pulled the girl up close so their bodies undulated to the crowd's applause.

"Hey, remember, unspoiled little girl, my Carmela," the dark haired leader who had been a threat to Matt, leaned close to him. "No screwing around, hear. You need a little action, you can see the old lady with the water pail."

"Want to go for a ride?" he whispered into the girl's ear. "Let's go up to Central Park. It's still early, have a cool walk near the fountains, sit under trees, have some fun." The girl looked at Manuel. He winked at her and walked to the other end of the street.

Matt drove the yellow truck past the open hydrant, held his hand on the car's horn until they rounded the corner and moved toward Central Park. Carmela dropped her hands onto her thighs, held her chin against the silver cross that teased her long ochre neck, and her eyes darted from the windshield to Matt Steele'e bare foot. His foot moved up and down on the gas peddle, his large toe grasped the peddle, then released it.

They wandered through the park, Matt pointing to the fountains and the expansive Sheep Meadow. Children were playing at the south end of the Meadow, sunbathers were still lying on their towels, a dog was chasing a frizbe, and a uniformed team was race walking around the perimeter.

Matt and the girl sat under the trees that gave them hunter's cover so they could watch the open grassy field without being discovered. Matt felt the girl move her thigh against his, felt her delicate hand touch his knee and then reach around his leg.

He put his arm around her shoulder, kept watching the Meadow, and pulled her close to him. Her hand left his knee, moved around his waist; she turned toward him and waited.

"Not supposed to do anything. Your friend will be...."

"He's not here." Carmela leaned her lips against Matt's chest.

He pulled her toward him, felt her cool body and realized she had dropped her shoulder straps. She pressed her hands under his shirt, pulled it up over his head and pressed her bosom to his bare stomach. They made love as the sun-filtered light hid their bodies from the sky. They moved in harmony as they had while dancing. Then they lay silent as she moved her hands up and down along his back as if to continue the lovemaking.

Matt buried his head in her neck, smelled the mixture of sweat and sweet rose perfume, then rolled away.

"You okay?" he asked.

"Why do you ask? Was beautiful."

"How's this going to be with Manuel?" Matt smiled. "He made me promise to bring you back unspoiled."

"Don't worry about Manuel. He won't know. Who's going to tell him?"

"I wasn't careful. What if . . . "

"I said don't worry. I take the pill, nothing can happen."

"You were terrific. Wasn't your first time, was it?" Matt reached around her.

"First time in Central Park," she said.

"So what's this about damaged merchandise?"

"Not damaged. Nothing happened. Look at those people on their towels. Anything happen. No. But you were pretty good too. Not like most white boys."

"Just a stud for undamaged merchandise," he quipped.

"No, really. You part Spanish? That'd be cool."

"No."

"Part Nigger?" she spit. "God, hope you ain't a nigger. Know you ain't a Jew. I know what they feel like."

"Told you just a skinhead stud. Good old American super stud for undam-aged merchandise. How about coming to the park with me tonight? Big party. Going to be fun."

"Have a date with Manuel. You come to our party. Big time stuff. In Manuel's place. You know, fun."

"No, have to go the park."

"You never hang around like that jerk you live with. He has his gang in there whenever you're not around. You know the kid with the boom box this afternoon, he has more than music in that box" She held her finger to her nostril. "And he brings magic to our party. Sells to your friend too. You must use some of that."

"Never touch any of that stuff. Could screws up your head. Can't have that. Thanks for a good walk in the park this afternoon. Cool dancing too. Tell Manuel that we had a fun walk and merchandise is in good shape for him." Matt spoke softly, but felt his fingers tighten around the steering wheel as he pulled into his regular parking space. "Maybe some other time. Maybe we can go to the Museum next time"

"No baby. Once is okay. Thought you would come to the party tonight, but no, once is enough." She reached across to kiss Matt. He backed away.

"Can't damage the goods." He smiled, reached across to open the door and brushed his hand across her thighs.

He watched her walk toward her friends, heard her talking about the wonders of Central Park, and what a nice gentleman the young Americano had been.

Friggin phoney, Matt thought, Just like everyone else. She's a fraud, Manuel's a phoney. The whole friggin world is like that. My old man was a miserable bastard who deserved what he got but wasn't a phoney. People around here pretending to be one thing and all they're interested in is what makes them happy, a drug here or there, a little roll in the grass. Don't damage the merchandise. Of course merchandise, he must sell her to anyone with the cash, that's how she knows what anyone feels like. Wanted to get me to that party so I could snort with them. Fuck him. I hated my father, hate all the damn hypocrites, hate the bastards trying to kick us out of the Park where we have fun, hate the old people who complain about the noise, hate the tight ass people trying to kick old people out of their apartments, hate the homeless who hang out in the empty buildings and piss in the Park, hate the Jews who come around to collect rents, hate the cops who tried to kick us out last week. We'll show them when we're back tonight. Hate that little bitch for making me feel like she was loving it this afternoon. Damn. We'll teach them how to make music, how to dance and have some fun tonight. We'll show them.

Police and firemen moved through the East Village shutting down fire hydrants. Water residue lifted in steamy clouds until the blacktop streets were dry and the early August night cooled empty spaces between buildings. Humming window fans, television sounds, and cooking odors that wafted from kitchen windows clung to remnants of the day's heat.

Tompkins Square Park, with its heavily laden shade trees and European style winding paths, was still alive. Screeching boom boxes, laughter from the end of the Park where private transactions were taking place, the chatter of homeless men and women who were getting ready for the night, and the loud outburst of punk rockers and their skinhead allies amended the Park's ambience. The Park outlasted a century of poor immigrants, absorbed the sounds of Ireland, Italy, Poland, Russia, Puerto Rico, and the dialects of Africa. While architects were planning Central Park and wealthy communities and College Communities beautified their private parks and fountains, this part of the City remained the squalid domain of the poor. Tompkins Square Park segregated the artist-writer pubs and bars from the crowded immigrant centers and is the boundary between upward bound college graduates who do battle in the burgeoning economy and the historical poor, the drug houses, the homeless and the uncomfortable sights of newly arrived ideas that have not become mainstream New York; it has remained a vocal battlefield for turf. The closeness of noisy bars that empty into the Park at closing time, adds to the sense that it is an area best left to itself.

Colored chalk writing has been bleached into the Park's sidewalk. The lettering *August 1988* was stenciled onto the sidewalk since the police disbanded noisy skinheads, punk rockers, homeless and young drunks. The small contingent of police had moved through the park to stop drug deals. They did not find any drug dealers in the park, refused to walk into the pitch of East 6th Street tenements with two priests who pointed to the deserted buildings, and dispersed the crowd that tried to re-entered the Park.

New chalk markings started to appear.

RALLY 8-7, PROTEST, PROTEST, PARK BELONGS TO US

Matt scraped his foot across the chalk marks, looked up at the flagless window, walked to the West Village, stopped for steak and salad, sat back with a glass of iced tea and watched the young girls walking past the restaurant alone, in small groups or with young men. He watched them move, watched them moving away and coming toward him, wondered how many of them were damaged merchandise. He hated his father, he hated Carmela, he hated the blacks and the Jews who had slept with her, he hated Manuel. Through the sweltering August evening, he soaked up hate, and he waited.

17

Tompkins Square

Matt navigated familiar alley shadows, bolted past the doorway where he had met the cleaning lady's explosive pail of bleach-smelling sewage, paused as a dull echo trickled through the alley, listened to his own heart beat, checked for secretive movements and sounds, continued to Eighth Street's exuberance and dimly lit pubs.

The day's heat engulfed the city in tenacious yellow haze under wet street-lights. Clinging shirts and shorts formed exclamation marks over white sandals of men and women who filled pubs and restaurants along the Tompkins Square Park frontier.

Matt edged into the crowded piano bar, girls smiled as he passed, pressed against him, and continued talking to their friends. He imagined being in Central Park with each of them. A girl pressed against him and stretched her hips like a cat trying to relieve an itch. She smiled at Matt, waited for his arm to reach around her, then shrugged and moved on to another muscular man who entered the bar.

"Whas a matta, kid?" the bartender slid the bottle of beer across the bar to Matt. "Lookin fer sompin special? Maybe some other kind of action? Doesn't happen aroun' here till laita."

"Screw off buddy!" Matt grimaced. "Just having a drink. Besides, I don't want to catch anything she's carrying." He meandered through several bars, sat on a crate at the end of a dismal alley where a cat screeched until a tom cat escaped her attack. A bottle clinked in a dumpster, rustling sounds and more clinking bottles interrupted the alley's compacting secrecy. Matt moved cautiously along the cool exterior brick wall of the bar toward the juicy breathing that was coming from something that may have once been human. There was a heartbeat pounding with the same resonating drumbeat coming from inside the pub.

Matt braced to confront whatever specter might have escaped campfires to capture his spirit; he planned to stomp it until it returned to whatever devil rock had released it; he would force it back to the native soil from which he had fled. His body ached to confront the ogre lurking in that dank place.

The thing moved erratically and Matt pounced onto it, rolled it to the ground, and set his forearms to severe its heavy neck. The thing offered no resistance, lay still making no sound, seemed to stop breathing, then tossed Matt back against the wall; it pulled Matt's legs forward, and landed on top of him with a crushing arm to his neck. Matt responded by slowly raising his leg and kicking the thing with the heavy toe of his boot. The thing howled, pulled away, and tried to get into the dumpster. A passing car's headlight outlined the veteran he had met in the park.

"What the hell you doing in here?" Matt gasped.

"Collecting beer and booze. I got as much right here as you, as anyone." The veteran disappeared into the darkness. "Going to be a big party in the park tonight. Always plenty left in these bottles."

"Screw those things. Get out of that garbage. You need beer, buy it."

"Don't be a friggin moron kid. You need money to buy them things."

"Come on," Matt leaned into the dumpster and helped the man climb out. "We'll go into Gristede's and get all you need."

"Won't let me in. Think I'll steal stuff."

"I said come on." Matt pushed the veteran. "We'll buy a bunch of stuff for tonight. Your friends and mine will have a party."

"I seen you a lot kid. Seen you with that guy with the flag. You don't look like his type."

"Come on let's get out of here, and I'm not anyone's type." Matt looked back into the alley. He was sure that ominous winds were forewarning him, posting a notice to beware of the dark, and be on guard.

He had held back from battering Tim earlier in the day. He remembered his vow to avoid Sean Donovan's drunken rages; he remembered accepting beatings to save his mother. He thought about going to the party with the girl and remembered his vow to keep his mind clear and away from easy temptation of drugs that would bring relief from loneliness and would bring uncertain friends. He swore he would not be the prisoner of any drug, dealer, or fraudulent offer of sex.

The market clerk watched Matt and the Veteran as they loaded the shopping cart with beer, bread, cheese, and ham. The clerk waited until they approached his counter, then shut the cash drawer. "Can't ring any of that stuff up unless you can pay," he glared at the veteran.

Matt stared at the clerk, "Ring it up, runt. I'm paying for this." He opened the brown envelope and flattened a hundred dollar bill on the counter. "Ring it up! And never talk to my friend like that ever again." He reached across the counter but did not touch the quivering clerk.

"Take this stuff to the Park." Matt turned to the veteran. "Don't tell anyone where you got it or who paid. See you there."

"Good thing there're no cops around anywhere tonight." the veteran smiled at Matt. "This sucker would've hit the alarm."

Matt left the store, was aware of the missing sound of police sirens, noticed the absence of police patrolling the street and protecting the outside of the Eighth Street bars. "Must have a big bust going somewhere," he thought. "Or a mega barbecue."

"Yeah." The veteran scampered past Matt. "Didn't think you were that guy's type. Never saw you go up to his place. He's moving anyways."

"No kidding?" Matt hid his surprise.

"Yeah. He's moving into that other place as soon as they finish putting in air-conditioning. Heard him with the builder. I think he owns a few of these old joints. Hey, thanks for the goodies. See you later. Gonna call you the supply sergeant. Those friends of yours say you're their natural born leader. Don't remember which building he's going into, but he's sure to have a big flag set up when he gets there." The Veteran laughed as he adjusted his belt. "Natural born leader. I'll tell that to the Jesus freak who hangs out in the park and next time I'll sure 'n' hell keep my back to the wall. Might be someone trying to knock me off in the dumpster. Or might be that flag guy trying to get some easy action. I gotta get to the Park. See ya later Sarge."

Matt heard the first beat of Jamaicanl drums coming from the bandstand, pushed open the glass doors, was about to jam the brown envelope back into the mailbox, withdrew all the money except for twenty dollars and wrote a note. *From now on, keep the rest of these. You'll need it for the mortgage. I'm heading out of here. I'm done doing boring stuff here. More to do like the catching up with Aryan groups, and the ideas of leaderless resistance, better than I've been doing. Now going to set it up right. Make contact with people in Oregon. You can use this twenty to get yourself a cop. Or try the veteran in the Park. He's noticed you.*

He stuffed the envelope into the mailbox.

Matt ambled into the Park and spun an old lady around as she was getting up from a bench. Punk rockers were clapping to the music and mixing with skinheads who had already arrived. The veteran was commanding the homeless cadre near a chess table.

Two priests, who lived among the homeless in Sixth Street's abandoned buildings, were talking to addicts at the south end of the Park. The last overheated joggers appeared and vanished behind the tree-hidden pathways that wound around the century-old sanctuary. Cooling night air conspired with damp heated sidewalks to shroud treetops in variegated mist. Cooking odors from bordering houses and restaurants filtered through the park's sweaty brackishness.

Skinheads, carrying wooden sticks and led by a beer logged Tim, swaggered into the park. Ragged homeless men formed a perimeter arc around the veteran. Reinforcing the myth that they were invincible, the skinheads paraded past their would be assailants and joined the rockers. The unassailed homeless continued their party.

"Hey Matt," Tim clasped his arm around his roommate's shoulder. "Hear ya got hold'a Carmela. Cool. Manuel get to you yet, or you going over there later?"

"You know I don't do drugs. By the way, I'm out of the place."

Tim jumped into the crowd of furiously mashing punk rockers. Tim looked back at Matt. "Better watch out for that spic. He's wanted to get a piece of you ever since you got here; a patient bastard. They get some pretty good stuff."

"We just went to Central Park," Matt whispered.

"Not what we heard," Tim shouted. "That's what she's for. Set you up, haul you in, then gotcha. Hey we had some fun up at Washington Square. Caught a couple of them sweeties. Not a cop around." Tim held onto one of the girls and disappeared across the path.

A sallow, hollow cheeked man stood on one of the tables near the two priests. A thick rope was tied around the waist of his baggy pants that were rolled up at the ankles. Skin clung to his neck, chest and backbone as if to hold in the last vestiges of blood cells. His gaunt face, hollow eyes, gray skin, and surrounding black hair augmented the spectral image. He held out a pair of thin branches tied to create a cross. Stands of colored yarn were stretched around the Cruciform's intersect. White and green yarn circled a swastika-like form at the cross's center.

The skinheads jeered at the Cross and laughed at the swastika. The man leaped from the table, spun into the dancers' midst.

"Come to Jesus," he cried. "Find your way. Let Him enter your soul." Still carrying the Cross high over his head, he marched toward the homeless group.

A series of wooden boxes had been set up on the Park north sidewalk. Speakers were protesting the forced evacuation of the tenements, the elimination of the low rents that poor could afford, leaving them with no place to go except the Park, leaving them homeless.

"Now," screamed one of the speakers. "Now we're even being kicked out of here. Cops will come like they did last week. Let's prove this part of the City is ours, let's prove that we're alive and well and won't let anyone shove us around anymore."

Matt had allowed himself to be used by his contact to keep blacks out of Wall Street; he accepted his task to indoctrinate young boys into the skinhead mode; he had delighted in his task to start trouble in the Park and to give police an excuse to enter it.

If those cops show up again, this time, they'd be in for a surprise. He had alerted skinheads to come to the Park for action.

Matt joined the dancers, pulsated against a thin, tattooed girl. Their bodies competed for dominance. Her green hair rubbed against Matt's chin as he stared at the window with the small flag flying.

Protesters, young people on the way to Village clubs, silent old men feeding pigeons, and joggers were listening to another speaker. "Folks, no cops here tonight. Not a single politician here tonight. Too hot for them, right."

The chant went up. "No more cops, no more cops, no more . . ."

Cooing pigeons fluttered in crevasses of decaying buildings. They had settled in this decadent place when falcons were imported to drive undesirable birds from midtown New York. They puffed out their bodies, protected young birds and lay there, eyes open, watching for intruders.

A muffled siren cruised into Greenwich Village's curved canyons as a sole patrol car ambled to a stop near the Park. Two policemen moved toward the soapbox speaker's stand. "You folks better move along. Causing a traffic jam and don't have a license to have this rally."

"Screw off," a woman's sharp nasal voice screeched from behind the skinheads. Two policemen twirled their nightsticks and withdrew when the crowd closed around them. People staggered from bars and started to gather around the speaker, or move toward the punk-rock music, or form their own groups, or move toward the south end of the park toward the drug dealers.

An armada of patrol cars, lights flashing, sirens blaring, squealed into St. Marks Place; the warm air gasped in subtle anticipation. The sound of sticks pounding concrete sidewalks and paved streets sent shockwaves through the neighborhood. Police in riot helmets, carrying shields and moving in solid lines, massed toward the speaker's stand. A bottle spun through the air, crashed into the street, and created the signal for police to charge into the Park. The bare-chested Cross-carrying ghost stood in front of the first onslaught.

"Think of Christ," he shouted. "Bless you all in His name." A policeman tossed him over a bench, then turned menacingly toward the punk rockers.

The speaker screamed from his box, "No more cops." He was sprawled onto the sidewalk, struck from behind and pulled behind a shrub where bone crunching sounds were drowned by moans screaming through the bullhorn he had used for the rally. Blood oozed from his mouth and skull as he lay quietly gripping the smashed bullhorn. The veteran waited for the police to move away, and then he pulled the speaker under safe shrubs, wrapped the head wounds with the speaker's shirt, picked up a long length of pipe, and waited for the next attack.

The rhythmic resonance of sticks pounding the pavement accompanied the panic of people running in every direction. The next line of helmeted police in unmarked uniforms, moved shoulder to shoulder, held shields in front of them, looked like a black-steel moving fence, advanced toward the fleeing bloody crowd. As the militia broke ranks they chanted, "kill, kill, kill."

They invaded the Park, striking everyone in their line of march. They pursued the escaping crowd; passing people were knocked to the ground; the homeless tried to defend themselves with the brass pipes they expected to use against the skinheads, but were over powered and bloodied; skinheads who did not run with the punk rockers were battered. Tim picked up a baseball bat, charged into the battle, two police toppled him, cracked his rib, handcuffed him and dragged him to a waiting patrol wagon.

Mounted police charged into the Park. A cyclist was tossed onto the pavement by a frightened horse; the bicycle was trampled; the man was kicked and knocked to the ground as he tried to rescue the remains of his books and backpack.

The priests, who had been in the Park, ran to the safety of Sixth Street along with the drug dealers they had been trying to rescue from sin. The ghostly Cross carrier raced around the Park, stopped in front of a charging horse. "Come to Jesus," he cried as the horse brushed past him. The Cross flew into the air. The man scampered after the Cross. A nightstick slapped at his back, his body's spurting blood flooded the green and white yarn that held the tethered crucifix. He held the Cross high into a breeze, shook the blood soaked strands so that blood seemed to be dripping over the Cross itself.

Police chased people along Avenues A and B and St Marks Place until the night was still. People, who had come out of the bars and their houses to see what was happening, either fled to safe havens or were beaten by renegade police. The sounds of the boom box screamed through the night; the echo of sticks beating the street and then crunching against skulls and bodies reverberated through the trees; the mantra of "kill, kill, kill" was whispered in hushed activity in Village bars.

Matt hoisted the man who had been pummeled from the bicycle and pulled him into a vacant building; then he charged into the Park, leaped onto the back of one of the horses, but was hit from behind by a charging horseman's whip. Blood dripped over his face and flowed across his eyes. The cyclist he had saved pulled him into the empty tenement and they sat quietly until the furor ended.

"What the hell was this all about?" the man asked.

"They want everyone out of here. What were you doing here?" Matt looked through his spread hand at the man he had saved.

"On my way to work at St. Vincent's emergency room. Funny, isn't it?"

"Yeah, a panic," they laughed.

"They're going to win." Matt grew silent. "This round is theirs." He thought of his home, of how that land had been taken, bought for trinkets, liquor, or stolen. He thought of Indians massacred by overpowering forces. He thought about the campfires and old Tomahawk's words "Take it all back, but beat them at their own game. Beat them, beat them, beat them." He thought of the wind that would have protected him at home. He thought of the smell of jasmine and wild blackberries in the autumn woods. He listened to the wind blowing through trees in the Park. He remembered the smell of rye whiskey that streamed through his nostrils when his father would beat him. He remembered the torment heaped on him by black and white students, he remembered the first meeting with the skinhead recruiter in Riverhead, and he remembered the bloody battle that had driven him from home. He hated his father. He hated blacks, he hated cops who had beaten him, he hated landlords, he hated drug dealers who tried to make him as dependent on their drugs as his father had been on alcohol. He hated the smell of his own blood. He hated hating. He listened to grandmother wind and welcomed her calming voice.

This Park's trees, or their ancestors, have been here for over a hundred years, he thought. My ancestors were there longer, thirty thousand years longer. These trees remember the amalgam of poor souls, Irish and Italians and Jews who lived near here and who came to this Park. They nurture memories of the poor from Chinatown and Puerto Rico and unnamed places. Those oaks and maples remember all the poor. And now, they know that the days when the poor could count on these trees for protection are over. The pigeons will move to some other desolate place. What the trees don't know is that, like the trampling of my people, their days are also numbered.

18

The Wind

Alphonse Palmieri sat quietly in soft leather seat of his air conditioned Cadillac listening to the weather report forecast that promised more of the heat that bloated the New York air. He knew there was only one person who could have opened the gate and back door to the fish market before him and he was uncertain about the coming confrontation. He locked the car door, walked toward the yellow pickup truck, ran his hand across the rear fender as if to delay going into the shop.

"Morning Al," Matt opened the back door. His clothes were wrinkled from having slept on a stack of burlap bags.

"How come you're here so early?" Al walked to his desk without looking at Matt.

"Moved out on the twerp. Getting ready to . . ."

"What the hell you doing with them flyers in your truck? And what you doing with them guns in your locker?" Al slammed a stack of posters on the floor.

"What were you doing in my locker? What is this some high school? My things are private. Remember you said you don't care what I do away from here?"

"But not this Nazi stuff." Al held up a book.

"That's mine. And it isn't Nazi. Nothing like it. It is plain old American. Good and true." Matt reached for the book.

"*Turner Diaries*. Fucking guy who wrote this would have all my customers lined up against a wall and shot, and probably me too. This what you believe? This what you do? At least the twerp says what he wants to, you hide it. No wonder you scared the Jews. Can't have that. Damn it. I liked you, would have wanted you for a son, and now this. Bring this junk into my place; bring those guns in here. Can't have it." Al turned toward the wall.

Silence hid the anger, fear, and rage that filled the room. Matt gathered the papers from the floor, tapped them into order, and placed them in the duffel. He lifted the bag over his shoulder and moved toward the door. "It's real American, like me. I was born here, my Mom was born here, so were her ancestors. My father was born here too. Name isn't Donatelli. It's Donovan. Irish name, not Italian. But I use the name Steele, because I come from my Mother's side. Goes back to before the beginning of this nation. That's why I can decide who is real American. So don't give me any of that crap about who I am."

"Where you going?" Al opened the desk drawer and handed cash to Matt.

"Keep it. I was going to tell you I was leaving." Matt tossed the bag into the truck, backed out of the driveway and sped onto the heated street.

"Good luck. Come back when you straighten out," Al shouted after the truck.

Matt stopped near the Tompkins Square battle scene. He put his head into his hands and sobbed. "Damn him. Why did he have to open the locker? Damn that high school and all those bastards who hated me. Damn those black kids who thought they were so good and could take me. Damn my old man for getting himself killed. Damn that idiot kid who brought me to the Riverhead meeting with the guy who hangs those little flags in his window. Damn the wind that torments me, that knows who I am. Damn those people who make a maid out my mother. Damn those Indians for not winning the land, damn them for not keeping me where I belong."

He drove toward the Holland Tunnel. "Got work to do. Get in touch with real skinhead organizations, learn about the real white Americans. Damn them all, they can't know who I really am.

Matt put his hand out of the open window to catch the warm breeze that rustled beads hanging from the rear view mirror.

19

Nowhere

Benito Palmieri introduced Gloria to the geography as they toured the community on mountain bikes. "Forge Creek," he waved his hand in a wide arc, "is proud of its hills, farms, Sunday cover dish suppers, and survival despite its isolation from New York and Philadelphia."

He pointed to the wooden bridge where Main Street turns abruptly and becomes a narrow shrub-lined road. "That's the end of town and that's the bridge to Nowhere. Look," he pointed in the opposite direction past the line of small shops. "That wide boulevard with its beautiful pear trees, seems to go on forever, slides up the hill, meets the War Memorial and the Five Corners."

"When was the Memorial built?" Gloria sensed the quiet old feeling about the town.

"Went up, let's see," Benito pursed his lips. "About ten years ago. They wanted to use the town for some movie and needed a monument so they brought it up from Missouri or someplace like that. Adds something to the place, don't you think?"

"Uncle Ben, you're kidding. When was it built?"

He motioned to Gloria to follow as they raced across the rattling wooden bridge and past fields with fresh rolled hay.

"What difference does it make?" he said. "One war's as good as the other. Men die, we say the words, build monuments, and people come to gawk. They don't even know the poor lads who died. No one around to really remember each one of them. See these fields?"

She inhaled the sweet smell of fresh hay.

"These fields know those boys. Some of them died here during the Revolution and others in the Civil War, others fought in other wars. The fields know who they are, the grass knows, the trees and the sky know. And that's more important than those monuments because these things last. No one comes here to see nonexistent old statues." Benito blew his nose.

Gloria put her arm around her uncle; they stared at the sign announcing the date for the hay auction.

"There's an exquisite little restaurant where we can have lunch. They serve crab cakes and wine that I think they make themselves. Illegal as hell but nobody cares." Benito was about to ride off.

"Where is this place," she laughed.

"Nowhere," he pointed ahead.

"No really where?"

"Nowhere. That's the name of the town. Perfect for this place, don't you think?"

They reached a small, unpainted converted barn. Flattened weeds filled cracks in the cement parking lot.

"That fading sign tells it all," Benito pointed to the glass front of the café. "See. *Welcome to Nowhere. Best food in town.* It's absolutely honest," he chuckled. "Except it's the best food in the county. Don't spread the word too far around. That would really spoil it."

Gloria made a mental note to come back often. It was not like the Palmieri Restaurant. The waitress with a missing tooth, the soft spoken farmers who frequented the café, and the extra attention given to Uncle Benito was a calming approach that Gloria had never felt before.

"Okay, Gloria. Time to chug along. Want to show you the other parts of town. Think I'll write about these fields, sort of set it up for my Veteran's Day column."

"They say that you write about old times as if you had been there yourself."
Gloria was not sure if she had offended Benito.

"In a way, they could be right." Benito was peddling slowly, his arms across
his chest, his knees maneuvering the handle bars.

They rode past the Monument, passed the wide concrete steps of the Christian
Science Church, and passed the iron gates of the Crandall Family Cemetery.
Markers, blurred by ancient winds, told of children who died of pneumonia,
and long forgotten farmers who had died of unknown diseases before the War
of Independence, and wars in which Crandalls died for their country.

They raced past the large yellow building that Uncle Benito shouted was the
oldest building in the county. He stopped, looked back toward the Soldier's
Memorial, pointed to a flock of migrating birds that had settled on utility wires,
and then rolled his hand as if he were painting the sky. "With all these beautiful
old things, you wonder why they had to bring in that gray stone tower with names
of men who were never here. Hey Gloria, take yourself slowly through each of the
streets. Start from the Five Corners, ride around, knock on doors, better carry
some dog biscuits. Meet the folks. Have some fun. See you later." He walked
across the old cemetery, passed through the back gate, and out of sight.

Gloria turned onto an unpaved road, tumbled off her bike into a mud pile.
The odor of a wood burning fireplace and a twisting wisp of smoke from the
chimney of the cabin at the end of the abruptly ended path was out of sorts
with warm September weather. Gloria battled with her bicycle as she pulled
herself from the puddle. Clanking sounds came from the cabin; the door flew
open and a gnome like man, wearing a heavy Irish knit sweater over a black
wool shirt and baggy jeans, walked barefoot onto the porch. "You must be the
new one working with Benny."

"Yes. My name is . . ."

"Gloria Palmer. I know all about you. You come here to work with Benny.
Part of the family, his, not mine."

Gloria thought she had fallen through a hole and would be confronted by
the March Hare.

"How did you know my name?" she looked around to be sure her exit was
not blocked.

"Benny tells me everything. Was here the other day to have those bikes fixed.
Goin' to be a cold night. Come on in before you freeze out here."

Gloria propped her bike against the porch, brushed her shoes on the faded welcome mat and stepped cautiously into the house. The old man scanned the dirt driveway as if watching for observers, then closed the door.

"I'll get you some paper towels so you can clean off some of that muck. You can get a cup of tea if you'd like. The water is hot. Nothing formal here. Help yourself. Guess Benny didn't tell you nothing about me. I have this here bicycle shop. I fix most of the bikes in town and most of those near about if I happen to like the people." He handed Gloria a roll of towels.

"Does everyone make the same entrance I did?" Gloria was beginning to like this elf.

"Did the old lady see ya? The one in the old house?"

"You mean the yellow one?"

"Yes! Any other old house up here? Did the witch watch you coming in here?"

"I didn't see anyone," Gloria looked out the window.

"She won't come out in the sunlight. Comes out in the morning or late, after the sun sets. Wears a big bandana and sweats, sweat suit that is, can't imagine she ever sweats. If you want to talk with her better get there before the newsboy because she starts watering the yard when she thinks he's coming. An old witch. Sorry but she is. You'll want to talk to her though."

"I will want to get to know everyone."

"You mean the old families. Lots of new people. I know who messes around and who drinks and who should be in jail. They all come here for their bikes and I get to know them. That tumble didn't hurt your bike. That old crow probably saw it and is still cackling."

"OK. My name is Gloria," she put out her hand and waited for the man's hand and name.

"Already told you I know who you are. Just call me Burt."

Gloria walked her bicycle to the paved road and checked the lettering on the mailbox that was nailed to a curly oak. "This is the private property of Burt Crandall. If you ain't the mailman keep your hands off."

"Can't believe I did that," Gloria shook her head. "Actually went into the house in this muddy camouflage."

Strands of light stretched under soaring white and mauve tinted clouds that were offset by flickering streetlights. Rustling pear tree leaves alternated verdant top sides with lime-colored and gray bottoms. Darkening clouds raced out of the western sky. Gloria sped along Main Street to the newspaper office, set her bicycle in the rack and took two steps at a time onto the loading dock. She leaned against the white washed brick wall, looked out at the neatly lined parking lot. A newly painted sign was marked with a capital G.

"Wonder if that's for me or if they're expecting God," she looked up at the small patch of blue sky.

"Have to get use'ta our sudden rain storms here. They'll just pop up across the river and wham your soaked." Tom Mosley, the janitor, spoke softly. "They're all marked, them spaces, for the regular staff. They'll be starting to get here soon. Mr. Palmieri likes to work at night, so they usually hang around then. He says that way they have lots of time to play during the day."

"I don't see any space marked for Benito, though." Gloria started into the building.

"He doesn't need one. Takes any of the spaces if he brings a car," Tom shook his head. "And who do you think is going to complain if he sets his wheels in the wrong space?"

"There's a shower in his office if you want to use it. That's okay. I'll be in later to clean up. Oh he said if you come in he'll be back around seven."

"Thanks. I fell into a mud pile and . . ."

"Yes, I know."

"How does everyone around here know what happens?"

"Had a call from Burt. He left a message for Mr. Palmieri."

"How come everyone calls him Benny and you call him Mr. . . . . "

"Because he's my boss. Wouldn't be proper. So I call him Mr. Palmieri and he can call me Tom. Don't have to worry about those nasty dirty clothes, Miss Palmieri. There's some clothes in the back closet. Never know how many people gonna show up here for a few days. He'll take in anyone who, well, who is down and out."

"I saw some of his friends when he came to Brooklyn."

"Oh no," Tom smiled for the first time. His grin revealed a row of yellow teeth intermingled with a hint of chewing tobacco. "Those were probably his friends. He's all over the place, and knows people in New York and even in

China. Keeps his self moving aroun'. Gotta get to work, mam."

"Tom," Gloria stopped his broom cart. "Please call me Gloria. And my last name is Palmer."

Tom looked quizzically at this young woman who was his boss's niece. "Yes Miss Palmieri, Gloria. Best lock the door when you're in the shower. And he keeps the dog biscuits in the lower desk drawer. Best to have them when you go visiting."

Benito Palmieri's office belied his eclectic personality. A long maple table was the center piece of the room. It was a ten foot rectangle on high dowel legs, built so that he could stand on it, walk around the galley proofs he would have spread in careful patterns, and arrange his final version of the weekly edition of *The Sentinal*. A flat wood door was set on thick carved legs to form his desk that was against the white wall. A worn leather chair was set on casters so he could glide around the room.

Two telephones, one black relic of the 1940s and a bright yellow phone with ochre push buttons, paid tribute to Uncle Benito's disdain for conformity. Gloria opened the sliding door that was painted the same antique white as the rest of the room. White tile walls were highlighted by black sink, commode, and a royal blue glass encased shower stall. Tom Mosley had understated the sizes and types of clothes in the oversized closet. Behind the clothes were shelves with colorful towels, wash clothes, and boxes of Irish Spring soap.

Gloria felt the warm shower water trickle over her, adjusted it so it felt like driving rain. She wrapped a towel around her hair, put on a baggy sweat suit and sandals. She was rubbing the towel over her hair when she noticed the office had three doors that looked like the cartoon answer to a bad joke about which door would lead to paradise and which to hell.

She opened the door that led to the chatter. Colored partitions divided the large white-washed room into low walled cubicles. A bizarre painted Haight-Ashbury type of '60s Volkswagen van, located at the far end of the room, identified the Art Department.

Wide aisles, allowing space for walking, chat areas, sitting space, and privacy divided each of the cubicles. The room was made over from the knitting mill that had dominated the community industry. Its setting close to the sheep-raising farms and the fast flowing stream had provided the resources for the defunct industry.

Red IBM typewriters on rolling carts and ornate walnut doors became an absurd dedication to formality in the fun oriented office.

The highly polished walnut receptionist desk was a 19th Century replica. The yellow plastic chair, softened with a thick cushion, met the demands of Irma Delong who, under five feet tall, had brought it in for her special needs. "Makes this damn place ergonomically correct," she had said.

Two short couches faced each other over a glass top coffee table and an arm chair was at the far end of the reception room. A conference area with two round tables and soft leather arm chairs was set behind a walnut partition. Two offices were located behind the receptionist desk for the convenience of working privately with clients or sales people.

Gloria risked opening another one of the doors in Benito's office; then she burst into uncontrollable laughter when the door revealed a mural of the road to Nowhere and a sign, "Ya shoulda peeked through the keyhole."

The third door led to the sales office with its charts, rate cards, telephones, typewriters, gray metal desks, and crisp white curtains over foot high windows. Gloria could not identify the source of her uneasiness while roaming through this room. She was surprised by the disarray of materials on each desk, the occasional plastic coffee cup, and the disorganized stack of advertising proposals. She wanted to review the sales contracts but could not find a chair.

"Don't bring any chairs in here," a bass voice bellowed. "Don't need them, don't allow them in here. These guys begin to get comfie they'll think their jobs are here, where no one's going to buy anything. So no chairs. That way they go out, I don't care if they go to some restaurant to use the bathroom. They have to meet people and make the sales."

"Sounds pretty hard boiled. I'm not one of your sales people. Gloria Palmer." She extended her hand.

The crew cut man took her hand. "Paul Scheuer. Glad to meet you Miss Palmer. Heard a lot about you from Benny. Hope I didn't sound too harsh. My staff does a great job, and they do have a place to sit down, out there in the lobby, in the conference room or down the street at Zarbo's Greasy Spoon. Benny'd have a fit if they were unhappy warriors. He'd punish me, send me to get ads from Nowhere."

"How often do you have everyone here and where is the accounting section? I would have thought it would be in here, you know, business office."

"Benny has them upstairs. Keeps my sales staffs down here. Had an elevator put in especially for the girls, so they don't have to strain themselves. He uses the stairs, usually takes them two at a time. My ad guys and gals have Friday morning deadlines. Usually take them to Skipper's for a brew or two Friday afternoons. You're welcome to join us anytime."

"Sometime maybe," Gloria tapped a stack of empty advertising contracts on a file cabinet, was about to open the top drawer when a low rumble ripped through Benito's office from the production room.

"Who the hell did it? Which of you lunk-heads did it? Some sort of practical joke? I'll shove that joke you know where."

"Ah you're about to meet one of the witches," Paul Scheur laughed. "Good luck."

Gloria straightened her back and walked into the production room. The partitioned room had come alive with clicking typewriters, two men huddled over a desk reviewing stories that had already been set, a balding man was tossing darts at photos that had appeared in earlier copies of the *Sentinal*. A tall woman stood in front of a corner desk, her hands on her hips, deep set brown eyes squinted over her pronounced cheek bones.

"Okay Tom," the woman's voice softened as she turned to Tom Mosley. "Here they are, so-called artistic turkeys, these pretend journalists, that sales jerk next door and none of them could get their fat behinds on one of those bicycles. So which one did it, which one put a bike in my place? Couldn't put it left or right, in spot one or two or ten but in my place." She was getting more intense.

"Guess it was me," Gloria broke in. "Sorry, didn't know . . ."

"Well why didn't you ask? That's what we do, here. We ask questions. That's what makes the paper so good. Now who the hell're you?"

"Gloria Palmer. Really sorry about the bike."

"Oh! Benny's daughter."

"No. Niece."

"Right niece. I'm Samantha. Samantha Crandall and don't hand me any books to review or try to tell me who's doing what to whom or ever did around here. And oh yes, I moved your bike to the end slot."

Must be the witch, Gloria thought.

Paul Scheuer put two thumbs up and closed the door.

Samantha Crandall slid into her leather chair, turned toward her typewriter, and began writing her column. She stopped, picked up a book, opened it to a page she had fly-leafed, pursed her lips, shook her head affirmatively, and continued typing.

Gloria closed the door, sat behind Benito's desk, and thought she had seen enough for the day.

"Hey Gloria," her uncle appeared in a terry cloth bathrobe, shaving cream on one side of his face, and a towel draped over his head. "Just getting in order, then we can go out someplace nice for dinner. I'll let the crew get everything ready for me to look at for tomorrow's paper."

"I think they expect you to be working with them. Tom said ..."

"Isn't Thomas a gem? Place would be a wreck without him."

"But," Gloria seemed puzzled. "He said you like to work at night."

"I do. It's still early. The crew gets here, does its work, then waits for me to find everything wrong so they can get it right. You know they have two copies. The one they show me and the one they know I want. Sort of a charade." Benito dressed in denim coveralls, a tee shirt, and sandals. "Let's break out of here.

"Do I get to use the elevator?" Gloria smiled in triumph having the information about the elevator.

"Yup. But the stairs are faster. Takes too long. As if you're still on the ground where you started, waiting to be where you're going, and not really knowing where you are in that elevator shaft. But, take your choice. As for me," he opened the back door, "I always like to know where I am."

20

Uncle Benito

"C'mon Glory, help me set this up, we've got pizza coming," Benito spread a white table cloth over the conference table. Paper stuff is in the closet, beer is in the refrig, and some wine in back of the closet. Want you to meet the whole staff."

"But," Gloria motioned toward the editorial room. "Don't they have to finish getting the paper out tonight?"

"It's really all done. They're just making sure I'll like what has been done and not make any changes." He winked. "I checked it out this afternoon. Only one change in an ad that was grammatically incorrect. I'll show you how to check it out and get you started on a great place to get human interest stories, but later, right now, their feast. We'll eat later."

"Okay kids," Benito shouted. "Break time. Pizza's spread on my conference table, meet Gloria, then you can show me the layout, and we can go to press. Meet my greatest critic, Samantha; she's also the book review and cultural attaché for the papers. I did tell you we publish the papers for twelve small towns in the County. Have you met everyone? Good. Have a surprise for you."

Benito reviewed the material for the Courier, looked over the top of his glasses at an ad he had corrected, nodded approval; the editors scooped up the pages that had been spread on the table and floor. The office was silent, cleared of the pizza, beer, and wine. Benito leaned back on his swivel chair, clasped hands behind his head, pursed his lips, and asked, "Well?"

"Okay," Gloria wished she had another glass of beer. "What's the surprise?"

"Hah! You need a place of your own. I have a great little house set up for you along the river front, near that old bridge. You'll love it. Used to rent it out but when the people moved out, I had it fixed up for you."

"How did you know I would come here?"

"Would have kidnapped you if you turned me down," Benito laughed. "Has great view of the river, sunset, and enough space for you to really settle in. Want to see it?"

"Sure."

"Before we go there, let's get over to Downesville. They're holding night court and thought you should see what happens there. Not everything is sweet and nice. We have our burglars and family violence and car thefts and well there is always a kid or two who get into trouble or are troubled. See it all at the court. Introduce you to Judge Charlie Feather. His family can be traced right back to the Native Americans who were here long before any of us. The Crandalls claim to be the first family to have settled here. Only three of them left now. Lots of Feathers around though."

"I met one of the Crandall's today at the bike shop." Gloria looked out the window at the bicycle rack.

"You met two. Samantha is a Crandall, Burt's sister. You ought to meet Jessica Crandall."

"You mean the one Burt calls the . . . ."

"Yes, he calls her the witch. They have their problems, the three of them. Used to be another sister, but she's gone now." Benito was out the back door, down the stairs, and opened the convertible top. He tossed a sweatshirt with a hood to Gloria. "Going to be a windy drive."

He glanced toward the dimly lit cemetery, bowed as one might genuflect passing a church, then turned toward Downesville.

"Uncle Benito," Gloria held her head back to catch the wind.

"Glory let's get something right. Call me Ben. Drop the Uncle stuff, makes me feel too old. Okay?"

"Ben," she smiled. "You know your office is really pretty barren. Nothing on the desk, nothing on the walls, and back at the house, not a single family picture. My father," she stopped, reached up as if to grab the wind. "He had family pictures all over the place and he despised all of them."

"Don't need them. Have all the pictures I need right here." He lifted his hand to his head, and then touched his chest. "They are there and protect me even when I don't handle the wheel." He laughed as he jiggled the steering wheel with two fingers.

"But Ben, you must have had, well, must have had someone."

"Sure. There have been lots of someones. I love to meet people and have lots of good friends. You saw some of them in Brooklyn."

"How come no family pictures?"

"I have the important images. I was even married once."

"Thought you said three times."

"Did I?"

"Do you have any children?"

Benito turned slowly into the Court parking lot and lifted the top of the convertible. "May rain again when we're inside." He rubbed his nose. "Yes I was married once. Her family didn't like me. Didn't like the way I dressed, the way I acted, the way I loved her."

"How could anyone not like ... "

"Oh it wasn't really me they didn't like. It was who I am, where I come from, and my name. Palmierie. One of them would say. You know *"eyetalian"*. They thought she should go with one of their good boys who owned a lot of land and came from a family that arrived on the Mayflower. Always claimed their family came on the next ship after the Mayflower or from the Virginia colonies."

"But what difference does that make?" Gloria put her hand on his shoulder.

"None to my girl. Her family thought we were all thieves or murderers and came to America because we were common criminal types that had to leave Italy. Would have been worse if I was a Jew." Ben opened the car door.

"You said you were married."

"They never wanted to admit that when their ancestors came here from England or wherever the hell they came from, they were kicked out because they *were* criminals."

Gloria looked at her Uncle.

"We eloped. Lived in Pennsylvania for a while and then came back here to the homestead when her parents were gone. That's when I started to buy property around here and started the newspaper. Her sisters and brother took her back into the family and put up with me. *Thank God he's not one of those Indians.* That's how they justified that. They still own a lot of this town and some of the land across the river." Benito leaned on the top of the car. "Figure it out yet?"

"The Crandalls". Gloria fumbled with the hooded sweatshirt.

"You got it. Let's get inside before it starts to pour. Can happen all of a sudden around here." They settled onto the back bench in the courtroom. Gloria scanned the countryside paintings that formed a cyclorama. Casement windows on the side walls were designed to allow both northern and southern light to fill the room during the day and reflected the thinking of early settlers who had designed the building to be used for prayer meetings. The new section of the Court House was added during the 1930's.

A clerk sorted papers near the Judge's podium; two lawyers, seated at a table facing the clerk, were busy laughing at stories about old cases; a guard asked all present to rise. Judge Charles Feather swept into the chamber, stepped onto the podium, sat in the high backed leather chair, nodded to the audience to be seated, and poured a glass of water.

Gloria was surprised that this handsome, dark-haired, high cheek-boned Judge did not seem to be more than thirty-five years old. She nudged Benito. "Thought you said he was old."

"Said he was from old family. Very impressive though, don't you think? Introduce you later. Important guy to know. Get lot's of good information, and he likes to have lunch in the Nowhere Café."

The two lawyers took turns representing the night people who had been arrested including the drunks, brawlers, burglars, shoplifters, and one woman who had been doing 85-miles per hour in a 30-mile per hour school zone.

The Judge spoke to each of the defendants, lectured them on their behavior, and then set the fine or sentence. He talked quietly so that the public had to strain to hear the proceedings and in order to maintain the defendant's privacy.

Gloria thought about Hawk as she watched Charlie Feather. Both were tall, had dark hair, those sharp facial features, and intense eyes. She wondered if the judge also had a dream beyond what he was doing and wondered if he would one day break free of his black robe and talk to her about football.

"Hey Charlie, want to introduce you to Gloria Palmer, my niece." Benito led the way to the judge's office. "Short schedule tonight, eh?"

"Nice of you to stop by, Miss Palmer," the judge extended his hand.

"Gloria noticed the array of family pictures displayed on the glass topped oak desk. She stepped across the thick oriental carpet to accept the judge's handshake. "Those are beautiful paintings you have behind your desk," she nodded toward the two large Native American canvases that blanketed the wall. "Are these your children in these photos?"

"Thank you," he said. "My wife does the decorating. And yes. This is my son Walter. He's on his way to become quite a hockey champ if he manages to get through algebra. And here's my daughter, Claire. She's intent on becoming an artist, notice the crayons. And of course, my son, Vincent who plans on being the first man on Pluto. My wife, Fran," he pointed to the large framed photo of the dark haired woman standing in front of a Pueblo. "That's where we met. How long are you planning to stay with us?"

"Not going to let her escape," Benito broke in. "Gloria will be covering the court from now on." He smiled at Gloria. "Going to be picking up where I left off."

"Thought my life was going to get easy," the judge put on a leather jacket. "I have to get moving though folks. Promised to get to Walter's game tonight. They play whenever they can get ice time. Stop by again," he nodded to Gloria, "I'll have the clerk issue a press pass for you, make things nice and easy. By the way, things are not always quiet like they were tonight. They get some cases they don't want to handle over in the County Court so they send them over here for quick quiet disposition."

"You mean high profile guys or with some money." Gloria felt her shoulders tighten.

"No. That's not my kind of stuff. I'm known to be fair but tough. That goes for anyone they send over here."

The steady windshield wiper pattern punctuated the unusual quiet during the ride back to the Village. Benito's coal black eyes reflected rain pelting the roadway in front of them. The determined wind reminded Gloria of Tern Harbor storm seasons. She wanted to speak, wanted to ask what her uncle meant by "going to pick up where I left off." She wanted to be able to read his mind.

He pulled onto the narrow driveway, the garage doors opened as if they knew who was coming, and as quietly closed behind them. "Come on Gloria, I'll get us some nice snacks and hot chocolate. Good on a night like this. How'd you like the Court?"

"It was interesting to see that there are some of the same kind of people here as back home. You know, good guys and bad." Gloria sipped the warm beverage.

"And lots in between. How'd you like Charlie?"

"I guess part of my job will be covering the Court, but that can fill about half a column. So," she folded her hands, "what's the rest of it?"

"You will take my job. That's what I have in mind. Are you up to it?"

"But I just got here, don't even know all of what you do and why you want me to . . . . "

"Easy. Just shadow me and let the staffs do their work. You know we have several papers, learn about the real estate. Should take you about a month or so. Not too different from Tern Harbor except we have heart." he added.

"But, I don't understand why ...."

"It's easy. I need someone in the family to take over while I am away. When I saw you in Brooklyn, I knew you could do it. After all you come from a newspaper family, and everyone in the family has real estate, including your father, so you must have some idea about how it works."

"But where are you going. What makes you so sure about me?"

"Because you have the Palmieri drive and courage and sympatico. And I need a vacation."

"Where are you going?"

He leaned back, smiled, ran his fingers through his hair. "Out West. Start in Sante Fe for a while. Visit the Native American places in the desert, then move on."

"How long a vacation? Sounds like about a month or two. That's about how long it will take me to learn my job," she smiled.

"Longer than that. I have a big project in mind." He moved to the closet. "Ever go roller blading? Lot's of fun and takes a certain amount of skill. Taking these with me." He spun one of the skate wheels. "When I reach Portland, in Oregon, I plan to start the adventure of my life."

"On skates?"

"Not just skates. Roller blades. Going to visit every Native reservation, conclave, group, Nation, in the Country. Will write about each of those places, about the people who I meet. That's my mission. An "eyetalian", will be visiting people who got here after the buffalo."

"That could take ...."

Benito spread his arms over his head. "That's why I need you here. Want you to take over where I left off. I need to be free to fulfill my mission. Are you up to it?" He looked out the window. "Look at that beautiful sunrise. Guess we talked right through the night. I need to shower and get ready for a busy day. Why don't you get some rest? I'll be back later and we can get you moved into your new house."

Gloria knew she could do this job, do it better than Steve Palmer; she thought about being a Palmieri instead of a Palmer. She wondered about Benito's desire to be free. Wasn't this freedom, having it all his way? She thought about being a Palmieri, about courage, drive, and sympatico. She thought about her cousin Gis, about Hawk, and about making love on the beach.

"Okay," she said. "I'll get some rest, then head for Forge Creek."

21

Matt

Matt Donovan Steele ran his thumb across the New Jersey driver's license expiration date, mounted new license plates on the yellow pickup truck, checked newspaper rooms for rent ads, drove to a gas station phone, rented an apartment in South Crossing, and dropped onto the bed to catch up on days of missing sleep.

Fifteen hundred miles had been added to the odometer since he had left New York. Matt stopped in Detroit to meet skinheads who had formed a disorderly group with their own "club house". They were too well defined, easily identifiable group with clear lines of leadership that held tight reigns on its members who moved unfettered through the Midwest creating terror in black and Jewish communities. Their passion for physical violence repelled Matt. He tried to explain that by causing physical harm to people instead of imposing lasting fear, the skins could be easily rounded up by police, and would provoke counter productive moves by their enemies.

He continued driving to Oregon and spent the winter and spring in a white supremacist conclave. He observed training of new enlistees to the cause of safeguarding "White America". He understood why individuals who leave the training camps must be completely on their own. The enclave had no name, would not be involved in any acts committed by trainees who left the camp, and would defend no one. There was no identifiable organization or leader. The single thread that each man took with him was that one day he would be involved with the retaking of America by the white community. When the time became right, they would know it, and they would retake the American government.

He traveled along Southwest highways through New Mexico and Arizona, felt his body warm and his spirit soar as he experienced the desert. His temples throbbed as he bypassed Indian reservations and was transformed; he knew how he would have lived had he been born on a reservation instead of on Long Island.

He slept under desert stars, dreamed of animals he had never seen, dreamed of chants he had never heard, shuddered in the cold night air, shielded his face from the stinging sand, and wondered at the wind blown plants that survived in this time nurtured wilderness. He sat cross legged behind desolate scrub under the blazing summer sun; felt his mind and body turning to mush; he heard the silent shuffling of ghosts of the long walks across New Mexico sand and Oklahoma brush; he smelled the rancid smoke of grass burning for thousands of miles along Oklahoma farmland; he heard the echo of thundering buffalo; he filled with guilt at having hidden his heritage, and he endured rage at feeling that guilt.

He wandered under the blazing sun, searched for any signs of life that would defy the broiling desert, fell delirious under floating shrubs that offered hints of shade then rolled under the truck. He woke in the midnight cool breezes, marched in a wide circle until bathed by the moon searchlight he fell into a squatting position, reached toward the sky, his hair covered his face as if to hide it from the stars, and he whispered to the four winds, "What do you want of me?" He fell prostrate into the desert rocks and pebbles until the morning when he saw the perfect circle he had scraped into the land during his nighttime march. He committed the smell of the desert and of mountains and sounds of the land to his reborn sense of himself.

As if to flee the wind-borne terrors of the desert, Matt denied sleep, drove east until he reached the Atlantic shore, and rushed into the ocean. He tore off his clothes, raced into the surf, rode the waves, and fell silent onto the sandy beach. He tossed his clothes toward the boulders that bordered the beach, leaned against the moss covered rocks and thought of home.

He drove to the motor vehicle bureau and re-established his identity.

As he rolled over in his new bed, he tried to purge nightmares of the past year, tried to expunge the dreams of Tompkins Square, tried to drive away what he had become, tried to remember what he would be like if he had never carved the letter N into his friend's arm. He fell into dreamless sleep and quashed the desert voices into hiding.

Sunlight woke him. He dialed the phone number of his crew cut mentor, looked at windows close to his apartment, and waited for the sleepy voice to answer.

"Who the hell is this?" the gravelly voice demanded.

"Back," Matt snapped. "Get rid of whoever you have there and meet me in the Park in an hour." He slammed down the phone and smiled his mirrored image. He knew he was now in command, that whoever is the meanest and demonstrates the most strength, wins. He knew what he wanted and he was going to manipulate Carl Gohrman to get it. He wanted a new beginning, to escape the past, to rekindle his ancient ties, to look in the mirror and see that the face of good had replaced evil.

He would extract the funds he needed from Gohrman, and escape the scouring demands of the winds.

The crew cut runner in jogging suit was sitting on the bench when Matt walked into the Park. He sat next to his former mentor, offered him a donut, sipped from his open container of coffee, then detailed a plan to continue the work of recruitment he had started before he went west "Sounds ambitious and on target." Gohrman munched the donut then stoked the bottom of his chin. "So what do you want from me? What makes you think this is so important that you can get me out of bed at this hour? What gives you the friggin idea that you can make any demands on me?" He threw the half eaten donut into the path of a startled squirrel.

"Because you have no choice. You are deep into this system, have deep pocketed connections who have the control and want to keep it that way, and you either do what they want or your flag flies up your ass." Matt lowered his head, aimed his well rehearsed pinpoint stare, and pointed his thumb toward the lightly fluttering flag.

Carl Gohrman extended his broad jaw toward Matt, waited, then, raised his eyebrows and smiled. "Good to have you back, Matthew. Good to know you are ready to get back to work. Now what is it you want from, let us say, from me?"

Matt was not ready for this quick surrender, thought Gohrman might suspect the truth, and knew it would not be easy to get away He maintained his stare at the man who had introduced him to violence and self directed rage; he wondered why he did not reach out to strangle Gohrman.

"How much money do you need right now?" The man was jogging in place and looking across the Park for other signs of activity.

"Two thousand to start," Matt stood in front of his mentor.

"Okay. The same old mailbox. Good to have you back, and I have an exciting, bold project for you. You'll find the information along with the funds in the usual place." The crew cut jogger put his left hand on Matt's shoulder, reached his right hand across to shake Matt's hand, pulled him close, ran his hand down along Matt's arm, and whispered into his ear. "But don't ever fucking threaten me again, don't ever try to get me up at this ungodly hour unless you plan to come upstairs and help me raise that flag." He nodded to another jogger and pulled Matt closer to him. "Get it. Don't threaten me or you'll always have to be looking over your shoulder, always have to avoid shadows, and always have to listen to fluttering leaves."

Carl Gohrman jogged out of the Park.

22

Even Jesus Pays

Matt opened the brown envelope he pulled from Gohrman's mailbox, fanned one hundred crisp twenty dollar bills, and the small lined pad covered with a swastika stamped on the first page. He read the scribbled message on the second page. *Continue the work in Jersey City and Hoboken. Spread the word further South, like waterfront industrial area, kids like to get into battles near bars with merchant sailors from foreign ships. Good practice and get them excited about foreigners, and any of those non-whites. Then have a big opportunity for us.*

The next note was troubling.

We're bringing in a major group, the Knights, klan to you, in North Carolina are interested in coming along with us, an important coup for our financial friends if we can pull it off. Go to Clarksburg, there is a map and directions on the last page, call the number and arrange a meeting. It is all set up, so finish the deal. When you are done, come to the skins' gathering in Vineland, New Jersey. They're coming from around the Northeast for a big bash. Let me know when the deal is done.

These people are true patriots and can be big help in our ultimate goal. You met with the Oregon people so you know what I mean. Don't drop the ball.

He fanned the stack of twenty dollar bills, lit a match to the note but kept the map and phone number, put the ashes in the brown envelope, and drew a phoenix-like bird on the back flap. Then he wrote one line across the front. "These are for you. In the night, in the day, in the sun, in the storm, always look over your shoulder, stay out of shadows. Know that you may never be alone or safe. Now who must listen to rustling leaves?" He addressed the envelope to Carl Gohrman.

He pulled his laundry bag from the closet and walked to the laundromat on the Main Street. It was quiet in the brightly lit store. The sound of humming washing machines and dryers was interspersed with Latin music coming from a radio behind the counter. A woman with long black hair was reading a magazine and did not appear to notice Matt as he loaded quarters into the washing machine coin slots.

He walked to the front of the store and put two quarters into the vending machine for a cup of watery coffee. The machine clicked and nothing happened. He pressed the coin return and heard the coins drop into the collection box. When no cup dropped, he slapped the side of the machine.

"Try another quarter; takes seventy-five cents." The woman spoke with a Spanish accent. "Says fifty cents, but takes you for seventy-five." She continued reading her magazine.

Matt slid another quarter into the slot and again waited. He kicked the bottom of the machine. "C'mon sucker." He shouted. A cup dropped and the watery brown liquid filled it close to the top. He reached in for the cup as another cup dropped and filled with coffee, then another and another. It was as if the Sorcerer's Apprentice had invaded the vending world.

"Son of a bitch." Matt laughed. "How do you stop this sucker?"

"Pull the plug." The woman shook her head.

"Where's the plug. Don't see any damned plug." Matt reached behind the machine.

"Pull the fucking plug," she hissed. "On top, near the ceiling. See that fucking wire, just pull it."

He stepped onto a plastic chair, reached up, and pulled the plug out of the ceiling fixture. As the chair toppled, he scrambled to his feet, leaned into the dispenser section, pulled the multiple cups so that hot coffee flooded across his legs.

"Looks like you have a prostate problem," the woman put down the magazine. "Here let me help you get dry. She wadded paper towels, rubbed them along his legs, and then pulled up close to him. "You can finish the job, toss your pants into one of the machines. No one around to watch except me. S'awright. I seen it before. And I can get you a decent cup of coffee from my thermos. Never want to drink that piss." She nodded to the vending machine. "You go behind the counter and hand me your stuff. Let me have some quarters. Don't be bashful, it's slow here tonight.

"Thanks," Matt smiled. "You have a name?"

"Sure. What name you like?"

"Really, what's your name? My name is Matt," he volunteered.

"Call me Abbey. I like that name. It sounds like the beginning of the alphabet. Yeah, Abbey. That's a cute backside you have, by the way."

"You wait here for guys who'll get hit on by that coffee machine?" Matt laughed.

"Usual crowd in here's scrubby, smoke cheap cigars, and drink from brown bags. No use for them. Come over to my place later. I'll get you something to eat. You look like you need a good meal. But I'll skip the Matt stuff. I call you Chesus."

"Jesus? Not me." Matt grinned.

"Pronounce it right. CHE-sus. Like it comes from the back of your throat and like your Doctor Zeus. Now say it right."

"Didn't come here for a language lesson."

"My first boyfriend was *Che*sus but I left him back home; he had no ambition. Not like here where he could have made something of his self. You look like you could make something of yourself if you had a decent meal," she shrugged.

"I don't . . ."

"I'll bet you do," she smiled revealing her tongue through tightly drawn lips.

"I never pay for . . ." Matt hesitated. *Was this woman one of the howlies that had been following him all his life?*

"This one's on me. We're both alone tonight, it's cold out and could use some company. You're folding that underwear like you're afraid to let me see that you even have any. Here let me get that done for you. When was the last time you had anyone do that for you?" She moved next to Matt, quickly folded his dry laundry, and repeated her offer.

"But you have to let me buy some beer." *He wanted to believe that she was too kind to be an enemy.*

———•———

Abbey's dimly lit apartment was comforting to Matt. Orange couch and chairs, faux oak tables, and yellowing lampshades retained the subtle odor of cigarette smoke. She settled drops of sweet smelling perfume into metal rings fit over light bulbs as if to tempt him to unquenchable loving. The smell of onions, garlic, and spices drifted from the kitchen accentuating the same steady beat of Latin music that had been playing at the laundromat.

"Hey Chesus," the woman called from the kitchen. "You like some chips, salsa? There's some good Spanish beer in the fridge. She arranged dishes with chile, onions, and cheeses.

"So why did you really get me up here," Matt scanned her body. "I never . . ."

"You never? Don't believe you never. Madre mia, a virgin?"

"I never pay for anything I can get for nothing."

"Wasn't going to charge you. Just alone tonight, both of us, and like to have a good looking Americano." She licked some salsa from her fingers, dipped a chip into the spicy dip and lifted it to Matt's mouth. "Go on my Chesus. Won't be your last meal. Won't be your first time."

They ate sandwiches, chips, salsa, and drank beer. She moved behind Matt, moved her hand across his neck and shoulder.

"So you going to tell me your life story or are we just going to go into the other room and have some fun," she squeezed her shoulders so that her cleavage swelled.

"Forget the life story," he grinned, reached across the table, touched her elbow, and nodded toward the bedroom. She moved close to him until he could feel her warm hands reach under his shirt. He buried his head into her neck and they moved to the bed that dominated the room. *Matt thought about the Spanish girl in Central Park, and wondered how this woman planned to set him up, wondered if she would to try to get him to use some drug, or find some way to steal his money,.*

They stripped each other, leaned onto the oversized bed, and took repeated turns at making love.

Matt saw his father's image rise above the battering surf and then crash against the barrier rocks. The fearsome vision melted as he buried his head into the woman's hard bosom; he reached under her, lifted and lowered her as if in denial of the thundering breakers. He felt her knees tighten into his ribs and they joined the steady rhythm of the drum beating out time for the Latin music. *He felt her trying to take charge of his body, thought the swelling surf had finally gotten him, and he thought she had been sent to be trap him in the heavy foam of the receding tide.*

"No," he wanted to cry out. "You're dead, gone, not going to hurt my mother or me any more and can't pull me down."

"Bitch," he shouted. Matt lay on the far side of the bed, turned away from the woman, and stared into the darkness. Her hand reached across his hip, slid along the center of his stomach, and gently massaged his thigh. He rolled toward her unwavering breath. "Bitch," he yelled again. "You can do this in your sleep, in your dreams."

He pulled her toward him. "This time I'm in charge. You'll never forget me." He pressed harder and faster into her. *He envisioned the surf crashing against the rocks, felt the wind challenging the high tossing water, raising it and forcing it back from the rocks, allowing only foam to fold in white shrouds onto the white sand beach. Everything went dark and quiet; one more breaker raised the foam over the barrier rocks until all the howlies that had been chasing Matt since his uncle George and he dropped their package from the boat, screamed across the unyielding beach. Gentle breezes dispersed the howlies, spread them into glittering sand crystals, and Matt pulled the sand close to his body.*

He closed his thighs around the woman who was sinking her nails into his back. The overhead fan groaned as it whipped warm air around their bodies. "Bitch." He cried out.

She turned away.

He closed his eyes, listened for any strange sounds, was prepared for sudden movement toward him, and did not allow himself to dream.

"Bitch," he whispered. "Brought me here into this devil's haunt. You won't forget me." He pulled her close to him and closed his eyes. His body stayed alert.

Matt slipped into the living room, checked his clothes and wallet, then moved silently back to the bedroom.

"You were terrific," the woman said. "No way I could have charged you. Only second time I ever did this with an Indian."

"What do you mean?" he snapped.

"You move so quiet like an Indian does in the woods. No one would even know you were there, except for the loving. Ay, ay, ay. So quiet and slow and ay, ay, ay."

"I'm no . . ."

"It'll be our little secret. S'okay. I knew another one like you. Lonesome, holier than thou Indian. Some politician, maybe a student, I think. Not too many around here, but he was good. You're better."

"Shit, I didn't use any protection," Matt wanted to change the subject.

"S'okay. I always do and you won't catch nothing." She held up a coffee cup. "You can help yourself. Hey, we won't see one another again, not like that. I got business to do. Besides I know you have important things to do, important person to become. I'm psychic. I know things. Besides, why spoil a good memory."

"Why do you even think I could be a friggin Indian?"

"Told you. Also that eagle tattoo spread across your chest. Rises up, like it should overpower a woman, or anything gets in its way. Like an old Indian picture I once saw. And told you, I'm psychic."

"Well you're wrong. Won't have anything to do with anything not white, not real American," he turned his skinhead stare at her, picked up the bag of laundry and headed for the door. He felt rage soaring through his neck as she seemed to taunt his hidden heritage.

"So it's okay for you to screw with anyone as long as it's in the dark and you don't have to see the color. Hey, don't forget me. Hey, my Chesus," she called and threw a paper dish of salsa at Matt, then slammed the door.

Matt remembered the brown envelope he had hidden in the laundry bag. He wiped the red mess from his shirt, smeared the image of a winged bird-in-flight across the door, lowered his head, repeatedly scraped his foot along the floor, and crashed his boot against the target. The door opened, the chain locks gave way to his powerful kick; he lowered his brow, pulled his fist against his chest, and stared at the frightened woman. "Matt," he whispered. He lowered his hand as he thought of the image of his terrified mother.

"Matt, Matt, call me Matt. You friggin left your *Chesus* at home."

"Yeah, well next time you come remember to knock; and bring money. Even *Jesus* pays."

Tears and rain flowed along matt's face as he ran into the street. He reached a fist toward the storm concealed street light and shouted, 'No more, no more. I won't be what I have been, won't be that anymore. I will be my mother's son, will banish phantoms. I will... will...will be free."

———

Matt sniffed the woman's cigarette smoke on the neatly folded laundry as he placed it in his own dresser drawer. He bit into a stale donut, fanned the stack of twenties that had come from Gohrman, and dialed the New York phone number reserved for emergencies.

"Okay," he snapped at the crackling answering machine. "Leaving for North Carolina. New deal when I get back."

He knew it would take more than just intelligence and bravado to spell out the terms of a contract with the man who had guided him into this life. It would take the confidence of experience, the habit of intimidation, and the drive for self preservation. It came from understanding that he who instills the most fear, wins. It came from memory of elders, gathered at campfires, repeating the stories of ancestors and recanting old Tom Steelehart's mantra "Beat them at their own game."

"And remember," he finished his phone monolog to the answering machine. "Keep watch over your shoulder, listen to rust leaves, and stay out of shadows."

23

The Most Fear

George Donovan fumbled with the log house door lock, cursed the persistently ringing telephone, pulled it from its cradle, and slapped it against his head.

"Hello," he waited for a response. "Hello. Who the hell is this?"

"George?" The voice was hesitant and questioning.

"Who the hell . . ." George stopped, looked out the kitchen window at the tumbling surf. "Matthew? Where are you? Are you okay? In trouble?"

"No. I'm fine. How's my mother? Why you at the house?"

"She misses you. Just taking care of the place for her. Still works for old man Palmer and lives there most of the time."

"Why is she still with that cheap bastard?"

"It's a job, and, she still hangs onto that myth. Where are you?"

"New Jersey. Been traveling out west. Heading to North Carolina for a little job but will be back in a few days."

"Matt," his uncle George hesitated. "You still driving that old piece of junk?"

Matt smiled. "Yeah. I sleep with it so much, was going to give it a girl's name, but was afraid we'd fall in love. Going to finish this job and have enough money to get a new truck."

"Matt, what did you do with the artillery?"

"Dumped it. Couldn't store it anywhere or keep hauling it around the country, couldn't get caught with it. Made my reputation so no one would mess with me, and then I pawned the guns. Why? Anyone looking?"

"Nah! No one even cared. Folks around here just figured he booted your backside out of here and took off." George prattled on about local happenings, about Matt's old friends, and the recent fall campfire.

"Those gatherings are losing attraction for tourists and more important losing interest for your ..." George stopped. "I was going to say for your people, but... And Matt, your Mom keeps waiting for you. That's one of the reasons she still works in Tern Harbor. Still thinks old Steelehart was cheated, that his family should come back together, and she still thinks you are supposed to be some kind of hero, leader of your people."

"I don't have any people," Matt barked into the phone. "Tell Mom I called."

He moved away from the phone booth then turned and talked to the dangling telephone. "Hey George! Right now I'm at a rest stop they named for a famous football coach. Imagine that, honored him by naming a place where people relieve themselves. Guess if I had been a big deal football player like my old man wanted they would name a place where dogs poop after me. I can do without any honors, or any of what you call my people."

"Matt," George stopped when he heard the buzz and then the message "If you want to make a call please hang up and try again."

———————

The yellow pick-up truck sped along the wide flat roadways of the New Jersey Turnpike, connected with Interstate 95, then moved through Delaware and Maryland, slogged along the beltway around Washington D.C., and picked up speed in Virginia. Matt stopped at a diner as he reached North Carolina, then drove off the Interstate and headed west. The cool, moist foothills were perfect growing country for the abundant tobacco crops. He spotted the vacancy sign for the Wilton City Line Motel, looked across the road to the white-washed single story bowling alley, showed the motel clerk his driver's license, and paid cash for two nights.

"We don't got any restaurant here at the motel but there's a snack bar across at the lanes, there's a diner in town but it closes at five so I guess that leaves the bowling alley. That's where most of the truckers stop anyway." The clerk watched Matt walk down the hall to his room.

The first large rain drops slammed across the road as Matt ran toward the bowling alley. He collided with a hitch hiker as they reached the bowling alley doorway.

"Saw you back on I-95, how'd you get this far?" Matt called to the boy.

"One truck ride all the way. Got lucky," the hitch-hiker mumbled.

"We're in for a long night of rain." Matt moved toward the snack bar. Men, using all six lanes, were watching him. The sound of pins falling and being reset, the bitter smell of stale beer in open bottles, and drifting cigarette smoke were interrupted by the abrupt appearance of crisply dressed waitress.

Matt looked back at the young hitch hiker. "C'mon," he said. "You look like you need something to eat. I'll handle it. C'mon."

Brent Wilcox sat quietly as they ate hamburgers and drank Coke. The teenager had been visiting his grandfather in Virginia and was heading home in Kentucky.

"What's your grandfather doing in Virginia?" Matt asked as he finished his French fries.

"Ten years." Brent answered with his eyes opening wide to see Matt's reaction.

"What for?"

"Being stupid," the boy snapped. "Broke into the back of a store and took a *tee vee* set. Stupid. He didn't even have a place to use it. Wasn't living anywhere. Told me that was cool, now the State of Virginia is finally giving him housing. That's what he said."

"Ten years are a long time for burglary?"

"Got him one of them guards," the boy glanced at the bowlers then told how his grandfather hated police and how the jail guards were pushing him around and even trying to sell him to the highest bidders. "Old man can get real mean," the boy nodded then continued. He told how his grandfather would get into bar fights and take on anyone fool enough to try him.

"Well, one of them guards shoved him into a wall, so the old guy turned and flipped the dumb guy. Broke his back. Got ten years but ain't nobody going to mess with him no more, none of them guards or any of them boys who want to try him on for size."

Matt understood. The one who instills the most fear, wins.

"So how come you got to see him?"

"He's my grandfather. Someone has to see him. He said it didn't matter that he stole anything because it was from some Jew store anyway, but that's not how the State of Virginia saw it. Just being stupid."

Matt thought of Vince Palmieri and how angry he had become when Tim trash talked his Jewish customers. He thought of the work he had done getting kids away from hanging out on corners in New Jersey to put up posters to terrify foreigners who were invading their towns. He thought of the ultimate violence his father tried to inflict on his uncle George. He thought of the wind and waves that engulfed his father's memory. He thought of his wandering across America, the time he spent with the white supremacists in Oregon, the spirits that invaded his soul when he passed the reservations, and he loathed the mixed emotions about his current mission.

"I took care of some things for the old man though," the boy was still talking about his visit to the prison. "Made sure some of them prison workers got home late for dinner that night. Put holes in some of them tires of those nice shiny vehicles."

"How'd they let you into the place with a knife?"

"Didn't have one. Pulled some nails out of the parking lot fence. Learned long ago to use things you find along the way."

Matt lifted his foot onto one of the chairs so the boy could get a good look at the boot with the steel toe. Matt thought of the skinheads he had taught to use these and thought this boy would be prime to be dragged into the culture. He pushed his foot under the table and decided to avoid further thoughts of pain these boots could inflict.

The boy was looking at Matt's tattoos.

"You know who I am," Matt stared at the boy.

"Guessed it when I saw the tattoos. Must have done a lot guessing from the number of lines and spots on that spider web. Saw some of the Indians at a powwow back home, had the same kind of stuff."

"Where you going to stay tonight? Can't keep going in the rain and I could use some help on a job I have in the morning. You can stay in my truck tonight, keep you and it safe. If you try to snatch it, I'll find you and you'll be dog meat."

"Better than hiding in here," he motioned to the bowlers. "Them guys look like they'd like to get hold of a young kid like me. Okay. But if I do some work, I have to get paid."

"Cool, kid. You stay in the truck, that's all you have to do, then hang in there in the morning when I meet some guy, and I'll get you some cash. Cool."

———

Sparkling frost crystals on the truck reflected the sunrise that glowed in ochre and pink strands across the North Carolina hills. Matt tapped the window to be sure the boy was still there and awake.

"Been up long before got light," the boy laughed as he exited the woods. "Had to do what I had to do. Couldn't wait on you."

They drove through the four corners that made up the town, stopped at the combination gas station, diner, and general store; filled the gas tank and got coffee and rolls then moved along the narrow country road until Matt spotted *Stillwell Farm*. The flat land had gone fallow and would allow nothing, including weeds, to grow.

"That'll have good crop of tobacco next time around," the boy marveled at the expanse of farm land. They continued over a small rise in the road and then saw a wide, low brown shed with long tables and bins.

"This is it," Matt said. "Now when I get out to meet this guy, you just sit here in the truck. Don't open the door for anyone but me. You see anything strange you beep the horn or if you see me coming fast, you start the motor. You know how to do that?"

The boy smiled as if to say he could drive this truck faster than anyone else over any kind of ground. "Yup!"

He was not sure why he trusted the boy, had found him in the rain, and the wind was somehow talking to him. Matt yielded to his intuition and besides, he thought, "there's no one else around."

Matt assessed the man in the straw hat waving to him from the shed. Henry Stillwell looked like any other farmer. He wore loose fitting Levi jeans, a denim shirt and jacket, yellow work boots, a toothy smile that was oversized for his narrow jaw, and a North Carolina Tigers cap. He extended his hand and welcomed Matt as they walked into the shadow of the shed.

"Glad you were able to find the place. Figured you Yankees might get lost once or twice, but the boys at the bowling alley said you seemed to know your way around. And that was pretty smart to protect your truck that way." Stillwell placed a chunk of tobacco under his lip then pulled it to the back of his cheek and rolled it around his molars.

Matt, his eyes fixed on Stillwell, was aware they were not alone. He saw the sparkle of light that indicated two or three shotguns in the woods alongside the shed. He was glad he had the boy ready in the truck and hoped he was on his side.

"Well I was glad Gohry was sending you. You did a good job for us last time he gave you a task?"

"Always try to be precise and quick," Matt answered as if he knew what Stillwell was referring to.

"Kept them boys off Wall Street and away from the money. All we would have needed was to have a nigger office down there."

Matt suddenly knew who had funded the Wall Street escapade. He wondered who was behind the other tasks, and who was behind Gohrman; he recognized that his New York contact was probably working on his own for whoever came up with money and that he used any group he put together – like the skinheads – to enforce white supremacy or hatred for anything including the establishment, cops, drug addicts, politicians, even other skinheads. He began to understand that Gohrman had helped provoke the Tompkins Square Park riot. Son-of-a-bitch, Matt thought, he's fouled up my life so he could make money, so he could keep his flag flying.

"Well let's get right to it. A job we have for you down here. Good you brought a helper," Stillwell motioned to the truck.

"Was told to check out how the skinhead kids could possibly work with the Klan. Wasn't told about a job."

"What Klan?" Stillwell scowled. "We ain't the Klan. They're just a bunch of old men and pimply faced kids these days, maybe wear them Halloween costumes for show once in a while, but they are not a viable thing anymore. Life has moved past them. We have more significant ways to meet our objectives. You were out there in Oregon so you have some idea."

Matt saw one of the shotguns move away from the shed and assumed it would be heading toward the truck. He moved closer to Stillwell. "I learned enough from them about not having a clear organization, so what have you got here if not the Klan? Why did I get sent here?" He moved behind the man so he could have a clear vision of the truck.

"Klan was too easy to identify. These days anything done, the FBI or some other goody two-shoes would be down here all over our backs as soon as anything happened. No, No! We're not going to go through that again. We educate our boys and then they are on their own, more or less. They become doctors, lawyers, judges, or congressmen and when the time comes and enough of them are in important places, well son, we are in control again aren't we? Well as we moved along, some of them black boys get themselves educated, became doctors and lawyers. And that's good because then they think they are white and then want to become us so they try to take on some political jobs. As long as they play our game, that's okay." Stillwell turned, spit a wad of tobacco juice splattering the table top, and slammed his calloused hand on top of it. He smeared the brown juice around while he gritted his teeth and watched Matt.

"So who isn't playing?" Matt didn't see any signs of the shotgun near the truck but he leaned closer to Stillwell so that he could grab him as a shield.

"We got us a *boy* who wants to be sheriff. Used to work here, part black and part one of those Cherokee types that infiltrated this part of the south. Mostly they stayed quiet but some worked their way up here. Well this boy isn't playing with a proper deck."

"And?" Matt started to relax.

"And he has to learn a lesson."

"Why do you need us?"

"Told you, first thing that'll happen is FBI, Friggin Bureau of Instigation, would be right down here. Need this to look like some drifter came through, got the boy to a motel, and stuck him."

"Is the guy gay?"

"Doesn't matter. We want him to look like one of them boys who likes white meat, if you get my drift, and like he got what was right so nobody'd care, but they'd all know, and that'd keep'em in their place. And that's where you come in."

"How would I get him to a motel room? I don't play with boys."

"Doesn't matter what you do or don't do. He'll hear that you have one of his girlfriends in that room and he'll show up."

Stillwell explained that the candidate was always getting in the way of the main industry. "Tobacco," he boasted, "used to be number one, but there are more profitable plants grown in these fields." He explained that under the tobacco, rows of plants that crush into big money stuff give corporate boys a big money machine. "Hell, Matt, you learned that on your Wall Street job and it doesn't stop here. We need to keep that cash crop rolling, get it. We can keep the pickers quiet by letting them light up on some of the happiness weed."

Matt knew how that worked. Starting in colonial days on Long Island, slaves and the Indians were forced to live in common houses and were kept from running away by encouraging use of drugs taken from plants they grew along with food crops. He remembered how the land was taken from the Indians for the railroad and farms and he remembered the campfire mantra, "Beat them at their own game."

Matt spotted the shotgun barrel in the woods near the truck.

"Hells bells Matt. We paid good money up front to your boy in New York, let's see, think that was about ten thousand. So I guess you can afford to pay for another night at the motel."

Matt asked for the details, the name of the man he would meet, the timing, and then he made a change to the plan. He told Stillwell that he would have his truck parked out front of the motel and he would signal the job was done by getting into the truck, flashing the lights and driving across to the bowling alley.

"Smart move." Stillwell put both thumbs up. "Do a good job, and we can get in touch with Gohrman. He said he knows how to contact you."

The shotguns moved away from the woods. "Yeah," Matt thought. "Like you are ever going to let me get out of this town alive. Who would care if the drifter who killed the candidate got shot? Yeah! Gohrman will be in touch with me alright." He heard the slow movement of a truck over a dirt road, shook Stillwell's hand, and walked slowly toward his truck, waved through the open window, and drove to the Motel. He told Brent Wilcox to hang out in the bowling alley, have a sandwich and something to keep him busy until it got dark, then to get back to the truck. "Climb in behind the seats, keep down and out of the way. When I come out we're getting out of here. Head back up to Virginia and then continue North. I can get you to Pennsylvania and you can catch a ride wherever you need to go."

"Can't go that way. Can't go near Virginia. Better if we head west, maybe southwest. Go through Tennessee, a lot closer to Kentucky."

"Not the way I'm heading."

"Safer, and faster. I know shortcuts these guys will never catch up. Remember," the boy wrinkled his nose. "I'm my grandpa's grandson. Taught me a few things. Trust it my way." The boy jumped out of the truck and vanished behind the bowling alley.

Stillwell's words echoed in Matt's head, "part black and part Cherokee." He wondered if Gohrman knew that his protégé was part Native American, if he had known what the real object of this task was, and he wondered if the Stillwell crowd knew Matt's mother was full blooded Native American? He suspected this was supposed to be his last task, that he was supposed to be the drifter, and that if he got gunned down, no one would care. He began to map the fastest route out of North Carolina.

The moon had risen quickly, as if it was in a hurry to see the night's action. A sharp knock on the door was a welcome relief to the monotony of waiting. "Door's open," Matt shouted.

The six foot, slender frame of Sam Coleman stood like a thermometer in the doorway. "Where you got her white boy?"

"Just me here."

"Where you got her? I know you are hiding one of our girls in here, think you can do anything to any of our girls you gotta think again. Where's she?"

"Told you, no one here. Look for yourself." Sam Coleman entered the room, closed and locked the door. "Don't try to break out."

Matt saw the cheek bones that spread high across the front of his visitor's face, then bulge wide under jack-o-lantern eyes. The thin nose over wide lips hinted at the generations of genetic mixture. He was thin but powerfully built and clearly had no weapons.

"Told you no one here." Matt stood across the room and looked out the corner of the closed window drapery. "We've got to talk. We've both been set up. You were sent here so you could be put out of the way and I was suckered so I'd take the fall and then be snuffed too. Solves these boys problem, and saves the ass of one son-of-a-bitch in New York."

Matt had never killed anyone or done physical damage unless he was attacked or threatened, and he was not going to start now. He had made up his mind to cut loose from Gohrman and get back to the Palmieri Market. He had made up his mind to move forward, never to have to avoid shadows, never to have to listen to strange noises in the night, and never to have to look back over his shoulder.

He explained what was supposed to happen to the candidate and he explained what he had been told by Henry Stillman.

"Couldn't have spoken to Henry Stillman," the man glared at Matt.

"Hey! I'm telling you who I spoke with!"

"Dead? Stillman's been dead for three months. Was supposed to help me get elected but he died kind of suddenly. Had a heart attack or something."

"More likely the something," Matt quipped.

"Got to be a new face they brought in so y'ad think it was the dead old man." Coleman leaned against the metal dresser. "Some big Corporation runs these farms and want it all their way. Won't scare me off. So okay, how are we going to get out of this mess?"

Matt would move the truck across the road. "That'll give you time to bug out the back and get away," Matt nodded toward the back door. He would wait three minutes and then take off.

"They'll expect me to head toward Virginia and then North. I have – other plans."

Sam Coleman pursed his lips, ran his finger across the bridge of his nose, smiled and said, "Got to make it look good though. Make it look like we had a fight, you have to get bloodied. Me too. Then you make it out of here and when they find me, I'll be down at Four Corners making a

police report about some bum who tried to slash me. That ought to screw them up long enough. Start them scurrying around looking for someone who came after me. Give you time to move."

Sam Coleman did not wait for an answer. He pulled the mattress off the bed, broke a chair against the dresser, then turned quickly and landed his gnarled fist against Matt's jaw. Matt slipped back, felt the blood trickle from his lip, turned, landed on Sam's back, placed his knife against the man's shoulder, and drew blood that soiled the white shirt. The image of his cutting the letter "N" into his friend re-surfaced as he struggled out of the door.

The yellow pickup truck was across into Tennessee before daylight. The radio news station made no mention of the sheriff candidate being attacked in North Carolina. Matt and Brent Wilcox raced over narrow roads through the Tennessee hills and into southern Kentucky.

"Thanks for the lift," the boy said. "Want to stay a while?"

"No. Have things to do. Thanks for showing me the roads. Good luck to your Grandpa."

24

Matt

Matt drove through lush Kentucky horse country, passed farms in Lexington, stopped in Louisville, toured Churchill Downs, the Louisville Slugger Museum, then crossed the river into Ohio. He stopped for food and rest then headed to Cleveland where he wanted to see a Brown's football game. Early season snowfall delayed his movement across Pennsylvania, next he moved south on I-81, headed east on the Pennsylvania Turnpike until he crossed the Delaware River.

"Hah! Surprise, made it across like Washington. Surprise Carl Gohrman, back alive." He planned to shout into the ear of the man who had sent him to North Carolina. Matt sat in the restaurant of a highway rest stop, waited for a waitress to pour coffee and take his order. He scanned the Sports Section of the *New York Post* that had been left in the booth.

"Isn't that awful," the waitress was looking at the front cover of the newspaper. "Heard about that on the late news last night."

Matt did a double take when he saw the front cover because he recognized the picture under the headline.

Broker Bludgeoned, Slashed. The picture was a close-up of the blood smeared window with the American flag fluttering upside down. Center fold pictures showed the bloody inside of the bathroom where C. Gohrman's body had been found in the bathtub, his throat cut, hands bound behind him, and his head bludgeoned with a heavy Eagle lamp. Pornographic photographs had been found strewn over the bedroom floor and all the pages had been ripped from his address book.

The news article identified the victim as a Wall Street Bond Broker, recently divorced from a Chicago real estate heiress. Carl Gohrman had been involved with the redevelopment of the East Village. His clients included a number of Hamptons socialites, and several Fortune 500 Companies.

Police suspect local drug dealers who might be upset by his interference, but are not ruling out the possibility that he may have known his assailant.

"What a terrible way to die," the waitress continued while tapping a pencil on the order pad. "Do you need a few more minutes?'

Matt ordered a standard breakfast, read and reread the article. "So they got him. Must have been looking for me. Good he didn't keep my name or any records in that damned book of his. Guess he won't hear me shout in his ear."

Matt paid the bill and saw the stand with the local newspapers. A small article indicated that police were looking for a group of skinheads who had spray painted a Synagogue and were probably on their way to a Vineland concert. State police were ready to disband the gathering at the first sign of violence. "Sounds like a place I'll avoid," Matt mumbled. "Those days are over."

25

Gloria

Gloria Palmer's name plate with white lettering on a black plastic rectangle was used as a paper weight on letters from Benito. He was on his first of ten sets of skates he had bought before leaving for Oregon, along with twenty pair of socks, but only two sets of coveralls and sweatshirts along with other necessary items. He packed necessary things into a backpack and shipped the rest to a distant destination.

Gloria learned the newspaper and real estate business without the benefit of an apprenticeship before Benito announced his departure.

"But, Benito, I'm a novice, don't know what I'm doing yet."

"You'll learn fast," he winked. "And the crew here can adjust anything you screw up. But don't let them know that you know what they fix. Just learn and let Tom Mosley clue you in to whoever is doing stuff behind your back. Watch out for the Crandalls. They fight like mad amongst themselves, but they have a common cause, keeping this place unchanged. That's an inherited trait."

She decorated the house along the riverfront, walked to the office every day, and was depressed about the lack luster river front stores that attracted few customers; she tried to get to know reluctant tenants who lived in the apartments over the stores.

"Uncle Benny," she sat next to him at the Greyhound Bus Terminal. He had decided to travel across the country by bus. "Benny," she repeated as he waived at a young child in a stroller. "That place where I live . . ."

"You can fix it up anyway you want. Make it comfortable." He said while watching for the arriving bus. "Bus is a good way to travel. Takes time, allows you to see things, and to think."

"But Benny, I mean everything around it. Those people who live over the stores need something better. The merchants need help, and the whole place needs an overhaul."

"Gloria," Benito looked directly at his niece. "Do whatever you like. You are absolutely in charge, but better check with Doris about the accounting and financing. And," he came closer to her. "Watch out for the Crandalls."

Before Benito left for the bus stop, he rode up the hill, stopped near the cemetery, and laid a single rose over a grave marker near the back fence.

Gloria was at the office earlier that anyone else, spent weeks studying old editions of the papers, old sales records, the financial reports prepared by Doris Hoeffner, and county and town maps. She developed her own plan for the newspaper coverages, set small pins along the map where businesses were servicing the communities, listed the range of potential businesses not advertising in any of the newspapers' editions, and wrote questions for the sales department.

She examined the news and special features and made copious notes for the editorial staffs. After handing out copies of her questions and concerns she gently suggested that the various town edition offices be combined at the Forge Creek location. The empty space on the second floor would be converted to editorial offices and the business office would be expanded and made comfortable to appeal to Doris and her staff. Samantha Crandall's book reviews would now appear in all the papers and any of her social commentaries would appear as a regular monthly feature. Gloria reformed the papers into a broad distribution that appealed to the advertisers from the Main Highway as well as regional malls.

She knew that she had to act before the staffs began to take control, continue the old ways, and obstruct changes. Her gentle mannerism, copied from her mentors at Palmieri's Restaurant and from her Uncle Benito, improved the quality of the newspapers, pleased and maintained the staffs, and neutralized Samantha Crandall.

Gloria visited local police stations, fire houses, and courts so that any important local news would get to her before any major papers had a chance to get the headlines. She featured stories about volunteer firemen and auxiliary police. She visited local health facilities to write the homey stories about the employees as well as the residents.

She asked Doris Hoeffner to come up with a plan to improve the accounting office facilities and suggested that it would be easier for the staff to be located on a first floor. Doris was overwhelmed that she was being asked to make the decision, and gushed that a first floor with a view would be wonderful. Gloria suggested a large office could be set up in a corner store along the riverfront. It would be bright, sunny, have its own parking lot, and could also be an auxiliary office for the newspapers. Doris beamed that it could separate her department from the local newspaper.

"But Miss Palmer," Doris stopped. "That location is kind of scrubby."

"Guess we'll have to clean it up. Will need some help with that and I was hoping for some suggestions."

Gloria had won an important ally.

"Well," Doris twirled a yellow pencil from one chubby finger to another. "Have to get changes through the village board."

"Will that be a problem? It will be a terrific improvement."

"Well, the board tends to listen to them up the hill."

"Why should the Crandall's mind?"

"Afraid it'll bring new people around. Next thing you know they will be afraid other stores will want change and they own most of the . . . ."

"I didn't know they still owned much Village property."

"Not the waterfront. That's Benny's, and some of the other places are in the estate he manages. They never forgave that part."

"But," Gloria hesitated. "Thought they got along. Noticed he visited the graveyard and sometimes went though it. And Samantha works at the paper. Thought they got along."

Doris shuffled papers on her desk. "Guess you didn't know. He was almost one of them. The family was furious when he married the younger sister. They lived out west for a few years, think on some Indian Reservation. Came back here after her parents died. Those folks never accepted him, but left property to their youngest daughter as well as the others. When she died, cancer I think, her estate was left to Benny and that sort of forced them to accept him. Property will do that you know."

Gloria sat warming her toes near the crackling fireplace. She sipped hot chocolate, thought about those fun times with Gis and Hawk. She thought about sipping beer and planning the future. She scribbled, crumpled the pages, tossed them into the fire, then settled on a grand plan.

She let her hand flow free and sketched the lines of the stream and the wide unyielding shrubbery that led to the weed covered hill. She drew lines across shrubbery, pasted a paper cutout over it, and drew the design of a park. She marked off areas for jogging, game tables, and just sitting around. She sketched a bandstand at the top of the hill and a children's playground near the river. She drew a set of large blocks marking the existing stores and apartments.

"Pretty pleased with yourself, Miss Gloria, aren't you?" she stuck her tongue out at the image in the mirror. "But, dummy, you don't know how to make it real." She grimaced when she thought the drawing looked too much like Tern Harbor. "I'll have it like a garden that is open to anyone who wants to come here. It'll be open to change like the seasons and like a garden with new flowers joining perennials every spring. Won't be like my father's place. This will be built to help the people who live here. We'll have a Chinese Restaurant, a Pizza place, and even a Thai Restaurant. It will be a fun community but not a tourist trap. It will not be another Tern Harbor. But I need help."

She called her Aunt Marie and asked for the name of the cousin who was an architect.

"Gloria honey, do you know what time it is? One o'clock, in the morning. Wait, I'll get my phone book." Marie listed two architects. "But call Nicky. He's cute and will work cheap if I tell him to."

Nicholas Gagliardo put together the river edge development plan in less than one month. The plan would maintain the building fronts, paint them so they would look like their original 19th century origins. The park jogging paths wound through low shrubs and perennial gardens, game tables were set at odd angles to create a free flowing system that would give the appearance of limitless space, the children's playground was designed to allow for climbing, jumping, and areas for children of varying ages. The Victorian styled bandstand could provide shelter during sudden rain.

Gloria reviewed the design with Doris.

"Well, that's going to take a lot of money honey, and, well, the houses belong to the estate so I guess that's how that part could get paid. Benny would like that and will approve, especially if I tell him its okay. Well, the village will have to cough up the rest for the Park. Now there's the problem, you see, you'll have to get past the Crandalls. Most board members bend over when the witch, you know who I mean, shows up."

Gloria had inherited her father's determination and cunning. "Got something from the old bastard," she mused. She started revitalizing the corner building for the accounting office. The building was repaired and painted according to the architectural drawings. Greg Smith was chairman of the Village Board, so she hired his son to do the painting and repair work on the building.

Greg Smith Junior was a tall, slender, muscular young man who had been captain of his high school basketball team. After school he had avoided college by starting his own handy man operation and was know around town for his charm, wit, and excellent work. He was also known to spend a good deal of his private time away from the Village to avoid getting caught and "hooked" by local girls.

He reviewed plans for the buildings with Gloria, set up a work table in the back of the corner building and drew up his plans for what he expected to be a long and profitable venture. He was gladly sworn to secrecy about the entire project and was glad he knew something that no one else in the Village even suspected. He would show up each day, wearing his usual white coveralls, sweatshirt and black knitted hat.

Greg erected scaffolding outside the building to hold supplies and on which he could move from side to side along the building. He chipped away crumbling plaster and paint, ground years of accumulated mildew, and raised his fists in triumph as he saw the old building's features appear. Gloria met with her contractor to review progress, crossed the old bridge and wandered through hard packed grass to view the Village.

Greg pointed out a few changes he would like to make from the original drawing, raised his arms as if he were shooting a basketball, and indicated the wide brush strokes he would make to create an image of newness along with the reconstruction. Gloria realized he was an artist intent on creating beauty and perfection. She looked at him as he spoke and thought of her mother's dream that Gloria would become an artist. Feathery snow flakes sparkled like holiday lights on the tall grass, Gloria brushed them from her contractor's shoulder, and they sprinted back across the bridge.

"Stop over to the house tonight," she said. "We can go over the plans then." Gloria was not sure what she had seen in Greg Smith, was not sure if he reminded her of the artist with the pony tail and tattoos who had come to the Palmieri Restaurant with her Uncle Benito; she was uncertain until he arrived with a roll of plans under his arm. Greg showed the paint colors he liked for each of the buildings and design changes he had drawn to make the street seem like it was back in the beginning of the twentieth century.

Gloria listened to Greg and thought of her high school boyfriend. She reminisced about a sandy beach, moss covered rocks, a starry sky, and the rolling surf when she fell in love with Connie. She thought about being on that beach looking up at the windows to see if her father was watching.

Gloria initialed each of Greg's changes, rejected a few of them in order to maintain the architects concepts, and she wondered if Greg had ever been with a woman.

"Ever been married?" she asked while he kept talking about the last building on the street.

"Nope. Almost," he said as he wrote a list of materials. "Got lucky." He blushed. "I didn't mean we did anything, got lucky when we didn't get married."

"A local girl," Gloria persisted.

"Sort of. We went together in high school. You know I was on the basketball team, right. And she was pretty, not a cheerleader or anything, just real pretty and she liked being with me; she liked being with the big man on campus. Yeah, that was me," He smiled as he lowered his head so that he was not looking at Gloria.

"So what happened?"

"We graduated. I didn't go to college so I could be near her and we could get married. I never did anything you know, never did much besides a little, well you know, but never really did nothing . . . anything." He made more notes on the equipment list. "Will have to price this stuff so we can get a budget."

"Well anyways, she got to using her Dad's radio and was making contact with all kinds of people on the highway and finally ran off with one of those truckers. Last I heard she was living with some guy in Illinois. As I said, got lucky," he chuckled. "Not what most of the guys mean. But I'm okay now." He said that he no longer went with any of the local girls.

"See a special friend though," he said. "Out of town friend." He did not talk about driving out of town every night to meet his "special friend"; did not mention that the girl was African-American and that they were deeply in love. "Kind of a secret."

Gloria wondered what it would have been like to get close to her cousin Gis or to Hawk. Connie sank into the background of Tern Harbor memories and Gloria knew that some of the plans she had were bringing back those memories.

"Greg," she said. "Does your Dad know about the work you are doing for me?"

"Oh yes. He wants to know if we are going to do any more work down here. I've kept these plans secret. Well, I told him maybe. He wants to be sure you order all the material from his lumber yard, that's my Dad, always a step ahead."

"Wherever you think we get the best stuff." Gloria knew Greg's father was Village board chairman, and that buying materials from him would win over an ally and cause a problem for the Crandalls.

"You won't tell anyone about my friend, will you Miss Palmer?" Gregg was distressed about his revelation.

"We both have our secrets now," she reached across the drawings and shook his hand.

26

Rabbit Hunt

The Village police station garage was set up for the anticipated overflow meeting. Eight leather chairs were arranged in a semi-circle around the oak table that was usually in the small back room where poker games lasted until cigars or beer ran out, or the click of coins and rustle of dollar bills stopped, and the short list of Village business was conducted.

Chairs were crowded into even rows to accommodate the crowd of Village residents called for by *The Village Sentinel*. Free copies had been distributed throughout the Village. A picture of the barren river front with drawings of the architect's renderings filled the front page. The headline, *Which one?* accompanied the article *Waterfront Park Planned*. A poll of local residents favored the changes.

A short letter to the editor read:

This village has always been a safe haven for our residents. We always maintained its integrity, safe neighborhood, and kept it from becoming a center for tourists who would come in and wreck the place your children call home. It has been a lovely home since it was first founded and should be that for your children and grandchildren. M.W. Crandall

Despite the published poll, Gloria was uncertain of the villager's reactions to change, their devotion to the Crandalls, and her acceptance as Uncle Benito's stand-in. She had to win the confidence and support of Village Board members who were devoted to her Uncle Benito and but feared the control of Crandall influence, money, and history.

Gloria fanned herself in the late afternoon heat. She had spent Monday nights sitting in Benito's chair playing poker with his old friends. She smiled at the thought of how easy numbers came to her, knew card combinations, knew how to recognize the way each player puffed his cigar and bet, raised, or folded. She knew how and when to lose, despite holding a winning hand.

She had learned how to gamble by watching an expert, her father, and had learned how to use the game as a weapon. The chairman of the board, who would sell the material for the riverside project, was already talking about the safe haven for kids. He would raise Gloria's bid. She would want to sing "You gotta know when to hold em, you gotta know when to foldem," and would try to hum using Kenny Rogers's whiskey sound. The members of the board enjoyed the fact that Gloria had filled Benito's seat and enjoyed the fact that she always brought those spicey chips to go along with the beer; they liked the idea that she didn't seem to really know the intricacies of poker; they liked the idea that she would improve the appearance of the village blight.

She looked at the round table in the police station garage, remembered her father's unmoving face as he would win or fold his hand; she pictured him again with his arm around a woman and holding onto a clammer; she saw the beauty of Tern Harbor. "I can be as tough as the old bastard" she whispered. "But this place won't be run by one person or family, and it will be free to develop new traditions. Those Crandall's are like apparitions who can only remember how things used to be, and pretend to know the future but create it in the black and white comic strip of the past. They have no idea of what the world is like now. They are ghosts who fear the present. She walked to the front of the room, turned to the empty chairs, "Let's make things beautiful, bring art and culture to the Village, not just the art of the past, but new stuff. Music can be a slow waltz, a rock anthem, Mozart, the Beatles, heavy metal, and just plain old jazz.

Gloria moved her hands as if she were dealing, put down her invisible hand, "Royal flush boys," she laughed. "I win this hand."

The afternoon sun rolled bands of gold and lilac across the flirting grasses in the fields along the dirt road to Nowhere. Gloria walked alongside her bicycle, stopped before going into the café, looked back to the river and inhaled the smell of fresh baked bread.

She crossed her arms, rubbed her shoulders, and wondered why she had ever started this project, why she would ask for a public meeting where she might have to confront the Crandalls. She wondered why she wanted to build something better than her father ever did and disliked the idea that she was as tough, tougher, than him.

Gloria ordered chile and beer, read the letter from Benito describing the perils of skating across the country. He promised to send a painting from Sante Fe where he claimed to have known artists who had settled there and he wrote about Native Americans with whom he talked. He asked how her writing was coming, wanted to know if she had met the Judge's family, and asked about the young contractor. "Good boy. Helped him with a few things, you know, especially with that girl friend of his."

"Didn't know he had a girl friend. Good for him," Gloria smiled. "Will ask him to write to Uncle Benny."

She sipped her beer, added onions to the chile and thought of those barbecues on the beach with her boyfriend Conrad. She stroked the bottom of the table and thought about damp moss on soft rocks.

Gloria flinched at the repeated sound of gun shots.

"Oh don't worry, Miss Palmer," the waitress smoothed her towel along the front counter. "It's that jerk Verne. Can't figure out you can plant stuff to keep rabbits out of the garden and away from the important fields so he pops away at them. Couldn't hit the side of a barn."

"Then why . . . " Gloria stopped.

"Macho idiot has to try to show off. Gonna shoot himself in the foot someday. Anything else Miss Palmer?"

Last magenta strands faded to shades of gray and teal along the horizon. The pale blue sky held last beads of light before yielding to the harvest moon.

Gloria rode slowly along the moonlit roadway until she saw a small figure dart across the road and into the golden cornstalks. A breeze folded the tall flowing grasses that reminded Gloria of rolling surf.

She stepped around the split rail fence, parted a row of empty stalks, walked around the tall grass, and followed the sound of the moving animal. The sound stopped near the edge of the flat flower field. The oldest graves were of children who died of disease before the nation was founded. Low faded stones marked the place where young men who had fought in old wars had been remembered and taller markers had been placed for those who had been returned from newer wars. The cemetery's faded gate post sign identified this as the final peaceful place.

The sound of the stream touched the memory of her tenth birthday party. She was once again stealing the clothes from those young boys in the bay, and watching that strange boy who stood up on target rock. She thought about her cousin Gis and was glad he was home from Europe and taking control of the Palmieri Restaurant. She wondered what had become of Hawk, had he found his way with his people, was he happy, was he free? She wondered why she was doing all this in this strange town, wondered if it was to get back at her father, wondered if it was to please her Uncle Benito, wondered if she could ever be free of her past.

Gloria stumbled over a low rock and fell into the tall grass. "Oh no!" she cried. Her hand landed into the soft coat of the dead rabbit. Dry blood surrounded shotgun wounds. The small animal she had followed darted across the field.

"Hurry," she shouted. "Find your way home. You're on your own now, baby." Gloria moved back along the road and over the old bridge, looked at the new old monument and the bright lights at the meeting place. Silhouetted men were standing in the driveway smoking and waiting for the meeting to begin.

She took her seat in the back of the room, moved her hands as if she was still dealing cards across the oak table, and waited for the meeting to begin. "May have to bluff, let them think I have a royal flush. Going to be my pot boys."

Burt and Samantha Crandall were perched in the front row, with Jessica Crandall slumped into the next seat. Gloria had seen her moving through the garden, had made several appointments to meet her, but she always called with an excuse to put off the interview. This was the first time the occupant of that yellow house up the hill had been this close and she did not seem the giant who ruled over the Village's oldest family.

Slides of the River Front Project were projected on a screen that had been opened behind the Board members. The architect talked through each slide, finished with the drawings of the children's playground, turned to the full meeting room and asked for questions.

"Well, where you going to have a place for bicycles, ya know kids have bikes?"

"And where you going to have a place for the kids to, you know, relieve themselves?"

"And how much all this going to cost?"

"Who's going to pay for the buildings? You know they don't belong to the village so why should we put up the cash for private property?"

The architect tried to answer all the questions as soon as they came, but deferred the questions of cost to the Mayor.

"Well, folks," the mayor broke in. "The buildings belong to the Sentinel Corp. so that's their bill, we're hoping people in the village would donate their time to build the playground, materials will be supplied at cost by Smith Lumber Yard, the Park fix-up is up to the Village maintenance folks, and out of their budget."

"Well, finally we get to the facts." The shrill voice from the front row brought everything to a stop. "You bring this whole town out to listen to your high felutin idea to change this village and then you tell them they have to do the work, they have to watch everything around here change and then you drop the bomb that they have to pay for it. It has been a good village, been that way since it started, and still good for all of us."

Coughs and silence wrestled through the room. The bank manager turned away from the Board when Jessica Crandall, his major depositor, wheezed her complaint.

Gloria reached under her chair, pulled out a paper bag, and walked to the front of the room. "Miss Jessica, it is so good to meet you at last. I'm sorry I was a little late getting here tonight."

"Hmph! Late getting here at all is putting it mildly, not like most of these good families who have been here," Jessica Crandall motioned to the people behind her.

Gloria stood in front of the three Crandalls thought they were the three headed dog defending the gates of hell. She looked at the men smoking in back of the room. "The first time I met Benito Palmieri, he was getting off that big yellow bus of his."

"I set the new motor into that thing, fixed it so it was better than any the kids ever rode in," Harry Tillard called out from the back of the room.

"And who do you think painted it? Me!" volunteered one of the smokers.

"I thought he was strange; then he spoke to me and I knew he was the wisest and kindest man I'd ever met. He convinced, I should say connived to get me to come here."

"Typical," murmured Jessica Crandall.

"First day here he took me for a bicycle ride through town and over to the Nowhere Café and then sent me off on my own. Oh yes he pointed out the Civil War Soldier's Memorial at the head of Main Street. Well I rode up the hill and fell onto Burt Crandall's place."

"Plopped on your face that day," Burt laughed. "Not too different from this here episode."

Gloria lowered her head, narrowed her eyes and aimed her most terrifying stare at Burt Crandall. Then she exposed the broad toothy smile that gave away her Palmieri heritage. "Fell on my face again this evening," she said. "Was across the Bridge visiting Nowhere Café. Heard repeated shotgun firing. Anyone here ever fire a gun?"

There was laughter and a flurry of hands, "During hunting season, or at targets at Hobie's range?"

"Well, I found out there's a guy over there who just fires anytime he thinks some rabbit is eating his carrots. Like Elmer Fudd. I was told he never hits anything."

"Must've been Bud. Blind as a bat."

"Well tonight he finally hit something. I was walking through those weeds near the old cemetery. Now that's something really old and should never be disturbed. Well I fell and my hand sunk into the cold flesh of the rabbit whose baby was circling her body. I scooted it away. That poor little bunny is now alone."

She waited for a few women to blot their eyes.

"I lay very still and looked at those old grave markers, rubbed the rabbit, and looked across the bridge and up Main Street to that Soldiers Monument. Now that's what people drive around here to see something old and we all know that it is only the relic of a movie made here in town. What we are proposing here is to do something in between that movie set and the real hallowed ground the other side of the river. Remember the founders and those soldiers who grew and were buried over there in Nowhere. We can have those old buildings look like they used to and have the River Front a place where everyone in the Village can come, have fun, play, and just hang out. It can be a place where the old buildings can house those poor folks who live there now. It can be a place where that funny bus of Benito's can be parked alongside someone's brand new Cadillac. That's all."

"Well, you know, we have those things now, don't we?" Jessica Crandall spoke while staring at the paper bag that Gloria had placed on the Oak Table. "We always have. Oh not so grand, not so they will bring in every kind of riff raff to our Village, but just the way the original founders made it. And the way we want to keep it. I know how people around here think."

Gloria held the paper bag in front of her, leaned against the table directly in front of the Crandalls. "I asked if anyone had ever shot a gun and I told you about that little rabbit. It's gone now. There are some who remember how it used to be around here for a century, in fact that is all they know. They tell us how things will have to be in the future here in this town because they expect it will always be the same, but they have no idea of how things are now. They couldn't tell you what movie is playing, what the Rock music is on the radio, what cigarettes you guys are smoking, or what music the kids are listening to. They are near ghosts, not yet fully ghosts, just sort of shades of the past. I hope we can begin to bring this Village back to life, not for a whole bunch of "riff raff", but for ourselves."

Gloria held her breath. "We can't just fire blindly at anything like Bud over in Nowhere otherwise, what you have is this." She was about to reach into the paper bag but placed it back on the table.

"Going to pull some more theatrics, I suppose," Jessica Crandall pointed toward the bag. "Pull the rabbit out of the bag I suppose."

Gloria reached back for the paper bag, blew into it, and then popped it with her fist. "No. Stopped home first and buried that poor dead thing in the garden.

It is where dear memories make the ground fertile. Like those who founded this place, like the poor boys who gave their lives and are buried over there," she pointed toward Nowhere. "And then new things flourish, making the landscape beautiful. That's what is intended here. Keep the old things alive, let them add to the landscape, and then expand it. The new park, if it comes to be, should have an old name. I suggest we call it the Isiah and Hannah Crandall Park. She moved to the back of the room, stood on the sidewalk talking to the smokers, listened to the loud voices from the meeting, the gavel pounding, and the call for a vote by the Board. There was a hum of activity as the Board voted, then the gavel signaled the end of the meeting. The architect carried his briefcase, opened his car door, smiled to Gloria, and signaled thumbs up.

"My pot boys," she said as she walked toward the river.

———•———

Reporting burglaries and accidents were routine and tedious until Gloria started to sketch defendants in Judge Charles Feather's courtroom, place them against the background of the historic building. She sometimes had dinner with the Judge's family, learned about the region's Native American folklore, listened to Hannah Feather sing old songs she had heard as a child, and wondered at the portfolio of Native American art the couple had collected. Gloria was intrigued by the Georgia O'Keefe prints that were on a stand in the corner of the living room.

"Had fun collecting those along with your Uncle Benny," Charlie said. "We hiked through New Mexico and Nevada. Did you ever ride on that bus of his?"

"Saw the bus, and some of his friends once at a restaurant in Brooklyn."

"Oh yeah. That was a real fun trip; I drove the bus, I guess you didn't notice me; a few days before, we went along in a fleet of limos scooping up artists. He did things off the top. Never the same. Different from the way things were around here before he arrived."

Gloria examined the O'Keefe prints, sensed the expansive mood of freedom, wished that she could be in a place where the artist had painted, and wished she could see the original paintings. "I'll have to visit that part of the country," she thought. "Want to wander through those hills the way Benito and Charlie did, want to feel the freedom of the artist, the hot sun and warm wind on my face, and escape the tangled web that keeps invading my dreams."

"Hey, Gloria, I have to get over to the court house early tonight. Long calendar." Charlie wore his denim pants and shirt that would be concealed by his judicial robe. "Oh, might want to hang around after the session. I'm performing a wedding ceremony. You'll find it interesting."

The usual cases, teenager driving violations, a burglary, two domestic violence, and a sexual abuse case were rushed through the court. The judge did not smile at anyone in the room except the bailiff and the court clerk. He had told Gloria that he never takes breaks during the sessions, that his genetic background enabled him to go long periods without drinking or having to use the facilities, and he expected the same from anyone in the courtroom.

Gloria was surprised when she recognized Greg Smith Junior, Tom Mosley, the court clerk, and a young woman who had the chiseled features of someone who might have stepped out of a travel poster from a Caribbean Island seated in the judge's office.

"Glad you could stay. We need another witness." Charlie Feather pinned a carnation onto Greg Smith's lapel and snapped an orchid onto the young woman's wrist. "You kids ready?"

Gloria sat behind Tom Mosley, set her hand under her chin to be sure it did not fall open to reveal her surprise. "So that's what Benito meant about looking after the young contractor, and that's why Greg never dated the girls in town."

The office door swung open and Greg Senior, along with his wife and three other people, boomed into the room.

"Not going to have any wedding," Greg Senior frowned. "Not going to have any wedding without us here. I'll stand up for my boy and Tom, you stand up for your girl. I brought some extra witnesses. And Gloria," he winked. "this poker hand belongs to my boy and his bride."

27

Matt

State and local police were alerted for violence when skinheads and other young people left the Vineland rock concert. Penns Corners Synagogue had been spray painted and monuments had been overturned in Saint Raymond's Cemetery. Rumors spread that groups from Detroit were the front edge of a white supremacist meeting.

Cameras were set up at the Turnpike toll booths and toll collectors were asked to report any suspicious vehicles.

Matt was uncertain about his destination but was sure it would not be Vineland. He watched the rear view mirror to be sure he was not being followed, kept within the speed limit, and observed all traffic signs to avoid problems with the state trooper car that was trailing behind him.

"Wonder if they have these guys on the North Carolina guy's payroll?" Matt inhaled and blew breath several times to steady his rising blood pressure, pulled into the Molly Pitcher Rest Stop, saw the troopers drift slowly into the same parking lot, then he moved quickly into the crowded building. He watched the police checking his truck, knew they were waiting for him; they suddenly raced to their car, pulled out of the parking lot and onto the Turnpike. He breathed easier, took his coffee to the truck, moved out of the parking lot, passed the patrol car, and glanced at a pony tailed man standing spread eagle with his hands against the car as one of the policemen patted him down. "Must have been hitchhiking. Jerk, should of known they'd come down hard on him."

Matt was aware of a black Chevrolet speeding up behind him and knew it was an unmarked Trooper. "Damn. Snagged." He pulled over and pulled out his wallet prepared to show his driver's license.

"Step out of the car, please," The uniformed officer demanded.

"Didn't do anything officer. I'm sure I was not speeding."

"Out of the car, now!" A second trooper was in front of the truck with his hand on his holster.

Matt opened the door and stepped out of the truck.

"Turn around please, hands against the vehicle."

"Didn't do anything. What's this about?"

The first trooper started to search Matt from his shoulders, through his shirt pockets and then patted down the rest of his body.

"Told you nothing."

"Shut up." The second trooper had his gun out of his holster.

Matt was getting ready to attack and run; he was sure these men had been sent from the North Carolina crowd. One of the troopers held him in place while the other searched the truck. The trooper ran his hand along Matt's foot then reach along his boot. Before Matt could turn, his hands were behind him and he was clicked into hand cuffs.

"Nothing, huh? Then what's this weapon for?" the second trooper clicked open the knife that he had taken from the truck. "This is a dangerous tool my friend, a hidden weapon. Going to lock up this vehicle, it'll be towed. You, my friend, are coming along with us."

Matt was pushed into the back seat of the unmarked car and driven to a local police station. The hitchhiker had arrived moments before. He was tall, sullen, his dark pupils filled the eye sockets so only a sliver of white showed near the lashes, his pony tail had been let down so that his hair hung straight over his ears and below his shoulders. His high cheek bones reminded Matt of some of the people he had seen around Autumn campfires, near the reservations, and he knew this man's genetics.

A woman looked into the station doorway to ask directions to the Turnpike and was spending a longer than necessary time talking with the neatly dressed desk sergeant. She thanked him for his help and commented on the sharp appearance of his uniform. His starched white shirt fit around his thick neck that blended into bulbous shoulders, and fit tight against his chest and stomach. The officer watched her leaving the building, rolled his tongue at the corner of his lips, raised and lowered his eyebrows and then turned to the two new men brought in by the State Troopers.

He signed papers, made an entry into a book at his desk, and sent Matt and the hitchhiker into the search room. Matt smiled at the sergeant as he was led past him.

"Watcha lookin' at wise ass? Never seen a pretty woman before, or maybe you like looking at me?" The sergeant spit through his front teeth. "Better really search everything these guys have."

The two men emptied their pockets into plastic containers, removed their belts and boots, and waited for the police to make lists of the contents their respective boxes. Matt watched through a window between the search and front reception room, as the sergeant ran his hand over the starched creases of his sleeves and then checked his appearance in a mirror. The sergeant turned quickly, saw Matt and scowled. "Still lookin'. Wait'll you get inside, they wait for cute white meat like you guys. Okay boys what do they have?"

"Nothing unusual. This one," the guard policeman pointed to Matt. "Wallet, cash, license, life savers, keys, and some toothpicks."

"What about the knife?"

"Oh yeah! We got that too."

"Wasn't he wearing an earring?"

"None here and he's not wearing one now."

"Friggin skinhead must have dumped it somewhere, or hidden it." The sergeant rubbed his thumbs against his forefingers. "What about the Indian?"

"Nothing. Some papers in a rubber band, two fifties and a bunch of singles, some college ID, probably found that or lifted it from someone."

"Any jewelry? These guys always know how to hide stuff."

"Nothing Sarge."

"Strip them. Do a strip search before they can get inside. Check for hidden drugs or anything else."

"Hey Sarge," Matt shook his head from side to side. "getting a little horny?"

"Strip them," the sergeant shouted. "Let them really know they been searched."

"Why don't you do it Sarge?" Matt taunted. "I could use a good . . . " He was cut off by the guard shoving him against the wall and telling him to strip. The stick jammed into his kidneys was enough to convince Matt to comply. The hitchhiker was already standing stripped, hands above his head, with his legs spread to allow full view of his body. He pulled his clothes back on while he continued to stare directly at the policeman standing in front of him.

Two guards moved their hands under Matt's arms, forced him to lean forward against a table so they could examine every part of him with their night sticks. The Sergeant took one of the night sticks, ran it along Matt's backside, then smacked it against the back of his knees forcing him to the ground.

"Sorry guy, stick must have slipped. Better watch it wise ass," he pulled Matt's head up. "Not so nice or easy when you get inside. You're lucky I'm wearing this uniform. Don't want to get it soiled by suckers like you."

Matt pulled himself up and got dressed. He looked across at the hitchhiker who was still staring at the policeman who had examined him. "Do we get our belts, you know to hold up our pants? And what about our stuff, oh yeah my truck?"

"No belts." One of the guards handed each of the prisoners his own property list, arrest papers, and a printed set of rules of behavior in the jail.

The hitchhiker was first to enter the jail. The yellow steel bars clanged open, he stepped between them and a second set of bars, the locks on the first bars snapped shut, the inner bars swung open, two guards told him to move into the large room reserved for visitors. Small round tables and metal stools were bolted to the floor.

Matt approached the first gate; it swung open and he was pushed between the steel bars that formed a two feet square cage. His breath filled his lungs, and for the first time, fear he had often instilled in others began to infect his back muscles. He looked at the hitchhiker who was squinting toward him and he regained his sense of self. He turned toward the sergeant who was smiling from behind the first gate. Matt returned the smile, turned toward the inner gate as it swung open, stepped into the reception area, and waited for the next command.

"Okay gentlemen. You're going to be here over the weekend, we're not going to have any loud noise or screaming or any bullshit from either of you, are we?" The Afro-American guard did not wait for any reply. "This way." He motioned toward the solid glass door at the back of the room.

Matt looked into the jail beyond the glass door, saw the open cell doors, and prisoners mulling aimlessly around the crowded corridor.

"Hey, I need to be in solitary, away from those guys." Matt saw the dark skinned prisoners looking at his tattoos and heard them commenting about the skinhead. The hitchhiker spoke softly to Matt. "Stand next to me. Anyone tries anything I know how to stop him."

"So do I. We'll watch each other's back. These guys don't look friendly."

"We're here for a few days. Take turns sleeping," the hitchhiker answered. "Supposed to let us call a lawyer or someone. Going to wait until they get us to a court. The sergeant seems like he would screw it up."

They entered the prisoner's corridor, were assigned to a large cell with four other men. Matt watched the group of black men who had been tossing their fingers as if choosing a new prize. One of them approached the hitchhiker.

"Pretty hair you got there man. Your friend here must like it, y'all gonna like to get close to him tonight." The group started to laugh and discuss the type of action they wanted to see. Matt repeated to the guard that he and the other new prisoner should be protected in solitary.

The guard closed his note book without taking any action and moved into the small office from which he could watch the corridor. Two of the men, who had been laughing, moved toward the hitchhiker; one of them reached toward his target's long hair. The hitchhiker was motionless and suddenly the black man was screaming in pain. Matt smashed the nose of the other man who was reaching for Matt's hip. Blood spilled onto the floor, the guards came running, pulled Matt and his ally from onrushing prisoners, other guards pulled the injured men beyond the glass doors. The man who had reached for the long hair was still screaming and unable to move his forearms while the other cupped his hands over his broken nose.

Matt and the hitchhiker were shoved into a small dank cell.

"Told them solitary," Matt smiled. "What did you do to the guy? I never saw you move."

"Broke both his forearms, an old Indian trick. Learned it when I was a kid and never forgot it. You did a good job on that guy's nose."

A guard passed them dinner trays of hot dogs and beans and told them that the guy with the broken nose was in for murder. "Knocked off some guy in an alley and then did the cop who was trying to arrest him. He's really yelping. Bled all over the Sergeant's shirt, and Sarge's not happy."

"Wouldn't like to have been held down for him," Matt and the hitchhiker laughed. "Where you heading when we get out of here?" Matt tried to open the conversation.

"New Hampshire."

"Cold up there. What's an Indian going to do in snow country?"

"Back to school. Been away for a while, but need to go back so I can really become something to help my people."

The cell door opened revealing the Sergeant in a fresh uniform. "You guys going to be separated."

Matt was pulled out of the cell and shoved into the next one. "Got my shirt full of blood, skinboy. See it," the man showed Matt a rolled up shirt that had blood stains circling through it. "See it up close." He pushed the shirt against Matt's face. "Don't like it one bit." The Sergeant smashed his fist against Matt's cheek, the smacked a stick against his stomach, and kicked his knee. Matt refused to make any sounds or to move against his attacker.

"Maybe you caught something from the blood squirting out of that guy you whipped. Oughta be more careful when you start a fight." The neatly dressed officer turned to leave, turned back and cracked the stick against Matt's other cheek. "Should have told you, don't like you skinheads. Hate those friggin tattoos. Like this one on your elbow." He slammed his stick against the spider web tattoo and cracked his large silver ring across the back of Matt's neck.

The cell door clanged shut, light flickered through the small glass window; Matt allowed himself to slump to a dark corner, tried not to sleep, tensed his aching body anticipating another guard entering the cell, or prisoners being allowed to come after him.

"They're done for now," the hitchhiker called from the next cell. "There's space under the wall if you need to talk."

Matt slipped to the bare floor, dozed with his eyes fixed on the glass window, waiting for any shadow that might interrupt the dull light, wishing he had a glass of water, and thinking of the woman he had met in the laundromat. He tried to focus on happy moments with girls he had known or with the pleasant sounds of wind blown tides rumbling onto the beach or of the smell of fish at Palmieri's Market. He wondered who he should call when they finally got his one call. He thought of home and turned that down; he thought of Carl Gohrman, and smiled when he remembered that he had been murdered; he decided to call the number that had been scribbled on the paper before he left for North Carolina. That would do it, someone at the lawyers' office would know who he was and would come to help him.

"You okay?" the voice from the next cell was above a whisper. "Tap once if okay."

Matt scratched his nail across the cell wall, heard the door swing open, scooted into the corner away from the light, and waited. The guard looked in, flashed his light around the cell, and then closed the door. Matt waited for the lock to snap. The guard opened the door again. "You boys going to be visiting with us over the weekend. No judges around and then you'll be transferred the hell out of here. Can't have you hurting anymore of our guests. Or having anyone getting you. Long time between here and Monday. Going to send you over to next county. Get you in front of some hard ass judge."

"Don't we get to call a lawyer or something?" Matt asked.

"Sure. The Sarge'll be back in tomorrow. He'll take care of it for you."

"Hey," the hitchhiker was lying on the floor. "Don't ask the sergeant to make any calls. He'll screw you. Wait until we get to the judge. That way someone will be watching and we'll be out of here."

"Who you going to call?" Matt lay on the floor and whispered under the wall.

"Friend."

"Lucky. You have one. I'll call a lawyer. They'll have to help me."

"Friends are better."

Day and night fused into the corporeal stillness of solitary confinement; time was marked by arrival of paper trays with hot dogs and beans for breakfast, lunch, and dinner. Neither of the men ate any of the food, fearing intestinal consequences of the jail menu.

Matt heard the cell doors open and hand cuffs click on his hitchhiker ally. A guard called "Step out here, skinhead." Matt hesitated, uncertain if he was leaving the jail or was to be battered by one of the sergeant's surrogates.

"Come on turkey," the guard demanded. "Getting you guys outa here before we have any more trouble. Heard who you busted up and if his boys find you and your boy friend, bye bye baby. Then we'll have to fill out all them papers. Move it," the guard snapped.

The police van ambled through the Monday afternoon downpour and traffic.

"Taking us to McDonald's?" Matt smiled at the hitchhiker.

"Hopefully to a place with a clean bathroom and a telephone. Where did you learn to fight like that, move so quickly, so silently?"

"Used to run through the woods, follow animal trails, hide from my old man; listened to wind rustling through everything around me; listened to burned out campfires; took worse beatings than these guys can hand out, and waited for my turn. Learned never to fear anything and always expect an assault. Learned how to take control."

"Like my people," the hitchhiker added.

"Quit the chatter," the guard sitting behind them shouted.

The van circled the old courthouse, backed into the driveway, and stopped near the back door. The two shackled prisoners were transferred to the Court marshal, and their property list was compared to the accompanying packages.

The marshal logged in the two files, lit a cigarette, shook his head, stamped out the cigarette, and lit another one. "Stupid bastards. Never finished this stuff, never got in touch with anyone for you, no lawyers or any one, always screw it up and make more work for us. We can make a call for each of you, collect. Start with you," he pointed to the hitchhiker who handed him a piece of paper with a hastily scrawled note. The marshal dialed the phone number, had a brief conversation, and seemed surprised by the response to the call. He turned to the hitchhiker. "Says he has to be sure you are who you claim to be. Says you know how to let him know."

"Tell him it's Hawk."

"Here, you tell him"

"Hello, Gis."

"Son of a bitch. Really you. What's wrong, what can we do, never mind, I'll get help there right away. Let me talk to the cop."

The two men learned that they were to be arraigned that night, one for hitchhiking, and the other for carrying a concealed weapon and resisting arrest. The marshal asked Matt if there was anyone to call. Matt told him to check his wallet for the card of *Nelson, Alexander, and Finch* attorneys. "Tell them a friend of Carl Gohrman's is calling Nelson, mention the Wall Street job, but don't tell them where we are."

The court officer repeated Matt's message to several people then hung up the phone. "They say they never heard of you and Mr. Nelson's secretary says he has no idea what you're talking about and never heard of anyone named Gohrman. Outa luck guy. Guess we'll have to get someone for you."

"Screw that, I can deal for myself. Did you tell them who you are or where we are?"

"Never got to that. And they didn't ask."

Matt threw a chair across the room. Two court officers tackled him, jumped on his back, and handcuffed him to a bench. Blood oozed from a gash on his cheek. Hawk's dark eyes punctured the room. His hand rose to his lips as if to say quiet to Matt, then that hand, clenched into a fist, was lowered to tap firmly against his chest. The two men became transfixed as if they were piercing each other's thoughts in the way that twin brothers might, or lifelong friends might, or as comrades in a battle might.

"Get him some band aides," one of the guards called.

"Forget it." Matt screamed. "Just get the hell out of here. Leave me alone." Matt slid into the corner of the bare room resigned to the fact that he was on his own, that he would not have a lawyer to fight for him or who might give away his location, that he was deserted by those he had helped, worked for, almost committed murder for, for whom he was no longer useful, and for whom he had become a liability. He ran his hand over his face, rubbed his hand across the dusty floor and drew lines across his face as if to hide from any light. He reached under his tongue, pulled out the thing he had kept hidden since he was arrested, stuck the pin through his earlobe and replaced the small clam shell earring.

Matt sat on the floor, his knees pulled tight to his chest, his back braced against the corner of the cell, and his head cradled between his fists. He moved back, raised his head, lifted one fist to his chest, and tapped it imitating the ancient beat of drums.

The clerk and the bailiff arranged files for the judge, filled water pitchers, pushed chairs neatly under tables, and sat back to wait for the for the unusual Monday night session. "Glad it's a short session tonight, wonder why they have a session just for these two cases?" The clerk poured coffee from a thermos.

"Something about they had to get them someplace quiet to avoid a big splash in front of newspaper people near Newark. One of these guys is Native American and the other guy got into some kind of to do with some African American prisoner. They don't want to turn this into another racial deal so they shipped them over here. Thanks for the coffee."

"Judge in yet?" Gloria Palmer asked as she entered the back of the court room. The bailiff accompanied her to Charlie Feather's office.

"Unusual for you to be here tonight," the judge was putting on his black robe.

"Had a phone call from one of my cousins in Brooklyn, and he suggested it would be interesting tonight. You ought to know he got a phone call from one of the guys on trial."

"Hope he's not some hot shot from the New York Post, or something like that."

"You know me better than that. Charlie, I have something sort of special to ask you." She explained her relationship with Hawk, detailed who he is, and that he was on his way back to Dartmouth when he got picked up.

"Well doesn't sound too serious," the judge laughed.

"Well," Gloria hesitated. "I think he got into a problem at the jail, was being attacked by a prisoner and may have fought back."

"Nothing about that in his file. You vouch for him?"

"Absolutely."

"Probably a small fine. He can handle that, right?"

Hawk and another prisoner were seated when Gloria and the judge entered the court room.

Gloria nodded to Hawk and glanced at the other prisoner. His collar was turned up to keep out any sudden draft; his face, hidden in lines of dust, was dropped onto his chest.

Gloria avoided eye contact but was oddly drawn to this stranger's appearance. His auburn hair, blended with a brown undercoat, hung loosely over his forehead and neck. His ears were hidden under the raised collar as if he would rather not see or be seen by anyone. Something about him triggered isolated flashes of time and memories that she had tried to repress.

She was a young girl again, hiding in her mother's room trying on makeup. Amanda was at the door as if to stop her and suddenly it was her mother, smiling, hugging her and holding her jewelry. "Someday, when you grow up, I will give you some of these things, and you can wear rings, and pins" and then her mother was gone; it was her tenth birthday party and Amanda was setting the party tables. Gloria was listening to the splash of waves against the red buoy, and suddenly the myth of the Indian woman impaled on the hill watching her lover falling under the surf invaded her daydream. Then, she was trying on her mother's jewelry and Amanda was calling her, "Gloria, Gloria, Gloria."

"Gloria," Hawk whispered to her. "My turn at bat."

Charlie Feather lectured the hitchhiker on the importance of obeying the law, on the dangers to the public and himself for thumbing rides on highways and any public roads. He fined Hawk fifty dollars, signed papers, and handed the file to the clerk.

"Now off the record," the Judge called Hawk to approach the bench. "Never again get dragged in front of me. I can't have any Native American breaking the law and thinking he can get away with it just because he's in front of me." Charlie Feather spoke as if he was addressing his ancestral chromosomes, then to calm his mounting rage, he broke his own rule and announced a break.

Gloria watched the back of Matt's head while Hawk was listening to the judge's private lecture.

Hawk hugged Gloria then sat on one of the court benches, put his head into his hands, and shuddered.

At the beginning of the break, Gloria held Hawk's hand, stared at him, and they talked. She told him what she had been doing; he told her about his travels through Indian reservations in Nebraska and Oklahoma. He told her about the time he had spent walking across the country, hitchhiking, working and getting his mind in order. Gloria asked if he was hungry.

"Have to wait to see the next case," Hawk did not move. "This next guy, did you see him?" Hawk nodded toward Matt.

Gloria nodded.

"You know, that guy who's sitting with his back to us? He didn't do anything but I think they're going to nail him. He's a, well he's been a skinhead. Don't think he is anymore, but that's what he's been and he got into a mess. But Gloria," he stopped. "Something about him that, I don't know, but I think he's at least part way one of us, mine, Indian. The way he moves, acts."

"Then wait here Hawk, just wait here. I have to do speak to the judge."

"C'mon in," Charlie Feather motioned to Gloria. "Have to cool down before next case. Have some coffee, just ordered some Chinese stuff, will be here in a few minutes. Your friend, okay?"

"Yes, thanks. You know, Charlie how I've been writing those articles about the court and the people who work here?"

"Sorry, Gloria, not interested in anything about me."

"No Charlie, I know that. But I've never done anything about the people who come in front of you. I'd like to interview your next case. How about it?"

"He's tough Gloria, been very quiet from what I hear and may not want to talk to anyone, especially a newspaper person. And, Gloria, he's one of the reasons these two were sent to this end of the county, keep things nice and quiet."

"Charlie you know you can trust me."

"Okay, but it has to be in the interview room, and a guard right there."

———

Gloria felt herself drifting back to Tern Harbor, trying to escape the odor of her mother's sick room, trying to remember the warm aroma of Amanda's kitchen, trying to forget the hidden moments when she would hold her mother's jewelry to her face, and trying to forget the way she had learned to play poker. She inhaled as if to remember the musty odor of the old basement under her father's newspaper office and was aware of the same odor as she entered the court house conference room.

The second man was handcuffed to a metal pipe in the corner of the old room. Hawk had said that he seemed to move and act as if he were part Indian and Gloria tried to make out his features. The old pine table, oak chairs, ash floors, and the walls' nondescript wood paneling filled the room with an aroma that commanded respect and silence. It was as if Matt had pulled the corner shadows around him, buried his head in the crevice of his chest and would only show one side of his dust covered face.

"My name is Gloria Palmer. I write for the *Sentinel* newspapers. Try to cover the people here at the court." She sat at the far end of the rectangular table and tried to see her interview subject. There was no response.

"My name," she started again, certain that it was a dumb way to try to talk to this man. She felt there was something she should be asking but was not sure what it was.

"I heard you the first time," he said and seemed to draw himself into one of the room's old fixtures.

"My friend Hawk said I would find you interesting and thought I might be able to help."

"Good intentions. Tell him I said thanks. No one is going to help, no one going to come, people I helped," he stopped talking and turned to look at the guard who had moved into the room. Matt suspected any of the guards might be infected by the North Carolina network, and he would not speak in front of them.

Gloria asked the guard to stand outside the room so she could talk with the prisoner and promised to stay far away from the shadowed side of the room. Matt turned to see the guard leave, then pulled his head up to look at this young woman. "What did you need to know except I was set up by the troopers and then beaten by guards in the jail and never given my one call until I got here. Justice? Yeah right jailhouse justice." The overhead lights reflected against the high cheek bones, broad chin, and muscular neck which rose to the ears that were hidden by the uncombed auburn hair. A glint of light sparkled against the tiny clam shell earring.

Gloria leaned forward, tried to get a better view of Matt's ear, and stared at the earring. "They say you had a knife in your boot."

"No. It was in the truck. Use it for cleaning fish at a job I used to have. The bastards rubbed it against my boot and said that's where they found it. The sucker could never have fit in my boot. If it was there, they would never have been able to find it."

"Where did you get that earring?" She was surprised at the anger in her voice. "Who did you rob to get it?"

"It's mine."

Gloria moved cautiously across the room, bent close to Matt's ear, "You stole it didn't you? I know that jewelry." She thought of her mother's room and remembered the small clam earrings with the ruby in the center that had been made for her mother.

"You stole them, I know. When?" She lowered her voice so that the guard would not crash into the room.

Matt stared directly into Gloria's eyes. "It's mine, part of a pair that belongs to my mother. I have this one to remind me of her, and who I am. Don't accuse me of stealing. Ask your friend about how often his people were accused of stealing. Anything else you need to know?"

"Yes. Prove you didn't steal it. Where are you from?"

The only sound was the hissing of steam from the radiator. Gloria was not sure this defendant would ever talk with her again.

"Riverhead."

"So that's where you stole it."

"Told you. Never steal."

"My mother," she said. "Before my mother died she gave them to the woman who raised me. She would never have parted with that jewelry."

"No she wouldn't."

Gloria moved back, leaned against the table and examined the man she was supposed to interview. She looked at the auburn hair, the features, the earring, and thought again about Tern Harbor. She thought about the bay and Target Rock, about the birthday when she saw the boys swimming and then saw the boy she did not know standing on the Rock. She looked back at the man in front of her and saw the same color hair. "Amanda is your mother?" she pleaded.

"Right Miss Palmer."

"But I've seen you before. Recently. But the name was different."

"Donatelli."

"You. Oh my God. You worked at the fish market. That's what the knife was for. I'll see you inside. I have to go." She brushed against the guard as she raced out of the room.

Popping sounds of the court recording machine resonated through the austere courtroom masking the tenor sounds of Judge Charlie Feather lecturing the man who stood in front of him.

"I usually talk to a few drunks who I've seen before, people who have been speeding or didn't pay parking fines, occasional men or women who beat their mates or kids, and occasional burglars. You're an unusual case. Do you understand why you are here?"

Matt nodded at the judge.

"Well let's see if we can figure it out. You were picked up with a hidden weapon, a knife stuck into your boot." Charlie Feather closed the file on his desk. "Then you got into an imbroglio in the lockup and spilled blood on one of the guards. Did you know that there have been several incidents this week, incidents involving desecration of a synagogue and a church, the beheading of a statue in a cemetery, all because of people like you?"

"You mean with tattoos or skinheads going to a concert? So people shift into automatic, blame those kids for anything that happens, and expect that they're out to screw things up. Just some kids out having fun," Matt murmured.

"But you're no kid." The judge leaned forward and spoke menacingly. "And you had a hidden weapon."

"No. The knife wasn't hidden, was easy to spot in my truck. Never had it in my boot and I never hit any guards. They did the job on me and I didn't do those other things."

The judge sat back, looked at the file, looked across the room to Gloria and Hawk, and then back at his file. "Two things I see here. First, you didn't get a chance to contact a lawyer until you got here, and second, there is a letter here from a friend of the court."

Matt maintained his stoic pose, wondered if someone who wanted him released had written to the court, if someone wanted him as far out of the way as Carl Gohrman, or could it have been the sergeant who wanted to get him back to the jail for a chance to turn him loose with the black inmates?

"Your honor," he stood erect, his fists clenched near his sides, and his lips pursed allowing air to come close to a whistle. "I'm not guilty of being anything other than what I am. I'm not guilty of what anyone else may have done and I'm not stupid enough to carry a knife when troopers are sure to be on my case. So what happens now?"

The judge leaned on the desk, looked past the courtroom seats to the old murals, pointed to Matt, lectured him about the seriousness of the charges, and talked about the absence of any State Trooper to verify the charges. He talked about a letter from Miss Palmer. Charlie Feather indicated that he had to find Matt guilty of the fight in the jail and that he would give him a nine month sentence, allow probation but restricted him to the county, and required proof of gainful employment. "Miss Palmer said she would offer you a job. First decision is mine." The judge hesitated. "The second one is yours.

Matt nodded, didn't look at Gloria, but felt the anguish of being helped by a member of the Palmieri family, and in the long run by his mother. Strange, he thought, what a hunk of jewelry will do for you. He signed papers that were put in front of him, was given instructions by the clerk, released by the bailiff, and was surrounded by Hawk's arms. As he looked at Gloria, he thought of the time he had been at Tern Harbor with his mother, had been told to stay out of the way, had seen the other boys swimming and decided to make it to the large rock. He remembered standing on the rock and showing off to the young girl on the hill, but this time it was his inner self that was naked.

"You guys have got to be hungry. I am. Let's get out of here and let these folks go home. And besides, we have a lot to talk about." Gloria called over her shoulder. "By the way what do we call you?" She continued without interruption and realized she was talking like Benito. "Too late for any place in the Village and besides you both look kind of grimy, so let's get over to my place" Gloria and Hawk talked about GIs, about the house in Brooklyn, and about dancing on the furniture in front of the fireplace. Hawk was looking at the dark landscape as they neared the Bridge to Nowhere and he spoke softly of his flight to what he had hoped would be his freedom and redemption. He spoke softly of his disappointment and decision to return to Dartmouth.

A dog was barking in the distance; across the river a bird was calling for its mate; gusting wind was rapidly clearing rain clouds. Gloria held the door so that Hawk could carry his bag into the house. Matt, standing close to the river bank, seemed to be allowing the wind to surround him, to fill his lungs, and to cleanse his polluted body. "Call me by my name, Matt."

Gloria brought blankets and pillows into the living room for her guests, made sure they were comfortable for the night, checked the towels and soap in the bathroom, and called them into the kitchen. "You guys find what you like in the refrig. I'm just having a cup of tea and going to watch you two eat." She watched as Hawk arranged his plate of fruit and vegetables and Matt was tentative about his choice.

"Go ahead," she said. "And by the way, you can call your mother in the morning and tell her where you are. I can't call that house."

"No." Matt snapped. "She's not to know anything about this. I'll contact her when I need to. And how come you can't call?"

She stirred her tea, glared at Matt as if to defy his question, and remained silent. Hawk sat back so he could see everything in the room. Matt gained confidence as he realized that he had gained an advantage and was not about to give it up. "The old man still pulling your chain?"

"Hey. I just saved your . . ." Gloria stopped.

"So that's what happened in that court room. Tried to figure why the judge . . . " Matt smiled. "Thanks."

"He's a good friend and was willing to do a favor, and anyway they didn't want to have any publicity. So it was a trade off. And I owe your mother big time. We'll talk tomorrow about what kind of jobs you can do." She kissed Hawk goodnight and ran up the stairs to her room.

Matt looked at Hawk, then the staircase, then back to Hawk. "I saw her once a long time ago and for some reason saw you hitchhiking and for some reason we got sent to the same place. You believe it was just coincidence?"

"More like natural force. I knew from that jailhouse battle that you had some of my blood. I heard the wind on the highway telling me something was going to happen but I didn't know I was to be a medium for you to come here. Not coincidence, natural force. Do you ever hear the wind?"

Matt crossed to the river bank, stretched his arms over his head and, staring defiantly at the star crowded sky, was enveloped by the mystical call of the wind.

28

Wind, Moon, Air

Seasons fused imperceptibly, winter to summer and forward to the next winter, as Matt mastered construction skills and convinced his tutor, Greg Smith Jr., that power tools could speed their work and make it more efficient. Nights were devoted to studying the plans for completing the River Front Project, books of Native American lore, finance journals, Shakespeare, and modern poetry.

Matt occupied the corner building's renovated top floor with its clear view of the Village, Riverfront, bridge to Nowhere, and that had easy escape access to the roof. He assisted in the first floor business office, learned how to send statements, track accounts receivable, and gained an understanding of Benito Palmieri's real estate business empire.

During his probation period, Matt became an important part of Gloria's team, a friend and ally. He avoided talking about home, recent years, and his mother's vision of his destiny. He became project supervisor for the River Front Project when Greg Jr. took over the management of the lumber yard. While reviewing the project progress and Gloria's plans for expanding the newspapers' influence, he introduced the idea of offering discounts to advertisers for signing long term contracts.

Matt borrowed the money from local business people to buy a bankrupt radio station and turned the nearly defunct station into the County's most listened to daytime station; local business clubs vied for his attention and membership.

Gloria and Matt's time was consumed with development of the newspaper chain, the River Front project, the radio station growth, and their developing friendship. Matt appointed Jesus Alvarez to be the crew supervisor for the River Front project.

Jim Platt stormed into Matt's office, dropped his hammer onto the floor, and leaned across the desk. "What the friggin kind of crap is that?" he blared. "Putting that black kid in charge. He can hardly speak English."

"Not black," Matt whistled back. "Anyway, he does the work, doesn't goof off, always shows up on time, and he's the one who can get the best work out of the crew."

"Hey, we both know what you used to be. I know what the hell those tattoos came from. So how come the nigger gets to be boss and not me?"

Matt leaned across the desk, renewed the terrifying skinhead stare, and then pulled the workman toward him. "I told you he can do the job. You don't like it, leave. And remember, I can still take out anyone who gets in my way." Matt had not forgotten his ability to inflict terror and the knowledge that he who inflicts the most fear, wins. Jim Platt picked up his hammer, rolled his hand over its handle, and then stormed out of the room.

"Oh yeah Platt. Pronounce his name Chesus!"

Matt brushed beads of sweat from his forehead, felt the pangs of remorse that were coming more often when he remembered what he had been, kept hearing his mother's voice calling him through the winds. "Yeah," he repeated. "you have no idea where those tattoos came from."

⎯⎯•⎯⎯

Gloria never mentioned Matt when she spoke to Amanda. Matt would speak to his Uncle George, get the news of home, his friends and family members who still gathered around the autumn fires. He would call his mother, tell her he was working in New Jersey, had started a radio station, and was working long hours, every day. He did not mention Gloria.

Hawk invited Gloria to visit Vermont for a ski weekend and suggested she bring Matt along. Neither of them had ever been on skis; they became conspirators in a local ski shop. They bought clothes, skis, and sun glasses. Gloria was particular about the colors and the way things fit. Matt was more concerned with turtle neck sweaters that covered insignia skinhead symbols emblazoned on his arms and neck, the spider web on his elbow that now hosted the long string symbol of his heritage, his past, and his genetic ties.

Gloria spent most of her time on the beginner slope, talking loudly to Hawk, learning how to fall, and finally moving to the intermediate slope. Matt waved to Gloria from the chair lift and spent the day on the upper slopes. Pulling yellow glasses over his eyes, he rocked back and forth and then pushed off into the falling snow, making turns as if he had been on this mountain since childhood.

"You cheated," she chided. "Said you were never on skis before."

"Wasn't. Just watched others and did the same thing. Like watching some old fishermen and then going out to catch fish; either you do it or you don't eat. So either you ski down the mountain, get that awesome charge, or you sit up there and freeze. Go on Gloria, bet you can really do a number on that intermediate slope."

Gloria was determined to prove she could make it down the slope without falling and was angry to have been provoked by the boy who had stood on the rock taunting her. She was unnerved by his insolence and would show him what a Palmer was made of. Her body tensed at the thought that she was capable of surpassing her father's determined ferociousness. She reached the top of the hill, shook off the instructor's assistance, dug poles into powdery snow, and bolted down the slope. Competitive winds buffeted her face, trees whistled shrill notes as she glided past them, the gray Vermont sky blended with the rocky outcrops of snowcapped peaks, and small figures formed a broken column at the bottom of the hill.

Suddenly she was on her back and snow filled clouds were all she could see. Skis broke away from her boots and tumbled over her, snow streaked around her as she pummeled toward the line of people she had just admired.

"Lookout," she yelled to the unsuspecting crowd, but the sound carried back up the trail and she was rolling into the line of skiers who were waiting to buy hot chocolate. She pulled them along the short incline in a vee formation like birds in flight. Laughter erupted as the skiers found their gloves, hat, goggles, and composure. Gloria wanted to hide and was sure she would hear about the event the rest of the day and evening.

At dinner, Hawk and Matt offered a toast to the great day of skiing. All the diners raised their glasses to Gloria.

"Very funny," she quipped, looked across the table at Matt, wanted to be sitting closer to him uncertain whether to spill her drink on his shirt or hold his arm.

"Hey you two," Hawk clinked a glass. "Trails are lit for night skiing. Going to be a real challenge, exciting, and fun. How about it?"

"I'll pass. Did enough sliding around on my rear for one day," Gloria finished her coffee. "Early night for me."

Matt and Hawk boarded the lift to the top of the mountain. They chattered about who would make it down first, who would be the first to tumble or break a bone, and who could hug closest to the trees while navigating the mountain.

"Look there," Hawk pointed at the lake that had been hidden by the daytime snow fog. "The moon bounces more light against that water than man-made light does against these hills. If everything else went out, you could find your way from that glow."

Matt knew the power of water, moon, stars, wind, and fickle woods. He looked at the lake, turned back to the hotel at the bottom of the mountain, took off his hat so he could feel the wind rustling his hair, smiled, and turned to Hawk. "On your mark, set, yah."

They leaped off their positions and raced to the first turn, skidded past the trees, leaped over a small hill, and crashed into the forest that had been hidden from them. They rolled to a stop, looked for each other, and then looked for their skis which were twenty feet down the hill. They sat there drinking from their canteens and waited for the lights to go out on the trail.

"See, I told you, we have enough illumination from the sky to see the trail and everything around us," Hawk informed the wind. "I learned good when I was at home, didn't I?"

They talked about their past as if they were old friends who had met in a pub after years apart. Hawk told of his foster homes before he went to Dartmouth, his goods friend Gis Palmieri, his mission to help his people, and his decision to return to college. "I finally felt my Native sadness. I didn't know my people any longer, and they didn't know me. I was never raised with them, always with white families and was separated; but the ancient blood is always there. I thought I would be home, but did not know the feeling of the hills, the forest, or the desert. Learning how to fight was easy, it is natural, the blood runs through my veins."

Matt talked about his home, his need to keep his mother safe from his father, his skinhead days, some of the things he did before he went to New York, and about his trip to North Carolina; for the first time he revealed the fear that police, conspiring with those out to get him, might spot his pickup truck. He talked about his new life, about studying Native lore and the history of his people on Long Island, and plans he had for developing a media giant along with Gloria. He spoke of growing up inheriting nature's ways with his mother's blood, running with animals, swimming with fish, challenging tall grasses, and then trying to become someone far away from himself.

Hawk asked why Matt didn't go home, asked why he didn't think about his people, and asked if he was going to get rid of the yellow truck.

"You're the second one who asked about that damned truck. Uncle George figured it was a piece of junk, so why do you think I should dump it?"

"So no one will follow you."

"Okay, then what do I drive? And yes I have thought about going home, bunch of problems there, but maybe someday."

"You ought to go, someday. Why do you think someone might follow you, just an isolated bunch who wanted to get someone out of the way?"

"There are more of them than you think. Not open, not so anyone can see. There's an underground network. They can get in touch, have cultivated strategies, and can direct political destinies without anyone even realizing it. They don't know my real name, just Matt something or other. But they know that truck. Should've gotten rid of it long ago."

"And someday you have to go home. Life changes you know. Doesn't matter who you were a while ago." Hawk inhaled the cold air as if to appear taller and block out the moonlight. "You can decide to be something, someone else. Who you may have become because of whatever you may have done, doesn't destroy the root that is stuck up your spine calling you back to who you really are and demanding that you decide who you will be next. I saw you standing by the river that night, and I know the winds call you. But you must decide."

"Sound like my mother."

"Maybe, maybe! But maybe more like those drums that beat with every surge of Native blood in your veins. Sooner or later you have to decide." Hawk slipped down the hill to find his skis. Matt pulled his skis out of the snow bank, stood stripped to the waist with his sweater tucked into his belt; his arms were outstretched as he howled at the sky.

"You're nuts," Hawk yelled. "You'll freeze."

"The moon, the wind, the cold air will protect me as I challenge this hill. Let's go."

Matt felt the cold air brushing his body, listened to the whistling of skis against snow, stinging ice pellets pounding in rhythm with his pulsating temples, and he heard Hawk's crackling words chasing him down the hill, "Decide, decide, decide". He thought about the excitement of the River project, the newspapers, and the radio station. He thought about his life in New Jersey, of the membership in Kiwanis, of his welcome within the community. He thought about having to go home, to fulfill his mother's dream, about the old myths around those autumn campfires. He heard those words "decide, decide, decide." He thought about Gloria.

Back in the hotel, Matt pushed back in a soft leather chair, listened to soft jazz on a walkman, was about to fall asleep, when he pulled the headset out of his ears, walked down the hall toward Gloria's room, lifted his hand to knock on her door, stopped, moved his hand forward. Stopped. And returned to his room. "Decide you idiot," he pounded his chest.

29

Letters

Gloria wished she was still in Vermont, walked across the bridge to the Nowhere Café, sat in front of the fireplace and reread letters she had received from Benito, Amanda, and copies of notes she had sent.

Dear Gloria,

Ruined another pair of skates and had to hitch a ride to Sante Fe. Wonderful break. Had a chance to look at the desert from the cab of an air conditioned truck and had the delicious smell of horses in the back, but they had already been delivered to a ranch in Nevada. Sante Fe is as beautiful as I remembered and had the chance to revisit the Museums. Rented a small house and will hang around here for a while.

Glad to hear you are having so much fun with the papers and your special project. How's that young fellow doing? Did I ever tell you that Georgia O'Keefe was a special friend of mine?

I try to take early morning walks in the desert, it is still cool enough and just the most peaceful and beautiful feeling. I may decide to stay here. How is the River Front Project coming? Will send you a package soon.

Love, Benito.

———

Dear Uncle Benito,

Have never been so happy. I love the newspapers, the real estate projects, and working with Matt on the Radio Station. I think I owe Hawk a lot for having brought him here. He has a special way with Veronica Crandall. He actually had her write a big check to help finish the Gazebo in the park.

I heard that Gis Palmieri is doing an amazing job with the restaurant and he is planning to get married in the Fall. By the way, did I tell you I was skiing this past winter? Still feel the bruises.

Yes, Matt is doing a great job and can I tell you something? I could really go for him, maybe, I will. Does that make you smile? Thought so. So how well did you know Georgia O'Keefe? Love you so much for having brought me here.

Gloria

Dear Uncle Benito,

Just got back from Vermont. Hawk graduated from Dartmouth and has decided to remain in New England. I think he is very unhappy. You know he had taken time, thought he was somehow going to be the new leader of his people, you know he is Native American, and anyway, he thought he would be able to help them find a new way of life and regain what was rightly theirs. I think he was terribly disappointed when he found out he was not really needed, or accepted as someone who could feel like he was part of them. He is going to stay in New England, perhaps be a ski instructor. He has this mystical feeling about Matt. It is strange, and eerie. Did I ever tell you about the myth of the lovers at Tern Harbor? It makes me feel like Hawk has

*something to do with it. I think I'm getting as weird as he is. Oh yes,
I received that package from you and am following your instructions
not to open it until my birthday. Not fair. Love,*
   Gloria

Dear Gloria,

**It was so good getting a note from you. Your father doesn't
look well. Still goes to the newspaper office and does everything
else, but he should probably take a break. Dyspeptic as ever. Not
sure why I stay here, except I have this old feeling for you and
for your dear mother. I promised her I would always be here
for you, both of you.**

**I had a letter from my son yesterday. He sent along a picture
and he looks wonderful. He finally sold his old truck and has a
little white convertible. Very cute.**

**How are you getting along running your uncle's business?
Do you think you might some day have one of your own?**

**Good to call me on Thursday or Friday nights as your father
is always out after dinner.**

Speak to you soon. Love, Amanda

The usually gentle stream was swollen by the morning storm.

A moist autumn aroma wafted across the landscape. Gloria sat
reading her mail and thought of her mother watching her in that
ridiculous dance class, of the small Main Street shops, of Belle's
Tavern green doors that barred her entry, and of her father's insipid
control over every important happening in that desperate village. She
thought about the old wooden bridge, the mock soldier's memorial,
late afternoon sun sparkling against the window of Clare's Dance
Studio, the new park and its walkways, and was sickened by the
notion that she had created Tern Harbor's astro twin.

"Damn him. He's still in control, even here."

Matt read the letter he received from his uncle George.

> *Hey Matt,*
>
> *Your Mom's been spending a few days out here now that the Summer people have pretty much gone and they're getting ready for the campfires (not too many folks come to them lately.) The woods seem ablaze with sumac and other berries as usual this time of year. Can smell the dry wood of those evening campfires and the low murmur of the Sound drowns out the soft voices that must be telling those old stories.*
>
> *Mom will be heading back to Tern Harbor soon. Doesn't talk much, but I have caught sight of her looking out to where the spray rises over the rock jetty, as if she expected someone.*
>
> *Oh yeah. Remember that Robins boy, used to be a friend of yours, making quite a name for himself, and may run for council or something.*
>
> *Well that's some of the news from here. I'm working in an art gallery in Riverhead. Write soon.*
>
> *George*

Matt tied his boots to the split rail fence, wrapped his shirt around his waist, and ran along the stream until it dropped into the large pond inhabited by splashing Mallards. Birds disregarded him as if he were invisible. He climbed the bank and fled past the tall grass, nettles, and dry thorny bushes that tore at his body and blooded his once calloused feet. He started to race over the surface of these defenders of the river bank as he had in the days when he would careen through the woods toward Mama Robins's protectorate. When he reached the end of the marshy woods, he looked past the brown and red bulrushes to be sure the road was empty. He covered his scratched body, found his boots where he had tied them, turned away from the cloud covered yellow moon, and walked in the darkness toward the Nowhere Café.

A car moved out of the Café lot leaving it in complete darkness that separated Nowhere from the rest of the earth. Matt moved toward the figure standing in the dimly lit café entryway, screeching insects guiding their mates homeward through the darkness, and Gloria and Matt's footsteps crunched the unpaved roadway.

"Damn," she lurched forward. "Lost my shoe and can't see a thing."

Matt lifted the moccasin, rubbed it against his shirt, and then handed it to Gloria.

"How did you find it? I can't see a thing in this darkness."

"Always able to see in the dark. Old training, maybe comes with my territory."

"It was nice meeting you back there. Nice having a few minutes without anything special to talk about, just things." She was relieved to be in the darkness so he could not see her blush.

He reached out and held her hand. "Better hang on. Don't want you getting lost out here. It doesn't get light until we get near the bridge."

Persistent insect chirping flooded the night.

"Want to come in for a cup of coffee or something?" she was still holding his hand as they crossed the bridge.

"As long as we don't have to talk about any business."

"I promise. I'll show you a present I received from my Uncle Benito. It's amazing."

Gloria pulled the wood frame from inside the cardboard box, leaned the painting against the back of the couch, lifted the white sheet from the front of it, and turned to Matt. "Well, what do you think?"

"That's one terrific painting. Takes you right out there into the desert. Looks like if you were there, you could really be free, living in the sun, quiet, still, no bugs screaming at you, no nothing. Quite a painting."

She slid the frame back into the box. "How come you..."

"No questions tonight. Remember."

"Wouldn't it be something if we could just disappear into that picture?" She held out her hand.

There were no more words, no more questions. Gloria inhaled the smell of the woods that had led them both to the Café. Matt thought of his escape from North Carolina, the trip through Kentucky, his desertion in jail, and the miraculous rescue by this girl who had once seen him standing naked on a rock that should have been held holy by his relatives. He remembered the Tern Harbor myth he had heard as a boy, thought of that painting and wished he could inhale the desert. Gloria remembered the soft touch of the moss covered rocks, looking up at her father standing in his windows, looking down through his binoculars. She thought of her first encounter with a boy, and wondered if her cousin in Brooklyn ever filled in all the letters on his "score card." She thought if she had a score card she would leave all the letters blank except the letter "M." They moved toward each other, turned off the lamp light and in the darkness, they were in love.

They were wrapped in each other as they slept under the puffy quilt. The only sounds were matched rhythmic breathing and occasional movement of hands over tightly drawn skin. Gloria's eyes sprung open with the hum of the telephone. She reached across what she knew were the skull, then spider, then black rose tattoos, and fumbled for the phone.

He rolled over so she was lying across his chest and he ran his face across her shoulder.

"Hello," she put her finger across his lips. "Who's calling at this awful hour?"

"Gloria, honey. It's me, Amanda." Gloria wrapped the quilt around her as she snapped on the lamp light. She smiled as she looked at Matt lying belly up on the bed, and then covered him with her bathrobe.

"What's wrong Amanda?" she spoke so that he would know who was calling. "Are you, okay?"

"I'm fine, but it's your father. He's in the hospital. Was down in the village last night and had a stroke. They rushed him to the hospital, and, Gloria, I think you have to come home. You're the only one who can give them any kind of instructions at the hospital, the only family."

"I'm on my way. Will you meet me at the hospital or shall I pick you up."

"I'm there now."

She rushed though the explanation to Matt as she prepared to leave.

"I'll drive you, go with you," he was dressed and raced down the stairs.

"But what will you say to your mother?"

"Destiny. Yeah. Destiny."

30

Steve Palmer

Steve Palmer, propped in the high backed wheelchair, rolled his head along the soft wool blanket that surrounded him, and watched white sails making their way to the afternoon regatta. He moaned when he thought of white walls, sheets, curtains, and nurses' uniforms, the hospital where for two months he was unable to speak or move, and was surrounded by unending clatter.

Furious at his living internment, he had refused to raise or lower the hospital bed by simply pressing the button with the fingers that he could move; he punctured the nurses' routines by periodically leaning on the call button. A nurse would enter the room, question his call, and when he would not answer she would leave, and wait for the next call. During those months, he exposed phlegmatic contempt for the foreign born aides who were temporarily in charge of his body. He clenched his bed rails when they cleaned him or touched his private parts without any more passion than a butcher cleaning a chicken.

Gloria surrendered to entrapment in Tern Harbor, asked Matt to take charge of the Forge Creek business operations, and finally asked him to buy her share. They met every Tuesday, sometimes near Tern Harbor, other times close to Riverhead, and other times they would drive as far as they could before nighttime. They would stop at quiet places. At West Point, they looked across the open parade grounds to the splendor of the broad Hudson River.

"Native Americans would see this spot and know the wonder of Nature. They'd live here in every season, fishing, hunting, finding food, and protecting themselves from their worst natural enemies. Other Indians, other men." Matt sat on the damp ground and told her about the beauty of the mountains in the Northwest, the Sierras, and the deserts of the Southwest. He talked of the expansive open space in the West and the invisible rope pulling him back to Long Island and what his mother called his destiny.

Gloria talked about Benito's letters and how he marveled at the wonders of the desert and that he was going to remain in Sante Fe. "I found Paradise," he had said. "And I'm not leaving."

"Sometimes," Matt leaned against her. "I think I've spent my life moving in every direction across the threads of a web, not sure whether I was the hunter or the spider." He told her about the meetings with the Supremacists, the trip to North Carolina, and he told her about the stories told around the old campfires. He started telling the myth of the terns, but she finished it.

He told her of how the Wind had caressed and captured him, talked about mystic powers that lifted him when he raced across open fields or through impenetrable bramble woods, spoke of Nature having devised the plan to place Hawk on that highway, and then the exhilaration of being rescued by her.

He said he would go back to Forge Creek to fulfill his promise to Gloria and she would return to Tern Harbor to keep her promise to her mother *He knew he would only stay there until his job was done.*

Gloria was sure her father had manipulated this stroke to ensnare her. She was determined to prove her strength and his weakness, forced him to initial papers putting her in charge of the *Journal* and appointing her a cosigner on the bank accounts. She told him the details of how she sold off the unprofitable printing section of the business, delighted in his anger when she set up a system for collecting rents by mail and for systematic maintenance of the properties. She had ramps built outside the house to allow for easy movement of his wheelchair.

"Nah," he repeated. "Nah!" understanding that he would be in this condition forever. His blood pressure rose and he spit as he tried to talk. She reminded him of the promise to take care of him that she had made to her dying mother, and assured him that she would be around to take care of things until he got better, and then she would add "assuming you get better." She would pause, wait for him to try to yell at her, and then wiped the saliva from his lips.

"Finally have him," she thought.

"She'll never get away. Keep her here," he fantasized.

They were both aware their game was being played on an unending chess board, without kings or queens, a game without champion until one of them would quit.

He refused to see anyone, would not allow anyone to see him as an invalid old man. He did not count speech or physical therapists as people. They were objects placed for his convenience to enable him to return to the world he had built. He began to mumble a few distinguishable words and after several months was beginning to grasp things with both hands.

Gloria watched anxiously as he struggled with interminable recovery. Each day, she or Amanda would push his chair toward the windows so he could see the Harbor and Long Island Sound. He would scrutinize boats sailing past the red buoy, would lean forward to see unwelcome clammers.

"Watching for Conrad, Steve?" Gloria would tease. "Don't think he can show up. Don't think he could make it. He is gone, Steve, remember?"

"Shoo-o-o-ot hm, f ee cms heer," he shook his head, moved his lips, and waited for Gloria to clear the spittle from his chin.

He convinced the physical therapist to place one of his rifles across his lap. The young man thought it might motivate his patient to move his hands and do his exercises in the long hours of staring at the bay.

Everything that centered around Steve Palmer slipped into routine. Gloria turned the digital clock so she would not see the three numbers 5:00 with the little green light next to the AM, splashed warm water over her face and looked at the woman staring back at her from the walnut framed mirror. She wondered how that round-faced girl who would raise her arms and spin to entertain her mother had lost that innocent smile; she examined each new mark that required blush and lipstick, checked the roots of her hair and raised her hands as if to spin like that young girl who once smiled back from that mirror, then reached under her blouse to adjust her bra. "There.

Ready for another day."

She opened her father's window shades, inhaled as if to suck air through locked windows into the sterile smelling room, dressed her father, moved him to the bathroom, pushed his wheel chair to the kitchen, finished a second cup of coffee while Amanda fed Steve Palmer, positioned the wheel chair in the corner of the windowed family room, waited for speech or physical therapists to arrive, and left for the scheduled business day.

Gloria became a Friday lunch regular at Belle's Tavern, and attended the bi-weekly Kiwanis luncheon, followed her father's ritual of attending Tern Harbor College's Anthropology class to select interns to work at the newspaper.

Everything became routine, everything except Tuesday.

The silent imbroglio between daughter and father was never as clear as during the winters when she would wrap him in warm sweaters and blankets, move his wheelchair to the top of the ramp at the side of the house, move slowly, then faster down the embankment to the edge of the cliff. The terror that he would once have hidden, burst into audible grunts and stiff clenching of his fingers. He would gulp cold air, and breathe rapidly when the chair stopped near the deck railing. He had his revenge when she brought him outside during the Spring, left him at the top of the ramp long enough to close the screen door. Suddenly the chair was rolling down the ramp and she could catch it just before it made the turn toward the deck stairs and Devil Cliff. They continued their game during icy weather and hot dry summers. Gloria grew more confident, angry at her father for still being alive, and furious at herself for the thought.

Steve Palmer learned to make sounds that could be understood when Gloria or Amanda was close. He let them know what he wanted and that he wanted Butch Moulder to visit. The mayor, visited his mentor every Thursday, would talk about town politics, praise journalism prizes won by the newspaper, and then he would entertain Steve Palmer with his handling of the rifle in military drill. He would replace the rifle across the old man's lap before he left.

College interns came to the house for dinner on Friday evenings. Gloria reviewed their work, then, with the young man or woman, sat close enough to her father for him to sniff their cologne or after shave but far enough away to frustrate his need to touch them.

Late afternoon iridescence shimmered along the Harbor surface. Gloria, holding a glass of wine, watched the flurry of activity as sailors prepared for their weekend fun. Suddenly, she was aware something was out of place, the wheelchair had moved out of the usual corner.

"Amanda," she turned into the kitchen. "Why did you move him?"

"Didn't touch him. He's been in there all day. Wouldn't even have lunch."

"Was that jerk Moulder up here? It isn't Thursday, so why . . . ?"

"No. Watch him for a while. Don't let him know you're here. Just watch."

Gloria was on her second glass of wine when she saw it. Her father, who had not been able to manipulate the wheel chair, had moved forward. He edged the rifle toward the floor, used it as a pole and inched forward. Gloria walked into the large room and applauded. "That was terrific," she returned his smile.

He lifted the rifle back onto his lap, trying to hide his ability to use it as a cane. The gun clattered to the floor. They both were still. She was uncertain about retrieving it for him; he shook his head and hands and tried to make sounds but only moved his lips. It started slowly, hesitatingly, then they erupted into nervous laughter; neither wanted to admit what part of the game had just been played or which of them had made the best moves. Summer brilliance turned to wintry shadows over the room in which they jousted without clear victories.

Steve Palmer, resting against the windowsill, leaned forward so that his nose flattened against the glass pane and contorted into a cartoonist's characterization of the man whose face raced ahead of his time. He remembered seeing young women and men on the beach. "I used to be one of them," he thought. "Used to be better than any of them. Had more fun. Would have known what to do on any one of those boats with some girls. I should have been a Palmieri, not had to prove who I was, I was a Palmieri. My name should have been up there in those neon lights at the restaurant." He pointed at the family pictures on the long piano. "You should have been kinder to me Papa. I could have made that business into something. Had to be as tough as you were, even tougher. I own more than you ever thought, and my family, yeah familia, familia, my family is right here with me. And not going away. See, old man, see. Look at what I made."

He pointed the rifle toward the window. "If this thing gets loaded, anything I shoot is something I own. But, shoulda been back there in New York, a Palmieri. See those pretty sweet things there on the beach? Delicious. Don't tell me you never went after them, old man. I know better. So what was the big fuss about me having a good time? Look. She's taking off the top. Wouldn't you have liked to see that? Old son-of-a-bitch." He pointed the rifle at the pictures and pulled the trigger of the unloaded gun.

Steve Palmer examined each line of ice crystals that were forming against the windows as if he was seeing his own face growing older; falcon-like, unseen from his perch, he waited for unsuspecting prey to cross the harbor entrance.

———

Butch Moulder, tanned from skiing, visited on Thursdays, had lunch, talked about local politics, the Tern Harbor Day plans, and asked if there was anything special his host needed.

Steve Palmer's slurred speech left their conversations in a frustrated monologue. During one of those visits, Steve pointed to the piano bench and said, "bullets."

Butch found the box of rifle shells. "You don't need these Steve. Could accidentally go off." Butch closed the bench before he left.

Steve Palmer was angry and distressed. He used the rifle as his ally, moved toward the piano, and took charge of the bullets. "Got them now," he thought. "Ever see that boy trying to steal my girl away from me, Ping, he'll be gone. Took this friggin stroke to get her back, never going away again. Ping, ping."

The gray afternoon settled on the black and white choppy waters below. The low murmur of a clam boat slicing past the red buoy woke Steve from his nap. "At last, you're out there. He raised the loaded rifle, and fired. The bullet crashed into the paneled wall, the sound roared through the room, and the rifle kicked back knocking him off the chair. Amanda raced into the room, tried to lift him, and called 911. Steve Palmer woke up in the hospital victim of another incapacitating stroke, with tubes stuck into his body, machines beeping, and those same foreigners who he had tried to keep out of Tern Harbor in charge of his body.

"That boy did this," he thought. "Get him next time. Get me out of here," he tried to scream at Gloria who was seated behind the beeping machine.

31

Giant Shadow

Warm gusts leapfrogged over the surf, then fanned the sputtering campfire when old men vied to recant ancient stories; men told of an alcoholic Indian turned into a rock that would scream for liquor when anyone passed close to it; other men told about giants who trod the earth to prevent strangers from damaging or stealing it. The last myth spinner was about to leap toward shadows to magnify his size but stopped in terror in front of the fire. Wind coiled around the flames, lifted dust over the high trees, and vanished into the gently lapping water. A giant figure emerged from the sheltering sumac, its shadow spread across woods that rimmed the conclave.

Harry Hart leaped over crackling embers, embraced his cousin Matt, and brought him into the orange light. "Hey, look who's back. The giant came to save the earth." Smiles, murmurs, and thumping of feet accompanied nods of welcome.

Matt had decided it was his time to listen to the old stories at the campfires, and invent a new one.

The cousins drank beer, watched seductive stars fade behind the pale blue morning sky, and talked about what they had been doing since Matt had left. They talked about old days when they wrestled until their mothers pulled them apart, and about the times they would swim into the Sound, catch breath, and hope they could make it back to shore without drowning. Harry emptied another bottle, turned to Matt, sat with the silence of those old shamans who experience every thought in the circle, and finally asked, "Why Matt?"

"I had to leave."

"No. Why become, you know, Mr. Tough guy who nobody could stand. Why?"

"Easy to get sucked in. Everything went down hill. Stupid fight and then cut up the Robins kid. I was odd man out, easy to blame things on the old man, made it easy for me. Met some wise ass rich kid, you know, the type who would get through school with no one ever really noticing him. Nice, smiling type. Did all his work, never any trouble, never in any special group, never best at anything. Then one day he finds himself important enough to get to a meeting with kids like himself. Then I meet him and he pulls me along to a meeting where some guy from New York makes a pitch that makes sense. Talks about everything and everyone who had been trying to push me around, punish me, gang up on me. Well I went all the way. Learned how to hate. Hate the nigger who was once my friend, hate the Jew teachers, hate, hate, hate. Learned faster than anyone else; learned how to win; learned how to be the biggest dick in town so anyone with any sense would stay out of my way. "Hate the niggers," that guy from New York said. "Hate the Jews, hate the Indians – Native Americans, hate foreigners. Made sense for a long time, until I realized that the one he really made me hate, hate, really hate, was me."

"But, that's us."

"Yeah! It took me a while to be able to get it. Took a special event. But it was quite a ride. Sometimes, I guess, you have to sink pretty low before you can come up for air. Like when we used to swim out there."

"We need you here, Matt."

"Why?"

"You saw the fire tonight. Bunch of old men whose old stories don't mean much to the few kids just hanging around. Most people think we are still just some cutsie relics of 'Native Americans'. We need something to bring us back to being a real people, a nation within a nation."

"What do you want to do, start a casino? They got it going in New England. Why try to get one here?"

"No, Matt. We need, more. Most of us still have to fight for anything we have, have to go hat in hand for loans. They still think we shouldn't buy liquor."

"Well, you never know, that old rock is liable to yell at you."

"Matt, come back to stay. You have more courage than all the rest combined; you've got that old mystique that your mother has been yaking about since you were born. They saw you cast a giant shadow tonight and were ready to accept you no matter what you've done. They know what you were like as a kid, and they know you go directly back to Old Tom Steelehart. They know how you always challenge the wind and water. They saw your giant shadow and that will spread like wild fire. Matt, come home."

They sat cross legged without speaking. Swollen clouds reflected gold, pink, and orange of the October sunrise. Matt leaped forward, ran toward the pebbly beach, threw off his clothes and jumped into the glassy calm of Long Island Sound. He turned toward Harry, "Come on, race you across the Sound."

"You're nuts Matt. Nuts." Harry was close behind his cousin. Their bodies rose above undulating swells, until Matt vanished then reappeared a hundred feet ahead.

"Matt. That's enough. Looks like a storm coming. Come on back."

"Come on, come on Harry. Or can I still kick your butt out here?"

Harry submerged, came up breathing hard, looked around and did not find Matt until he felt the hand grab his ankle and pull him under. First claps of distant thunder greeted them as they surfaced laughing.

"Fun's over. I'm heading back, come on."

Matt turned. "Never swam out in a storm when we were kids. Let's do it. Little breeze not going to frighten us now, you know that old lady wind watches over me."

Harry headed toward the shore. "Hey Matt, look. That German Shepard is tossing our clothes around, running off with something. Looks like someone calling the dog. Shit, he's running with my pants."

Matt moved through the increasing fury of the dark, green, impenetrably black waves, challenged kettle drum sounds of the raging tidal wave battles where the Atlantic Ocean meets Long Island Sound. With the first crack of lightning, he arched above the pounding water and sailed under the speeding surf until he rolled onto the pebbly beach. He looked up, hoping to see a girl waving his clothes. A large dog, holding a shoe in his mouth, was standing at the edge of the woods in front of a tall African American man. Matt recognized the man who used to be his friend. The dog and his owner turned and disappeared into the woods. He turned to his cousin Harry who was wearing a tee shirt.

"Damn dog shredded my pants and don't know where anything else is." Harry tried to cover himself with the bottom of the shirt.

"Wear mine," Matt faced toward the closing streak of lightning. "We could have made it further out, kid. Maybe in another storm. Okay Harry. I'll come home. Going to stay at my mother's house, have to see my uncle George, he wants me to see someone.

———————

Matt studied the oversized barn. The bright red roof was the only new thing about the unpainted clapboard house at the end of an East Marion side street. A concrete driveway led to the back of the old structure; the steel and concrete loading dock belied the pre-revolutionary building's age. Haphazard spindly birch trees separated sections of the parking lot.

The tall, thin man who answered the door struck a direct contrast to the random stacks of the *Orient Weekly Times.* Sidney Ackerley wore a gray suit, white shirt, purple tie, small lens glasses, and brown sandals. The office was modern and crisp looking as the newspaper publisher himself.

"Glad you took the time to stop by. George told me you might be here."

"George said you were interested in meeting me. I always liked the looks of this big barn, used to imagine all kind of weird things that could happen here. Never thought it was a newspaper office."

Matt expected the place would smell of hay, animals, and moist earth above a root cellar. He guessed bats and owls once shared the wood rafters waiting for their turns at night hunting, instead, he recognized the smell of newsprint and ink. Sidney Ackerley described the changes he had made to the barn, how he had created the printing plant, newspaper offices, his own private space, while maintaining the basic integrity of the property.

"We do everything here, have it all, including the printing plant. We do everything here. Always have. Can I get you a cup of coffee or tea?"

"No thanks, but I am not sure why . . . "

"George told me about your paper experience in New Jersey and got me interested. George and I are good friends."

"He's my uncle, but, I'm not like him." Matt tried not to squirm.

"Hah! Neither am I. But he is still a good friend. I've bought a few paintings from his shop. He does quite a job. Rents from me you know."

"Mr. Ackerley, George mentioned you had an offer for me?"

"Yes, yes. First let's get something straight. I've been here for a long time. I remember your mother as a little girl, and her parents. I knew your father and what he was like. Notice I said 'was'. I know a lot more than was ever printed in the paper. You know this has really been my whole life, but it's time to give it up. Did you know we used to set the type by hand? It was better then, not the typos that you get today with all these computers. Well, I told George I was looking for someone I could trust to take it over; then he told me about your success in New Jersey. I didn't think they had any decent small papers there."

Matt waited for his host to continue.

"I figured you'd be back sooner or later. What do you say, want to take it over? There's a catch. I also own some property, a few houses off the main road in Orient, some empty land, maybe hundred acres, this building, and a few gas stations in Riverhead. You'll have to take over the whole shooting match. So, well?"

Matt lowered his eyebrows so he could take charge of the meeting as well as get a clear look into the Sidney Ackerley's face. "Do you know who I am? Who I really am?"

"Told you I know your mother, know all about those campfires, and know all about old Tom Steelehart's whole family history."

"Mr. Ackerley, I'm a former skinhead."

"And I'm a Jew."

"Cool."

They eyed each other, made small talk about the community, the single track railroad meandering through land where Native Americans lived before Europeans arrived and claimed it for one king or another.

The former skinhead tried to fathom why this old man would offer all he had spent a lifetime building to someone who had lived in an alien and destructive world. He focused on Sidney Ackerley, tried to imagine a green printer's shade lowered on his forehead emphasizing a finely sculptured nose. Matt inhaled to capture the smell of newsprint; imagined a room with someone setting type while another ran a page proof and another tied bundles of papers. Instead he saw this fastidiously dressed man, his nails clean, hair carefully combed to disguise the almost barren head, and smelling of some non-distinct men's cologne. This man might be playing some sort of game, but for some obscured reason, Matt could not pinpoint it, he trusted George's friend.

Sidney Ackerley had measured Matt Donovan Steele, had done his research, knew about the football and the school problems, knew about his career with the newspapers in New Jersey and his relationship with Gloria Palmer. He knew about Matt's development of the New Jersey properties, his ownership of the radio station, and his good relationship with that county's business community. He stared at Matt and waited for the opportunity to ask about the missing years when Matt left Riverhead and resurfaced in New Jersey.

"How about a cup of coffee? I prefer tea myself." Sidney Ackerley had the reputation of being the perfect host.

"Just a glass of water, thanks." Matt listened to the clacking of the train moving east. He thought of how that land was taken, granted to one or two connected Englishmen who threw their lot with the English King: he thought of how that land had been divided, measured, and then sold to farmers who in bad years could not pay the mortgage. He thought he should look at the old foreclosure records preserved by the Riverhead Town Clerk; he wondered how many of his ancestors were victims of those nefarious actions, and remembered the words of old Tom Steelehart, "Take it all back. Beat them at their own game." He felt the pounding in his temples as he recalled his mother's mantra that it was his destiny to lead the people to their proper glory.

"Why would you trust me, offer me all this?"

"Not giving you anything my dear boy. I will hold the mortgage. You screw up and you're up the creek. But I don't expect that. I know about you, remember I've known your family for a long time, and I know what you can accomplish. This newspaper is stagnant, like all the other little town gossip sheets; unless they grow, they'll die. Too late for me to do it, too old. I know that something is burning inside of you. I can feel it, have good intuition. By the way, what were you doing when you left here? Not why did you leave, not interested in that."

"Worked at a fish market, then did some executive stuff." Matt stopped.

"I mean as a skinhead."

"Told you exec stuff. I was an organizer."

"Hmmn. Then why did you stop?"

"You figure things out after a while, sometimes it's too late, and sometimes you sink so low you think you'll always be there so what the hell; then somehow, you get pulled up."

"Sounds very aesthetic. Ummmn how did you get into it?"

"Easier than you think. Fall into it at the right moment, have a hate brewing that matches the teaching, need to get back at the beatings you got, need to get back at the people you think have harmed you or are out to get you, and it's just easy, but I got out before it was too late. Decided I won't spend the rest of my life looking over my shoulder. Always look forward, look danger in the eye, draw my life from it."

"That's why I'm making you this offer. You're the one I can trust. I think we're going to be friends. If you like, talk it over with your mother. That's okay." Sidney Ackerley prided himself on knowing how to close a deal and he had played one of his trump cards.

Matt stood toe to toe with his host, knew exactly what his mother would say, knew he had no choice, stared at this old Jew who had suddenly become his benefactor. He thought he should run, speed away, and go back to New Jersey. The sterile nature of the room swelled around him, the trees beyond the parking lot swayed in the rhythm of an aqua show chorus, the soundproof room seemed like a hushed audience waiting for a decision.

He thought of Hawk screaming on the mountain, "Decide, decide, decide." Matt knew that his mother would be silent and that stillness rolled over him. He knew the power that had just been thrust at him from this man who lived among people hostile to his faith, lived in a place where German submarines once landed men who would have killed him, a place that hosted a training camp for Nazi sympathizers before and during WW2, a place where rampant bigotry was buried under the mask of respectability.

He knew this place was stolen by English, Spanish, and Portuguese scavengers when high tech was cannons and muskets over axes and knives. It is still a place where being a Native American, an Indian, is considered a show thing for the respectable old families whose ancestors had commingled blacks and Indian slaves in common work houses, allowed them to smoke self grown drugs so they would not revolt or run away from farms close to the reservation where they now allowed them to sell tax free cigarettes.

He knew the decision had been made long ago. This old Jew, this friend of his uncle, had presented a non-decision. It was destiny.

Sidney Ackerley covered their clasped hands. "Deal. And I know you're a Donovan but have taken the old Steele name. I know about all that so you should know something about me. The name Ackerley was convenient when I settled here. Name was Ackerman, but business people did not like to accept anyone with that kind of name so it became Ackerley. That way I win at their game." He twirled a pencil between his thumb and forefinger.

32

The Old Building

Tern Harbor Rail Road Station was the same as it had been when Gloria had attempted her escape. Commuters' cars were in the same places, marked with the same annual parking stickers; commuters were waiting for the same trains, some were talking to friends with whom they have spent hours on the 7:04 or 8:22; some were holding white capped coffee containers carried from the muffin shop that had been in the same place as long as anyone could remember; new commuters replaced those who had occupied the same window or aisle seats until they retired. Women, dressed in neat pants suits, carried briefcases denoting a higher rank than secretaries arriving by subway from Queens or Brooklyn. Athletic types locked bicycles to the racks provided courtesy of the Tern Harbor Cyclery that had grown from the small Main Street shop to occupy a two story building near the *Journal* office. Seasons, weeks, times of day could be identified without looking at a calendar or clock but simply checking the number of cars in the station parking lot.

Store front decorations are drawn from the same pallet each year. Colors reflected appropriate holidays, street light poles had proper flags, holiday parades started at the same time with the same order of March. Everything was the same. Tern Harbor Day format was easy to organize; it had the same staff, the same type of vendors and contests, the weather was always perfect, Steve Palmer and Butch Moulder had always been in charge. Only one thing that had changed, Gloria Palmer had replaced Steve Palmer.

Tern Harbor resembled a town built around toy trains that could be changed by the child playing with the setup, but limited by the village pieces that came in the box of toys. Gloria thought of her father playing with those toys, controlling their every position, setting them up according to his will, and she thought of her days with the Palmieris in Brooklyn and her building the newspaper and organizing the town in Forge Creek. She wondered if she had become one more of her father's toys, extending his train set, and then finding a way to wreck it, to call back one of his toys, and she was afraid of becoming a willing part of his game. She imagined seeing everything through a spinning kaleidoscope. The *Tern Harbor Journal* started as the center, then crystalized, was replaced by the Palmieri Restaurant, colorful images of Belle's Tavern and the Band Stands in Tern Harbor and New Jersey. Jack Greeley was pointing to headlines in the newspaper, Sally Bastone was commanding waitresses and watching carefully if anyone got too close to Billy, Butch Moulder was pinching any blonde who got too close, and her father's wheelchair would move to the center obliterating the town in which she was now identified as the "Boss."

Belle was chattering while cleaning the bar and refilling a beer mug. The *New York Times* was running a feature about Brooklyn's growing art colony and the in-eateries. Top rating had gone to the old time Italian keepsake, *Palmieri's*. A picture of Gis Palmieri, his wife and twins covered a four column description of the restaurant history and menus.

"Think I'll have this page made into a poster and mounted in my father's room." She winked at Belle.

"The old fart still up to his gurgling tricks? I heard he was going to put in an appearance at Tern Harbor Day. Moulder's been gloating. Says he talks with him all the time and is promoting the idea to get a big turnout in Steve's honor."

"In a monkey's behind. He does visit with Dad, but I'd hardly call it conversation. Can't imagine what Butch ever expects to get from him. Matter of fact, never thought he ever did anything without expecting something in return. Maybe that's why he pinches all those backsides." They both laughed. "Ever pinch you, Belle?"

Belle stopped laughing, poured another glass of beer and slid it across to Gloria. "In a monkey's ass. He'd of lost those fingers and the stump would be stuck up his."

Gloria counted on Belle for a good laugh, salty language, and a place to hide before going home.

"Hey Gloria," Belle became serious. "I hear that you sometimes have interns up to the house. Old man ever see them there?"

"I make sure he does. Sometimes I make sure he sees the kid who delivers clams on Friday, or the gardeners when they are working without their shirts on. I have that pretty Spanish girl come in to clean every few weeks. He still has therapy, which means a massage from that handsome gay guy. But you know, Belle," Gloria drank the last of the frosted jug. "Sometimes I think I should cut it out. It's time, don't you think? Maybe he's suffering enough just being stuck in that damned chair, still thinking about the past, with nothing going on in his life except when Butch Moulder comes to visit."

"Gloria. Sally is worried about Billy. Thought you could talk to him, or to her. She'd listen to you. She knows how good you have been to everyone around here since Steve's stroke. She'd listen to you."

———◆———

Gloria walked into the diner kitchen, put her finger over her lips to stop Sally Bastone's endless barrage of orders and commands. Sally had been waiting for this moment when she would confront Steve Palmer's daughter, chat with her, or plead with her for help.

Gloria was uncertain, at first, how to begin. Her talk with Belle had been unsettling. For the first time, she was uncertain about who she really was. She was not Gloria Palmieri, the young woman who had grown into woman-hood at the restaurant in Brooklyn, the woman who had taken control of the newspapers and real estate when her Uncle Benito decided to leave New Jersey forever, the woman who had dreamed of a card of conquests like her cousin in Brooklyn kept before he was married. She was Gloria Palmer, daughter of Steve Palmer. She had been Steve Palmer's daughter when she attracted friends at ballet school, or in academic classes in school, or when she was at Tern Harbor Day carnivals.

"Sally," she said. "Understand you have some sort of a problem, about Billy." She was on her way now to do something she never could have done before, something her father would never have done. She was going to try to help someone who had nothing to give back.

Sally Bastone told her landlord's daughter the thing she had never shared before. She told her about Steve Palmer's monthly visits, about his attempt to collect rents any way he could and the fear he instilled into Billy. She told Gloria how he had supplied the athletic equipment, how he had watched Billy work out, how she had made sure she was close by so that Steve Palmer could not put his hands on Billy. She told Gloria about the one time she was late and found Steve Palmer standing over Billy, helping him with the weights and then rolling his hand across Billy's stomach. She told Gloria how she had picked up a chair and tossed it at her landlord. She cried as she told Gloria that her Steve Palmer would go after any person who would give him what he wanted, "anyone. Billy, clammer, blonde, buxom blonde, or flat-chested brunette, one of the young cops, anyone." She had never told anyone about how Billy was terrified at the beginning of the month, like a woman's anxiety waiting for her period, and even how he was terrified at the idea of being close to Steve Palmer. Sally turned to Gloria and told her how she thought Billy needed to get away from Tern Harbor, but close enough so he would feel safe. Sally thought it might be good if Billy could open a small diner somewhere quiet, somewhere he could begin to earn his own way. Then she stopped talking and the two women cried.

———•———

Gloria changed the meeting place for Tuesday, drove to Sound Beach, sat at the Sound Beach Restaurant bar until Matt stepped up beside her, put his arm around her and they moved to a table overlooking Long Island Sound. A gull floating on the water, rose up slightly above the glistening surf and dove after its prey. Matt told her that he had purchased another newspaper, had set the fifteen newspapers into two groups, and would soon be establishing a third regional group. He told her about how his cousin Harry had brought together key members of the Native families and they had formed a private bank and told her about the old properties he had in Orient.

She told him about Sally's son.

"I need someone to take over the renovation of an old building before it collapses. You think Billy Bastone could do that. He could live there, set up a café, and that would be really cool."

They had lunch, drove to Orient, and made love in the old building that would become Billy's Café.

33

Devil Woman

Steve Palmer propelled the wheelchair away from the cold fireplace when Gloria came home late on Tuesday night. It was as if he had been waiting for a teenage daughter to arrive late from a date.

The accentuated sensation that she was his controlled daughter, that everything had been handed to her, everything had come easy because she was his property. She was the prisoner of a silent guard, incapable of action, and she knew what she had always wanted, his love. She wanted to hit him with his "damned rifle" when she thought of his love, a love that had always been denied.

"Why," she whispered. "Why did you always go outside, why never here, never give us your love?" She did not expect an answer or reaction. "Why did you always interfere when I found my own way?"

He turned toward her, his head lowered, his eyes narrowed, trying to sear through her. He raised his hand and pointed his shaking finger at her. He pushed it forward, again and again, formed a fist and pounded his chest. "Mine," he blurted. "Mine."

He pushed the chair violently toward the piano, swept his arm as far as he could reach and knocked over the family pictures. He turned back to Gloria and with venom spewing from his lips, pointed his finger at her, pounded his chest, and coughed, "Mine." He rolled back to the window, leaned his forearm on the windowsill, his chin on the other hand and stared, in catatonic state, at the harbor entry. He watched the reflected image of Amanda entering the room, fixing the pictures of the piano, whispering to Gloria and then leaving.

Gloria spoke softly, told him she would be going out early in the morning but that Amanda would be there to help him.

No, he nodded. "No! No leave," he seemed to be pleading.

"I have to be free of you for a few days," she shouted. "What you going to do," she taunted. "What if I have a baby?"

He pointed his thumb and two fingers at her and seemed to be firing a gun.

Gloria felt an emptiness she did not remember. All she ever wanted, she thought was his love, and now all she wants is to be free of her jailer.

"No leave," he mumbled.

"Amanda will be here." Gloria dimmed the lamp lights.

Gliding terns screeched near the small island beyond the harbor. A flat boat floated at anchor while the young clammer surfaced to breath, returned to his digging in the shallow sand, came up again, and dropped a handful of clams onto the boat. He scrambled aboard, yanked at the motor, and moved into the night.

Steve Palmer reached for the mounted spy glass with which he had once watched Gloria and Conrad, searched the bay, tried in vain to find the small boat, turned toward the red buoy, target rock, and the steep cliff. He scrutinized the harbor entrance as if he were a sentry on watch for approaching enemies; he stiffened when he saw a woman's face mirrored beyond the dark window.

"Devil woman," his breath fogged the window pane.

34

Sidney Ackerley

Sidney Ackerley's stark white boat, *The Osprey*, slipped quietly past the entrance to Gardiner's Bay, rounded Orient Point, then picked up speed moving through Long Island Sound toward fishing grounds off the coast of Rhode Island. Ackerley invited Matt to join him for a day of fishing and to discuss business. Tufted leather seats, arm rests fitted with beverage holders, swiveled to allow the fishermen easy mobility.

"Doing a good job with the newspapers, Matt. Thanks for being so prompt with payments on the notes. Heard you've been doing quite a job putting together that private bank." Ackerley was busy casting his baited line.

Matt flipped his sun glasses down from his forehead to cut the sun glare and hide his occasional sideways glance at his host, thanked Sidney Ackerley for advice on how to leverage increasing property values so he could invest in more small town papers along the North Shore. Together with his cousin Harry, he had been successful in gathering the regional families that had Indian blood and molding them into a powerful economic force. He used his natural powers of persuasion to convince them that it was to their advantage to remember who they are, to come to the annual meetings and campfires, and to form the private bank from which any of them might borrow for worthwhile investments. He impressed on them that an individual's growing wealth was not as important as the effort to revitalize the communal sense that had been stolen from them. He reminded them of Old Tom's intonation which would become their silent motto, "Beat them at their own game."

They all agreed that no one was going to give them anything for nothing. They joined in a pact to reestablish themselves privately as a true Nation within a Nation. They became an efficient, functioning amalgam and were buying land with money borrowed from their own bank.

Matt found it hard to believe the success he was having with the newspapers and was afraid that he would wake up and find himself back in a jail cell in New Jersey, waiting for a sheriff to smack him with a night stick.

He did not answer Sidney Ackerley, laid his fishing pole on the deck, opened a bottle of beer, and steadied himself against cavorting swells that jiggled the slow moving vessel. Lines of light and darkness blended the Sound into a sweet tableau that seemed unaware of dragons that might be lurking, buried in the sand below a turbulent eddy. Matt pulled in his line, avoided the possibility of snagging an unwanted canvas package, more comfortable with the wind than with this part of the Sound.

"This is quite a boat you have Sid. Don't think I've been on one of these before. Did I ever say thanks for all you have done for me? Well, thanks. This is a far cry from the old boat my Mom has at her place. Never been used; don't know why she keeps it. Old time thing."

"Used once that I know of," Sidney Ackerley cast his baited line.

Matt suspected that Sidney might know about his father. He had a glancing picture of the gray day George and he were on that old wooden boat with the package they dropped into the Sound. "Never saw it used, Sidney!" Matt was emphatic.

"I knew your Mom as a little girl and as a lovely young princess. Knew young people and the old ones and I handled a lot of paper work for people around here back then, even your Mom's folks. You know about your mother's house, don't you?"

Sidney, conscious of Matt watching him, talked as if he was alone.

"Yes, she inherited it," Matt didn't know where Sidney was going with this.

"Well," Sidney continued. "Amanda's mother and father were pure blooded Indians, imagine that, pure. Entire line never mixed with any other, never wandered from their ancestral roots. When they died, she inherited that log house. Not just the house but all the land, you know, from the end of the bay, along the ridge to the Sound, and the other way through the wooded area along the main Road to the beach along the Old Indian Path. All in all close to fifty acres, that's a lot of waterfront property my lad."

Matt was growing restless, waiting for the shoe to drop.

"Imagine that, she grew her own vegetables, all the time she worked for other people. Never wanted to sell any of the land, could have made out pretty good too. Always seemed to have enough to keep herself going and kept pretty much to herself. Those days fishermen worked pretty much on their own, would go out drop their nets, and scoop up the fish that might be running. Most of them were a bunch of boozers. One of them just showed up one day. Had his own wooden boat, people used to say he just dropped from the sky. Well he didn't."

"Where's this heading, Sidney."

"Amanda met this fisherman. He was as hard a worker as she was. Name was Peter Eagle, yes. One of the boys who had been born here and finally came back. He was as independent as the rest, would do clamming when fish weren't running, and got to be known by most people as the quiet guy who didn't put up with any, pardon my talk here, didn't put up with any crap."

"Well this lovely woman fell in love with this handsome young fisherman Peter Eagle, this Native American kid.

"Hold the phone, Sid. You're making this up. Mom married my Dad and he was no friggin eagle, no damned hard worker, and big a drunk as anyone around."

"She fell in love with Peter Eagle and they were going to be married. He was as independent as he was strong. And that's when things started to go wrong. The Corporate fleets started pushing their way in and Pete got into a fight with them over where he could drop his nets. Got into trouble with the big corporate boys and one day his floundering boat washed up onto the shore. Amanda found him, his throat cut and her name written with his own blood on the side of the boat."

Matt felt a tingling in his legs, wanted to go below to use the bathroom but didn't think he could move without stumbling. He began to wonder why

Sidney Ackerley had really asked him on this trip.

"She was real upset, had no one to turn to. I told you I knew a lot about that boat. Well, you see, Amanda needed someone to help her with her parent's estate when she inherited it and figured I could keep my mouth shut. When she stood there at the Eagle kid's funeral, I could see she was suffering, I held her hand, she looked at me and I knew."

Pain lashed at Matt's belly as if he had been hit by a random bullet, or clubbed by police on horseback in Tompkins Square, or strung up in North Carolina. Fear, which had always been his ally, turned against him and he remembered the days when his father would beat him for crying.

"She couldn't tell any of the relatives about her condition and then by some stroke of bad luck she met Donovan at the pub where she was working. Didn't take him long to find out she owned all that property so he made a play for her. She decided to marry him and hide from everyone that she was carrying Peter Eagle's child. I was never invited to the wedding. He didn't want a, well didn't want a Jew there."

Matt watched the quiet water glistening in the hot sunlight. He felt a tug at the line that was bobbing off the starboard, pulled in a sand shark and threw it back.

"Why," he screamed. "Why didn't I know? Why didn't she ever tell me? Who else knows?" Tears streaking along his cheeks, he rushed at Sidney Ackerley who was standing against the polished cabin door. "Who else knows?"

"No one."

"Then how do you . . . ?"

"Because I helped her when her parents died. Helped settle the estate so she didn't get screwed. Like I said I held her hand when they buried that poor Eagle kid and looking at her, I just knew. Never told anyone, until now. I promised to keep the secret."

"Then why now, why tell me now?" Matt still had Sidney Ackerley pinned to the door.

"Because she wanted me to. Do you think I would have broken my promise to her? You can let go now."

Matt released Sidney, and felt his shoulders and body relax. He leaned over the side of the boat and threw up.

They tied up at the private dock, and drove to Billy's Café. "You did a great job with this old building, turning it into that café. Has become real popular place." Sidney Ackerley tried to change the subject.

"Kid did it mostly himself. I just gave him a helping hand, a favor for a friend of mine, you know how that goes!" Matt turned to Sidney. "Thanks Sidney for helping my mom. Guess I owe you more than I knew. But why did she want me to know now?"

"What has she always said from the moment you were born? Think about it. Destiny! Think about it."

Matt gunned the motor of the white convertible and headed for Tern Harbor. When his mother answered his light tapping at her door, he embraced her, tears rinsed their cheeks, they sat quietly in the dimly lit kitchen, he held her hands as they looked into each other's eyes. Then he took a handful of cookies and left. He parked near the beach, looked up at the Palmer house, saw light gleaming on a rock jutting out from the hillside, and listened to the bell on the red buoy. He tossed the last of his mother's cookies into the air where it was caught by a tern in flight.

35

Amanda

Steady moaning and thumping, like shudders battered during a storm, brought Gloria rushing to her father's room. Her pale yellow pajamas cast a ghostly image in the curved hall mirror. Steve Palmer had tossed his pillows to the floor, was trying to grasp the spindles of the walnut headboard, but only succeeded in rocking the bed against the wall. He pulled in deep breaths, gasped rapidly, and then repeated his desperate motions.

Amanda swooped into the room; the two women wrapped the hallucinating man in their arms, pulled his quivering body from his invisible target, replaced the pillows, and tended to their patient. Amanda brought a damp cloth and towel from the bathroom; Gloria washed his sweat drenched face, gently dried his head and neck, adjusted his enveloping covers, and then offered him a glass of ice water.

His breathing returned to its normal pattern. He raised his fingertips and moved them along his cheek and eyebrows. Long lost memories floated across his daydream. Young girls were with him for slow sensuous days; they massaged his face and body. He opened his eyes and saw the two women who could not satisfy his reverie, one his daughter, the other a sentry planted by his wife to record his every deed, as if she would someday reaffirm his own father's judgment.

He called out in garbled tones, as if to warn that someone was there. He reached for Gloria as if someone was trying to take her away.

"No Dad. No one coming," Gloria held his hand. She was sure that her father was beginning to remember old things and imagine new ones, waited until he was asleep, leaned forward, kissed his cool forehead, dimmed the lamp light, and left the room.

Amanda prepared two cups of coffee and pushed a plate of cookies toward Gloria.

"He did hear someone tapping. My son was very quiet but he must have heard him."

"He thinks any man he doesn't know is out to steal me away. I think he's really losing it, hardly sleeps, wants to watch out that damned window all the time. Thank God he can't get at those bullets. He'd probably shoot his toe off."

"You know Gloria, he knows how much he missed when you were young. He just didn't know how to love you."

Gloria dunked a cookie into her coffee, then dropped it into the cup. In one moment she thought of his women in the boat house, his nights of gambling, his attempts to keep and control her. She began to think of him as a sad, tired old man who had missed the mark in his life, had filled himself with things, with all the things that had vanished along with his youth, with the love he never had from his own father, Gloria's grandfather with a broad smile that engaged guests to his restaurant but spelled danger and terror to his eldest son. Suddenly, she felt the sympathy that had drawn her to kiss him and wanted to rock him so he could feel safe.

Gloria felt the same overwhelming loneliness since her mother's death. She looked up at the woman who had protected and nurtured her and wondered how Amanda had spent so much time in Tern Harbor, away from her own son. Gloria wished it was Tuesday night and she could be held close by this woman's son.

"I know about my father, Amanda. I missed his love back then, lost my teen years, lost my early twenties, kept blaming him."

Amanda started closing windows. The first trickling rain drops smacked against the screens like frantic June bugs.

"We're in for a heavy storm, Gloria. Going to rain for a few days."

"Amanda, I have to stay here with him, but it feels like a prison. I do all the things I should, take care of the business, the real estate, everything like that and do a damn good job. I fulfill my social responsibilities, joined the men's tribe – you know Kiwanis, watch over the Tern Harbor Day, do it all. But all I ever dream about, ever want is to be free. Now I've learned to love that sick old pirate and that keeps me here, keeps me from being free. You could leave, could have left anytime. So why...?" She hesitated. "Why didn't you spend more time with your son?"

Amanda pulled back, unwilling to discuss her need to stay at this house, with this family, away from her growing son.

"Freedom's not always what it's cracked up to be, not always a choice," Amanda spoke softly. "Sometimes it comes with the wind, sometimes, with love, sometimes in mysterious ways, and sometimes it doesn't come. Now eat one of those cookies without drowning it."

They shuddered at the approaching storm. Gloria started up the stairs. "You know, Amanda, I feel tremendous freedom on Tuesday nights."

"Be careful about too much freedom," Amanda disappeared into her private part of the house.

———

Ghosts lingered in the hallways of Amanda's memory.

She had been challenged with a simple question, why! She had heard that word, freedom, as if it was a fragile cup that could simply be replaced if broken. She knew why, and she understood freedom.

How can one have freedom, she thought, when one has to find a way to survive, to eat, to feed a child, to protect a child, to live with everything taken away. Her father and mother had died when she was young. She had to take care of the land that had come from old Tom Steelehart. She was silent and alone. Missing years melted away as she thought about her log house.

She remembered the beautiful young man with whom she fell in love. She waited to see his fishing boat pass the bay, waited for him, waited on the beach, and dreamed of the day they would be married.

She was on the beach lighting a beacon fire, watching the sky for ominous signs of storms, then had returned to the house to wait for Peter Eagle. He would sail past the cove, haul the day's catch to the wholesaler, clean his boat, and then walk along the beach to meet Amanda. She waited, put more wood on the beacon light, then left the door open, and fell asleep.

At daybreak, she found the boat drifting in the bay. She ran through the water, swam to the boat, climbed aboard and saw the blood scrawled name, Amanda. When they found his body, she kneeled next to him, cradled him on her lap, and cried ancestral sounds she had never heard.

Amanda's goblins rattled her windows, tested the doorway, and chattered with the rain soaked trees. Only minutes ago, she had been working as a team with Gloria, holding Steve Palmer, and bringing him back into the present. Amanda repeated why, why, why.

She could have opened her secrets, could have told the true stories after the old men told myths around the campfires. She certainly could have made them stop and listen.

None of the relatives' children were allowed to come to the birthday party for her one year old son, Matthew Xavier Steelehart Donovan in July 1968. Amanda's relatives were cautious about being close to Donovan, afraid of his alcoholic tirades, unwilling to look at her darkened eyes that they knew were caused by beatings, afraid one of them would put a knife into him, and make their cousin into a widow.

He tormented her for having this child who could not be his, refused to renounce the boy, afraid it would deny his manhood. Donovan would disappear for days, then weeks at a time; the yellow truck would crash over the dirt road to the clearing and he would collapse onto the bed, sleeping for days. When awake, he would wrap his belt around his fist and slam it into Matt. He swore he would make the boy into a man, not let him be "one of them pussy Indians who hang around, not be one of them fairies who can't handle a football or a good fight, make everyone think he is as good as me."

Amanda taught Matt the ways of her people, ingrained the love of nature, infected him with her love, and while he slept, whispered about his destiny. They became spiritually one.

Donovan forced Matt to fight by beating him, taunting him until he fought back, whipped Amanda until Matt stood between them and took the whippings intended for his mother. Donovan laughed and then grew increasingly angry. He started to beat Matt instead of Amanda when she was away working; forced Matt to play football and become a star on his high school team, reserved the right to inflict pain, taught Matt to withhold tears, taught him to initiate fear. He would not tolerate anyone injuring his son on the field without having Matt retaliate. When the coach instructed one of the players to spear Matt in the back, jam his helmet into the small of Matt's back, causing the cracking sound that drove the boy to the ground. Donovan charged onto the field in his alcoholic fury; he crashed into the coach, slammed the man's head against a cinder block, stood over his bloody body, and roared with laughter. He dragged his son home, tied him to a post and whipped him for crying.

In the silence of her Tern Harbor bedroom, Amanda grimaced as she recalled the weeks away from home, away from her son and husband. She had convinced herself that Donovan would not be so angry and would stop beating her son, if she was not around.

"Why?" she cried out. "How can she ask me why? She talks of freedom, that's all she wants is freedom. Oh what a word, oh what a desire, to be free."

"To be free," she spoke to her image in the window. "To be free, my son had to become strong, had to know the ways of nature, had to be able to set things right, had to become the brave natural leader that he was born to be. He had to learn to be good, but how could he be good without knowing the face of evil. We both knew the face of evil there in that log house. My son had to sit in the back circle of the campfires, listen to old men talk of evil spirits turned into rocks that remained in enduring anguish. He would hear about moveable winds and seas washing across the land bringing new life, protecting nature's wonders, allowing us to wander forever free.

He had to learn that freedom is born when we can endure and overcome the torture and awful things created by evil. Those things will be covered over by nature, but how would my son know what is good if he never looked into the face of wickedness?

"Why? Gloria asked me. "Because he could have no freedom without fulfilling his destiny, what he was born to do for his people. Freedom, oh freedom."

Amanda fell asleep dreaming about her name written in blood on the side of a boat, and dreaming of her son who had confronted demons until this young woman had rescued him and led him home. She dreamed of her son reaching for the sky. She dreamed of freedom.

36

Marking Time

Thumb nail scratches along the arm of Steven Palmer's chair resembled marks on a prison wall. Slivers of time, separated by his organized mind, began to congeal like enchanted snow crystals forming into an ice block. His images, once clear, began to conspire with hideous characters, as if they would review his actions in suspended time.

Steve Palmer wondered how long it might be before he would have no relevance to current time, when he would not recognize his daughter, Amanda, Butch Moulder, or the beauty of Tern Harbor that he had carved out of his misbegotten inheritance. He tracked time by scratching the chair; recognized time of day by the food that was brought to him, the daily functions performed on his body and the disgusting help with bodily functions. He recognized days by their regularly scheduled visitations. Monday and Wednesday were therapist's mornings, Thursday lunch was Butch Moulder, summer and autumn Sunday afternoons were reserved for regattas, Tuesday was Gloria's day to work late, and Wednesday morning she made a final check of the weekly edition.

He dreaded stormy evenings when the harbor would be empty, fishing boats would have returned early, and he had trouble spotting the flat bottom clam boats. He watched them carefully, holding up his binoculars to look for the clammer who he heard leaving early in the morning, and who he suspected was hiding in the bay tormenting him.

He did not remember the night's activity, his attempt to get to an open window, his dream of aiming a rifle out the window, or the two women who chased away his nightmare.

Butch Moulder opened a bottle of Coca Cola for Steve Palmer's lunch. He gossiped about Village politics as if Steve had met the new cast of politicians, spoke kindly about Gloria and her contributions to the coming Tern Harbor Day Festival, mentioned the upcoming elections, and then dropped in the word that he was being considered as the Republican candidate for Congress. It was all part of the same patter but he noticed Steve Palmer jolt back at the announcement. "Wish you were around and about, Stevie, out there to lend a hand, even write a check. Was sort of hoping you could give Gloria the nod to help, you know to have a congressman," he winked.

"Hmmm. Hmmmm." Steve Palmer twitched his lips sideways into a rare attempt at smiling. Butch had given him a knobby walking stick capped with a silver handle. He tapped Butch with the stick and waved it at a black lacquer box on the mantle. Butch opened the box and saw bullets for the shotgun that had become adjunct to the wheel chair. He understood that his friend wanted to load the gun, but was unsure of his purpose, and closed the box without bringing out the shells.

"Ru-u-u-n," rasped Steve, more of a question than a statement and angrily waved the stick toward the box.

"Next time," Butch used the technique that had kept him in office for so long.

Steve turned angrily toward the window signaling their lunch date was over. He waited for the door to close and the car to leave the parking lot. Amanda cleared the trays, adjusted the blanket that kept his feet warm, and left the house to walk along the beach. He moved the chair toward the fireplace, maneuvered the box to the edge of the mantle, and tried to pull it onto his lap. The box tumbled to the floor, the chair fell over and Steve was sprawled in front of the andirons. He scratched his way toward the contents of the box which was spewed onto the carpet, was about to grasp the bullets when Amanda came into the room. She reset the chair, lifted Steve onto it, adjusted the blanket, and moved him back to his earlier position. She repacked the lacquer box, fit it into her pocket, and left the room. He resumed his sentry position; his eyes scanned the harbor, his hand clenched tight around the single bullet he had salvaged.

He dozed, imagined he was looking through the spy glass at a young clammer skimming flat stones across the water, imagined he saw his daughter Gloria who had grown into the woman who now controlled his town, he imagined they were looking up laughing at him, he imagined his father, wearing his white suit and hat and showing that wide, toothy, terrifying smile, was standing with them. He imagined he could aim his gun and with a single shot eliminate two men and then swoop down on a rope and bring Gloria to safety. Low rumbling thunder woke him. He looked down at the empty beach, glanced furtively between the red and green buoys, then at the harbor entrance searching for late returning clam boats.

<hr />

Gloria brewed the first pot of coffee before anyone else arrived in the office, signed the few letters that had been left on her desk, wrote checks, and left a "well done" note for Tom Greeley. She was on the 6:10 A.M. train to New York, made arrangements to meet her aunt Marie at the new Dolores Delgaddo Spa, "Deedee's" the popular name, where she would have a massage, have her hair and nails done, and look at the latest fashions before lunch. They wandered through the Whitney Museum, the walked to the Plaza for high tea.

"Okay, Gloria, what's up? Why the sudden rush to relax?" Marie checked the clasp of her bracelet.

"Just needed a fun day away from that place. Began to think I really like it and," she hesitated. "And him."

"You're being brain washed. Must be something you ate."

"No Marie. It just seems that the more I take care of the place, the newspaper, and really him, the more accustomed to it I become, and it's frightening."

"Better get a guy. I'll have to fix you up with a nice Italian boy. Shame that one who used to work in the fish market left, didn't turn out. I saw him once. Good looker, but must have been something wrong. Alphonse never talks about it, so who knows. We'll find one."

"That's okay, Marie. I can find my own. Your guys all seem to have score cards." They both laughed.

"You have one, don't you? I can see it in your eyes." Marie held Gloria's hand. "When do we meet him? God I hope he's not one of those Orthodox Jews or a Southern Baptist."

"None of the above, Marie." She tried to change the subject. "You know Dad's in that wheel chair and once he tried to get down the ramp by himself. He thought it was a lot of fun when he almost crashed over the side. I had the whole ramp system changed. It goes down a little at a time, comes to a deck, and then goes down a little more. No quick runs anymore and it makes it easier for anyone moving him. I checked it this morning and they're almost finished building it."

Marie pretended to be interested. "You should really take a trip, love. Maybe we can go on a cruise or maybe go to Italy. Can meet some good guy there."

"Yeah, but they'll either have score cards or wind up in a seminary."

The Long Island Railroad left Pennsylvania Station through the tunnel under Manhattan and the East River and emerged on the Queens side. It was greeted by darkening clouds, thunder, and lightning. Drenching rain swallowed the streets as the train sped past the local stops to Hicksville and then moved on to Tern Harbor. Gloria raced to her car, found the parking ticket on the windshield. "Damn," she thought. "Forgot to get one of those daily parking stickers." She drove to the empty newspaper office, made a pot of coffee, left a message on the answering machine that she would have dinner in town, and that she would get some more work done.

37

Bill Robbins

Matt started the day with his regular run along the beach, swam in the choppy Sound, and checked the wind for sailing weather. He drove along the Main Road through the small villages to the new Riverhead office. His uncle George worked together with his cousin Harry to administer the combination of the real estate and media corporation.

"Hey Harry," he called as he ran up the stairs to his office. "Anyone coming in to suck up, today?"

"No, someone here to see you. I think you should see him. The guy's getting to be important and, well he has a big following, commands a lot of votes, and well . . . I think you should see him."

"You sound funny about it Harry. Should I hide when he gets here? Do we owe him money? Is he Mafia?"

"No. Some one, uh, you know."

"Okay. Enough of the guessing game."

"Robins. Bill Robins."

Matt stopped. Ran the letter opener across his desk, made the invisible letter N, and looked at his cousin. "When? Why?"

"Why, first? He's director of some program in the High School and wanted to get you as a speaker. Thought it better to let you make that decision. And he's been waiting for about half an hour."

"Well get him in here. Does he remember me?" Matt tapped his desk.

Harry shrugged, "What do you think?"

Bill Robins looked very different from the man who had been walking in the woods with his German shepherd dog. A suit and tie exaggerated his height and build. He extended his hand across the desk as if to take possession of the moment.

Matt walked out from behind the desk, took the extended hand. They stood silent for a few minutes. "Welcome home Matt. Meant to get up here before this, but wasn't sure if I would be, you know, welcome." Bill smiled.

"Saw you down at the beach with your dog. I think you guys owe Harry a pair of pants."

"Well, let's call it even then." Bill Robins rubbed his covered forearm.

"How's your mom?" Matt attempted a smile.

"Still cleaning other people's houses. Your mother still working for old man Palmer?"

Matt thought of the Afro-American woman who had tossed a pail of water at him in the alley near Tompkins Square Park,. "Yeah! She's still there."

He imagined his mother sitting across the table from Gloria, gossiping about the weather, fussing about the quality of vegetables from the market, waiting to hear complaints from Steve Palmer, and both sharing secrets about him, secrets about how he was born, secrets about the tattoos he had burned onto his body as a skinhead and was now having covered with expansive tattoos depicting ancient Greek mythology. His mother had her secrets, Gloria had hers, and he had his.

"Yeah! She's still there."

They faced each other as if each was in an isolation chamber, waiting for the question that would bring them instant wealth or sudden defeat.

"Understand you work with kids. That's great. Teach journalism or something like that?"

"No Matt. Nothing like that. I work with kids who are about to drop out, kids who think they're tough. Think they know it all and can make it without finishing school, without learning something. Some are ripe for gangs. Some may be trying to form their own. My job is to try to get their heads screwed on straight." He walked closer, stared into his eyes, and put his hand on Matt's shoulder. "That's why I'm here. Want you to come talk to them, maybe act as a mentor for one or two."

"Do you know what you're asking of me? Not sure I could do that."

"Matt. You were tough those last few years in school, left here and became somebody. Look at what you have now. Must be something you can teach these kids, someway you can help them."

"Billy," Matt automatically used his friend's old name. "You really don't know what I did, why I left, what I became. Sit down. This is going to take a while."

As they sat facing each other, Matt pulled open his shirt and to expose his tattooed body. "See these, he pointed to the remaining Nazi symbols that identified him as a skinhead. The double eagle branded across his chest had been altered to hold an American flag on one side and Native-American head-dress on the other. A small swastika still sat in the middle of a black rose. The spider web, that adorned his elbow, was punctuated with huge teardrops each of which indicated an act of violence.

"That's what I became. See the rose, that's a black rose, the flower of death. Meant to really strike fear. Remember I knew how to do that, still do. Meant to inspire the poor suckers who bought into what I was selling."

Bill Robins sat on the edge of his chair, wasn't sure if he should stay or make a quick exit, rubbed the single scar that he knew was pulsating on his arm, and did not move.

"Was once a good guy," Matt continued. "Only thing I had to battle was Donovan. Only thing I had to put up with was him. Put up with his screaming about all the people who were taking stuff from him, taking jobs, the blacks, he called niggers, the Jews who were buying up property in the Hamptons and cheating him, he called them kikes. Had to listen to his rages, his hate, his pounding my back and learning to hate. But I didn't know what to hate until that one time when we, when I, when it happened. Slashed that letter onto your arm, had to keep watching my back so your friends wouldn't beat me. Then it happened. The meetings where they lectured us on hate gave direc-tion to my anger and they recognized me as a natural born leader. That's what

I became, Billy. When I left here, that's what I became until they were after my ass because of something I wouldn't do. Wouldn't do it because I remembered who I am, and what's inside just boiled up, and I discovered who I really am. All the Donovan screaming and beating can never change that." Matt felt the anger flushing through his system.

Bill Robins pulled his chair closer to Matt. "I should have come to you myself back then. But didn't know enough, didn't have anyone to talk to me. God, I feel guilty. What ever happened to your old man? He just seemed to vanish?"

"Don't know, don't care." Matt knew there were secrets too dark to discuss.

"Ever kill anyone?" Bill sat back in his chair.

"What a dumb question. Wouldn't be sitting here talking about it if I had, would I?"

They sat quietly assessing each other. Matt opened a desk drawer, withdrew and opened a pen knife, extended his forearm, and carved the letter I along the delicate skin that had been left void of any tattoos. A gentle trickle of blood clung to the new scar; he reached for Bill Robins's hand, slammed it against the oozing blood, and held it tight to stop the bleeding.

"There, now anyone can know who and what I am. They call you nigger, they can call me Injun. Now we are even."

Bill Robins held his friend's arm until the bleeding stopped then got up to leave.

"Billy," Matt whispered. "When do you want me there?"

38

Chris Verity

Anyone who lives in Tern Harbor for a few years recognizes threatening storms without watching the weather channel. It was an unusually dark evening for late summer. The screeching of children in the park, the familiar high pitched music from ice cream trucks, and the movement of tourists in and out of the antique shops were missing. Gloria welcomed the silence. She was able to sit back, have a cup of coffee, and plan the next issue of the newspaper. She plugged in a *Grateful Dead* CD and tried to read the *New York Times*.

She tried not to hear the insistent tapping at the front windows, gave up in frustration. Butch Moulder, dressed in white shorts, yellow sport shirt, and blue denim deck shoes was smiling in through the glass door.

"Getting rough out on the Sound," he wheezed. "Got the boat in and tied up, sent signals out for everyone to get in quick. You know there are some amateurs out there who probably think its fun to sit out this kind of storm. Just makes a lot of work for the Coast Guard."

"Yes, I know Butch," Gloria was distressed to listen to the obvious.

"Saw your Dad today. Had great visit. That's a terrific thing you did, changing that ramp around. I wanted to get him out and down to the hilltop where he likes to sit, but he wasn't up to it. Checked it out though, Terrific the way you can get right down to the patio, can see out from the hilltop. Best view around."

"Anything else Butch? I really am busy."

"Just going to dinner. Would you like to join me?"

"Thanks, Butch, but I'm sure Amanda will have prepared something."

He backed away from the doorway, said good night, and walked down the hill toward the bank ATM machine. Gloria watched as he punched all the keys and waited for his cash.

A gust of wind punched the bills from his hand and Butch stomped one foot on some of the money, dropped to his knees to trap the loose cash, and stretched forward to gather scattering bills. As he reached for the last twenty dollar bills, his shorts slipped below his hips revealing the bottom of his sun tanned back and the top of his pale backside. A voice called out his name; he turned and was shocked by the flashbulb explosion that indicated his picture was taken. The woman who had called sped away on a bicycle. He thought of expletives he rarely uttered, adjusted himself and his money and disappeared around the corner to his favorite restaurant.

Gloria wished she had taken that picture or had called to the woman to get a copy.

———•———

Chris Verity had been hung over when he left for work at 4 AM. He doused his head with cold water, moved into the deeper clam beds, pulled in his long rakes twice as fast as usual, filled the canvas bags, and disregarded storm warning flags and horns.

Circling rain pellets forced him to seek shelter in the old duck blind. He raised the motor, tossed the anchor into the shallow sand, and walked through the knee high water to the blind's protection. The anchor broke loose, Chris swam to catch the boat before it could float out toward the Sound, lowered the motor and struggled to get it started. He could see the thin line of sky far to the east and guessed that would be the last blue sky he would see for days. He climbed back onto the duck blind, tied the boat to one end of the old wooden structure, and leaned back to catch his breath.

He saw the sparkle of the brass spy glass that was often aimed in his direction from the house on the hill, but was surprised that it was swinging idly without the old man near it. Then there was something at the edge of the cliff, something resembling a huddled figure, something unworldly that he hadn't seen before. He could barely make out what looked like a wavering long broom handle, or a cane, and then he recognized the shape of a rifle. Thunder and lightning flashed like rock concert strobe lights. The figure holding the gun became a blur against the dark cliff and Chris thought he must have been mistaken. He set up the small lantern used for times when he spent nights on the boat. More strobe light effects captured Chris's attention as he heard the loud noise. "Hey that's not thunder," he said. He moved to get a view of where the sound came from and avoided the single shot that shattered the lantern.

Lightning crashed in front of the hilltop house and Chris saw the rifle bounce off the hill and into the choppy bay. He was sure he saw something like a ghost tumbling off the cliff, thought of the lady in the myth as the storm grew more violent; the wind and rain flooded his boat which clung to its tether; Chris crawled into the back end of the shelter, fell asleep until the criss-crossing of Coast Guard and Harbor Patrol lights in the bay woke him.

39

The Code

Autumn blinked into an early snowfall and frigid winter. Trees and shrubs, straining their sinews to support snow and ice, bowed toward the frozen waters along the harbor shore. Everything in Tern Harbor was unchanged. Shops were filled with weekend tourists, Christmas decorations were in place the day after Thanksgiving, and the Tern Harbor Day committee regular meetings were held in the Harbor Lounge. The Palmer family was again the official sponsor and the *Tern Harbor Journal* was printing articles about past winners of the festival's race.

Everything was the same, and everything was different. Steve Palmer was dead. Gloria had cleared the old furniture from her father's room, removed the sailboat racing painting from over the fireplace mantle leaving a dark rim where the frame had touched the wall, three holes needed filling where she had unbolted the brass spy glass from the windowsill, and the ramps which had been built to accommodate the wheel chair had been dismantled. She began to entrust the organization and editing of the newspaper to Jack Greeley and had completed working with the lawyers to settle her father's estate. Gloria was uncomfortable knowing that, as the sole heir, she was now a very rich woman and caged by responsibilities to the town, newspaper, and her father's life work. Occasional letters from Uncle Benito bridled her with envy. She wanted to despise Steve Palmer for being more of a jailer in his illness and death than he was when he was alive. She knew that it was easier to hate him when he was alive, than now that he was dead.

───

The Native American East End Association flourished, held annual meetings before the autumn campfires, placed interim decisions in the hands of the executive board with Matt Steele as presiding officer. He developed two media groups along the North Shore of Long Island, followed Sidney Ackerley's advice on snapping up papers that were near death and turning them into powerful influential tools sought after by local politicians. He controlled small business properties in each of the towns between Orient and Riverhead. The Association's private bank helped protect the environment through acquisition of the true wealth of the Nation within a Nation, land. Matt had convinced the families that those with a trace of Native blood would always be considered Indian; he repeated as a mantra that no one was ever going to return the land to them simply because they are of Native background. He rallied the families around the idea that they had to be totally self-reliant and that they must win their ancestral rights by playing the interlopers game. He had accomplished almost all he had set out to do, turned the leadership of the Association private bank over to his cousin Harry, moved his uncle George into management of the real estate, and spent much of his time building the media empire.

There was something left to do. He had been nurtured on his mother's repetition of the myth that the lovers had to be freed, that the wind would always find him, and that the fickle sea would call him until a night when great white clouds would come and he would know what he must do. He was wrapped in the mysticism that had ruled his mother's life. He waded into the Sound during the wildest storms, waiting for a revelation, stood on the beach waiting for the wind to whisper in his ear, or launch a sand storm against his body so that he could understand what it was that he must do. The wind had always protected him, shaped him so that he had no fear, and he waited for it to call his name.

"I've done everything," he shouted. "I brought the families back together. So what more?" He swam into the cold water, stood buffeted by the cold winter wind stinging his defiant wet body, stare up at the blackened sky illuminated by constellations, and waited for an answer.

Gloria crossed her ankles on the low table in front of the warm fireplace, sipped a cold beer, watched the television weather man reporting about a new snowstorm racing toward them, and then switched channels until she found an old movie. She reached for the telephone, tapped at familiar numbers, and waited for Matt to answer.

"Hey," he said.

"Hey. Watcha doin?" she snuggled into the couch.

"Just came in from climbing through the snow on the beach. Could use something hot to drink."

"Could use some company and need some help hanging a picture."

"I'll be there ASAP." The white convertible moved effortlessly along the well plowed highway and made record time to Tern Harbor.

"Did you have time to make a pot of coffee or did I get here too fast?" He shook fresh snowflakes from his hair.

"That's the saddest sight I've seen in a long time," he said, nodding at the missing painting's outline.

"Wait there, wise guy. You're going to help me hang another picture." She opened the cardboard box she had received from Sante Fe. The card from uncle Benito was very simple, *"Happy Birthday, glad you were able to unload all that stuff in New Jersey and get free, here's a birthday present I should have sent you. An old friend once allowed me to buy this and I know you will love it."*

She slit open the tape along the top and pulled out the simply framed oil painting. "There," she said "that ought to cover that mark" Then she looked carefully at the painting. It looked like a desert that was at once standing still and moving with the mountains in the background. Gloria thought she could float through the warmth of the desert sun and the coolness of the distant hills which were cast in snow mist. Neither Gloria nor Matt spoke.

"My God," she fingered the artist's signature. "It's an O'Keefe, an original

O'Keefe. I always thought of her flower paintings, forgot she lived in Sante Fe. What do you think, Matt. Isn't it beautiful?"

He lifted the painting over the mantle, stepped onto a chair, and felt the back for the wire hanger. He located the hook that was still on the wall, slipped the painting over it, and jumped backward off the chair.

"There," he said. "Did I hang it right side up?"

"Don't be funny. What do you think?"

"I was out there. Saw that desert, those mountains, the people who should have been there. Yes, she must have understood what the land should be. See, over that little rise, beyond the hill. See there's just a little bit of life still being pushed along?"

"Do you think she would have put me into that picture if I was there?" Gloria stood next to the mantle. "And if she did, what would she call this picture?"

"Probably *See the Tourist*," Matt fell back on the couch to avoid Gloria's shove.

"And if you were there, and she put you into the painting, I know you'd probably be that little thing behind the hill, what would she call the painting, or what would she call you?"

Matt cranked open the window and inhaled the cold night air that hovered over the Village silhouetted against a virginal snow blanket. He stared at lights reflected on icy trees, was alerted by two figures weaving along the dock toward the unstable-looking harbor master's shack, watched them break the lock and slide into the small room. He saw a flame shoot out the makeshift chimney.

Matt bolted out the door, raced his car engine, and sped along the slippery road to the dock. Gloria saw the flame sneaking along the outside wall and reaching the roof, called the fire department, and watched the white car scream to a stop within feet of the burning shack. He knocked snow from the top of a trash can and charged the blazing shack, repeated the action until the door fell open. He pulled a blanket from the trunk of his car and wrapped it around the two young men who had been huddling on the floor of the smoke filled shack.

Volunteer firemen followed the tire tracks on the dock, took charge of the gasping men, and tried to check Matt for injuries. He maneuvered through the blowing snow that had covered the blacktop road.

Gloria was waiting in the driveway with a plaid blanket and hot coffee. She wrapped the blanket around his shivering body, and commanded him to sit in front of the warming fireplace.

"What were those guys doing there? Did they get burned? How did you know the shack would give way when you charged it?" She was massaging his shoulders.

"Didn't know what would happen, figured those young guys might be hanging close to the floor. The fire was burning the roof and I just took a wild shot at it. Had to do something. Those guys were probably drinking beer or something like that. Think one was that clammer."

He became pensive. "I remember what it was like when I was a kid, fell into a deep hole and no one was there to pull me out. Felt like I was in that burning shack all the time. Just had to do it. Someone should get after them when they are doing better, keep them from falling away."

Matt listened to Gloria breathing behind him, turned, held her close, and felt her hands move along the outline of the tattoos on his back. She felt his cool hands circumnavigate each rib until he had pulled her close. They were buried in each other's necks, kneeling near the opened windows, and were aware of the idle snowflakes that were harbingers of drifts that would paralyze the sleeping village. They were unaware of the constant jangling of the harbor bell.

Low blue fireplace flames cast elusive shadows over the oil painting. Hidden truths were on the verge of emerging as the sand seemed to shift beyond the hills.

A nun on the Public Broadcasting channel was talking about art in the Louvre. Matt and Gloria, snuggled on the couch, were falling asleep in each other's arms.

Matt whispered onto Gloria's cheek. "She would call my name the wind."

"Who?" Gloria sighed as she fell asleep.

Matt didn't answer. He listened to the howling wind stampeding ice pellets against the side of the house, delivering a coded message. He committed the cadence to memory and fell asleep.

40

Four Directions of the Wind

Butch Moulder chose Tern Harbor Day to announce his entry into the primary for the vacant Congressional seat. He anticipated support of the Republican town leader, the regional Kiwanis clubs, and people he had befriended as the funeral director, and during his tenure as mayor. Certain that Gloria Palmer would help with a substantial check and endorsement from the *Journal*, he busied himself making the rounds of business organizations and preparing to make the announcement from the deck of his boat.

Gloria had spent the winter planning something else. Uncle Benito's gift painting and note had unleashed her boldest desires to be free. She decided to sell the newspaper and the properties, invest the proceeds so that she could travel, visit Benito, and at last be free of her Tern Harbor imprisonment. She turned to the one person who she could trust to maintain the properties free from further development, and whom she dreaded leaving behind.

That wintry storm had tapped its message to Matt and he understood it when Gloria unveiled her plan and offered him the package. He merged the newspaper with his regional group, asked Jack Greeley to assume general management of the group, and prepared to announce the merger with the Tern Harbor Day issue.

Jack Greeley received a package of photos taken of Butch Moulder at the ATM machine. The brief note with the photos suggested the mayor was caught in one of his best poses. Jack decided not to run these on the front pages of the papers but to allow one photo to be buried near the obituaries along with the continuation of the story announcing Moulder's run for office.

Butch Moulder was about to make his speech when he was shown the newspapers and knew his candidacy was done. He stared at the *Tern Harbor Journal* headline announcing the sale of the paper, saw the photo of the auburn haired person he recognized from Steve Palmer's funeral, moved toward the clam chowder contest, and put his arm around the blonde judge who was sampling the chowder. He didn't read the *Journal* article about the sale of the Palmer properties.

————

Chris Verity made an unusual Tuesday evening stop at the Palmer house and thanked Matt for having saved his life that night on the dock.

"I got some special stuff for you. I get real big chowder clams in a private place, off the old duck blind. Found it by accident. I had to fight off those damned birds. Was out there today and got a few whoppers. Friggin birds were so excited, I thought they were going to crap all over me and my boat. But I got what I wanted and thought I'd bring them up to you as a sort of thanks and welcome aboard." Chris refused any payment and left.

Gloria had called from Brooklyn said she was heading out to Sante Fe. "Can you come into town," she asked. "Dinner, maybe a show, maybe stay over?"

"Not tonight. Promised to do something here. How about tomorrow?"

"Promised Marie to go shopping."

He promised to call her so they could get together later in the week. He knew it was an empty promise, that he had to let her fly free, that he was bound to this place.

Matt placed a pot on the counter, started to open the large clams so his mother could make her clam chowder. He tried to slip the clam knife into the muscle of the largest clam but it would not budge. He poured fluid and clams from the opened shells into the pot.

He was about to toss the reluctant clam into the garbage when the regal blue sky, disguised by curtains of stars, cast an incandescent glow across the harbor. Cloud strings bordered the northern horizon. Hints of bright color, impervious to the screeching of the terns, laced the heavens.

Matt had broken the code and understood the wintry message that had come with sleet the night he knocked over the fiery shack.

He sprinted down the hill, swam to target rock, cut into the muscle of the recalcitrant shell, and found glistening powder that he had never seen before. He lifted the shell in front of him, faced the four directions of the winds, was about to drop the contents into the bay when a swirling gust lifted the powder like a bird's feather in flight. The powder floated toward the stars accompanied by a flock of silent terns.

Matt watched the flight of rising clouds and knew ancient Warriors had reclaimed the missing lovers.

He stood on Target Rock, his eyes searched the heavens, and his arms stretched toward emerging constellations. He whipped around, searched the vacant hilltop, listened for any sounds, as if on the lookout for someone waving a white shirt.

Epilogue

It was the wind that gave them life. It is the wind that comes out of our mouths now that gives us life. When this ceases to blow we die. In the skin at the tips of our fingers we see the trail of the wind, it shows us where the wind blew when our ancestors were created.

IT WAS THE WIND, NAVAJO, 19TH CENTURY

The elders say, "the longest road you're going to have to walk in your life is from here to here. From the head to the heart." But they also say you can't speak to the people as a leader unless you've made the return journey. From the heart to the head.

PHIL LANE, JR., YANKTON SIOUX, 1992

From *WORDS of POWER*
Fulcrum Publishing